BENEATH THE
mountain
SKY

MCBRIDE BROTHER
LUMBERJACKS

BOOK ONE

USA TODAY Bestselling Author
GWYN MCNAMEE

BENEATH THE MOUNTAIN SKY

© 2025 Gwyn McNamee

Cover Model: Camden; Photographer: Wander Aguiar

Cover Design: Y'all That Graphics

Editing: Stephie Walls at Wallflower Edits

To anyone who ever forgot your dreams but continued to fight until you reached them...

1

KILLIAN

There's only one thing more beautiful than McBride Mountain blanketed in the pre-dawn mist.

And I *don't* think about that other thing.

I don't think about *her.*

Because *I can't.*

If I allowed myself to indulge in those memories every time my mind wanted to wander to Willow, I wouldn't be able to get out of bed each morning. I wouldn't be able to come out here each day to the mountain we loved, where we built a life together, and do my job for all the people who depend on McBride Timber for their livelihoods.

And truth be told...I wouldn't be able to keep breathing.

Not without her.

So, no matter how badly I may want to, I can't dwell on the gaping hole she ripped in my chest when she left me and this place, when she turned me into this person I've become—one I hardly recognize.

This man traipsing through the thick woods with an axe—and a chip—on his shoulder is so many things I wasn't before.

Bitter.

Resentful.

Even quicker to anger, which a lot of people didn't think was possible.

I've become something that can be summed up in a single word: miserable.

Instead of obsessing over what I lost, how much I'd love to have her at my side to watch the sun rise and burn off this fog, what I wouldn't give to see that early morning light hit her face and brighten it the same way her perfect smile did, I concentrate on the bitter mist engulfing me and the rest of the Blue Ridge Range this morning.

Damp.

Chilly.

Clinging to my bare skin the same way it does the ground and the trees all around me.

An ethereal haze—almost like I'm in another world, even though we're less than a dozen miles from the homestead and cabin.

Yet it's another world out here.

Remote.

Wild.

Filled with the kind of feral creatures people often accuse me of being.

Maybe I should just stay out here...

That would be easier on everyone, I suppose, to disappear into the wilderness with my regret, into a world where I can live with my failure without interference from anything or anyone else.

But like my bitter mood this morning, this pre-drawn haze won't last long.

As soon as the sun hits the horizon, the fog will start to

burn off, and the heat of early summer will descend on the mountain.

Bright.

Warm.

All the things Willow was and I never could be.

My favorite time of day to be out here, trudging through the trees, alone save for my thoughts and ever-present axe.

Quiet.

Peaceful.

Only my footsteps on broken branches and leaves littering the forest floor, the birds starting to chirp at the lightening of the sky, and animals scurrying about after sleep break the otherwise silence of the crisp air.

It almost makes it possible for me to forget that I have nothing to look forward to once we complete our task today. That I will return to the timber yard and finish out my day, then return to the cabin I once shared with her and find it cold and empty. That I will have to sleep in the bed where I made love to her and sleep alone.

I can *almost* pretend I haven't spent the last 372 days since she left wandering around in my own sort of fog...

Almost—but not quite.

Her face continues to pop into my mind the deeper I push through the trees and the higher I climb up McBride Mountain.

My hand tightens around the axe handle, eager to use it to work out some of the tension that has only grown since I woke this morning.

I try to concentrate on scanning the area for the goal of today's expedition—the perfect tree for Liam. The one he says he needs to create his next project. Once we find it, I can put my axe to work, and hopefully, decimating something will make me feel better.

At least for a few minutes.

"Killian, wait up!"

Hell.

Pausing with a groan, I turn back to Liam, watching him thread through the massive trunks and step over a fallen log I just navigated with his own axe slung over his shoulder.

He hustles to catch up, releasing a little annoyed huff. "You got somewhere to be or something?"

I raise a brow at him.

Considering *he's* the one who dragged us all out here this morning, when we should be at McBride Timber supervising the final details of the big lumber shipment that needs to go out later today, it's a bold question.

"What?" He shrugs, tilting his head slightly to the side and offering his boyish grin. "They can handle things 'til we get back. And you're kind of rushing..."

"Fuck off." I shift my axe to my other shoulder. "I'm *not*."

I am.

My annoyance at being pulled away from work, plus not being able to wallow in my misery alone because I'm stuck with Liam and Connor, is enough to make me want to get this over and done with as quickly as possible.

Liam gives me a little frown that makes him look like the adorable toddler who used to follow Connor and me around to places he had no business being at that age, instead of the twenty-three-year-old young man he is today.

"Yeah, you *are*." His gaze drifts behind us to the path we wove through the trees. "And I think Connor would agree."

Connor trudges forward, still a good hundred yards back and looking seriously perturbed at either my pace or at having to come out here today at all—probably both.

Running a hand through my mist-dampened hair to keep it out of my face, I scowl at Liam. "Sorry. I didn't know you two still needed a leash like people put on their children sometimes."

He playfully bumps his shoulder against mine. "Mom never used that on us."

"She should have." I poke him in the sternum, directly over the swirl of ink visible in his half-unbuttoned shirt. "Especially on *you*."

Liam gapes in mock offense and presses a hand over his chest. "I'm offended on both my behalf *and* hers."

I wave him off. Not really annoyed anymore, just eager to get moving. "Yeah, yeah, yeah." Turning back, I call to the straggler. "Come on, Connor, let's go."

Our brother mutters something from behind us that gets instantly carried away by the breeze rustling the leaves, but even without being able to hear it, I'm confident it wasn't very complimentary.

So little of what Connor says ever is these days.

Maybe my attitude has been rubbing off on him...

There are certainly enough people around here who seem to think that's the case, if the comments on Raven's posts on the McBride Mountain Community News page are any indication.

The way she portrays Connor and me, warning people away from us and our volatile moods, we might as well be wild sasquatches waiting in the forest to attack unsuspecting hikers and tear them limb from limb.

I have been known to rip someone a new one...but they typically deserve it.

Connor finally catches up with us, releasing a huff that has nothing to do with exertion.

We've done hikes far worse than this, faster and harder, before and often, scouting for areas to log and hunt, but he, like me, prefers to choose when we go instead of being *told* we are by our insistent little brother.

I scan the surrounding area before rotating back to Liam. "Where did you say you thought you saw this 'perfect' tree?"

Apparently, the only *one* specific tree in the entirety of the

Blue Ridge Mountains he can use to make his next rocking chair happens to be in a copse, nowhere near town or anything resembling civilization.

Go fucking figure.

Liam motions ahead of us vaguely. "It was up near the river. A grove I stumbled upon last year up here." A glimmer of anticipation flashes across his green gaze, making him practically tremble. "I've been eyeing it for a while, waiting for the perfect project."

His genuine excitement is enough to make some more of my annoyance ebb, and I do my best to push away all those thoughts and memories that plagued me while I was hiking alone.

I step over a fallen log in the direction of the river that flows down the expanse of McBride Mountain. Liam walks beside me where the trees will allow it, with Connor trailing behind.

Liam smacks me on the shoulder. "Thanks for coming with me, by the way."

"Did I have a choice?"

A slow grin pulls at his lips. "Not really. I would have dragged you two out here, kicking and screaming, if I had to."

Connor snorts. "I would've liked to see you try, little brother."

Liam tosses him a dirty look, but there isn't any malice in it or their words. Pushing buttons, testing limits, and throwing verbal barbs have always been our love language—but it hasn't come to *physical* blows in years.

Mom would be proud.

At least, of that.

Not of what I've done.

Not of what I've become.

Acid churns in my stomach, imagining the verbal lashing she would give me if she knew how I destroyed things with Willow as the three of us continue higher up the mountain, weaving through the endless towering trees and dense foliage toward the sounds of the river finally starting to filter to us.

I push away a low-hanging tree branch with my axe so Liam and I can pass around it and almost allow it to sling back and smack Connor, but aggravating him even more isn't a good idea. "Which side of the river?"

It's an important question since I don't particularly feel like wading through the still-chilly water this early in the morning. Especially when I know we'll be out here for hours, breaking down this tree into manageable-sized logs to get it back to Liam's workshop on the makeshift sledges we'll put together with the materials stuffed in the pack Liam carries.

A task that would have been far easier if he had chosen a target that wasn't in such a hard-to-reach part of the mountain.

This portion of our home is completely wild.

Harsh.

Desolate.

Without a hint of civilization that you'll find as you descend closer to our homestead and eventually the town.

And it's pristine.

Exactly as Mother Nature intended it.

This is why the McBrides settled here almost two hundred and fifty years ago.

This is why I stay even when the bad memories threaten to overtake the good.

This...and the two men with me right now.

The promise I made to Mom before she died to look after them, to take care of them, to ensure they were okay, is one I intend to honor. I never broke a promise to that woman while she was alive, and I have no intention of doing it now that she's passed on to somewhere better than this Earth.

That means staying, even when it doesn't feel like home without Willow here, even when the place I've lived my entire life somehow seems foreign and all the things I once loved only seem to irritate me.

Like being out here now helping Liam.

Liam smirks, likely already anticipating the bitching and moaning that would ensue if he were to tell us it was on the *other* shore now, rather than back near the homestead, where we could have used the bridge to cross the river and make our way up the mountain on the proper side from the beginning. "This bank."

Good.

Because the river up here isn't anything I want to tangle with.

We push through another few dozen yards of trees before we reach the west bank. Rushing waters cascade over and around giant boulders, creating bubbling and churning rapids. Farther down, closer to town, McBride Falls tumbles down into the swimming hole so popular this time of year to cool off in the afternoons. But this early, no one would be there, and there's certainly no one up this far on the mountain.

This is the type of spot I would bring her, though...

Willow's face flashes before my eyes.

What she would look like lying spread out on the thick, green grass along the shore, laughing and smiling.

Panting and gasping.

Coming undone in my arms.

My fingers twitch, imagining how wet she would be and how soft her skin would feel under my rough hands.

I clench them around the handle of the axe so hard my knuckles ache, fighting the descent of the dark cloud I've perpetually lived under that always surrounds me whenever I think about her.

Liam smacks me on the shoulder. "You okay?"

"Yeah." Because I would never admit to him or anyone else

how bad it's gotten in the past week since the anniversary of her flight from McBride Mountain. "Let's go."

We wander along the rocky bank, pushing farther north and west until Liam points to the left. "I think it's just over there, but it could be up a little more."

Connor scans the vast expanse of trees, taking in the landscape and the endless possibilities, then glances in Liam's direction. "Let's split up. Cover more ground. Signal if you find what we're looking for."

We all nod our agreement.

It will be the fastest way to locate this grove—and the hickory Liam has his heart set on using to build his custom chair. If he weren't so damn good at it and the end results weren't so beautiful, I would have told him to cut down any of the millions of trees within easy walking distance for the project. But knowing him and the extent he's going to in order to get this, it must really be something.

Worth the effort to see him happy.

Connor sets off directly to the west, and Liam heads into the woods a dozen yards to the north, both disappearing between the trunks while I take a moment to scan the river as far as I can see up the mountain.

The sound of the rushing water floats through the air, and I stand absolutely still, waiting for that raging torrent of emotions that threatens to drown me when I'm alone to come like it always does.

It starts with that tightness in my chest.

A feeling of simultaneously suffocating and drowning while trying to draw in air.

But before it can completely overtake me, a splash of pale-red color catches my eye near the opposite bank, fifty yards upriver. Not a color I would usually see out here. Not natural.

Instead of stepping into the woods like Connor and Liam to

continue the search, I move toward the water with slow but deliberate steps.

What the hell is that?

It wouldn't be completely unusual for an animal carcass to end up in the river after a coyote or bobcat got to it, but the hair on the back of my neck stands on end as I move even closer.

There's something there...

Lodged up in the roots of the tree protruding into the water...

"Fuck."

I drop my axe onto the ground and rush into the frigid rapids.

The sharp sting of the icy swirl against my skin makes me grit my teeth, but I fight through the natural instinct to head back to dry land.

Because that isn't a wild animal in the river.

I can just barely make out an outstretched hand, dark hair floating in the water, face turned away from me. The rest of the torso and limbs are beneath the surface or tangled in the tree that prevented it from drifting farther down the rapids.

What the hell was anyone doing up here?

There is absolutely *nothing* for hundreds of miles in almost every direction except one—toward our homestead, the falls, and the town. But that's a good eight miles from where we are now, and whoever this is clearly entered the river farther up to have ended up here.

My boots slip on the slimy rocks on the bottom, but I manage to keep my balance, arms spread wide, as I work my way across the expanse toward the opposing bank, fighting the current that threatens to drag me down.

"Fucking hell."

Teeth chatter at the chill seeping into my bones, but I force myself to keep moving.

Each step feels like barely advancing, yet I finally make it close enough to grab the end of the log. My grip on the wet wood helps me battle the current and get a better footing.

I inch my way along the fallen tree until I can grab the hand floating in the water.

Pale, clammy skin.

But it doesn't have the cold, stiff feel I would expect from a dead body.

The heat barely registers against my palm...but it's there.

Holy fuck.

Whoever this is.

They're alive—though barely.

I push forward along the log toward where the person is pinned in a *V* created by the massive tree roots. My feet slip on the rocks again, but I regain my balance enough to grasp the thick, dark hair and shift the head back to ensure it stays out of the water, so whoever it is can breathe.

But it's *my* breath that catches at the face that tilts up at me.

Covered in cuts, scrapes, and mottled bruises...

Blood trickling from a nasty cut over one dark eyebrow...

Normally pink lips now holding a deathly blue tinge...

Lips I kissed every day for five fucking years...

"Willow?"

WILLOW

Beep.

   Beep.

   Beep.

   Beep.

The pitch-black abyss surrounding me ripples...

God, what is that?

Onyx shifts to gray, then returns to impenetrable black again.

I float in it for a few seconds.

Struggling to cling to it.

Beep.

Beep.

Beep.

Beep.

The noise pierces my skull.

My brain thrashes against my skull violently, desperate to escape to somewhere *quiet.*

Back to the darkness I've been floating in so beautifully.

Beep.

Beep.

Beep.

Beep.

I try to raise my hands to press them over my ears, to drown out that infernal racket clearly sent by Satan, but something tugs on my arm.

A wave of nauseating agony rolls through me.

Lancing my side.

Slicing and stabbing at various places across my body.

What the hell is happening?

Beep.

Beep.

Beep.

Beep.

I attempt to swallow, but it's so dry I can't make it work right.

All trying does is cause more *bad.*

Scratchy. Awful. Pain.

Fuck.

Beep.

Beep.

Beep.

Beep.

Groaning, I roll away from that incessant sound, putting my back to it in a vain attempt to block it out. But the movement brings more agony that roils my stomach and makes acid fill my throat.

I choke on it, coughing violently, only making the throbbing in my side worse.

"Willow?" The sound of something metallic shifting across a hard floor comes from directly in front of me. Sharp. High-pitched. No better than that damn beeping. "She's awake. Go get the doctor."

That voice...

The familiar, deep, silky sound permeates the darkness that's still trying to drag me into it, where I would willingly go if it stopped all this hurt. It cuts through the thudding in my head. Washes away the pain for a brief moment. My heartbeat picks up, that horrible beeping sound increasing its pace in time with the thumping against my ribs.

Beep. Beep. Beep. Beep. Beep. Beep.

"Willow?"

Killian...

He's here.

His eyes. Those crystal-blue orbs, always filled with so much love and affection, flash across my closed lids. I want to see them. Need to. My aching body yearns to feel his arms around me, to have him hold me...

But moving again is completely off the table, given what just happened.

Beep. Beep. Beep. Beep. Beep. Beep.

A warm, rough, calloused palm brushes along my cheek. Gentle. Reverent. "Willow? Can you open your eyes? Can you look at me?"

It seems like such a simple request.

And I *want* to.

I want to see him *so damn badly.*

I *need* to.

It feels like it's been an eternity since I've laid eyes on him...

Yet when I try to lift my lids, to see his strong, handsome face, that smile that he reserves only for me, they refuse to move.

Why are they so damn heavy?

"Willow?"

The plea in his voice makes me want to try again.

I somehow get them half-open, despite them weighing a thousand pounds, but the immediate blinding lights make the stabbing headache a thousand times worse.

Wincing, I clamp my eyes shut and try to swallow again, barely managing to wet my parched throat. "Lights..."

"Someone turn off the fucking lights!"

Killian's voice booms, filled with so much authority and tension. A command he expects to be followed by whoever else is here.

And they'll do it.

Everyone always does what Killian asks, even if he isn't the nicest about the way he does it.

He has always been grumpy and short with people, but they know he doesn't really mean it. And he's never that way with me. Certainly not like *that.*

He sounds angry.

Frustrated maybe?

I try to shift again, to move closer to him, to reach out and offer my touch that always seems to soothe him whenever he's lost in his own head, suffocating with the weight of all that he carries on his broad shoulders. Just as he does for me when I need it.

But *everything* hurts.

Every limb.

Every muscle.

Every damn inch of my skin.

Every fiber of my being screams at me to *stop* moving.

That incessant beeping picks up.

Beep. Beep. Beep. Beep. Beep. Beep. Beep. Beep. Beep.

What is that?

Killian's thumb brushes softly over my cheek. That familiar scrape of hard-earned callouses soothes some of the tension in my body. "Willow, can you hear me?"

I manage an almost imperceptible nod through the pounding in my skull and hear his sigh of relief over that horrible beeping.

What the hell *is that?*

Nothing on the homestead makes that sound.

Certainly nothing in the cabin.

Yet, it's somehow familiar, even though I can't quite place it.

"Did somebody get the doctor?" Killian again, panic rising in his voice. "Someone *get* her. Now!"

Panic?

No.

Killian McBride doesn't panic.

Ever.

So strong.

So steady.

So confident in himself and everything he does.

But not now...

What did he say?

Doctor?

"What—" I only manage to get out that single word before the dryness in my throat prevents me from speaking anymore, and I cough again. A sharp stab in my side doubles me slightly, and I press my hand against it, groaning at the discomfort every little movement creates.

"Can someone get her some water?"

People shuffling.

Footsteps approaching... "Is she allowed to have it?"

Liam...

Liam's here, too.

That's good.

He always calms things down, especially when Killian is out of sorts.

And it sounds like he is right now.

I try to settle down into the bed that doesn't feel quite right.

Not our bed.

Ours is soft and comfortable and smells like Killian—like the clean, crisp mountain air, leather, and freshly cut wood. This smells...sterile. Like chemicals. And the sheets are scratchy on my aching skin.

Definitely uncomfortable.

Something else brushes against my forehead.

Not his hand.

His lips, maybe?

Soft and warm.

Loving.

I groan and try to shift closer to him on the bed. My body screams in protest, a piercing pain in my ribs making me wince again.

"Here."

Liam again.

He always takes care of everyone...

Killian's fingers tip my head up, and something presses to my lips. "Water. Take a sip."

I open my mouth, and a straw slips slightly into it.

Water.

Yes, that would be good.

So thirsty.

I take a short pull from it.

Cool liquid coats my desert-dry throat.

God, does that taste good...

Killian's hand slides away from my face, and he pulls the straw back. "Not too much." Feet shuffling again. Murmured voices I can't quite make out. "Willow? Can you open your eyes?"

His voice wavers.

Unsure.

Unsteady.

Not at all the way he usually sounds.

That alone is enough to get me to make another attempt to see what's wrong, what has him so upset.

I finally manage to get my lids to lift, and Killian's face is right there, illuminated by something behind me in the relative darkness of the room.

Thick, long blond hair falls over his temples and to his shoulders, disheveled and unkempt. Rough and rugged.

Just like the man.

A muscle in his clenched jaw tics while he examines me.

Those icy eyes sweep over my face, narrowing with concern. Taking in every minute detail, as if he hasn't looked at me every single day for the last five years and known me my entire life before that.

Almost like he's seeing me for the first time.

Heavy lines at the corners of his eyes and dark smudges beneath them make him look somehow older. Exhausted. Almost...haunted. "Willow?"

"Hi..."

The corners of his lips twitch slightly, melting away a bit of the tension from his features. "Hi."

He releases a long exhale that sounds like he's been holding his breath for days and cups my cheek again, slowly grazing his thumb across it. Goosebumps break out across my skin at the soft touch coming from such a strong man, clearly filled with so much tension.

I shiver slightly, every part of me aching or stinging or screaming out in some other way.

His brow immediately furrows, distress darkening that azure gaze. "The doctor's going to be here soon."

Doctor?

It takes a moment for my foggy brain, still tinged with that warm, welcoming darkness, to process his words.

Oh, the beeping...

That's why the sound is so familiar.

I peek over my shoulder at the machines lined up behind my hospital bed, monitoring my vital signs. An IV line runs to my left hand, which explains the tug on it when I moved. But nothing explains *why* I'm here, or why the hell it feels like my entire body is revolting against me.

My head throbs as I struggle to remember what might have put me here, but all that comes is that same pitch black that surrounded me before I woke.

I turn back to Killian, wincing at the ice pick slamming into my temples. "What happened? Why am I in the hospital?"

He glances behind him, and I follow his gaze to where Connor and Liam stand. His brothers look just as nervous and concerned as he does, shifting on their feet and averting their gazes. Liam runs a hand over his short, reddish hair while Connor presses his lips together, his dark brows narrowed over hard eyes that focus on the foot of my bed and not me.

Neither one of them has ever been uncomfortable around me before or afraid to speak their mind.

Confusion shifts to unease bordering on panic.

What is going on?

No one says anything, and before anyone can or I can ask again, a woman in a while lab coat enters the room and flicks on the lights. I wince, and her soft hazel eyes immediately fall on me over the rim of tortoise-shell glasses, and she offers a genuine smile. "Willow, nice to see you awake."

I try to sit up, but Killian places a gentle hand on my shoulder, keeping me prone. "Don't try to move too much."

What happened *to me?*

He's obviously terrified, and if I'm in the big hospital in Asheville, that means it wasn't something Doc Broward and his nurse, Amy, could handle at the McBride Mountain Clinic.

All I see when I try to remember how I got here is a vast, empty black hole.

The doctor approaches the bed on the side opposite where Killian sits and takes a look at the monitors and something on the tablet in her hand. "I'm Dr. Sommers. How are you feeling?"

I attempt to process the question and take stock of my body. The aches. The stabbing pains when I move. The throbbing in my head. "Like shit."

She chuckles softly. "I would imagine so, given your injuries."

"Injuries?"

Killian squeezes my shoulder. "You're okay. Right, Doc?"

Dr. Sommers presses her lips together and meets my gaze after giving him a reproachful look. "You have quite a few bumps and bruises, lots of scratches and scrapes, and the cut above your eye needed stitches, but you were lucky that the only things broken were a few cracked ribs."

"What?" Panic seizes my chest, wrapping around it and tightening until my breaths feel more like a slow trickle of air instead of filling my lungs. "Wh-what happened? Was I...in a car accident?"

She exchanges another look with Killian that I can't quite decipher.

He cups my face, turning it back toward him. "What do you remember?"

"I..." I try again, but there's still an empty abyss where my memory of whatever got me here should be. "I don't...I can't...

the last thing I remember is being at the Memorial Day Festival, watching you do the carving demonstration. I was with Raven." Darkness encroaches again, and I shake my head to try to keep it at bay, but I immediately regret the move when it makes those daggers stab into my brain again. "And that's it. I don't..."

Killian's eyes widen, and he glances at his brothers.

Their earlier nervousness has shifted into something else.

Fear.

My lips tremble along with my body. "What is it?"

Killian's throat works, his Adam's apple bobbing as he peeks up at the doctor. "Um...Willow, that was a year ago."

No...

I try to push myself up, but the doctor gently presses on my shoulder, keeping me down.

Killian pulls his hand from my cheek to shove it through his long, unruly hair, pushing out of his chair to his feet. "We just had the festival again last week, Willow. And you weren't there. That was a *year* ago that you watched me..."

"What?" *No. No. No. No. No. No.* "That can't...that can't be right."

That can't have been a *year* ago.

Connor and Liam exchange a look, as if neither particularly wants to intervene, but Liam steps forward, giving me the kind, reassuring smile he typically sports that always makes people feel at ease.

He rests his hand on mine on the bed and squeezes gently. "I'm sorry, Willow, it is. That was last summer."

Last.

Summer.

"Oh, my God."

Dr. Sommers types something on her tablet. "You don't remember anything from the past year?"

"I..."

No.

No.

No.

No matter how hard I try, I can't get past this solid wall of *nothing.*

The memories of the festival and everything before are crystal clear.

I can picture the way Killian's tan work pants hung low off his trim hips that day. How those delicious abs and sinfully perfect Adonis belt tempted me to look even lower. The sculpted muscles of his back and chest bunching and flexing as he demonstrated wood carving for the excited crowd of locals and tourists that packed Main Street that afternoon. The way his eyes drifted over to meet mine, and he gave me that lecherous grin that promised as soon as we got home, he was going to get cleaned up and then get *very* dirty all over again.

But after that...

Absolutely.

Nothing.

"There's like...this black hole." I squeeze my eyes closed, wincing at the thumping of my brain against my skull. "I can't see anything there. Not after the festival." Releasing a frustrated groan, I force my eyes open. "It feels like that just happened yesterday..."

Killian's gaze softens as he stares down at me the way he always has—like I'm his entire world. Like the sun revolves around *me* instead of us around *it.* I remember *that.*

Why can't I remember anything else?

God, that was a year ago?

The fact that I can't remember anything and they're all looking at me expectantly makes me bristle. Something is very wrong. Full-blown panic threatens to choke me. "How-how did I get here?"

Killian retakes his place in the chair next to the bed and

pulls my hand into his. It feels the same, but it trembles now in a way I've never felt from this man. "I found you in the river, Willow."

"The river?"

An image of the main waterway that cuts a path across McBride Mountain flashes through my head.

The lifeline for the wildlife in the area.

But also incredibly dangerous in places.

Definitely not anywhere I would venture on my own.

Killian nods.

"But...how did I...?"

He shakes his head. "We don't know. You were hypothermic. I don't know how long you'd been in the water, but I pulled you out and we got you into Asheville to the ER as quickly as we could."

What?

That's something I should remember.

How I got into the water.

Being swept downriver.

Killian's pulling me out.

But there is *nothing.*

I glance up at the doctor. "Why can't I remember?"

She offers me a soft smile. "The good news is, we did an MRI, and there doesn't appear to be any damage to your brain, and your bloodwork has all come back normal. Given how you were found in the water and that gash on your head, you likely have a concussion, though. Your body shows that you were battered pretty badly on your way downriver. You've obviously suffered trauma, and with a traumatic injury, it's not uncommon for some parts of the brain to shut down so it can focus on healing. The memories should return. Eventually. You just have to give it some time and give your body a chance to heal."

Time to heal.

But apparently, a *lot* of time has passed.

An entire *year* just *gone*.

So much must have happened in that time.

We had so many plans—

My gaze immediately drops to my left hand, where my engagement ring has sat on that all-important finger since Killian proposed, searching for the wedding band that would be with it if Killian and I had finally gotten married like we had planned last July.

A few cuts and scrapes mar the otherwise bare finger where it rests on top of the hospital blanket.

No wedding band.

Not even my engagement ring.

As empty as my memory of why it's gone.

2

WILLOW

My stomach tenses along with every sore muscle and joint in my body. That pulsating agony pierces my temples as I try to remember *anything*.

Did it come off in the river?

Or...

Was it already gone?

I never took it off.

Not even when I was making candles.

It was a part of me as much as the man who gave it to me.

The harder I try to figure it out, the more I have to choke back the bile rising in my throat.

I wouldn't have taken it off.

Never.

Killian watches me carefully, so stock-still that he almost appears like he isn't breathing. His massive chest doesn't move. Those intensely blue eyes don't waver from mine, but I see fear swimming in them.

He has the answers.

And I need them.

Not being able to remember feels like floating lost in space with no tether to get me back to Earth. Spinning endlessly in a dark void. Spiraling out of control with no anchor to anything tangible. No lifeline. Except *him.*

Killian has *always* been my rock.

Even before we were together, the McBrides felt like home. *He* felt like home. A safe haven. The only person who could ever calm my fears and help me escape the turmoil in my life and head.

That's what I need now.

I need him to do what he does best—take control and wipe away my uncertainty and confusion.

"Wh-what happened since the festival last year?"

Connor and Liam both shift nervously and give Killian a long, knowing look, then offer me tight smiles before they slip out of the room, leaving me alone with the doctor and the man I *should* be married to by now.

"Ms. May..." Dr. Sommers offers me a kind look and a pat on the hand, as if she can sense my rising panic and doesn't want it to boil over. "It's best if you just relax and rest right now. Don't try to strain your body or mind. Give yourself the opportunity to heal. In the meantime, we'll keep you comfortable when it comes to the pain, and you should be able to go home tomorrow."

Home...

I let my gaze meet Killian's again, but before I can ask him anything else about the massive gap in my memory, rushed, frantic footsteps pound down the hallway, and a blaze of blond hair flies through the door.

Familiar green eyes meet mine, filled with frantic concern.

Raven's jaw drops. "Oh, my God, Willow!"

She rushes toward the bed and elbows Killian out of the way. The man twice her size, who absolutely could have stood his ground, knows better than to get between Raven and me after all these years. Especially when she gives him her *don't mess with me or you'll regret it* look.

Even *I* fear that one.

Raven throws her arms around me, and I wince as the pressure and movement pull at both the IV in my hand and at my damaged ribs.

She doesn't seem to notice, just buries her face against my neck, wet tears hitting my skin. Her body trembles, and she squeezes me far too tightly, as if she can't believe I'm really here, in her arms.

When she pulls back, she searches my face. "What the hell happened?"

Her accusatory gaze cuts to Killian.

He holds up his hands with a defensive scowl, his ice-hard glare carving through her like the blade of the axe he usually carries. "Don't look at me like that. I found her like this in the river."

Raven's blond brows fly up. "The *river*?" Her focus slices back to me. "What the hell? Last I heard, you were in Charleston."

Killian shifts his stance, angling himself closer to me, physically inserting himself between Raven and the bed, forcing her to retreat a step. "Charleston?"

What?

My confusion matches Killian's.

I flick my gaze between their stare-down, trying to process what's happening, but my drugged—and apparently damaged—brain can't seem to grasp what they're saying.

Even attempting to remember brings more agony.

"Why the hell was I in Charleston?"

I struggle to find even a single memory to prove it's true.

The thudding against my skull gets even worse, and I raise my hands, the IV tugging on my left one as I rub at my temples.

But it's no use.

It's all blank.

Absolutely blank.

Raven shoves Killian's chest, and he retreats enough for her to sit on the edge of my bed and take my hand in hers. Squeezing it, she glances at Dr. Sommers rather than answering my question, almost as if she's afraid to. "Why doesn't she remember?"

The doctor continues typing on her tablet, barely peeking up at the soap opera unraveling in front of her. "Trauma like she's suffered can cause temporary memory loss. It should come back with time and rest."

She keeps saying that, but the vague answer doesn't do anything to ease the panic at having a year of my life missing.

I watch her face carefully, trying to gauge her level of concern when I ask the very important question no one has yet. "Should come back. But *when*?"

"That's not an easy question to answer." She finally fully looks up and offers me a sympathetic smile. "For most people, it takes a few days or weeks. For others, it can be months, even years." Her gaze darts to Killian. "And there are some rare cases where people don't ever recover those gaps in memory. Though, those are few and far between."

Don't ever recover...

A vise tightens around my ribcage.

I might not ever remember the last year...

Dr. Sommers smiles, tucking her tablet under her arm. "I'll come back and check on you before my shift ends. Press the call button if you need anything. And you"—she points between Killian and Raven—"need to clear out of here. She needs to rest."

Killian grunts, reinserting himself closer to me with his hip touching the top of the bed. "If you think I'm leaving her, you're out of your fucking mind."

The doctor just glares at him, seemingly undeterred by his attempt to physically intimidate her. "Do I need to have security come for you?"

A low growl slips from his lips. "Let. Them. Fucking. *Try.*"

He widens his stance and crosses his massive arms over his barrel chest, making his T-shirt pull taut across bulging muscles and tattooed biceps.

An immovable force.

My heart flip-flops the way it always does when he goes into this protective and possessive mode. When he stakes his claim on me and ensures anyone else around knows I'm his—and he's *mine.*

Raven offers her most innocent smile to the clearly perturbed doctor. "We'll just be a few minutes, and then I'll go." She knows better than to argue with the woman who very well can get her thrown out, even if Killian would be more difficult. As a reporter, she understands what it means to choose her conflicts carefully and how to get what she wants. "I promise."

Killian continues his stare-down with the doc. "*I'm* not going anywhere."

Silent tension permeates the air, along with that infuriating beeping that is no longer drowned out by our conversation.

Beep.

Beep.

Beep.

Beep.

Finally, Dr. Sommers seems to realize she's going to lose this battle with Killian and releases an annoyed huff before she leaves the room.

Probably wise.

Killian McBride isn't the man you want to have this kind of argument with because he never breaks or bends. And Raven isn't much better. She doesn't get intimidated; she intimidates when necessary. Which is what makes her such a damn good reporter and best friend.

Raven squeezes my hand as soon as the door closes behind the doctor. "So, you don't remember where you were or how you ended up in the river?"

I shake my head and glance up at Killian. "The last thing I remember was the Memorial Day Festival...last year."

Her pale-pink lips part as she gapes at me for a moment, then whips her head toward him. "Oh, my God." She clears her throat, gaze darting between us almost frantically. "Um..."

Killian offers her an almost imperceptible shake of his head.

Anyone else might have missed the motion.

But I know him too well.

I know his body and how he moves.

I know his moods and how to read them.

I know every inch of this man.

And the vibes he's giving off now...

Something is very wrong.

Something he doesn't want me to know.

Something he doesn't want Raven to tell me.

"Umm." Raven bristles, shifting nervously on the bed and giving me a tight smile. "Well, I think I can help fill in some of the gaps."

Except whatever Killian is trying to keep her quiet about...

"What do you mean?" Killian's deep voice echoes around the room, vibrating with his anger. "You told me you didn't know *where* she was when I was looking for her."

Looking for me?

Raven's earlier comment about Charleston flickers through my head as she scowls at him. "I fucking *lied*, Killian. She told me she didn't want to see you again. I was going to protect my best friend, not help *you*."

Protect me from what?

My stomach pitches, and I have to fight to keep bile from making its way up my throat again.

"What are you two talking about?" I start shaking, the fingers of my free hand curling in the scratchy hospital bed blanket and tightening. "What's going on?"

Tears well in my eyes the longer they don't answer.

My question just *hangs* in the air.

Neither Killian nor Raven says a word, both simply staring at each other like they're waiting for the other to break first—or daring the other one to try it.

Finally, Raven throws up her free hand. "Oh, this is ridiculous, Killian. It's not like she isn't going to find out."

Having them talk about me and *my life* as if I'm not sitting right here makes me want to scream. "Find out *what*?"

Raven squeezes my fingers tightly, ignoring the fury radiating off Killian. "Honey, you left town the day after the festival last year."

Left town?

I look at Killian. "*What?*"

His clenched jaw matches the granite hardness of every muscle in his body, and he shifts uneasily on his feet, arms still crossed over his chest.

He doesn't want to explain and hates being backed into a corner like this.

He's exposed with nowhere to hide. "We...had a fight..."

A fight?

Pain stabs at my temples again, and I squeeze my eyes closed, trying to reconcile his words with *anything* in my memory.

We *never* argue.

Like...*ever.*

What could we possibly have fought about that was bad enough to have him acting like this?

That was bad enough to make me leave McBride Mountain?

I open my eyes again and meet his tentative gaze filled with utter anguish that I have only seen on his face once before—when his mother died. "I left?"

Raven glares at Killian, who finally moves from his imitation of a statue and turns away, scrubbing his hands over his face and through his hair, tugging on the long, blond strands like he always does when he's frustrated.

He doesn't seem inclined to shed any light on the situation.

He can't even *look* at me.

But my best friend won't leave me hanging.

She tightens her grip on my hand, casting a hesitant look at him before refocusing on me. "You called me to come up and help you pack. You were...borderline hysterical. Said you had to leave. That you couldn't stay any longer."

Killian's shoulders tighten, back still to me.

But I don't have to see his face to know how upset he is.

The tension practically radiates off him.

"I tried to get you to tell me what happened, but all you would say was that it was over between you and Killian, that you didn't have a future on McBride Mountain."

Those words ring in my ears, almost as painfully as trying to remember.

But they don't feel *right*.

Not when the last memory I have of him is the love in his gaze and touch and of the future we were planning together.

"But *why*?"

Killian spins to face us now, his hands fisted as if he's fighting the urge to destroy something. "It doesn't matter."

Raven sneers at him. "It very much *does*."

His gaze drifts to me, and the apology soaking those azure eyes tells me that whatever happened between us, he regrets it deeply. "Please, Willow, you don't need to be worrying about this right now..." He shoves a hand through his hair roughly. "Later, when you're feeling better. We can...we can talk."

There's a plea there.

To let it go for *now*.

Under any other circumstances, I wouldn't.

I've always had to push Killian to open up, to break free from his natural inclination to shut down and keep everyone out—even those he loves the most. And I was the only one who could ever do it without getting snapped at and paying the consequences for poking the bear.

But bone-deep exhaustion threatens to drag me back under the longer this goes on.

And that incessant pounding in my head only grows.

Right now, I don't have it in me to *push,* not when even breathing and *thinking* hurts.

I tear my gaze from his to focus on Raven and what she said earlier, which makes more sense, coupled with this revelation. "So, I went to Charleston?"

She shakes her head. "No, we loaded up your truck, and you said you were heading to Asheville, to those friends you met at that market."

"Julie and Rob?"

"Yeah." She nods. "You stayed with them for a while before you went to Williamsburg."

"Williamsburg?"

Killian snarls. "What the hell, Raven? First, you said Charleston, now it's Asheville and Williamsburg. Where the hell *was* she?"

Raven glares at him, then turns back to me. "Over the last year, you've sent me maybe half a dozen different things. A birthday gift, a Christmas gift, a few postcards. It seemed like you were spending a couple of months in one place and then moving on. Hitting up local markets and selling your candles in various shops. You always sounded so happy when you wrote, and I didn't think there was any reason to worry, as long as you were."

A shadow falls over her as Killian shifts closer to the bed, blocking out the light and looming over Raven in a way that would intimidate someone who wasn't so used to dealing with him. "So, you don't *really* know where she was before today?"

His question fills the room, along with a thousand other unspoken ones.

Raven pulls her lip under her teeth and shakes her head. "No." Her eyes meet mine. "The last postcard I got was from Charleston a few months ago."

Months?

Shifting his weight, Killian scowls deeper, his brow furrowing as if he's trying to process all this information just as I am. "A lot can happen in a few months..."

And a year, apparently.

Killian issues a frustrated growl, shoving his hands into his hair again. "None of this makes any fucking sense. Why would she come back to McBride Mountain and not tell anyone?"

I suck in a long, slow breath, that same question battering my brain.

Even if I wasn't in Charleston. Even if I had moved on to somewhere else. Even if whatever happened with Killian kept me from wanting to see him, I would have driven straight to Raven's the moment I pulled into town. "I wouldn't have..."

Raven seems to understand exactly what I'm saying, tears brimming in her emerald eyes as she squeezes my hand. "When are you getting out of here? When can I bring you home?"

"Tomorrow, but—"

Killian moves again, towering over Raven, who is half his size at best—David and Goliath going head to head again in a battle I can sense in the air. "She's not going to your place."

His tone offers no room for argument.

Raven gapes up at him. "Excuse me?"

He thrusts an outstretched finger toward the door. "That

doctor isn't going to get me to leave her bedside, and there's no way in Hell she's not coming home with me."

KILLIAN

Raven glares at me from where she sits beside Willow, clutching her hand possessively when it should be *me* doing it.

The woman who has been a thorn in my side since basically the day she was born appears to want to continue that placement—and fester in the wound she created by not telling me where or how to find Willow over the last year.

So many arguments.

So many times I tried desperately to get *any* information about how to find Willow.

Only to get nowhere because of Raven.

Her pink lips that have spewed so many horrible things about me and everyone else in McBride Mountain on her little website twist at me, her jaw tightening. "She *broke up* with you, Killian. She *left* you. She's *not* going back to your place."

Fucking hell.

Raven isn't wrong about what went down—or the fact that Willow's leaving me was completely warranted. But rage boils in my blood at the thought of letting her out of my sight again. It reignites from the simmering fury that's been there since the moment I found Willow in that cold water and pulled her from it.

Even now, cataloging her injuries mentally and seeing them marring her still-too-pale skin makes me want to punch through a fucking wall, to burn down the world until I find whoever's responsible for this—

Except it's *me.*

That fight...

Willow had every reason to leave and believe what she told Raven—that she didn't have a future with me on the mountain anymore. She had every reason to want to stay away. But coming back and ending up in the river like that, so far into the remote area of the mountains that even Connor, Liam, and I rarely venture there, doesn't make any sense.

And seeing her with Raven confirms for me that something else is happening beneath the surface of how things appear.

Even if she wants nothing to do with me and didn't want to see my face again, she wouldn't have returned without going straight to Raven. She would have run to her best friend the moment she crossed past the "Welcome to McBride Mountain" sign.

Which means there's something bigger going on here.

Something that could be very dangerous.

Especially to the woman sitting in that hospital bed.

That means I *won't* cave about bringing Willow home with me.

Not a fucking chance.

Not when we don't know anything.

Not when she doesn't have her memory.

Not when she's so vulnerable.

Not when—since the moment I saw her face in that river— my heart started beating again for the first time in a fucking year.

I won't let her out of my sight again until I know she's safe and I've unraveled this mystery.

Unless that's what she wants...

I tear my focus from Raven and redirect it to the woman in question, who watches us with wide gray eyes, one with a bandage above it where the skin over her eyebrow was split open and had to be stitched closed.

"Willow, I won't force you to do anything you don't want to" —I swallow the emotion clogging my throat at having to even ask her this—"but would you rather come home with me tomorrow or go to Raven's?"

The mere thought that she might not trust me, might not want to come to the home we shared, is enough to make me hold my breath in anticipation of her response.

All the agony I've suffered the past year, knowing I lost the greatest thing in my life because of what I did, rushes over me, washing away the relief of having her back. Because I could lose her again just as quickly.

She could say no.

She could want to go with Raven.

Some subconscious part of her might still hate me and want to stay away.

Her uncertain eyes shift to her best friend and then return to me, searching mine, though I don't know what she's looking for because I don't even know what's there.

Anger.

Fear.

Full-on hysteria.

Everything happened so fast.

This morning, I woke up thinking I was going out with Connor and Liam to fell a goddamn tree, but instead, I found the woman I thought I would spend the rest of my life with, the woman who left me and shattered my heart a year ago, practically dead in the fucking water.

And now she can't even tell me how she got there or explain any of it.

"Please, Honeybee..."

There's only one woman on this planet I would get on my knees and beg for, and it's *this* one.

If I have to drop to this shitty linoleum in front of Raven, knowing full well it will end up on her gossip page tomorrow, I would still do it.

And using that nickname for her might have been playing dirty, but when it comes to her, I'm willing to do anything.

Willow looks at Raven and squeezes her hand, giving her a soft smile that pulls at her split lip. "I...I want to go *home*."

The way she says the word finally allows me to draw air into my lungs again.

She means the cabin.

Our home.

The place we shared that's been so cold and empty since she left it.

Raven's gaze softens until her glare flicks to me. "Are you sure? You left him for a reason..."

I flinch at that, squeezing my eyes closed, rocking back on my feet slightly at the blow. But when I reopen them, Willow isn't looking at me with any sort of mistrust or anger.

There's a soft yearning there.

Because she doesn't remember the fight or what I said.

Willow gives me a smile that tugs at my heart in a way nothing else ever could. "Killian would never hurt me. Not in a million years. I need to go home. I need to go where I feel safe."

Fuck.

I've spent a year wanting her back, wanting to hear words just like that, but now, I can't even enjoy them. Not when she can't remember and would despise me if she could.

Raven appears torn between arguing and caving. "And that's with him?"

Willow nods, wincing slightly at the movement in a way that makes me want to climb into that bed and pull her into my arms. And I would, if I weren't afraid of hurting her—and of the doctor actually calling security to try to physically remove me.

Not that they could.

But it would cause Willow undue stress to witness their vain attempt.

"If you're sure." Raven leans in and kisses Willow on the cheek, then rises to her feet. "Do you need me to bring you anything?"

She glances at me, and I run a hand through my hair, rubbing at the back of my neck. "She took most of her stuff with her. I only have a few things. She'll need the basics— clothes, toiletries..."

Raven offers a nod. "I'll drop it off at your place tonight."

"I won't be there."

Her annoyance hardens her gaze. "Then I'll leave it with Liam."

I nod my agreement, not about to get into *another* argument with her by mentioning she could also leave it with Connor just as easily. Knowing the animosity between those two, there's no question about why she didn't mention that possibility.

Willow gives her a smile, and a single tear trails down her cheek. "Thank you."

"You don't have to thank me, hon, just get better. I'm so glad you're home."

Raven leans down and hugs Willow again, more gently this time, then turns and slips from the room, letting the door close behind her and leaving me alone with Willow for the first time since I pulled her from that river.

Those first few minutes flash through my head...

Before Connor and Liam heard my screams and came rushing from the woods to see what had happened...

When I had her laid out along the shore, searching her for injuries and trying to get her to wake up.

I don't think I breathed during those moments.

I don't think I did anything but pray.

And someone heard me...

She's lying in this bed.

She's *here*.

She's *okay*.

Mostly.

But I can see that she's really *not*.

Even after a year apart, I can still read her.

And she's terrified and lost right now.

I slowly lower myself into the chair beside her bed again and take her hand in mine.

So small.

So soft.

So cold compared to my own.

I bring it to my lips and brush them across the back of it, inhaling that scent that's all Willow that somehow still clings to her after everything that's happened today. Sweet honey and lavender. "How are you doing?"

The tears flow down her cheeks now, over the bruise on the left, the scratch across the right, to where her bottom lip is split near the corner.

Each injury painful to even look at.

She shakes her head. "I don't know. How should I be?"

A little strangled sob slips from her mouth, and I squeeze her hand when all I really want to do is pull her into my arms and hold her tightly.

"I'm so sorry." I stare at our entwined fingers, including the one that *should* be wearing my ring. The ring she left sitting on the nightstand beside the bed we shared when she cleared out and left me and McBride Mountain behind. "I wish there was something I could do. Anything."

Literally anything.

I would give every penny I have, my own life, to save her even one more minute of the suffering she's going through right now. To alleviate the pain I see in her eyes. To wipe away those tears permanently.

"It's not your fault." She releases another sob. "I don't think..."

Because she doesn't *know*.

And I can't tell her.

Not now.

Not when she's like this.

Not when it would break her even more.

I release a heavy sigh, filled with a year's worth of regret. But she doesn't need my apology right now when she doesn't even know what went down between us.

What she needs is reassurance.

"Your memory will come back eventually, and you'll be able to tell us where you've been, what you've been doing, and what happened to you. How you ended up back on the McBride Mountain and in the river."

Her bottom lip quivers. "What if...what if I can't?"

Fuck.

Those words do more damage than any axe ever could, splintering me wide open as tears start to form in my own eyes.

I lean forward and kiss away the one trickling down her cheek. "Then *I'm* going to find out what happened to you, and I'm going to make things right. I promise."

"Don't make promises you can't keep, Killian."

That blade cuts into me again, slashing deeper.

If she only knew what she said really meant...

How I've utterly failed to do just that, and it sent her running from me.

I need her to remember where she's been and what happened to her, but I dread the day the memory of our fight returns.

Because once she knows what I said to lose her, it will change everything, and I will lose my second chance with the woman who still holds my heart.

3

KILLIAN

The narrow, winding gravel road up the mountain to the McBride homestead takes every bit of concentration to maneuver, yet I can't seem to keep my eyes on *it* instead of *her.*

Willow sleeps in the passenger seat, her temple resting against the window in exactly the same position she's been in since almost the moment we left the hospital—even after she insisted she wasn't tired as I helped her climb up into the truck.

I knew she was lying.

Twelve months may have passed, but that time can't erase the hours, days, weeks, months, and years I spent learning this woman.

Her desires.

Her wants.

Her needs.

And right now, she needs sleep.

Time to heal, like the doctor said.

I glance over at her every few minutes to check on her.

Every time we go over a bump, I wince, knowing it probably hurts her, but she barely moves or reacts to the very rugged road that was never designed to be comfortable for anyone going up it.

She's so exhausted from her ordeal that the pain it must be causing her to get jostled on this shitty road doesn't even register—or maybe it's just the pain meds the doctor gave her that are keeping her asleep through the two-plus hour drive.

Of course, Willow didn't want to take them. Tried to say she was fine, even though I saw every twinge, every wince, every cringe as she struggled to get out of bed and dressed, even with the help of the nurse. But knowing we'd be coming up here, how long it would take, and how difficult a drive it is, I'm relieved I finally got her to relent.

I couldn't bear to see her in any more pain than she's already suffered.

Because of me...

The closer we draw to the turnoff to the property, the heavier the guilt weighs down on me and the stronger the anxiety ripples beneath my skin.

For the past year, I've prayed she would return. That I'd have an opportunity to apologize. That I might get a chance to beg for her forgiveness and receive at least that, even if she could never forget what I said or take me back.

It's all I've wanted.

The *only* thing I've wanted for so damn long that it was basically all I thought about.

Having her *back.*

But not like this.

Never like this.

Seeing her in so much pain, so confused, so frustrated, makes my body vibrate with a barely contained rage.

At anyone else who may have had a hand in this.

At myself.

At the fact that we have nothing to go on.

Sheriff Briggs didn't find anything near the river during his initial cursory search after we found her, and since Willow still doesn't remember, his talk with her this morning before we left the hospital didn't offer any helpful details.

Which means I need to get out there.

As much as I don't want to leave her—even for a moment—I know this mountain better than anyone.

If there's something to find, Connor, Liam, and I will find it.

Just like I found her.

The truck rolls over another bump in the dirt road, jostling the cab. Willow shifts restlessly in her sleep, her soft brow furrowing, eyes scrunching closed, and I reach over and rest my hand on hers atop her thigh, twining my fingers through her much smaller ones.

She instantly relaxes, releasing an almost relieved sigh.

Fuck.

My heart stutters, skipping a beat with the knowledge that I still have that effect on her. After all this time and everything that happened between us, I can still calm her nerves and quell her anxiety. I can be the balm she needs to soothe whatever pain she feels and the hero to chase away the demons in her dreams.

But it's only because she doesn't remember.

It's only because—to her—everything's still great between us.

She still thinks things are perfect because they were that night after the Memorial Day Festival last year...

The next day changed everything.

The next day is what got us *here*.

As we reach the turnoff for our land, I reluctantly tug my hand away to turn the wheel and pull through the narrow archway of trees that lead up onto the mountain, to the homestead that's been in the McBride family for nearly two hundred and fifty years.

It takes almost fifteen minutes for the forest to finally open up to reveal the large clearing holding my cabin, the main barn, my workshop, Willow's workspace, and the rest of the smaller outbuildings, along with the livestock pens.

Sitting on the site of the original cabin that occupied this space, this one, almost a hundred and fifty years old, and has housed generations of McBrides, was *our* home.

Where *we* lived.

Where we were so happy.

I could have built something bigger and more modern, the way Connor and Liam have deeper onto the property to have their own spaces, but there was always something about this old place—the history, knowing my ancestors hand-hewed all the logs and built it with their bare hands.

Leaving it would be nearly impossible for me.

And Willow understood that.

She understood *me*.

If only I could have trusted that...

Instead of parking the truck in the safety of the barn, where it would be protected from the storms that like to pop up in the afternoons this time of year, I pull up in front of the small, one-story structure held together by chinking, pride, and the sheer will of the men who built it.

It's more important to make things easier for Willow than to keep this truck dry, and being closer means less of a walk for her—which seems wise, given her condition.

As soon as I put it into park and turn it off, Willow jerks awake, her hands flying out around her. Startled, she presses her palm to her chest, as if she can't catch her breath.

"We're home."

Her head whips in my direction, and her sleep-hazed eyes

meet mine, a relieved exhale rushing from her lungs. "Did I fall asleep?"

I nod. "The whole way."

She rubs her eyes, yawning so hard it makes *me* wince, afraid she'll split open the healing cut on her lip. "I'm so sorry. I'm just—"

"You don't have anything to apologize for, Honeybee. You're exhausted. Stay there, I'll help you out."

I climb from the truck, agitated even more than I was a few seconds ago.

The old Willow would have argued.

She would have insisted she could do it on her own because she *could*.

The woman I've been in love with for what feels like my entire life has always been so fiercely independent. Even up here, which isn't necessarily true of all the women on McBride Mountain. Some men here still have a very antiquated idea of what a woman's role should be—keeping the house and raising the children...and that's about it.

But not me.

Not after seeing the way Mom stepped up after Dad died.

I may have only been five, but watching her take over McBride Timber, adopt Connor and Liam as a single mom, and become the matriarch of the mountain in her own right demonstrated how strong and resilient people say "the weaker sex" really is.

Willow is no different.

At least, she wasn't.

Through all her mother's issues with alcohol and addiction, Willow found safety here with us, but she never once asked for help or admitted she needed it.

She's too proud.

Too fucking strong.

When this was her home with me, she never hesitated to

help with anything on the homestead: caring for the animals, handling the chores so they could get done quicker, even setting up her own organic candle-making operation that became so popular with the locals and the tourists before she left that she couldn't keep up with demand.

And she never once asked for anything from me except to assist in building her workshop—though, that was more of me insisting when I caught her trying to lay out where she was planning to pour a concrete slab and realized what she was up to.

It still stands there—filled with all her honey harvesting and candle-making materials but somehow empty because she hasn't been here.

A reminder of what could have been, what should have been, if I hadn't been such a fucking idiot.

So, having to help her—not because it's the gentlemanly thing to do but because she *needs* it—doesn't sit right.

I tug open her door and reach in to assist her out of the lifted truck. She clenches her jaw and winces, pressing her right hand against the left side of her ribcage as she steps down.

My hand on her hip steadies her. "You okay?"

With gritted teeth that suggest she's anything but, she nods. "Yeah."

Broken ribs are truly awful.

Every little movement can irritate them.

I can't even imagine how uncomfortable she must be from that alone. Not to mention all the bruises that cover her body and the scrapes and cuts in various places caused by the jagged rocks and sticks in the river that abused her on her way down it.

It makes me want to go find each and every one and obliterate them with my fucking axe for what they did to her—inanimate objects or not.

I loop my arm around her waist carefully, kick the truck

door closed behind us, and ease her up the two steps to the front porch of the cabin.

She stares up at it, a wistful look in her steely eyes. "It feels like I was just here yesterday."

In so many ways, it does.

I can still physically *feel* the pain of that argument. I can *see* the look in her eyes that told me it was over before I stormed out of the cabin. It might as well have happened for *me* yesterday, too, the same way Willow's mind makes her feel like it did.

Fighting my desire to drop to my knees and beg her never to leave again, I give her a tight smile. "I wish you had been; then maybe none of this would have happened."

I wouldn't have walked away.

I would have stayed.

I would have pleaded and done whatever was necessary to make her *stay*.

Before Willow can question me any further about our argument, I turn the knob and urge her inside in front of me, closing the door behind us.

She steps in on unsteady feet, my hand still at her hip, keeping her secure. Her eyes scan the interior of the cabin, from the kitchen with the small table that seats four to the right, and over to the stone fireplace, leather couch facing it, and the old recliner to the side, then to the bookcases that line the far left wall that I haven't touched since she left.

She glances at me, brows raised. "You haven't changed anything."

I offer a shrug. "I liked it how it was."

The thought of changing anything, erasing any of the memories she and I shared here, was too painful for me.

I'd rather have them.

I'd rather let them haunt me because at least I'd have her in some form, even if it was as a ghost.

She steps in farther, slipping from my hold, wandering to

the couch, and resting her hands along the plush leather back. Her gaze remains locked on the fireplace and the space in front of it where we spent so much time—sitting, talking, reading, fucking...

The silence that fills the space between us makes me shift uneasily on my feet.

It was never like this before.

Tense.

It was always just *easy.*

Before that day...

I clear my throat, needing to break the tension that starts to feel suffocating. "Raven will be here soon."

She peers over her shoulder at me but doesn't say anything.

"Liam brought over the bag of clothes and other things she dropped off. They're in the bathroom."

Willow finally seems to snap out of whatever haze she's in. "Oh. Tell him thank you."

I give her a tight smile. "I will. You need to rest, but I thought maybe you might like to take a bath first."

Her eyes brighten, her lips curling slightly into the first genuine joy I've seen on her face since she woke up. "You remembered..."

I can't fight the grin that pulls at my own mouth. "How could I forget?"

Almost every single night for five damn years, she sank into that tub with bubbles practically overflowing. And the nights that I would climb in with her are some of my favorite memories, and the most painful ones because they were when we were at our happiest.

Before I fucked everything up beyond repair.

The look Willow is giving me tells me she's remembering exactly the same thing I am—without the pain of the year-long absence of it.

I tear my eyes from hers and glance toward the bathroom. "I

checked with the doctor and confirmed it's fine, as long as we don't get your stitches wet, and I still have some of your bubble baths under the sink. I'll go run it for you."

Then get the fuck out of here as soon as Raven arrives.

Not only will imagining Willow in there be far too much for me to bear, but I need to be boots on the ground looking for any explanation for the madness we've found ourselves in the center of.

There are still enough hours of daylight to meet Tony and hike up to the river where I found her, to search more than he was able to himself with the minimal resources of our tiny sheriff's department.

I start to walk past her, but she reaches out and grabs my wrist, stopping my advance.

Her small, warm fingers curl tightly around me, and every fucking nerve in my body flares to life at the simple contact. "Thank you."

My gut twists. "Please stop doing that."

Her brow furrows, pulling at the cut above her eye. "Doing what?"

Looking at me like I'm a man who deserves to be looked at that way.

Looking at me like I'm a man who didn't destroy you.

Looking at me like I'm the only one you want.

"Thanking me."

Her lips part slightly, and a surprised half-breath floats from them. "You saved my life—"

That familiar anger I've felt since I found her flares in my blood again. "I didn't. Not really. Because if you hadn't left, you wouldn't be in this position. Whatever got you back here, whatever put you in that river, it never would have happened if I hadn't destroyed everything we had."

Her gaze softens. "What *did* happen, Killian? I've tried, but I just..." Her hand tightens on my wrist, and that same little electrical charge that I've always felt when our bodies connect surges through me. "I can't remember."

"Maybe it's because you don't want to. I sure as hell wish I could forget it."

An agony far worse than anything she's suffered physically flashes across her steely gaze. "You want to forget me?"

Fuck.

"God no..." I tug out of her hold, rubbing my hands over my beard. "That's the last thing I want." Holding her gaze while I say this feels like falling down a hole I won't ever be able to claw my way out of. "I've spent every day since you've been gone thinking about you and wishing I could take it back."

Tears pool in her eyes. "But you're not going to tell me what happened?"

I clench my jaw, fighting the desire to just say, "no," like I want to. "Later. When you're feeling better."

I stalk to the bathroom, knowing full well that's a conversation I will put off as long as possible.

Forever, if I had my way.

I have her back.

It may not be how I wanted it, but it's a second chance.

An opportunity to fix things.

And maybe, just maybe, save what I lost.

WILLOW

The sound of the running water draws me toward the bathroom even though Killian's tense parting words should act as a warning to stay away and give him some space.

I've never been particularly good at that.

It's one of the reasons he and I ended up together in the first place.

People always gave him a wide berth, hoping to avoid being snapped at. He always preferred to spend his time alone —in the woods with his axe. Felling trees was his outlet for the tension he always seemed to carry with him, the weight that seemed to rest on his shoulders, even when we were younger.

But *I* was never scared of Killian McBride.

And for some reason, he never barked at me the way he did others.

Maybe it was because I hung around the property so much when I was younger and saw him grow into the man he became. Because I knew that Connie could never raise a son who didn't have a good heart, despite what he might portray to the outside world.

I slowly pad toward the familiar scent of my favorite lavender and honey bubble bath and find Killian sitting on the edge of the huge cast-iron tub, running his hand through the water to encourage the bubbles to build higher—just the way I like them.

He remembered.

It shouldn't matter so much, but the way my heart skips a beat when his eyes move from the tub up to mine tells me that whatever happened in the past year hasn't changed the way I feel about this man one bit.

Even if I can't remember it, my heart remembers *him*.

I step in cautiously, unsure how to even approach this man when I used to so easily run into his arms. Run my fingers through his hair. Trail them across his rippling muscles and inked skin.

He rises to his feet, wiping his hand on a towel as he assesses me. His eyes move over my face—from the bruise on my cheek to the bandage over my eyebrow. Then his gaze dips to my torso, zeroing in on my ribs.

Killian shifts uneasily, rubbing a hand on the back of his

neck as he glances away. "Can you...uh...get undressed by yourself?"

Almost as if in response, my ribs throb, and the thought of trying to unbutton this shirt, get it off my arms, and then bend down to remove the sweatpants I came home from the hospital in is enough to make me wince. I could barely tolerate it with the assistance of the nurse at the hospital. Alone, there's no way the pain won't be unbearable, even with the meds Killian made sure I took before the drive home.

His lips twist into a scowl. "That's what I thought..."

He steps up to me, keeping his gaze locked with mine as he slowly drags his fingers over the top button of my shirt, popping it free. My breath hitches, and he goes absolutely stock still. His hands hover over the next one, then he clears his throat and resumes making his way down the row until the material splits, exposing my breasts in the bra Raven brought me—along with all the bruises and scratches covering my torso.

His jaw tenses.

A muscle there tics wildly, matching the tempo of my racing heart.

His hands tremble as he carefully brushes the fabric over my shoulders and down my arms, tugging it free from one side, then the other. It flutters to the floor, along with any ability I might have had to appear unaffected by this.

My knees shake as hard as his hands do.

Killian's fingertips slowly graze the waistband of my sweatpants, but he keeps his eyes locked on mine, never once looking down—giving me that little bit of privacy, even if he's seen me more naked than this thousands of times.

The last time he undressed me, it was fast and frantic, and he had me bent over the back of the couch, pounding into me without reservation or restraint within sixty seconds of us walking through that door.

This man is different.

Whatever happened between us has left him unsure—something Killian McBride has *never* been a day in his life.

He draws in a slow breath, as if it's a struggle for him to suck in air with the tension permeating it, and it reminds me that I've been holding mine. I follow his lead, inhaling long, slow, and deliberate breaths, which only succeeds in making my ribs ache even more.

There is no way I would have been able to get out of these clothes and into that inviting hot water without excruciating pain if I had attempted it on my own.

Killian always knew what I needed and gave it to me.

And it seems that hasn't changed.

But it did.

Because I left him...

Yet, he's still here. Doing *this*. For me.

After sleeping at my bedside all night in an uncomfortable plastic hospital chair, refusing to move to the more comfortable one in the corner. Wanting to be near in case I woke and needed him.

He slips around my side, running his rough palm across my stomach and hip. His warm breath flutters the hair on my neck as he settles behind me. "Can you do your bra and panties yourself?"

I try to reach back for the clasp that one of the lovely nurses assisted me with before we left the hospital, but that simple movement tugs at my damaged ribs, making me hiss.

Killian's hand quickly wraps around my wrist, holding my arm steady, preventing me from trying further. "I'll get it."

My breath catches at the gentleness with which he holds me for a second too long before releasing my wrist and unclasping the bra.

I let it slide from my arms and onto the bathroom floor.

His hands shift back to my waist, fingers tenderly caressing the bruises and marred skin around the waistband of my sweat-pants and underwear. "Reaching and bending down to get these off would be agony…"

So is this.

I've never mastered the way my body responds to Killian, but today, it seems even more out of control. As if every fiber of my being knows I haven't experienced it in a year and craves his touch the way my lungs do oxygen.

A shiver races along my spine, and Killian slides his fingers under the elastic waistband of my pants, along with the thin fabric of the underwear beneath, and draws them down my legs, his warm breath floating over my bare skin.

Goosebumps pebble.

My knees tremble.

He urges me to step free, then tosses the sweats and panties onto the pile of clothes on the floor, leaving me completely and utterly exposed.

Killian stays at my back, but I don't miss the way his breath hitches.

Only when I glance up at the mirror and meet his gaze in the reflection, it isn't purely the normal heat there when he looks at me. All I see is anger clouding his eyes, making the normally bright blue darken like a wild sea. Conflict rages there, churning violently as he holds me steady with his arm around me and with his gaze.

A moment passes.

Another.

Until he finally slides his arm free and grips my elbow, urging me toward the tub filled with bubbles about to overflow —exactly how I like it.

With Killian to lean on, I manage to swing one leg over the edge and then the other. I sink into the hot water with a satis-fied groan as Killian releases his grip on my arm. Instead of backing away and slipping out of the bathroom, he slowly lowers himself to his knees at the head of the tub.

I peer over my shoulder at him. "What are you doing?"

He reaches to the ledge beside the tub and grabs a bottle of shampoo from it, giving me a half-grin. "You need to wash your hair to feel clean and comfortable, and you aren't doing it on your own without causing yourself unnecessary discomfort and potentially getting your stitches wet."

Tears immediately well in my eyes, emotion clogging my throat. I have to turn away quickly before he sees me completely fall apart.

This is the Killian I know.

The one I remember.

Kind.

Thoughtful.

Caring.

Always dropping to his knees to give me everything and anything I ever wanted or needed—even when I didn't ask for it.

I don't know a version of this man who would do something that would make me *leave* like that.

My hot tears hit the water.

Hopefully, the steam rising from the surface will conceal them enough that he won't notice. But knowing him, he will, no matter how hard I might try to hide them.

He does me the great kindness of not mentioning it as he grabs a cup from beside the sink. "Tilt your head back."

I do as he asks, closing my eyes and letting it fall toward him.

Hot water cascades over my hair, shoulders, and into the tub. He repeats the process until my thick locks are thoroughly soaked, and my tears are mostly gone.

Silence lingers in the small space, the sole sound him lathering the shampoo in his large hands before he sinks his fingers into my hair and starts massaging my skull as he works it in.

"Oh, God..."

The moan slips from my lips before I can bite it back, and he immediately stills.

"Shit. I'm sorry. Did I hurt you? I know you hit your head. I wasn't thinking. I—"

"No!" I reach up, not even caring about the stab in my side with the movement, so I can wrap my hand around his wrist. "Keep going. I'm fine. It just...feels so good. The hot water and your hands..."

Killian was right—soaking in the near-scalding bath was exactly what I needed to ease all the aches and pains that were bordering on unbearable by the time we got up the mountain.

Slowly, his hands return to gentler movements, working in the shampoo.

All the tight muscles and bruised parts of me relax into the weightlessness of the water. Knowing he's washing away the last remnants of that river and anything else that might have clung to my hair helps me take what feels like my first truly deep breath since the moment I woke in that hospital.

He urges my head back gently into the water to wash it, then resumes the same treatment with the conditioner, gliding his fingers through my hair to work out any snarls without tugging too hard.

Like it always has, those bubbles and the soft scent of honey and lavender help soothe more than merely my battered body.

It helps clear my head.

At least, somewhat.

That massive black hole still fills the space the last year should in my memory, but I'm slowly able to process everything that's happened since Killian found me in the river.

All the conversations with the doctor, the sheriff, Raven, and Killian...

And one thing has become abundantly clear—I need *answers*.

Not more questions, which is all anyone seems to have right now.

But where the hell am I going to get them?

Killian rinses the conditioner from my hair, threading his fingers through the smooth strands in a rhythm that causes a low hum of contentment in my chest.

Almost instantly, he stops.

His hands slide away, and I sense him retreating from the tub. "I'll leave you to enjoy your bath."

My eyes snap open in time to catch him tossing a towel onto the rack, his shoulders tense, jaw locked tight.

He pauses for merely a second at the jamb but doesn't look back. "I hope it helps."

With that, he closes the door with a deafening *click*.

It somehow feels like he was closing the door on something else—whatever this electricity still sizzling between us is, the feelings I can't pretend to ignore when—for me—they were alive and well only a few days ago.

None of this makes any sense.

And finding the answers just may destroy the one person I've ever loved in this world.

4

KILLIAN

"Are we really not going to talk about it?"

Liam's question cuts through the peaceful silence of the forest—previously broken by our own footsteps through the brush—and I scowl at him as he walks next to me along the western bank of the river.

"Talk about what?"

He snorts and gives me an incredulous look, his green eyes narrowing the same way Mom's used to when she was waiting for us to crack. When she *knew* there was something we were hiding, something weighing on us, and it was only a matter of time before we had to get it off our chest. "I don't know, the fact that your ex-fiancée showed up half-drowned in the fucking river and is now at your place?"

Fucking hell.

Leave it to Liam not to know when to let something go—or not bring it up in the first damn place.

"There's nothing to talk about..."

Absolutely nothing.

Not a fucking thing.

Certainly not the way my hands still tremble from touching her.

Not the way her scent still lives in my lungs and every breath.

Definitely not the way my heart finally started beating again the moment I saw her, even in that broken condition.

If I breathe a word of what I'm feeling, it will unleash a tidal wave I won't be able to stop, and Willow has already almost drowned once.

I won't put her through that again.

Sheriff Briggs and Connor motion to us from the other side of the river, indicating that they still haven't found anything, so we keep moving, just like we have been for the last three hours, searching the banks, the rocks along the shore, the trees and branches that hang out into the rushing waters, and as far into the woods as we can go with the limited daylight we have left, trying to cover as much ground as possible.

Liam stares at me instead of focusing on the ground in front of him that he's supposed to be searching. "Really? Nothing?"

There isn't any point in trying to avoid his inquisition.

Not when Liam is a true *master* at getting under someone's skin and making them open up, whether they want to or not.

Even as a child, when he would follow Connor and me around the mountain, trying to do everything his big brothers could, he never stopped talking.

Never stopped questioning.

Because he always cared about everything and everyone so deeply that he needed to know what made things tick.

"Look, Liam, I don't know what you want me to say."

His coppery brows rise. "How about that this situation is fucked up? Or that you don't know what the fuck is happening? Or that you're confused? I don't know." He throws up his hands, one clutching his axe, just like mine is. "*Anything, something,* because this not talking is really weird, Kill."

"When have you ever known me to be a chatterbox?"

He releases an exasperated sigh. "That's not the point. You have to have *some* feelings about this." We keep walking, scanning the ground, the river, anywhere there might be a sign of where Willow could have come from or how she ended up in the water. "I saw the way you looked at her yesterday when you found her...and you didn't leave the goddamn hospital at all."

"Should I have?"

The thought of leaving her, of walking away like I did that morning she left me, never even crossed my mind as an option.

Liam sighs. "I'm not saying that."

"Then what are you saying?"

He shifts his axe to his other hand, twirling it absently as we continue our way along the river. "Well, that it's a little complicated, isn't it?"

Understatement of the fucking century.

"Yes. It is."

Liam looks to the other bank where Sheriff Briggs and Connor continue to scour—though, nothing has given us any clue up to this point. "She really doesn't remember that you guys broke up?"

The annoyance and anxiety building in my body finally reaches the boiling point.

I pause and turn to face him, waiting for him to stop before I let myself go. "Are you *trying* to piss me off? Because you're succeeding."

He holds up his hands again. "No. Just trying to get you to open up a little bit, bro, because all the tension you're holding onto? It looks like you're about to snap."

Snap.

That's a much better analogy for what I'm feeling like—a

rubber band pulled taut and then stretched even further until it finally lets go.

"I might."

He offers me a genuinely concerned grimace. "I don't want you to snap at *her* because you can't process all your feelings. Isn't that what got you into this position in the first place?"

"Fuck." My shoulders slump. "You're an asshole, Liam."

I never should have told him what happened between us. Never should have told anyone. But a few too many beers and a broken heart did me in when it came to the man standing in front of me.

He always was the easiest to open up to, the easiest to talk to, unlike Connor, who's always been emotionally shut down since the moment he came to live with us at age two.

Though, I think most people would say I'm that way, too.

At least, I am *now*.

It was always so easy with Willow.

To be around her.

To love her.

Then why did you let her go?

"How about we stop talking about my love life and just concentrate on figuring out what the fuck happened to Willow?"

Because that's all that's important right now.

Addressing the consequences of my fuck-up might be painful, but my suffering is nothing compared to what Willow endured.

Liam sighs, glancing up at the building cloud-cover. "Fair enough. For now. But don't think I'm going to let this go forever. It's not healthy, you know—not talking about things..."

"Yeah, yeah, yeah."

I bump my shoulder against his as I walk past, pushing northwest along the river, searching for what would be the most obvious and easiest path. "She was barefoot."

When I pulled her from the river, she wasn't wearing any shoes or socks. The current could have pulled them from her feet, but given the state of them—the scrapes and cuts—it was as clear to me as it was to the hospital staff that she was making her way through the woods without them.

Running from something?

Or someone?

Liam nods, pressing his lips together into a firm line as he scans the water's edge. "I know."

I turn the other way, toward the dense woods, surveying every inch of the ground. "She would have looked for the path of least resistance..."

Willow isn't familiar with this part of the mountain.

No one is.

But she's spent her entire life in the area and enough time in the remote woods with me to know how to travel through dense foliage without getting hurt.

My gaze catches what appears to be a game trail cutting between two trees at the edge of the forest. "I found her, what, a mile downriver?"

"Yeah." Liam moves closer. "But that doesn't mean it's where she went in."

It could have happened closer to here, the current bringing her downstream until she got caught up on that tree.

"I'm going to follow the game trail. You stay along the shore and search for any signs of where she might have gone in."

He nods. "I'll meet up with you."

I set off down the game trail, nothing more than a beaten path created by deer and other wildlife on their way to the river, looking for any obvious human activity that could have been Willow.

Several yards down the trail, I draw to a stop.

A bare footprint exactly the size of Willow's feet in the soft ground makes me grit my teeth.

It rained two nights ago, which means she was cold and wet before she ever made it to the river.

Tightening my grip on my axe, I push forward until a flash of color up ahead draws my attention, the same color of red as the tattered shirt she was wearing when I pulled her from the water.

She definitely came this way...

"Liam!"

He can't have gone far, and up here, sound carries.

It takes a few minutes before I hear his thundering footsteps, and he appears behind me. As soon as I know he can see the same thing I do, I reach out and tug the tiny scrap of cloth off the branch.

"She came this way." Motioning toward the footprint and holding up the scrap, I incline my head back toward the river. "Signal Tony and Connor to get to this side of the river. We need to be searching over here."

"On it."

Liam bolts off the way he came to alert Sheriff Briggs and Connor that we need them over here as I move farther down the game trail, my heart climbing into my throat.

What the fuck was she doing up here?

I picture the McBride Mountain area on the map.

The town near the base.

Our homestead halfway up, about as far as is livable comfortably, where the land can be flattened at least somewhat for crops and structures. Any farther up and the slope gets too steep to really build anything, and the trees and temperatures start to change.

No one lives up here.

There's nothing but wildlife.

And, apparently, the love of my life.

But *why*?

The question has rattled around my brain so much in the

last two days, and I still don't have an answer. Not one logical explanation for why she would have been back on the mountain, let alone all the way up here.

None of it makes any sense.

Yet, she *was here.*

I push farther along the game trail, finding additional signs that this was definitely how she came through the woods. Another bare footprint pressed into the soft earth, broken sticks and branches, as if she were stumbling and grabbing them for support or they snagged her along the way.

It must have been incredibly painful.

This hike is no joke, even with the proper gear.

Doing it barefoot...

"Christ..."

I always knew she was tough.

Determined.

This proves it.

I continue to follow the trail until it finally opens into a small clearing.

All there is up here is vast green grasses and wildflowers surrounded by towering trees—with no sign of which direction she came from.

"Shit."

My grip on my axe tightens, the familiar feel of it in my hand doing nothing to calm me like it normally might.

Fuck! Fuck! Fuck! Fuck!

I turn and slam it into the nearest trunk, driving the blade in hard and deep, working out some of the rage and growing frustration on the poor, unsuspecting pine.

Each swing sends woodchips flying.

Over and over.

I slam the head into the tree as if *it* were responsible for all this instead of myself.

Only the sounds of hurried footsteps and voices floating down the trail finally stop my violent outburst.

Liam, Connor, and Sheriff Briggs emerge from the treeline, all eyes immediately landing on me and the gouge I made in the trunk beside me.

Liam raises a brow. "You good?"

My chest heaves from the exertion. All my muscles twitch. My palm flexes around the axe handle, tightening my grip. "Fucking wonderful."

Connor steps out farther into the meadow and turns, scanning three-sixty around us. "Where the hell was she coming from?"

I shake my head. "I don't know. There's nothing up here."

Tony nods—if anyone knows the mountain as well as us, it's him. It's literally his *job* to know it and all the people on it. "There isn't."

But there has to be...

Otherwise, there wouldn't have been any reason for Willow to *be* this high on the mountain.

Running the back of my hand across my sweaty forehead, I scan the clearing. "Can we get dogs up here?"

Dark brows rise under his sheriff's hat. "Why?"

I pull the scrap of fabric from my pocket and hold it up. "Maybe they can scent her. Follow the trail deeper into the mountain, figure out where the hell she came from."

He scrubs his hand along his stubbled cheek. "I can try to get a few up from Asheville, but—"

"Do it."

"It could be expensive."

I tighten my hand around the axe again. "You think I give a fuck about the money? You know I'm good for it."

One thing the McBrides are never short of is money—though, we don't let it control our lives. Don't go around spending it the way the tourists do when they come through town, as if their entire worth somehow depends on what car they drive, what phone they have in their hand, and what other material possessions they can accumulate.

That's not what this has ever been about. The money we've made through McBride Timber over the generations came from the place of wanting to help everyone find a place to call home, the way we did here. Establishing a town, a safe place. It was born of necessity, not of greed, and we got lucky to have expanded over the generations to supply lumber to a large swath of the East Coast.

"I'll pay for whatever we need, just get someone up here. You still have the clothes she was wearing when she was brought into the hospital?"

Sheriff Briggs nods. "In the evidence locker."

"And we have this." I hold up the scrap. "It wasn't in the water, so that should help, right?"

"I guess." He offers a slight shrug, rubbing his jaw again. "But I'll be honest, I don't know a whole lot about using the search dogs."

"Me, neither. But at least it's a clue."

Liam looks to the sky. "Sun's about to go down, and we've got at least five hours to get back to the homestead."

"Fuck."

I scan the meadow, seeing the true vastness of what we're facing as the sun starts to settle behind the treetops, drawing long shadows. Frustration twists deep in my gut, and I turn to meet Connor's gaze.

Without even having to say it, I know he understands.

He inclines his head. "You want to stay."

I nod. "Just another hour or so. Check the perimeter of the meadow to see if she came across it from another direction and left any visible evidence."

Sheriff Briggs gives me an annoyed look. "I don't want to have to send rescue up here for you, too."

I scowl at Tony. "I've headed every search and rescue team you've ever had on the mountain, so I hope you're fucking joking."

He snorts and holds up his hands. "I know better than to joke with someone who doesn't have a sense of humor, Killian."

Liam inclines his head to Sheriff Briggs. "I'll head back with him so he can make the calls tonight and hopefully get the dogs up tomorrow. You two be careful."

"Always."

For anyone else, staying up here in the dark would be a surefire way to get lost—or worse. But for Connor and me, it won't be a problem.

What will be is turning away and returning without answers.

Tony and Liam set off using the game trail to backtrack to the river, while I join Connor deeper into the meadow.

He watches me out of the corner of his eye, a question there.

"Not you, too."

One of his black brows rises. "What?"

"Liam was giving me shit on the way up here...about Willow being back."

"And?"

Asshole.

I scowl at him. "I don't need it from you, too."

He shrugs, trying to appear innocent—a look that absolutely does not fit him. "I didn't say a word."

"You don't have to. I know that look."

His deep caramel eyes widen. "What look?"

"That judgy one you always get."

"I'm not judgy."

"Yeah, you are." I point my axe at him. "And you're judging me right now."

"I'm not." A long sigh falls from his lips, and he holds my

gaze for a moment. "I'm just worried about you. I know what that woman did to you by leaving, and I don't want to see you go through that again. It's been a year, and you haven't recovered."

I growl low at him, taking a threatening step in his direction. "You idiot. It isn't about what she did to me by leaving; it's what I did to make her leave in the fucking first place."

Turning, I walk away from him before he can continue to argue with me about it. Before he can push me to do something stupid like deck him—or worse.

He's always taken my side.

On everything.

Including the argument that broke us up.

But he's wrong in that, and I've known it since the day it happened.

I was just too proud to admit it to anyone but myself.

Until I saw her in that water.

***

WILLOW

Lightning flickers across the jet-black sky, the crack of thunder rolling so intensely behind it that it shakes the cabin and rattles the glass in front of me.

It's the kind of storm that always sets every nerve in my body on edge and makes my stomach turn. The kind that sent me running into Killian's arms for comfort and safety, even though I knew the power and awesomeness of the squall wouldn't touch us in this place.

But I don't move back from the window.

Not even as the sky rips open and the driving rain pounds the glass.

"Shouldn't they be back by now?" I chew on my bottom lip,

then wince at the bite of pain where it's split, releasing it as I glance at Raven, where she sits in front of the fireplace, enjoying the fire we started when the temperature started to drop as the front moved in. "It's really coming down out there."

The maelstrom swirls outside, the wind buffeting the cabin, rain pounding the roof and soaking the ground.

Raven offers me a tight smile that doesn't quite reach her eyes—well aware of my storm phobia and how uneasy I would be regardless of the current situation. "I'm sure they'll get back soon. The McBride brothers know better than to be out on the mountain this late, this dark, in this kind of weather. The storm probably just slowed them down a bit."

That fact alone makes the small dinner I managed to eat threaten to come back up.

"Come sit down." Raven waves me over and pats the spot beside her on the couch. "You're going to drive yourself crazy standing there, watching for them."

It isn't *them.*

It's *him.*

As much as Connor and Liam became like *my* brothers over the years, they aren't the ones I've spent every moment thinking about since I got out of that bathtub and was very—embarrassingly so—disappointed to see my best friend in the kitchen making me tea instead of Killian.

Thunder rolls again, making me shudder.

I release a heavy sigh, then wander over and plop down next to her, wincing at the pain in my side and pressing my hand against it. "Shit, I have to stop doing that."

Raven offers a soft smile. "You keep forgetting that it actually hurts."

"I know..."

And as the day has worn on, the aches and pains have started to return with a vengeance.

Those blissful moments of relief the hot bath offered wore

off the longer we waited for Killian. The fact that I refuse to take any more pain medication doesn't help. But I can't bring myself to.

I hate the way it dulls my senses, makes my brain even foggier than it already is.

It's bad enough not having any memory of the last year of my life, but not being able to think clearly isn't something I would be able to handle right now. As it is, I feel like I'm teetering on a tightrope over McBride Falls, and all it would take is one swift wind to blow me right off it and back into that water that almost took my life.

Raven hands me one of the books from the stack next to her on the end table. "Here. Something to do instead of worry."

I glance down at the title.

Wuthering Heights.

I snort. "You think reading about the tragedy of Heathcliff and Catherine is going to make me feel any better?"

Her laugh floats through the air. "Better than this one."

She shows me the front of the book she's had open for the last couple of hours.

Romeo and Juliet.

I roll my eyes. "Not much better."

She grins and returns her attention to the book. I watch her for a few minutes, reclining in the corner of the couch with her feet up and eyes on the pages in front of her.

Rain continues to pelt the roof and windows, blown by the blustering wind.

Raven may appear relaxed, but being in this cabin has always put her on edge—because of the man who lives here. "Did you two argue again when you got here?"

She sputters slightly, then clears her throat. "Umm. I plead the fifth."

Which means they did.

"Why do you two always have to be at each other's throats?"

Even in school, as children, they were always going at it, trying to one-up the other when verbally sparring. And when Killian and I evolved from friends to something more, it only seemed to get worse.

Killian's protectiveness of the mountain and everyone on it never jibed with Raven's desire to expose details of people's private lives she considers important enough to broadcast. For her, it's news. Information essential for everyone to know. But to him, it's personal attacks.

She smirks. "You have no idea. It's ten times worse since you left."

My hand tightens on the book, and I swallow through the nerves. "How come?"

Anything to do with why I left?

An annoyed sigh slips from her lips as she closes the book, clearly seeing through my attempt to get the deets from her since she won't spill, and neither will Killian. "Because he was pissed I wouldn't tell him where you were. And..." Raven glances up at me, looking sheepish. "I may have published an article on the site—well, a few of them—about what a dick he is and how people should avoid him."

"You what?"

It's no wonder his animosity toward her rolled off him in waves at the hospital.

Raven holds up her hands defensively. "I don't know exactly what happened between you two, so don't even ask, but whatever it was, it was bad enough that you left. I lost my best friend for a year, so he isn't my favorite person on the fucking mountain."

The unsteadiness in her normally level voice bears the weight of the time I've been gone and how much she's missed me.

"I guess that's fair..." I fiddle with the book, turning it over in my hands. "I really didn't tell you what happened between us?"

I've been dreading asking her all day, putting it off while we sat and chatted over tea and dinner, and she caught me up on what she's been doing the last year since I left.

But I have to know what she does—what Killian clearly doesn't want to tell me.

Raven's gaze softens, and she shakes her head. "You really didn't. You called me up here, and you were in tears. I asked where Killian was and what happened. You said he stormed out and that you were leaving and going to Asheville. I thought you meant just a trip, but then you started packing everything...and I couldn't convince you otherwise." She releases a little sardonic snort. "Believe me, I tried, begged you to stay with me, to give yourself some space from whatever happened between the two of you, but it was like you had made up your mind and there was nothing I could do or say to get you to stay."

I tighten my grip on the book, her words settling over me heavily. "So, it must have been really bad..."

Because I tell Raven everything.

Always have.

She knew the moment I started looking at Killian and seeing him as more than the gruff, grumpy eldest McBride brother. She knew the first time he kissed me. She knew when I finally fell—hard. She knew when he proposed and that I said yes without even thinking about it.

Yet, I wouldn't or couldn't tell her whatever happened with the man who was my life and future that would make me leave him and my home forever.

"Yeah." She nods, her blond hair spilling over her shoulder. "I'd say so. I'm worried about you being up here with him. Whatever happened wasn't good, and you don't have any memory of it, which means that, to you, it feels like the two of you are together, that everything is hunky dory, and it sure as hell isn't. I don't know what that man did to you."

I scowl at her. "You've known Killian your entire life. Do you honestly think he would ever do anything to hurt me?"

She shakes her head. "Of course not, but he's a man."

Thunder cracks again, almost as if in warning.

"What's that supposed to mean?"

She snorts. "Oh, come on. You know damn well how inconsiderate they can be. How oblivious they can be to how what they say and do can affect us. You need to be recovering. You need peace and quiet. You need to be comfortable—"

"I am. Here. This is my home."

"It *was*."

As per usual, Raven isn't wrong.

Her blunt advice and ability to cut through the bullshit to the heart of the matter are precisely why she's such a good friend—and why she pisses so many people off so damn easily.

"Killian and I obviously have a lot to talk about. A lot to work through. And maybe this will give us the opportunity to do that."

She sighs. "That's what I'm worried about, hon. I don't want you to get hurt again after everything you've been through."

"We don't know what I've been through."

"You're right, we don't, but—"

Heavy footsteps sound on the porch, and my heart leaps into my throat. The front door swings open, letting in a howl of wind and driving rain—and the man I've been waiting for.

Killian steps into the cabin, drenched from head to foot, his long blond hair darkened and plastered to his head and shoulders, T-shirt clinging to his sculpted muscles. His eyes sweep over the room and find mine, anchoring me in place with the intensity of the shimmering blue before I manage to break free from the hold.

I leap to my feet and race across the room, throwing my

arms around him, not even caring that he's soaked—and now I am, too—ignoring the screaming objection from my ribs and several other parts of my sore body.

He stiffens, his entire body rigid, a wet, immovable wall of uncertainty for a second before he finally relaxes.

His strong arms wrap around me and tug me up against him tighter. The movement pulls at my sore ribs, but I don't mind the pain. Not right now. He buries his face along my neck, inhaling deeply as a tremble wracks him. Matching the way my own body shakes, even though I'm in his solid hold and can both *feel* and *see* that he's all right.

"I was so worried..."

Far more than I should have been.

Killian can take care of himself.

He's always been the one watching out for his brothers—and just about everyone else on the mountain.

But I can't stop shaking, and the tears flow before I can stop them.

Thunder rumbles outside, and his large, warm palm settles onto my back, holding me steady, grounding me in the way only he ever could. "I'm okay, Honeybee. Everyone's okay."

I want to believe his words, but the weight of everything that's happened in the last few days finally crushes down on me, making it impossible not to feel like I'm crumbling. "Y-you scared the sh-shit out of me."

Killian sucks in a sharp breath and releases it slowly, one hand sliding up into my hair to cup my head and hold it against his chest while the other presses into my lower back. "I'm sorry."

He brushes his lips across my temple, and I lean into it, relishing the feeling of being back in his powerful arms.

Like I've missed it...

My memories may tell me it's only been a few days since we

were together, but deep down, somewhere, I know it's been a year.

I've longed for this.

I've needed this.

I've needed him.

He finally pulls back slightly and takes my face in his palms. Those familiar rough callouses scrape over my sensitive skin, wiping away my tears as he locks his turbulent gaze with mine. "I'm okay, really. Just wet."

The rain continues to pound on the roof and ping off the windows, a reminder of the deluge he hiked through to get home. In the pitch black of night that rivals the darkness I floated in before I woke.

Raven clears her throat behind us, and he tears his eyes from mine and looks over my shoulder at her. I follow his gaze, one of his hands sliding away from my cheek.

She climbs to her feet, tossing the book onto the couch. "Well, I guess I'm not needed here anymore."

The annoyance in her tone makes me cringe.

Raven stalks to the kitchen, snags her purse off the counter, and stomps toward where we still stand. She pulls on her shoes and assesses us for a moment before huffing and moving toward the door.

I meet her concerned gaze. "Drive safe..."

Stopping beside us, she narrows her eyes at me. "Be careful." Then she glowers at Killian. "Keep your fucking hands off her."

The heat of his hand still at my cheek seems to grow with her warning, but Killian doesn't release his grip on my face as she tugs open the door and stalks out into the rain to make her way down the mountain to her place in town above Claire's Bakery.

Killian kicks the door closed behind him without even

looking at it, keeping his eyes on me the entire time—as if Raven wasn't even here. The same intense focus I recognize and have always craved that makes heat flood my core and warms me, despite my now-wet clothes.

His gaze dips to my lips, and I shiver in anticipation.

But instead of kissing me, Killian clears his throat and steps back from me, putting enough space between us for the reality of the situation to slam into me.

You just threw *yourself at him...*

"I'm sorry. I didn't think about..."

Jesus.

He isn't my fiancé anymore.

He isn't my anything.

It might feel that way to me, but I *left* him.

"Don't apologize for worrying about me." The corners of his lips curl slightly. "I love that you did, but you don't have to. You know this mountain is my home. I know it like the back of my hand. Nothing would happen to me out there."

"This coming from the man constantly reminding everyone how dangerous McBride Mountain can be."

"That's true." He nods slowly. "But it doesn't apply to me."

"Oh, really?"

His lips quirk. "Really."

The steady *drip, drip, drip* of water falling off his clothes and body and onto the wood floor finally drags my focus down to the puddle forming around us. "You need to get out of these clothes."

He nods and retreats another step, and I instantly miss the warmth, shivering as the cold, wet front of my clothes cling to me. I retreat, giving him some space, and he bends down to untie his muddy, wet boots, peel them off, and set them onto the plastic mat beside the door.

The hands that just held my face so gently reach for the

hem of his shirt. He tugs it up over his head, revealing the body I memorized. Rippling muscles, peaks and valleys of abs that descend to the belt of his jeans. Tattoos covering almost every inch of exposed skin—even a few new ones.

Christ.

If anything, he's only gotten more beautiful in the time I've been gone.

He tosses his shirt on top of his boots, keeping the wet clothing on the protective plastic as much as he can, but it still drips from his jeans onto the floorboards. "I don't want to walk through the house like this."

"Oh."

I quickly turn around and close my eyes, giving him some privacy, even though I know his naked body as well as I know my own.

The sound of his button popping and zipper lowering stiffens my spine, and heat coils low in my belly at the sound of his jeans hitting the pile near the door.

"I'm going to go take a shower, then I'll be back."

I nod, squeezing my eyes closed as tightly as I can so I don't unintentionally—or intentionally—ogle him. But as he brushes past, that scent of fresh rain and cut wood and mountain that's all Killian washes over me, and I can't help it.

My eyes flicker open, and I see him gloriously naked from the back.

Firm ass.

Massive, muscled thighs working as he stalks down the hallway toward the bathroom.

Tattoos ripple across his back and arms, but as he reaches the bathroom, he glances over his shoulder at me.

I quickly close my eyes again—but not before I catch his half smirk—and heat floods my cheeks.

The door clicks closed, and I release a heavy breath, the

dull throb between my legs reminding me that I almost died, and I may have broken up with the man for some unknown reason, but it certainly doesn't mean that I'm not still attracted to him.

In my head, it was yesterday that he had me bent over that couch, pounding into me after the Memorial Day Festival—because I lied and didn't want to tell *everyone* my last memory was of getting railed rather than of the festival itself. But after that, going to sleep that night, it's blank...

What went so wrong?

I can't imagine anything that would explain what Raven says happened—that I would rush to pack my things and leave the mountain for *good*. That would make me stay away for an entire *year* without ever coming back to see her or try to clear the air with Killian...

Releasing a heavy sigh, I make my way to the couch and settle into the corner while the sound of the shower running in the bathroom and the rain pounding against the roof and the glass fill the silence, punctuated by the occasional pop and crack of the wood in the fireplace.

Flames leap and dance, casting long shadows across the pine floors.

I stare into the fire, racking my brain, diving deep into my memories, trying to make more come to the surface.

Pitch black greets me.

My temples throb.

But I keep going.

Pushing.

Trying to delve deeper.

A flicker of another flame.

Different from this one.

Smaller.

My heart pounds.

My skin heats, growing clammy—

"Willow, are you all right?"

I jerk at the sound of Killian's voice as he steps into the living room.

His brow furrows deeply. "Shit, did I scare you?"

Shaking my head, I wrap my arms around myself. "No, I..."

"I'm sorry." He takes a tentative step toward me, running a towel over his still-wet hair in a pair of gray sweatpants and a white T-shirt that clings to his pecs. "Where were you?"

"I don't know." I clamp my eyes shut, trying to bring back the memory. "I was just looking at the fire and then..."

Releasing a frustrated sigh, I let my lids flutter open.

"Did you remember something?" Killian stops in front of me, squatting to my level. His eyes search mine, filled with concern and something else. "Willow..."

"I...it was another fire." I shake my head. "Not here, but I don't know where it was...or when...or why it would come to me now."

Killian reaches out and pulls my hand into his. "It'll come back."

And what if it doesn't?

What if not knowing is my new reality?

"Did you find anything today?"

His jaw tightens, a muscle there ticcing wildly as he stares into my eyes, holding my gaze. "Yes. Part of a trail you must have run down before you got to the river."

"Trail? From where?"

"We don't know. It's an animal trail, nothing humans should have been on, but I found your bare footprints and a scrap of the T-shirt you were in. Tony is going to call to get dogs in from Asheville to try to pick up the scent, figure out where you came from."

Tears pool in my eyes and begin to trickle down my cheeks. "Why would I have been up there?"

"I don't know."

I shake my head, my body trembling as that flicker of flame flashes through my head again, somehow sending an icy chill through me, despite the warmth it should bring to mind.

"Neither do I, and that's what scares the fuck out of me."

5

KILLIAN

Lightning sends another vibrant flash through the living room, and thunder cracks immediately after it and *close*, shaking the cabin and violently rattling the glass in the window frames.

On and on and on...

The storm continues to rage, just as it has for the last several hours since I came home—almost as if the mountain sky is as agitated as I am tonight and can't settle into any semblance of quiet calm.

Lying in the recliner, I alternate between watching the light show and the fire, the flames crackling and popping, filling the silence save for the sounds of the storm.

It should be peaceful.

But each clap of thunder and flash of light that fill the cabin merely seem to enforce the fact that I won't be able to find peace again until I figure out what happened to Willow.

With so little to go on, I'm not holding out much hope of getting a restful night's sleep anytime soon.

How can I when her world has been upended and I can see her spiraling?

How can I when I'm spiraling just as badly?

The bedroom door opening issues a low creak that echoes through the high A-frame cabin ceiling almost as loudly as the following crack of thunder.

I freeze, my right arm tucked beneath my head, and watch the hallway, waiting for her to appear with my heart in my throat.

Having her back here, in this space we once shared, where we planned our future together, without knowing what's going on in her head, has left me more rattled than I care to admit even to myself.

On edge.

Vibrating with an intense, writhing tension only made worse by how badly I still want this woman I can't have right now...or maybe ever again.

Willow comes out slowly, her arms wrapped around herself, emphasizing how thin and frail she's become since I last saw her in this cabin a year ago.

The flickering light from the fire illuminates her features as she steps farther into the room, and even with the red scrapes and cuts, the bruise on her cheek, and the bandage covering the stitches over her eye, the woman still takes my breath away.

Every bit as beautiful as the last time I saw her before she disappeared.

Her gray eyes meet mine, and the hesitation I see there makes my stomach twist violently.

My Honeybee has never hesitated when it came to me before. Always so confident. So sure of what she wanted. Never afraid of my moods or reputation.

But not tonight.

Tonight she's shaken.

I hold her gaze, waiting for what feels like an eternity for her to say something. "Can't sleep?"

She shakes her head and approaches slowly. Another flash of lightning brightly illuminates one side of her face, and her flinch at the sharp crack of thunder contorts it violently.

Of course...

"The storm keeping you awake?"

Willow shakes her head again and makes it to within a few feet of me. "I mean...yes. But it's more than that." Her lips twist as she considers her words, as if she has to choose them carefully around me. "It's just...weird."

"What is?"

She glances behind her toward the bedroom. "Sleeping in that bed without you..."

Fuck.

I squeeze my eyes closed, letting her words wash over me and sear my skin like acid.

The pain real.

Powerful.

Intensity I couldn't have predicted I would have felt.

They're precisely what I would have killed to hear any time over the last twelve months, if she had come back to me.

Because I know that feeling all too well—how wrong it is to be in there without her.

That's why, half the time since she's been gone, I've ended up falling asleep in exactly this position out here rather than torture myself with the bed I shared with this woman.

Where I still smell her, despite replacing the sheets.

Where I still feel her beside me, despite her side of the bed being long cold.

Where I still hear the echoes of her gasps and moans as I slid into her.

And for her, we shared it only days ago.

In her mind, I should *still* be there, holding her through this kind of storm that has always unnerved her so much, despite spending her entire life on this mountain.

The sheer agony of the reality in which we find ourselves threatens to tear me apart, but I force my eyes open to find her watching me carefully, as if she's not sure if she should turn around and retreat to safety or if *I'm* the harbor she's seeking from the storm her life has become.

God, I wish it were the latter...

"You need to get some sleep, Honeybee."

My voice wavers slightly with the issued warning, but it doesn't deter her.

She continues her approach and settles on the arm of the chair, though somewhat cautiously, still holding trepidation in her gray gaze. Her slender fingers, covered in cuts and scratches, trail over the warm, worn dark leather. "I can't believe you still have this thing."

I can't fight my smirk. "Did you really think I'd ever get rid of it if *you* couldn't make me?"

The corners of her lips curl up slightly. "I guess not, but I understand why you still have it. I was always half-joking when I suggested it was too ugly to stay in the cabin."

And I always knew that because she knew what it meant to me.

"It's the only thing I really remember about my dad, other than him teaching me to swing an axe."

Willow gives me a sad smile that darkens her eyes and pulls at that cut on her lip. "Sometimes I wish I had known mine, but I feel like maybe I didn't miss out on all that much." Her throat works hard, like she's fighting emotion she doesn't want to let out. "Mostly because of your mom."

A knife slices through my heart at the agony in her voice for the woman who took her under her wing and gave her what her own mother couldn't. The one who stepped up to raise

Connor, Liam, and me all alone in this wild place and always kept her doors open to anyone who needed help.

Against my better judgment, I let my left hand drift down to cover hers on the chair arm. "She loved you, you know? Like you were one of her own."

She nods, tears pooling in her eyes. "She did have a habit of taking in strays."

"You weren't a stray."

A little laugh fills the night, followed by another crack of thunder that makes Willow shudder. "Yeah, I was."

"You had your mom..."

She snorts. "Yeah, and she was Mother of the Year."

"She had her issues, no one can deny that, but she loved you and did the best she could. My mom just"—I shrug—"was there to help pick up the pieces and fill in where your mom couldn't step up."

"She did that for a lot of people."

"I know."

More than I could possibly count.

Everyone in McBride Mountain knew they could come to her for anything they needed—money, a warm place to sleep, advice on life or love, or just a warm, motherly hug.

Willow assesses me in the firelight, her gaze roaming over my face before it connects with mine again. "You got that from her."

"Got what?"

Her eyes soften into a look I longed for so much over the last year. "Your big heart."

The way she says the words rips said organ in two.

If I had as big a heart as she believed, none of this would have happened.

She never would have left.

I may spend most of my free time helping people on the mountain and in town, donating my skills and money where it's needed across this vast swath of North Carolina wilderness, but none of it could ever be enough penance or wash away the sin of what I did to Willow that day she drove away from me and this place.

No one has been able to get close.

Nothing has brought me joy since the moment she left.

I would give up anything and everything I own if I could have had her back this entire time, if I could retract those words I said to her. And the way she's staring at me, I know I won't be able to put off having the conversation about it much longer.

She deserves to know the truth about that as much as she does about what happened to her.

Outside the window, lightning streaks across the sky again, and another rumble of thunder rolls through the house.

Willow shudders again, this time clenching her eyes.

"You never did like the storms up here..."

She reopens her eyes and gives me a tight smile. "No. Something about them, the volatile power they possess, it just scares me."

I trail my fingers over hers lightly, wanting so badly to twine them together. "Why?"

Her slender shoulders rise and fall, then she presses her free hand against her ribs with a wince. "I guess because it's not something we can control, and I don't like feeling out of it."

"Like you do right now?"

She swings her legs toward me more fully, a tear trickling down her cheek. "Yes. How can I when everything is so *fucked up*?"

The way her voice breaks on those final words makes my hands itch to pull her into my arms, but I can't do that.

I don't trust myself.

And I won't ever put her in that position.

Another sharp crack of thunder makes her wince even harder than tweaking her ribs did, and something clicks in my head. Something that's been bouncing around in the back of my mind since I first saw her bare footprints pressed into the damp ground.

"There was a storm that night, before I found you in the river..."

She nods, swiping at her tears. "I know." Her voice cracks. "And I wouldn't have gone out in it if I had any other choice."

Whatever happened up there, it wasn't good.

It sent her running outside during a storm she was terrified of, with no shoes, improper clothing...

Pure wrath floods my veins, heating my blood and solidifying my resolve.

Tears continue to fall faster, and I finally can't take it anymore.

I glide my hand up around her hip and tug her toward me gently, giving her every opportunity to resist or say no. But she accepts the invitation and slides into my lap, resting her head to the crook of my neck and snuggling tightly against me in the spot she fits so perfectly.

This.

This is what I've been craving, what I've been needing.

All of her pressed up along all of me.

The familiar feel of her in my arms again, her scent that somehow hasn't changed over the last year invading my breath and giving me life in a way oxygen can't.

All of it envelops me in the knowledge that she's safe, as long as I have her here.

With me.

A little sigh falls from her lips, fluttering warmth against my neck. "What do you think happened to me?"

It's a question I had hoped she wouldn't ask because I don't want to have to give her the answer—the one that's been forming, even though I haven't dared to voice it.

Because I don't want it to be true.

It opens up a world of horrific possibilities.

Yet, I know Connor and Liam must be thinking the same thing, as well as Sheriff Briggs, given everything we've discovered.

But saying it to her when she's still so shaken and fragile feels like dealing another blow she might not survive.

I run my hand gently down her back, and she relaxes into me, resting her hand over my heart, directly on top of the tattoo of McBride Mountain. "I think you left McBride Mountain with every intention of never returning because of me."

She stiffens in my arms but doesn't say anything as I continue to trail my fingers up and down her spine.

"I think, at some point, something happened that made you come back. Some reason you didn't tell Raven about. Maybe because you hadn't planned to stay very long, or maybe to surprise her. And I think something happened that brought you up to that secluded part of the mountain, but..." I swallow the lump in my throat that attempts to prevent me from speaking what might be the ultimate truth. "I don't think it was by your own choice."

Willow tenses again and lifts her head, the tears really flowing now, leaving streaks down her pale cheeks. "That's what I'm afraid of. What if...what if someone..."

I pull my hand from her back and cradle her face in my palm, brushing away the tears. "If there was someone else involved in this, if anyone laid a hand on you, I swear to fucking God, I'll slice him apart with my axe while he's still alive so he can watch it happen and then rip his throat out with my bare hands."

WILLOW

The absolute menacing threat in his words and the sincerity of it swimming in his blue eyes should terrify me. It should make me wary of the type of violence Killian is capable of. I should fear it and him. But the promise settles over me like a warm blanket, comforting me the same way being in his arms does.

Even if it shouldn't.

Given how things apparently ended, this is the last place I should be now—in the arms of the man who drove me away in the first place.

After five years together and a lifetime of friendship before that, whatever it was had to have been bad.

Maybe unforgivable.

I left the only home I've ever known, the town and the mountain, my best friend, and the man I loved, without telling *anyone* why. It was too painful for me to even reveal to Raven. And it drove me away from my life.

Yet, since the moment I woke up in that hospital, he's been nothing but the man I always knew him to be.

Protective.

Loyal.

Kind.

Caring.

Sweet.

Moody, certainly...

And gruff.

Even violently rough around the edges, but it's impossible not to be growing up the way he and his brothers did up here on the mountain.

Fighting to maintain their family legacy after his father died when he was so young, his mother stepped into a role she never intended to take. She had to run McBride Timber, be a mother to a little boy, then she took in Connor and Liam, and also mothered the entire mountain.

He had to be tough. He had to step up, too.

They all took care of each other, and now, he's doing the same for me, even though I left him. So, I can't feel threatened by this man, despite what Raven might think. Despite the potential warning signs screaming that I wouldn't have left if I hadn't needed to. I can't be afraid when he says things like that to me because that type of anger and intended violence would never be directed at me.

His promise to eviscerate anyone who may have had a hand in what happened to me isn't a threat.

It's hope.

The kind I *need* right now.

I relax even more against him, his strength and tight hold on me grounding me in a way no one and nothing else ever could. "You really think you can find out what happened?"

Please, God, let him succeed.

I want to believe his promise, pray that it's true, but it's hard to know if that's possible when I still can't remember anything.

We have nothing to go on.

Absolutely nothing.

He brushes my hair away from my face and tucks it behind my ear, cradling my other cheek in his rough palm. "I do. We already found part of your trail today. And with the dogs Tony is getting, we should be able to follow it farther into the mountain. We should be able to find answers."

That same thought that has plagued me since the hospital returns, the one I haven't voiced because it's too painful to consider.

What if I don't want the answers?

What if I want to pretend that none of this ever happened and go back to my life with this man?

The life I had before, the one that feels like it was yesterday instead of a year ago, was happy. I could so easily fall right back into that life, that routine, the love I shared with this man.

Why can't I just do that?

Almost as if he can read what I'm thinking simply by scanning my face with his fathomless blue eyes, Killian gives me a sad smile. "I know how scared you are, terrified of what we might find. I am, too, but we have to know what happened. Where you've been. Tony already got all the postmarks from the stuff you sent Raven over the last year, and he's checking into it, trying to track where you've been and locate any former residences, friends, credit card usage, anything. We're going to solve this mystery, Honeybee."

"And then what?" The question comes out before I can stop it, but it's the only thing I can think to ask because solving the past doesn't help me figure out my future. That's as murky and black as the abyss I fall into trying to look into my memories of the last year. I can't see what it looks like. "Then I go back to whatever life that was? Go back to hating you because of something I don't even remember instead of loving this life we had together here?"

His eyes shimmer as another flash of lightning illuminates the room, and he looks so torn. Like the war raging inside him rivals the one happening in the sky outside. "I wish I could tell you we could go back, but we can't."

Following thunder rattles the entire building, like even the mountain is angry with the situation.

Tears slide down my cheeks again. "Why not?"

"Because I'm not the same person I was then, and neither are you."

Wherever I've been, whatever I've been through...of course it's changed me. Once I get my memories back, I'll realize how much. But lying here with him in his dad's old leather recliner, in a position we've spent so many hours in before, with a storm raging outside that rivals the tempest currently blustering in my head, I can't imagine wanting to be anywhere else than where I am at this moment.

And I certainly can't fathom wanting to be with anyone other than the handsome, difficult, grumpy, gruff man whose calloused hands move so gently to wipe away my tears.

"You still seem like the same person, Killian."

He shakes his head. "I'm definitely not. Losing you changed me, Willow, and not for the better. I've been..." Killian glances away, focusing on the deluge outside, continuing to drag his hand up and down my spine, the same way he used to soothe me to sleep during storms all those years. "I became a man I don't like seeing in the mirror. One who's angry all the time. One who's quick to argue, quick to temper. I snap at people. I don't want to do all those things everyone expects of me anymore." He releases a long sigh, heavy with whatever burden he's been carrying since I've been gone. "It has been like I'm suddenly not in control of my emotions anymore. Like any ability I had to rein in those darker parts of me left when you did."

"You were always hotheaded..."

He finally returns his gaze to mine and grins, and the genuine affection in the act, the humor underlying it, despite how serious his words were, is enough for me to see that he really hasn't changed that much. "Yes, I was, but this is different." His rough fingertips skate over my cheek reverently, and those fierce eyes lock with mine. "I've been adrift, lost without you as my true north."

My heart shatters into a million pieces at the familiar words and the pain with which he says them. "You always said I was that."

"Because you were. You always guided me away from the places my mind wanted to go to somewhere brighter, happier, to you as my home."

A small sob of frustration slips from my lips. "Then how did we get lost?"

"Do you really want to have that conversation right now?"

Looking down at him with his long blond hair spread out behind him on the dark leather, his soft, warm gaze locked on me, powerful arms wrapped around me, his firm body supporting me, his heart thumping beneath my palm, there's only one answer I can give him. "No."

Right now, I don't know if I can handle the truth of whatever broke us up.

Living in denial for a few more hours won't be the end of the world, but not being able to look at him the same way might be.

I lower my head back into the crook of his neck, inhaling the scent that's all Killian—fresh mountain air, leather, and freshly cut wood—and he tightens his grip on me, squeezing me gently, careful to avoid my sore ribs as he adjusts me to be more fully on top of him.

The storm keeps raging outside. Lightning flickering across the dark room. Thunder alternates between sharp cracks close to the cabin and low rumbles that spread across the mountain. The sounds of the storm that kept me awake as much as his absence from the bed are suddenly not so scary anymore.

Not with him here holding me like this.

Slowly, I let myself start to drift toward the darkness encroaching on the edge of my vision. My eyelids grow heavy and droop until a sudden crack of thunder that sounds more like a gunshot jerks me up.

Pain sears my ribs, but it's the flash through my head of a similar sound echoing through the woods that makes my heart thunder. I gasp, pressing my hand over it, trying to catch my breath as a panic I've never felt before engulfs me.

"Willow, what is it?"

Squeezing my eyes closed, I try to analyze the image I saw

for only a split second, to figure out where it came from, what it means.

"I...don't know." The anxiety continues to rise, though, threatening to steal my ability to breathe as bands tighten across my chest. "I can't get past that darkness. It's eating all these memories, but there's something there. Something important. Something I need to remember."

Something that sounded an awful lot like a gunshot.

And for some reason, my gut is telling me, deep down, that if I don't remember, it could be catastrophic to that future I can't see.

6

WILLOW

The bell over the door at Claire's Bakery jingles again as someone strolls in off Main Street, and I jerk toward the noise, my entire body tensing.

On high alert.

Every muscle vibrates with unease, which only makes the pain in my side—and everywhere else—even worse.

"You okay?"

I glance at Raven across from me at the small marble-top table, her fingers poised over the keys on her computer keyboard, gaze narrowed on me.

Definitely not okay.

Since the moment she picked me up from the cabin this morning, I've been on edge.

Jumpy.

Flinching at every little sound.

My gut twisting anytime anyone walks into what was once my favorite spot for a cup of coffee and a pastry, which just also happens to be where Raven does most of her work, at this back table tucked into the corner since her apartment is right above us. It's the perfect location to watch the hustle and bustle of downtown McBride Mountain—and gather intel for her site.

I *should* be okay here.

It should feel like as much of a safe haven as the cabin does. *Should.*

And I don't have the heart to tell her it doesn't when she's trying so hard to make things feel "normal" and ensure I'm comfortable.

I force a smile. "Yeah..."

Raven's gaze softens. "Do you want to go home?"

Shit.

I hate how well she can read me sometimes.

Apparently, I suck at hiding my discomfort with basically *everything* right now.

But I still have to *try.*

If I don't at least make an effort to do the usual things I used to, to see if any sights or sounds trigger my memories, then I may never recover them.

I shake my head. "No. Thanks for bringing me along to your 'office' while you work."

She snorts and purses her lips, returning her focus to whatever is on her screen and typing away rapidly. "What I wouldn't give for a *real* one again."

Her disdain for the fact that Old Man Murray finally decided to close our tiny town paper three years ago still lingers even now, despite the fact that she's done *very* well for herself as a freelance journalist and with her social media page to keep everyone local up to date on the goings-on here in McBride Mountain.

I scan the large windows that give a wide view of Main Street, watching people occasionally walk past. "It's good to see town and everyone..."

And I really do mean it, despite how jumpy I am.

As much as I love the cabin and the feeling of familiar comfort it provides, without Killian there, it just isn't the same. Any tension that exists between us—given our unusual circumstances—doesn't seem to in any way affect that he still feels like safety.

Like *home*.

He still carries that protective instinct, the one that made him incredibly reluctant to leave me this morning, especially given the flash of memory I had last night and the subsequent meltdown he held me through.

But the opportunity to head out with his brothers, the sheriff, and a dog crew from Asheville means a chance at finding answers both of us so desperately need.

Something he couldn't pass up, despite his trepidation.

Raven glances up at me, like she isn't sure she believes my statement about how great it is to be here.

I take a sip of my black tea with honey and shrug. "I knew it would be a long day of doing nothing but worrying and letting my mind run off to dark places if I had stayed there."

Very dark places...

That same darkness that has overwhelmed my mind since the moment I woke.

Thick.

Inky.

Immovable.

Something about it gives me goosebumps and sends a shiver of dread down my spine each time I try to delve into it. And without Killian at the cabin, that's exactly what I would have done. Here, with Raven, I'm surrounded by familiar sights, sounds, people, and even though I'm jumpy as hell, it's better than the alternative.

I take a bite of one of Claire's famous chocolate croissants and issue a groan of approval as the buttery, rich flavors dance across my tongue. "I've missed this. They taste exactly the same."

Raven snorts and grins. "I should hope so. I think if Claire changed the recipe, there would be a town-wide revolt."

I return her smile and glance at the woman in question behind the counter, her graying hair tied up in a bun at the top of her head. She bustles behind the display case, pulling out various confections for the few people in line—Betsy O'Brien, her children who have grown shockingly since the last time I saw them, Jake Swanson and his wife, Maureen, and a man I can't quite place but know I've seen around town before.

Several sets of eyes peek over at me, but as soon as they see I'm looking, they dart their gazes back to the display case.

My stomach sinks. "People know already..."

Raven follows my line of sight, and she releases a little sigh. "This is McBride Mountain. Everybody knows everything about everyone else. You should know that."

"I do, but..." The man looks over at us again, and my skin prickles at the way he examines me. I quickly look away. "I don't even know what happened to me, and now, everyone's speculating about it."

Raven pushes her laptop away from her and leans closer to me across the table. "Look"—she glances at the people in line —"obviously the rumor mill has already started churning, which I expected it to, given the way you made your reappearance. So, you have two options. You can ignore it, or we can get ahead of it."

Ignoring it sounds amazing.

Just burying my head in the sand, pretending everything is normal, and getting back to the life I had before...all the things I can remember. The ones I can't recall don't need to control my life.

Theoretically...

But Killian said that wasn't possible last night.

And he might be right.

Raven sure is about this.

This is McBride Mountain, population 536.

There are no secrets here.

And this small town loves nothing more than to spread rumors and make their own leaps when information isn't readily available.

Like now.

"How do you recommend getting ahead of it?"

She holds my gaze, uncertainty in hers that I normally don't see there. "Let me post an article."

"You're kidding."

Her hands fly up defensively. "You would be able to have the final say about what goes into it, but I feel like the town needs to know *something* besides what the whispers are saying."

"But we don't even know what happened." I can count the number of actual *facts* on one hand. "What are we supposed to tell them?"

She offers a half shrug. "Exactly that. We don't know what happened. Maybe it would help draw out some information that we don't already have from someone who doesn't even know they have it."

"Killian said Tony is interviewing everyone he can think of and making calls."

Her head bobs, causing a strand of her blond hair to fall from the messy bun pulled up at the top of her head. "I'm sure he is, but you know there are a lot of people who don't come into town often and never leave their homesteads unless they absolutely have to." She taps her computer. "My site is how they get all their news and know about what's happening since the paper shut down. Almost everyone has conceded they need power and the internet these days, and they're willing to check the site frequently. While some people do know you're back and how Killian found you, there are going to be even more who *don't* know. Or they'll get their information from someone who doesn't have the *right* information. We can control the narrative, if you'll let me do it."

She has a point there.

I haven't been gone long enough that the way McBride Mountain works has changed. Everybody is in everybody else's business. And of course, a body found in the river would be front-page news if we still had a local newspaper.

Raven's site has become basically that, and she isn't wrong about trying to get ahead of it. It might be a way to curtail all the crazy stories people are making up...and potentially get some information we wouldn't have otherwise.

I release a heavy sigh and nod. "Okay. Let's do it."

Her brows fly up. "Really?"

Something tells me I'm going to regret this.

"Yeah."

She tugs her computer closer, and the excitement vibrating beneath her skin is enough to make her tremble in her chair. "You're sure?"

I nod again—more to convince myself than to reassure her that I'm actually one hundred percent on board with this idea. "Yes."

"Okay, well"—her fingers fly across the keys—"let me type up a quick draft and then we can discuss it, make changes, until you're comfortable. Is that okay?"

Her green eyes flick up to meet mine, and an ache forms in the center of my sternum. Like I'm looking at something I thought I'd never see again. Maybe I didn't think I would ever come back to McBride Mountain or have a chance to sit with her here like this again while I was gone.

Emotion clogs my throat, so I nod.

"And here." She slides a bag across the floor to me. "In the meantime..."

"What's this?"

"All the notes and postcards you sent me. You said you wanted to see it all. I already gave Sheriff Briggs the dates and locations to run down."

"Oh..."

That vise constricts around my chest again.

This is all that exists of the last year of my life.

Our only clues.

The sole ties I have to the life I led when I left McBride Mountain.

My hand shakes as I grab the bag, pull it up onto my lap, and empty the contents onto the tabletop.

Handwritten notes.

Postcards.

A birthday and Christmas card.

Raven gives me a half grin. "I didn't bring any of the gifts. I figured if you needed to see those, we could head up to my place before I take you to the cabin. I thought the notes might be what you were really after."

I nod, the tremble in my hand so bad that I have to pause and fist it for a few seconds before I lift a postcard from Colonial Williamsburg and flip it over, noting the postmark and the date.

October of last year, months after I left here.

My familiar scrawl fills the space.

> *Hey, Rave.*
> *Miss you. The candles are selling really well here. It may be my best setup yet. Something about this city speaks to my soul. The history is fascinating. You'd love it here. I miss you.*
> *Love, Willow.*

"That's definitely my handwriting."

Raven looks up from where she's been typing, her brow furrowing. "Why wouldn't it be?"

I chew on the inside of my lip. "I don't know. I was kind of thinking...wondering, I guess..." The thought bounces around my head, but it seems so off the wall and unfathomable that voicing it makes my mouth go dry. But Raven continues to watch me until the intensity of her stare draws the words from me. "I was wondering if I was actually the one who sent you all these things."

Her hands come off the keyboard as she rests her elbows on the table, her wide eyes searching mine. "Why would you wonder that?"

Everything Killian said last night comes rushing back. "Killian and I are starting to suspect that maybe I wasn't up there by my own choice." She doesn't immediately reject the idea, so I push on. "It stormed the night I went into the river. Why would I have willingly been out in a storm like that, running barefoot, anywhere, let alone on such a remote part of the mountain?"

Raven nods slowly, as if she's processing the idea. "I see where you're going with this."

"And if I wasn't up there by my own choice, of my own free will, then who's to say I was the one who sent all these things over the last year?"

She reaches out and clasps my hand. "But you were. *Look* at them." She rifles through the stack to find one particular note and flips it over to show me, leaning closer as a family with small children hustles past us on their way out of the shop. "You sent this one with a damn vibrator, for fuck's sake."

"What?"

"On the anniversary of the day I lost my virginity." She waggles her blond brows. "*No one* else would have known that."

Relief floods through me like a tidal wave.

She's right.

Her first time wasn't anything to get excited about—hence the vibrator—so it wasn't something she told anyone. Except me. Of course, Micah McConnell would know, but he would be the last person to remind her of his failure.

"You're right..."

I clutch the note and can't help the smile that pulls at my lips as I read the words I wrote to her.

Figured you could use this as much today as you needed it fifteen years ago. Happy Pop Your Cherry Day!

It's exactly something I would say.

I toss it back onto the pile and run my hands through my hair—more confused than ever. "So, what does any of this mean? I clearly sent you all these. I was clearly traveling, but somehow, I got back here. Why would I return without telling you or contacting *anyone*? And why would I be up where not even the McBrides go and out barefoot in a storm?"

"You haven't remembered *any*thing?"

"Only a few flashes. Something with a fire and lightning, maybe thunder or a gunshot, but I don't..." I shake my head, squeezing my eyes closed as my temples start to throb with the struggle to bring up the memories. "But everything else is just black."

A gaping, endless abyss of *nothing.*

Raven offers me a soft smile. "Maybe the boys will find something today that can offer some insight."

It's meant to be reassuring, but the hesitation in her voice tells me she shares the same concern I do—that I might *never* remember. That there might not *ever* be answers.

"I sure hope so. It's only been a few days, but there's this giant hole that I can't fill. And part of me doesn't want to because I'm afraid of what I'll find."

Her brow furrows. "Are you and Killian okay? Are you sure you don't want to come stay with me?"

I should have known she'd ask again.

With their history and how I apparently left things with Killian, it's only natural she'd be worried about me being cooped up with him in the cabin.

Sleeping in the bed we shared...

And she has no idea I woke up in his arms this morning, still snuggled up on the recliner where we fell asleep...

With his warm blue eyes watching me as my eyelids fluttered open.

"I don't know. Things are...weird."

She snorts. "I would expect so."

"To me, it feels like..."

"Like you're still together?"

I nod.

"Just be careful with him, Willow." She shakes her head. "He isn't the same person he was a year ago. And even if he was, that's the man who sent you running."

"I know."

She purses her lips, suddenly looking very serious. "He could be as dangerous to you as whatever you can't remember."

KILLIAN

"Send. Them. Back. *Out.*"

My words come out more snarled than spoken, more feral animal than human, bearing the weight of the desperation currently simmering in my veins.

Sheriff Briggs stares me down, arms crossed over his barrel chest, mimicking my posture as he takes his stand against my demand. "Killian, you know I can't do that."

I issue a low growl and step toward the man I seem to have been at odds with all day, despite the fact that we've been friends since we were in diapers. "*Yes*, you *can*." I point my axe in the direction we know Willow came from. "Send the fucking dogs back *out* there."

Tony scowls, his dark brows dropping low over even darker eyes. "They're not *my* dogs, and according to the handler, they've lost the scent. There's nothing more we can do."

It's the same bullshit he's been telling me for the last ten minutes, and hearing it again only seems to aggravate the already-festering wound our fruitless day of searching has created.

"Fuck. *That*."

He holds up a hand. "I understand you're frustrated—"

"Frustrated?"

I step away from him before I do something stupid, like take a swing. Getting into a fistfight with Tony when we were young, hormone-fueled teenagers was one thing; decking the sheriff is another.

That would end up with me in a holding cell until Judge Byrne decides to roll in—probably around 10 a.m. on Monday. Something I have no desire to experience when it would mean leaving Willow. Instead, I shove my hands through my hair and tug on the strands, struggling to get that sharp bite of pain on my scalp to somehow stop the anger and frustration boiling over into something more.

"We've been at this all day, Killian." Tony drops his hand when I retreat a few steps, offering a sympathetic tilt of his lips. "We got farther than we thought we would, but it rained that night and almost every afternoon since. We can't expect fucking miracles."

"I don't need fucking miracles." I grit my teeth and release my grip on my hair, turning away from him. "I just need some *fucking* answers."

Tony sighs. "I understand."

"Do you?"

I twist back to face him, and several sets of eyes land on our confrontation from across the meadow where we set up our base camp for the continued search.

The team from Asheville stands with the dogs halfway across the wildflower-filled field, taking care of them after they've spent the day scouring the mountainside, trying to follow what little trail seems to remain of where Willow came from.

They look exhausted. Lying on the grass, panting heavily. Enjoying treats and a bowl of water.

But their failure feels like it's my own.

"She's been gone a year, Tony." I suck in a sharp breath, fighting against the threatening sob that wants so badly to slip out. "A fucking *year*. How the hell do you think she ended up in that fucking river up *here*?"

He has the decency to look contrite. "I wish I could do more."

Wishing will get us nowhere.

"You can!"

"I can't, Killian. The dogs can only do so much. It was a long shot. We knew that, with the weather and time not on our side."

Fuck. Fuck. Fuck.

And all they got us to was the end of the game trail we already discovered with nothing for hundreds of miles and no sign of where she could have come from.

The trail ends here.

Along with any chance of finding out why she was in this spot.

Adjusting his belt, Tony removes his hat, rubs his hand across his head, then reseats it. He moves to stand closer and drops his voice slightly, probably to dispel any belief that we might be actually arguing. "You know I've had people digging into those postmarks and the information Raven gave us."

I nod.

"Well, I radioed in for an update. So far, no one's come up with anything."

"What do you mean?"

"I mean, we haven't been able to confirm that she was actually *in* any of these places. Yeah, there are postmarks and dates, but nothing else we can find. I've checked with the police in every city she was supposedly in. They don't have any records of her in any way, shape, or form. No business licenses if she was selling her candles, no W-2s if she was working for someone else and getting paid. Not even a 1099. She hasn't filed taxes in a year. She hasn't rented an apartment where they did a background check on her. No signs of her vehicle. Nothing."

The revelation settles on my shoulders, adding to the reality already weighing me down. "So...you're thinking the same thing I am."

He glances around the meadow and who's around us. "That maybe she was never *in* any of those places?"

Hearing the words from his mouth makes my stomach tighten, even though I've been wondering how it was possible for her to have spent a year away and never to have contacted me, Raven, or anyone else except via random written notes. But the sheriff confirming it somehow makes it real, makes it so much worse.

The gifts and notes could have been decoys, designed to keep Raven from looking for her...and she may never have set foot in a single one of those cities.

Connor and Liam leave their discussion with a few other members of the sheriff's department who joined the search today and cut across the clearing toward us, eyes narrowed on the conversation.

Of course, Connor already has that look, like he's ready to

intervene if he needs to—and defend *me* to the death, even against the man who is the law up here, despite the name of the mountain.

Liam just looks concerned, prepared to try to talk us down. By the time he reaches us, his reddish brows cut deeply over his green eyes. "What's going on?"

I sigh, shoving my hands through my hair again. "They're not going to send the dogs back out."

"Shit." Connor looks over to the Asheville team, who seems to be packing up, preparing to hike down the mountain. "They're done?"

As the sun starts to set, it's exactly what we should be doing, too.

We don't want to get stuck out here again like last night. But at least there's no storm heading our way this time.

Vibrant shades of orange, pink, purple, and blue streak across the sky.

I wish I could enjoy them.

But I can't.

I couldn't enjoy anything while she was gone, and now that she's back, it's almost worse.

The uncertainty.

The wondering.

The constant worry that we're missing something important.

Liam claps me on the shoulder, squeezing gently. "Head home. Go check on her. I know how worried you've been all day."

I scrub my hand over my beard. "She was terrified last night..."

He raises a brow. "The storm?"

Connor and Liam know her almost as well as I do. Which means they understand her astraphobia, and the fact that she wouldn't have been out here during a storm like that the night before we found her in the river if she'd had a choice.

I shake my head. "No. I mean, that was part of it, but she had a flash of a memory."

Tony's eyes widen. "Maybe you should have fuckin' mentioned that sometime today!"

"It wasn't anything she could pinpoint. Fire, and then a feeling, something having to do with the lightning and thunder, maybe a gunshot. She says they're just flashes, no real substance to them, but I suppose any memories are better than none." I release a heavy sigh. "Unless maybe what we suspect is true."

I look at Connor and Liam, because we've already had this conversation earlier this morning when I collected them from their cabins on our way up here.

The more we look at the facts that we do know, the more it becomes evident that Willow wasn't up here alone.

Something or someone drove her to that river.

Scanning the clearing and the diminishing daylight, I resign myself to the fact that we aren't going to get anywhere else tonight, especially with the dogs and the handler already heading out of the clearing to travel down the mountain in front of us.

"Let's start back. If we can't do anything more with the dogs tonight, I might as well see if she's had any luck remembering anything today."

Tony nods his agreement. "Is she with Raven?"

I nod. "Yeah."

Connor grumbles, already stalking toward the game trail and the way to the river, the easiest path down the mountain. "I can't believe she hasn't posted some bullshit gossipy story about her yet."

I flash a dirty look at his back. "They're best friends."

He glances over his shoulder and raises his dark brows.

"Like that would stop her? You've seen the stuff she posts about us, about anyone else on the mountain. That woman's a goddamn terror."

"I don't disagree with you. But I also don't think she'd ever intentionally hurt Willow."

Not the way I did.

She may be pushy and abrasive.

She might set Connor, me, and just about everyone else in town off with her stories.

But she's been a great friend to Willow.

The sole person who has stood by her through thick and thin her entire life.

They might as well be sisters.

Connor can hate her all he wants, but Willow needs her. That means I have to set aside my animosity toward the woman, and he needs to make an effort to do the same.

For Willow's sake.

And ultimately, that's all that matters now, giving her what *she* needs to get better, to rebuild the life she lost.

Whether answers come or not, Willow will need everyone she loves at her side, and that includes Raven.

It just might not include me anymore. Not once I'm forced to come clean with her about why she left and how badly I hurt her.

In the dark last night, wrapped in my arms, she may have wished we could pretend the last year never happened and go back to how things were before, but that can't happen.

The truth will come out eventually—on all fronts.

And it will undoubtedly mean nothing but pain for Willow.

7

KILLIAN

Raven looks up from her computer as I step into the cabin and close the door softly behind me.

My gaze immediately moves over the small space, my eyes seeking out Willow the same way the rest of my body and my heart do, but there isn't any sign of her. "Where is she?"

The feisty blonde who looks less than pleased to see me points down the hallway. "She was exhausted and went to bed hours ago."

I wince at the reproach in her voice.

Like I somehow abandoned Willow when I was really out trying to *help* her.

Just let it go.

It doesn't do any good to argue with Raven right now, not when I'm as exhausted as it sounds like Willow appears to have been. And I have to follow my own advice when it comes to the woman on my couch and do what's best for Willow, which means at least pretending to get along.

I reach down to untie my boots and toe them off as Raven closes her computer, slides it into a bag, then climbs to her feet. "How was she today?"

She releases a long sigh. "Okay, I guess? She had me take her to town."

My back stiffens as my blood runs cold. "It isn't safe."

A blond brow rises sharply at me, and Raven crosses her arms over her ample chest. Her toe starts tapping as she gives me the same how-dare-you-question-me look she always has. "You think it's safer for the two of us up here alone at your remote cabin than it is on Main Street with dozens of people around us? Most of whom have known us our entire lives."

"*Yes*." I don't mean to snap at her, but it comes out harsh all the same. "Because we don't know what the fuck happened to her, or if any of those people were involved in it."

Raven gives me an incredulous look. "You can't be serious."

I grunt and give her my back as I stalk into the kitchen, tug open the cabinet above the stove, and pull out a bottle of whiskey and a glass. If she weren't standing right there, judging me already, I'd chug it straight out of the bottle, but I don't need to give this woman any other ammunition against me.

Ignoring her glare, I pour myself a shot and down the entire thing, slamming the glass harder than I should onto the butcher block counter.

"Did you guys find something else?"

The waver in Raven's voice from behind me is what finally gets me to turn around and face her. She's one of the most stubborn, pig-headed, relentless women I've ever known, and she has never, ever, sounded so scared.

It causes a twinge in my chest that I hate to have when she's been such a pain in my ass.

She loves Willow.

She's worried about her.

"No." I shake my head. "The dogs were only able to track

her for a few more miles in the woods beyond where we got previously, and then they lost her scent. The storms over the last couple of days wiped away everything."

Raven winces. "Shit."

I lean against the counter, running my hand through my hair, and I drop my head back to stare at the ceiling—the parallel logs running nearly perfectly straight. Still supporting all the weight effortlessly, even though they've been here for so many years. All that hard work standing the test of time. For some reason, seeing it makes me angrier about the situation.

They built *this* without the help of any modern tools or equipment. They settled this area without roads or cars. The McBrides logged this mountain without the advanced equipment we have today. They made it work, and with everything at my disposal—men with boots on the ground, technology, time —I can't even figure out what the fuck happened to Willow.

"She didn't come back and go up there on her own." I drop my head to meet her gaze again. "We all know that, right?"

Raven nods. "I showed her all the stuff she sent me. She confirmed it's her handwriting. The notes *had* to have come from her."

Fuck.

I tighten my grip on the edge of the counter, hating what I'm about to say. "That doesn't mean she wrote them willingly."

"What?"

"I'm starting to think...fuck." I scrub my hands over my face, then turn around and pour myself another drink, unable to look at Raven as I say the words that have been batting around my head the entire trek down the mountain. "What if someone forced her to write those notes? What if someone sent those gifts to you to ensure you wouldn't look for her?"

"Jesus Christ. You don't think that's possible..."

I shrug, down the drink, and glance over my shoulder at her. "I don't know. I've just been trying to think of all the possibilities. And it's very weird that she never called you or insisted you come visit her. To not speak with her or physically *see* her for an entire year?"

Raven shakes her head. "No, it's not. You know how close we were. In one of the notes, she said that if she heard my voice, she'd want to come back. That definitely sounds like her."

"Maybe. But she also never contacted *me*."

Her brows fly up. "You really wonder about that? After what you did?"

I slam my palms against the counter, my earlier annoyance with this woman now switching to full-blown anger. "You don't know what I said or what I did, so stay out of it."

"I can't." She crosses her arms again defiantly. "She's my best friend."

And she's my fiancée.

The words *almost* come out of my mouth before I can stop them.

We aren't together anymore. Not like that. Maybe we won't be ever again. But last night, it sure felt like she was still going to marry me, that we were still on our way to spending the rest of our lives together as we had planned.

I clear my throat, forcing away what I want to say. "Well, I've got her now, so you can go."

Raven scowls at me. "I swear to God, Killian, if you hurt her any more than she already has been, I'll fucking kill you myself."

"I believe you."

And it's that devotion to Willow that prevents me from truly *hating* Raven, even if I might not *like* her.

She stalks away, closing the door behind her far quieter than I expect her to, given her mood.

As soon as I hear her car start up and pull away, I pour myself a much-needed third drink. The amber liquid in the glass blurs as I stare down at it, tears pooling. I squeeze my eyes closed before one falls.

You can't cry.

You have to be strong.

In control.

I suck in a long, slow breath and release it just as slowly, then down the drink and hiss at the burn before I silently make my way back to the bedroom to her.

Just like I have so many nights before…

Only on those nights, it was to delve under the sheets with her and get her to make that little whimper that always undoes me.

That won't be happening tonight.

Or any other time soon.

The door stands cracked at the end of the hall, nothing but the soft sounds of her rhythmic breathing audible in the darkness. I ease it open and find Willow curled in the center of the bed, wrapped up in the comforter. A thin sliver of moonlight from the window on the far wall reaches her, barely illuminating her face. But it's enough to see that it isn't as calm and peaceful a sleep as I hoped to find her in.

Her brow furrows.

Her eyes move frantically behind the lids.

All I want to do is climb in and hold her.

Tell her it will be okay.

Slay whatever demons chase her in her dreams.

Seeing her there in our bed, smelling her in this room again, it's all I *can* think about.

But I can't do that.

It was dangerous enough pulling her onto my lap in the chair last night. All day while conducting the search, I relived each moment of having her in my arms.

The press of her body to mine.

The scent of her invading my breath.

The feel of her soft puff of breath against my neck.

I can't allow anything else to happen.

It isn't fair to her, knowing that she would hate me if I told her the truth.

I start to pull the door closed, but her violent scream slices through the night air. Willow bolts upright in the bed, frantically lashing out at someone or something that isn't there.

"Willow?" I launch across the room, at her side in a second, pulling her into my arms. "Willow, *wake up!*"

"No, no, no!"

Her cries wrench from her throat as she punches and tries to push me away. But she's no match for my strength—or resolve.

I hold her steady with one arm wrapped around her as I take her face in the other and squeeze her chin, twisting it up toward me. *Ensuring* the first thing she will see is *me* and not whatever is chasing her in her nightmare.

"Willow, wake up. Open your eyes." I shake her gently. "Willow!"

Her eyes finally fly open along with her mouth on a surprised gasp. She frantically tries to pull from my hold before the stormy gray finally finds my gaze and holds it.

"Honeybee, I've got you."

Willow sags against me, and her sob tears through my heart as she buries her face in my chest, wrapping her arms around my neck and snuggling close.

I lean back on the headboard and tug her fully across my lap. "It was just a dream."

Instinctually, I squeeze her tightly, but she stiffens.

Shit.

Her ribs.

"I'm sorry—"

She shakes her head, her lips and body trembling. "I don't think it was a dream."

Her words freeze me in place with my hand pressed to her back, holding her close. "What do you mean?"

A hiccupped sob slips out as she struggles to speak through her hysteria. "It was too real. I've never had a dream like that. I think...I think it might have been a memory."

WILLOW

Silence fills the room for a few moments while Killian holds me as I try to gain control of my breathing and fight back the sobs that continue to wrack my body.

He gently rubs his hand up and down my spine, giving me time to process while being the rock he has *always* been to me.

Last night, he called me his compass, directing him to true north, but really, that's what he's been for *me*. Through all the turmoil in my home life, he was there. A friend. And then, he became more.

He became *this*.

After several minutes of the sound of my crying and ragged breaths, he leans back and cups my face gently, searching my eyes. "You want to tell me about it?"

I shudder.

Of course, I knew he would ask.

How could he not when we've been trying to get me to remember, praying it would happen?

There is no judgment in his gaze.

Only understanding, even though I haven't told him anything yet.

He would let me say "no" and just keep holding me if all I want to do is cry. He would give me space if that's what I asked for. He would do anything I want in this moment.

And as painful as it is, reliving the panic coursing through my system...I *want* him to know what I saw.

I swallow through the final sob, taking several deep breaths to gather the strength to tell him. "It was storming. Thunder. Lightning. I was soaked. The ground was cold under my bare feet. Rocks dug into them. Branches kept catching on my clothes and cutting my skin. I—"

So cold.

So wet.

So loud.

So dark without the moon.

I squeeze my eyes closed, simultaneously trying to force the vision of the dream to come back with clarity while not *wanting* to remember that fear I felt.

The frantic panic.

It consumed me in the memory.

A kind of all-out terror I've never experienced before, even during everything I went through with Mom, never knowing if I would find her dead or if one day she would not come home.

Nothing compares to what I felt during that dream.

What's starting to seize me again now as the flashes return.

So vivid.

I can *feel* the bite of the rocks. The scratch of the branches. Hear the crunch of the twigs under my bare feet and my own panting breaths as I race through the forest along a narrow trail.

It's so *real.*

Only Killian's firm grip on me and his familiar touch remind me I'm safe in the cabin with him. He keeps running his hand soothingly along my back, keeping me grounded. Keeping me *here* while allowing me to explore *there.*

"I was trying to run, but it was so hard..."

I fell.

Several times.

Stumbling over fallen logs I couldn't see in the near pitch black that overtook the thick trees.

But I didn't dare move out of them to where the flashes of lightning could make it easier for me to see—because it would also mean it would be easier to *be* seen.

That thought makes me clutch my chest.

It feels wrong.

Empty.

Like something's missing that should be in my hands, that should be pressed to me.

"I think I was carrying something. Something important. And then..." A sob works its way up my throat as the visions from the dream flash again. Something jerked me backward, stopping my progress. My scream. "And then someone grabbed me."

I open my eyes and find Killian watching me intently, his beautiful gaze filled with so much concern.

And *anger.*

Red.

Hot.

Fury.

His Adam's apple bobs as he tries to tamp down his rage so he doesn't scare me. Because he never directs it at me. Even when he feels like he's out of control, he can rein it in around me. Find his center. But now he trembles as if he's on the verge of losing it. "That's all you remember?"

I nod.

He presses his lips together, brows drawn low in contemplation. "It might not be a memory. There isn't anything you just described that you couldn't have picked up based on the information I've told you we've found. You might be piecing together all of that subconsciously and forming it into a dream that you are mistaking for a memory."

Even before he finishes saying the words, I'm vehemently shaking my head. "No. I don't think that's what I'm doing."

It makes sense what he's saying.

My brain is still trying to process the emotional and physical trauma of whatever I went through, and to do that, it could be grasping at the tiny pieces of evidence Killian has found and using them to create a story that might not be real.

But deep down in my gut, I *know* it is a memory.

He tucks a strand of hair behind my ear, letting his fingers linger at my temple. "How can you be so sure?"

I place my right hand over my chest again, clutching at something that isn't there—a gaping hole where something should be. "Because I can feel it *here*."

"Feel what?"

"The weight of whatever I was carrying." My voice breaks as I try to figure out a way to explain this to him when I can't even understand it myself. "I can feel it as if it were really there when I was running...and now...it's not."

All that remains is the empty, hollow feeling that matches the dark abyss my memories have disappeared into.

Killian's gaze softens, the last of his anger washing away on a wave of some tender emotion I recognize but am too afraid to act on. "I'm so sorry, Honeybee."

He tugs me up against him, burying his face in my hair, and I let myself relax into his hold, like I did last night. Just like I did for so many nights through so many years.

It feels like home.

Like where I'm supposed to be.

I'm safe.

It doesn't make any sense.

Why would I leave McBride Mountain?

Why would I leave this?

Him?

I brush my hand over his chest, feel his heart thudding

under my palm and centering me, pushing my own heartbeat back to a normal rhythm. Slowly, the panic brought on by the memory dissipates until the warmth permeating my palm replaces the knowledge that I no longer have whatever I was carrying.

My fingers brush across the neckline of his T-shirt, tracing the tattoos on the bare skin there. The ridgeline I know so well —an exact depiction of McBride Mountain with the central peak right at his throat.

His breath hitches, and he stills, his hands tightening around me gently.

Being here like this with him, back in his arms, feels so right.

This energy between us still so powerful.

So *real.*

And I know it's going to shatter the moment to tell him what I decided while he was away today. But I have to do it, no matter how bad the backlash might be. Especially after the fear and panic of that memory, I *have* to go through with it.

I keep my gaze trained on his ink, tracing the peaks and valleys of the place that has always been home—the mountain *and* him. "Raven's going to do an article about me coming back."

"What?"

There it is.

The incredulity in his tone.

That vibrating anger tied to his dislike of Raven and anything associated with her.

I push back slightly so I can look up at him. "I want her to."

"No, you don't." He clenches his jaw. "I know you can't remember it, if you had been following the site over the last year, but the stuff she posts? It's no better than a fucking gossip magazine."

"This won't be." I take his face in my hands, running my

fingers through his beard. "People need to know that some-thing might be happening on the mountain. That there could be danger... Don't they?"

A muscle tics along his jawline, and I can see the debate raging in his agitated gaze. "We don't know that, though, Honeybee. If we get everyone stirred up for no reason, it could cause unnecessary panic."

"You know I don't want that, but what if someone else was involved? What if..." I struggle to swallow, trying to work through both the jumbled mess in my head and what my *heart* is telling me. "What if I tried to come back to you, to Raven, and what if someone stopped me?"

His entire body stiffens underneath me, every muscle going tense and hard as stone. "Why do you think that?"

The tears burn in my eyes. "Because this feels right, being here with you. I know we argued about something. I know I left. But would this still feel right, even if I couldn't remember? Wouldn't I know, deep down, that something was wrong between us if I hadn't forgiven you? Hadn't gotten over what-ever you said? Whatever happened?"

Killian is quiet for far too long, so long that I start to think he is going to shut down completely.

"It isn't something you can just get over, Honeybee. What I did, what I said, it was unforgivable."

"I don't believe that."

"Why?"

"Because I know you, Killian McBride. I know the kind of man you are. I know how your mother raised you and your brothers, and you may be rough around the edges, but here"—I press my hand over his heart—"you're a good man, and you're always doing the right thing."

"You have way too much faith in me."

"Maybe you don't have enough."

He shifts me off his lap, setting me on the mattress, and

climbs from the bed, releasing a heavy sigh as he shoves his hand through his hair. "Try to get some sleep."

"You're leaving?"

He glances back at me. "I'll be right in the other room if you need me."

I want to beg him to stay.

I want to tell him I *do* need him.

But the look in his eyes tells me it would only make things worse, harder for him if I did, so instead, I simply nod and let him walk out, closing the door behind him and leaving me in the room in the bed we once shared with nothing more than the memory of the nightmare that may or may not be real.

8

THREE DAYS LATER

WILLOW

Everything is exactly as I left it.

After all this time, I expected cobwebs, dust, and any number of animals to have infiltrated my work-shop and filled it with nests, but all my candle-making supplies are still stacked in neat rows on shelves.

No cobwebs.

In their place are entire buckets filled with honeycomb waiting for me to process it for the pure wax I use for my creations.

When Killian told me he kept things exactly as they were in the cabin, I never anticipated it would extend out here.

Not to *my* space.

Not when he didn't know if I'd ever come back.

I now know how *that* feels because he disappeared on me.

The past few days with him have been tense in a way things never were before, filled with all the unspoken things between us. And this *need* I have for the man who has been there for me through every dark moment of my life, including the dreams that have haunted me. Yet when I woke this morning, before the sun even came up, he was already gone from the cabin, out taking care of the animals and all the other tasks the homestead requires before he heads into McBride Timber.

He left, like he has every night after my nightmares have come.

It could be his absence.

It could be that I'm just starting to feel better.

Either way, I'm restless.

Unable to eat breakfast, pacing the cabin until I finally couldn't take it anymore and had to come outside.

This property has always felt like home since the moment I first set foot here when I was twelve years old. Connie knew I needed a safe place to land, and she gave it to me on those days and nights it wasn't with Mom. And today, my feet lead me to the small structure to the left of the barn that has always been one hundred percent *mine.*

Killian built it for me when he realized how impractical it was for me to keep using the kitchen to process the honeycomb and make my candles.

When *he* knew I needed my own safe space, the same way his mother did all those years ago.

The man is giving me whiplash.

Doing sweet things like this—maintaining the hives, collecting a year's worth of honeycomb for me so if I came back, it would be here and ready. He cared enough to look after something he knew meant so much to me, yet he's fled from the bedroom every night.

Each time I wake screaming, assaulted by another memory, he's right there to hold me, to make me feel safe, but as soon as I've relaxed and calmed down, it's like he can't put enough distance between us.

Like he doesn't trust himself...

I release a frustrated sigh and set to work pulling out what I'll need to start purifying the wax to make candles.

Despite the pain in my ribs, moving feels *good*.

After days of just sitting around the cabin or at the bakery with Raven, I need to do something normal, something I would have done any other day before all of this happened.

I need to do something I love, and because of Killian, I still can.

Those damn tears threaten to come again, and I wipe them on my forearm as I pull out one of the large metal buckets of beeswax and light the flame on my burner to get water boiling.

I pour it in from a few reused milk jugs waiting on the floor —another thing Killian ensured would be ready for me—and wait, examining my scents, trying to figure out what I want to do today.

Lavender...

Jasmine...

Sandalwood...

But my gaze keeps drifting to one tiny bottle in particular.

Killian's scent—the one I made to mimic what clings to him.

I release a heavy sigh and pull it out, despite *really* not needing a reminder of how complicated things seem to be between us right now. Fingers wrapped around the stopper, I pause and try to prepare myself for what will happen when I pull it.

But nothing could ever prepare me for Killian McBride.

I pop the cap and take a long inhale of the crisp, woodsy scent I created—and which happened to become my best-selling candle.

Different memories flood my head now than those that have plagued me through the violent flashes.

Happy ones...

Because so many of mine are wrapped up in that man.

Nights spent in his arms.

Days spent hiking and enjoying the mountain.

I close my eyes and inhale again, allowing his scent to do to me what it always does. When the sound of the water boiling finally draws my eyes open, I actually feel relaxed for the first time since I woke in that hospital bed. I grab my giant wooden spoon and start stirring the beeswax, watching it slowly melt, the little bits of dirt and other impurities separating from the beautiful gift from nature that I need to create a batch of candles.

Being out here, doing this, always gave me an outlet, the same way carving does for Killian and building chairs does for Liam.

Creating something beautiful from something most people might overlook or even discard. Finding beauty in something Mother Nature gave us and utilizing it to create something else beautiful.

A shadow slips across the door behind me, blocking out the sun, and I whirl toward it to find Killian leaning against the doorjamb, arms crossed over his chest, making his dark T-shirt pull taut across sculpted muscles. "I thought I might find you out here."

"Oh, hi." I shrug, feeling like somehow I've been caught doing something I shouldn't and need to apologize for being in what used to be *my* space. "Just needed to do something normal."

His gaze softens as he steps in and makes his way over to the counter...and me. Those warm blue eyes I get lost swimming in rake across every inch of my body, taking in the exposed bruises, lingering on my side, even though he can't see the damage to my ribs. Like he's examining me for any signs that being out here and doing this has aggravated my injuries in any way.

He stops beside me and lifts the scent bottle to his nose.

A grin pulls at his lips.

And hell, he's fucking beautiful.

It's so rare to see Killian like this—with his guard down. If anyone else saw it, they wouldn't believe he's the same man they know. The one Raven has warned them about when he's in a foul mood. This Killian is the one I fell so easily in love with.

His voice dips low as he sets the bottle back down. "That's familiar."

Oh, hell.

So are the butterflies fluttering through my chest at being this close to him. At hearing the fluctuation in his tone, so full of promise...

I nod, clearing my throat awkwardly, suddenly uncomfortable around the man who has been my comfort zone for so long. Because I don't know *what* we are anymore. Friends. Former lovers. Jilted betrothed. Potential mates. None of those labels feel right. "It should be; it's yours."

He leans against the counter and watches me stir the wax, that smug grin still playing at his lips. Because he knows as well as I do *why* I chose that scent to make today. "I have to go into the yard, take care of some things before I go up the mountain again tomorrow."

The subtle reference to where he's going without directly referencing *why* is appreciated, but my gut still tightens. "Okay..."

Those all-seeing eyes of his roam over me again. "I don't want to leave you alone, and Connor and Liam are already down there."

That concern in his voice somehow both warms my chest and raises my hackles.

"I'm okay to be up here alone, Killian."

I can't rely on other people to watch over me like babysitters, to always be here if I have a meltdown. That isn't realistic.

It's been a week since Killian found me, and their lives and schedules have already been affected enough.

His jaw hardens. "It's not you I'm worried about, Honeybee."

Every time that nickname slips from his lips, my heart stutters a little.

When he first called me that, we were young. Still in elementary school. So oblivious to anything that existed beyond our isolated world on the mountain, to the pain that could come to us from things on it and outside it.

The worst things we experienced at that age were scraped knees and bee stings.

"You really harvested all this honey and maintained the hives while I was gone?"

I earned the nickname due to my ability to handle the hives without getting stung, but Killian has never been so lucky.

They seem to sense he's a predator at heart.

They're on guard when he's around.

So, the fact that he put himself in that position to keep things running smoothly speaks more than his words ever could.

The corners of his mouth quirk up slightly. "That surprises you?"

"How many times did you get stung?"

He chuckles, leaning in slightly, until we share the same breath. "Too many to count."

I can't help grinning at him and the playfulness in his words, despite knowing how miserable he is when he's in that position.

His gaze dips to my lips. "I think I should drop you in town with Raven."

Immediately, my shoulders tense, that warmth evaporating quickly.

Something about being back there over the last few days

I've spent with her has left me uneasy, a feeling almost like I've been being watched.

It's probably just my self-conscious brain knowing that everyone is aware of what happened to me, but something about hiding out up here in the workshop all day sounds like the far better option.

But I need to shake it off.

I *can't* hide forever.

Especially not if I want to regain my memories.

I finally turn off the burner to let the water cool so the wax will re-solidify on the top, letting the "gunk" I don't want in it sink to the bottom, then rest my hip against the counter and face him. "Okay..."

Killian watches me, eyes narrowed, and this close, he isn't missing *anything*. "You don't look so sure about wanting to go down there. Did you and Raven have a fight or something?"

I bark out a laugh at that. "God, no. You know how we are. We might bicker about something, but we never really fight."

He smirks. "Sounds familiar."

Just like Killian and his brothers, we may not share blood, but Raven and I are sisters in the way that matters. Always there for each other. Through thick and thin. Even when we're annoyed or angry.

"It's just...I don't know." I tug at the hem of my shirt, staring down at a fraying thread. "I feel like everybody's watching me, staring at me."

"They probably are."

I jerk my gaze up to meet his again. "What?"

"You're a beautiful woman, Honeybee. Every man on McBride Mountain sees that, and every woman is probably jealous."

He pushes off the counter and brushes past me, his shoulder gently bumping mine. Heat radiates through me from the contact, the most delicious warmth that always comes with his touch—intentional or not.

Or maybe it's the compliment that did that.

"I need to leave in an hour." He pauses at the door and glances back. "Will you be ready?"

I nod. "Yeah, I'll just do this batch and then get changed."

His eyes rake over me from my leggings to my tank top, lingering on the yellowing bruises visible in various places. "You look perfect in that; don't change a fucking thing."

With those words, he stalks out, and just like every night when he's left me alone in the bedroom we once shared, I feel like a part of me is walking away, a part of what I need to make things right.

KILLIAN

Liam jogs to catch up with me as I stalk across the timber yard toward one of the massive piles of logs destined to become firewood to be sold in town. "Hey, what are you doing?"

"Going to chop something with this." I lift my axe, clenched tightly in my right fist, not bothering to slow down on his account. "Maybe a lot of somethings."

He raises a reddish brow at me. "We don't have to do that by hand anymore, you know."

I scowl at him. "I know..." But after my conversation with Willow this morning, I'm antsy, unable to concentrate on anything in the office, or any of the projects I'm supposed to be monitoring today, before I disappear tomorrow out on another hike for answers. "I just need to work off some tension."

A corner of Liam's lips twitches. "This have anything to do with me seeing you come out of the bedroom where Willow was sleeping this morning?"

My footsteps falter slightly, but I manage to catch myself before I do something stupid like fall over onto my axe. "What were you doing in the house that early?"

He smirks, his green eyes glittering mischievously. "I stopped by the diner last night. Snagged some of those bear claws Willow likes so much. I thought she might want one for breakfast."

I was so rattled by realizing I had fallen asleep with her in my arms last night after the final time I went in to comfort her through a nightmare, that I didn't even bother stopping in the kitchen for my typical cup of coffee and bite to eat. I just bee-lined for the door and high-tailed it out onto the property to do exactly what I'm on my way to do right now: some manual labor designed to rip my hands open and work out some of this constant buzzing that's vibrated through my system since she returned.

Liam continues to keep pace with me, clearly not intending to drop the line of questioning. "I saw you leave."

"Where were you?"

He snorts and grins. "Still in the kitchen. You looked pretty fucking determined to get away, so I didn't stop you."

Jesus Christ.

I scrub my free palm over my beard as we reach the log pile. Of course, Liam's right. We have machines that can do this. Plenty of employees who would do it by hand if necessary for any reason, to make the job go quickly.

But quick and easy isn't what I want right now.

It isn't what I need.

I grip my axe tightly and set a log up on the massive stump that's been here so long that Dad would've used it, too, maybe even my grandfather. "You might want to step back."

Liam doesn't deserve the warning with the way he's ribbing me, but he grins and holds up his hand, retreating a few steps so the pieces of wood that fly free won't hit him.

He crosses his arms over his chest and watches me as I swing the axe and slam it down.

One piece flies to the left, the other coming to rest mere inches in front of Liam—which means it definitely would have hit him had he not moved.

I point my axe at him. "I wish that would've hit you."

He smirks again and shrugs. "If you didn't want me in your cabin, you shouldn't have left it unlocked."

"I didn't." I've been locking it every single night before I go to bed to ensure Willow feels *safe*, even though I'm confident the homestead is. "You must have used your key."

Another nonchalant lift and fall of his shoulders. "Shouldn't have given me a key, then."

"Fucking smartass."

I shake my head, set up another log, and send it flying.

The familiar motion comes as easily as breathing.

Muscle memory I don't even have to think about.

Just do.

After so many years, felling trees by hand around the property and up into the mountains to help clear paths to get our machinery up to do more of the major logging operations, I could do it with my eyes closed.

I could do it asleep, the same way Willow can with her candles or bee tending at this point. Only, I destroy things while she *creates* them.

Two sides of a very different coin.

Liam continues to watch me, crossing his arms over his chest, like he's waiting for something from me, some sort of offer of information I have no plans on giving him. "I saw Willow was out in her workshop this morning."

My swing falters and misses the log, slamming down into the stump, and Liam barks out a laugh that carries across the timber yard, melting away into the sound of the machines, forklifts, and semi-trucks pulling away with loads destined for dozens of different cities across the eastern seaboard.

He chuckles low, shaking his head. "You're really twisted up about her, aren't you?"

I growl at him as I jiggle the axe head free from where it's lodged in the stump. "You pointing it out doesn't help very much."

He nods slowly. "Look, I know things are complicated between you two, especially given how things ended."

The tension that I had started to work away returns at the mention of our breakup, so I throw another log on the stump and send the pieces flying again.

Trying to ignore him and what he just said.

"And anyone who sees the two of you together knows that this is the real thing, Killian, so tell her the truth, and do it sooner rather than later, if you want any chance of having a future with her that you blew last time."

Well, fuck.

I drop the head of my axe onto the ground as he turns his back and stalks away toward the office.

He's smart enough to know to avoid a full-blown confrontation about this, and given my mood, that's what would have happened if he had stayed and pushed.

The last thing I needed was another Liam insight at this moment, especially when I'm feeling so conflicted over my continued attraction to her when she's broken, bruised, battered, when I know she would feel differently about me if she knew the truth.

"Fuck. Fuck. Fuck. Fuck. *FUCK!*"

Right now, all I want to feel is *pain*. The burn of exertion. The sting of my palms when I overwork them on the axe handle.

It's what I need.

I shatter two dozen more logs before my muscles start to really feel the effort.

Then I keep going.

And going.

Working well into the afternoon, until the sun has moved across the sky, and all the men start to trail off toward their trucks to leave at the end of the day.

The door to the office opens on the far side of the property, and Connor steps out, eyes narrowing on me as he makes his way across the yard. When he reaches me, he stands almost exactly where Liam had been, crossing his arms over his chest in the same pose, watching me splinter yet another log. "You've been out here for hours, Kill."

I snarl at him, set up another log, and let it fly.

He ducks to avoid getting hit with one half of it.

"I. Fucking. Know."

That was the whole point.

My intent.

To come out here and work myself so hard that I can't feel anything but the aching muscles and sore hands.

"Well, did you know it's almost dinnertime?"

Shit.

I mean, the signs suggested that. The movement of the sun. All the employees leaving. The ache in my back and shoulders.

"Are you planning on feeding Willow tonight?"

Guilt slams into my chest.

I've been doing my best to make her comfortable, cooking her favorite meals, comfort foods that I know she'll enjoy. But I spent so long in my head today that I lost track of time.

"I have no idea." I run a hand through my sweat-soaked hair. "I'll go to the diner, pick up something to bring home."

He nods. "Good idea. We'll join you."

Before I can object, Liam steps from the office, turns to lock the door, and jogs toward us. "What's going on?"

I finally arch my back, stretching out the aching muscles. The burn feels good. Somehow, it's a relief from the other pain that's been eating away at me.

Connor inclines his head toward me. "We're headed to the diner to snag dinner."

"Great." He grins. "Meet you guys there."

Fucking great.

I sigh.

There will be no getting rid of them now.

Even if I would have rather enjoyed a few more minutes alone to figure out what I'm going to do when I see her again and have to fight this urge to pull her into my arms and kiss her senseless.

This morning, I got dangerously close to doing just that in her workshop.

Get your shit together.

It's easier said than done.

And today's little meltdown should have helped.

But it doesn't feel that way as I wander toward my truck, my axe still clenched in my hand, and set it across the passenger seat as I start it up and let the engine rumble. Connor and Liam both pull away, but I pause for a second, letting my head drop to the steering wheel and tightening my hands around it, too.

Liam's right.

I really am wrapped up in my head.

Messed the fuck up over this woman.

I want to give her everything, the life that we should have had, but I can't, not even when she looks at me like she has every time I've gone into that room to comfort her.

Like I'm her white knight, her hero, not the one who destroyed her.

"Fuck, fuck, fuck!"

I slam my hand against the steering wheel, and the horn blares, jerking my head back.

"Fuck."

I throw it into drive and pull out of the yard, pressing the button to close the massive gate behind me.

Instead of turning right to head up the mountain toward home, I make a left to go down into town, hitting Main Street a few miles from the McBride Timber yard.

My carving work lines the road on either side.

Each piece handcrafted with care.

Statements about this town, this place, the people who live here, and the wildlife we have to protect, along with the mountain.

Claire's Bakery, the church, the courthouse, Town Hall, the police station, and the library around the town square, the bait shop and sporting goods store, the grocery and general store, the old newspaper building, now abandoned, and finally, Wilson's diner.

Connor and Liam's trucks stand parked in front, with a familiar car between them.

Shit.

My hands tighten on the wheel, and I pull into a spot and climb from the truck, then make my way in past the bear with a picnic basket I carved for Elaine a few years ago.

The bells above the door jingle, and she smiles at me from behind the counter, inclining her head toward the corner booth where Raven and Willow sit with Liam, while Connor stands facing them, feet planted wide and arms crossed over his chest —looking pissed the fuck off.

"You might want to deal with your brother."

"What's going on?"

She shrugs. "Arguing with Raven again?"

Hell.

I stalk over to him and bump his shoulder with mine, interrupting whatever he was saying. "Hey, what's going on?"

Raven glares at Connor, her green eyes hard as emeralds, while Willow watches with a slight smirk on her lips.

Her amusement matches Liam's. He leans back beside her in the booth, fighting a grin as he watches Connor and Raven's battle of wills.

Connor doesn't even look at me, refusing to back down from the staring contest he's locked in with the blonde, who seems to get on his nerves even more than mine. "Raven and I were just discussing her most recent article she posted today."

I raise a brow. "Which is?"

Raven drags her gaze from him and offers a saccharine-sweet smile laced with contempt. "An exposé I think you might be interested in."

Shit.

Which means it is something I very much will *not* appreciate.

"Oh, yeah?"

She nods. "It's all about relationships, how keeping secrets can sour them."

Acid and fury crawl up my throat as I fight the desire to rail at her.

This fucking woman...

She's calling me out the same way Liam did earlier, demanding I come clean with Willow. But it's only been a week, and Willow is still weak. Traumatized in ways I can't even imagine.

Raven isn't there every night, hearing her scream. Feeling her trembling. Getting soaked with her tears.

Demanding the truth from me when she doesn't even understand the depths of what Willow has suffered is enough to make me cross my arms over my own chest, mirroring Connor's stance.

Because I actually agree with him.

I let my gaze drift to Willow, who watches me with wide

gray eyes and one dark brow raised at me. She's waiting for something—an explosion or the truth.

Maybe both.

But when I do come clean and discuss what happened between us, it sure as *shit* won't be in front of a captive audience like this or anywhere public.

All eyes in the diner are already on us.

Elaine's from the counter, pretending to wipe it down while watching us from the corner of her eye. The McMahon's in the opposite corner booth, him glancing over his shoulder to see the fireworks while his wife who faces us leans forward and whispers to him. A young couple—clearly out of towners passing through on vacation—casting furtive glances our way. And the few other town residents sitting at the counter, each peeking over between bites of their food.

The last thing I need is an audience for a showdown with the woman who is essentially the news source for the community.

"Sounds like you're just stirring up trouble again, Raven."

She leans back, crossing her arms over her chest and tilting her pink lips into a smug grin. "Trouble's my middle name."

"Believe me...I fucking know."

But somehow it's the dark-haired woman across from her who's causing me all the trouble right now.

I need to get my fucking head on straight so I can concentrate on what's important: the search tomorrow, finding the truth.

What happened in the past between Willow and me can wait.

At least for a while.

9

ONE WEEK LATER

WILLOW

For the first time in a week, I step out of the cabin with a sense of purpose.

The last several days, nothing has been able to drag my head away from those dark places it wants to go.

Not in my workshop, making candles.

Not going into town with Raven, while Killian spent his time hunting the mountain for clues or taking care of his responsibilities at McBride Timber.

All I've felt is listless.

Lost.

Like I've just been going through the motions.

Walking around the streets I know so well and seeing them all for the first time, through the eyes of someone who's suddenly suspicious of everyone and everything.

Nothing has changed in the year I've been gone, not really. It never does in a town like this. But the way people see me has. People I've known my entire life now give me tight smiles instead of the genuine ones they always offered me. Lifelong friends avoid eye contact because they don't know what to say, and I can't blame them.

They've all read Raven's article.

They all know what happened and that I can't remember.

Dr. Sommers said it could take time, but after two weeks, I still don't have anything resembling answers.

All I have are these bits and pieces that keep coming in strange flashes that leave me breathless and terrified. And despite everyone telling me that all I need is "time," the longer this drags on, the worse it becomes.

This feeling like some massive weight is sitting on my chest, suffocating me.

I have to get my memory back.

It may have felt like it would be simple to just return to the way things were and forget any of this ever happened, but the past two weeks have proved that isn't possible.

Killian still alternates between hot and cold, affectionate and aloof. Holding me so tightly when I need him, then quick to slip away with longing looks that break me almost as badly as the nightmares do.

He has changed.

Whatever happened between us, it's made him afraid—not of me but of himself.

That alone is enough of a reason to want the truth.

And there's only one way I can think to find it.

Face what's up there.

I close the cabin door behind me, head down the two steps off the porch, and make my way across the homestead toward the barn.

Killian should be at McBride Timber right now.

He should be doing his job, managing the several dozen employees who depend on his business for their livelihoods. He should be checking stock, sending shipments, even running the saws like he loves to so much, even though he doesn't need to do it anymore.

He *should* be doing his job, but he's too afraid to leave me alone here, too scared I'll have a meltdown while he's gone.

And considering what's happened during every one of these memory flashes, he's probably right.

I can't seem to bring myself out of them. Can't get back to the here and now without *him*. His warm arms and reassuring words keep me grounded.

The familiar sound of his axe slicing through the air and chopping into a heavy piece of wood hits me, and a smile pulls at my lips.

Whenever he got angry or stressed about anything, I always knew I could find him out here, either chopping endless amounts of firewood—more than we would ever need that he would just end up donating to someone in town—or carving something.

His beautiful wood sculptures line Main Street, standing sentinel in front of the various businesses and the entrance to McBride Mountain.

An eagle in front of Claire's Bakery, clutching her famous croissant in its talons. A bear in front of the diner with a picnic basket. A mischievous raccoon in front of the grocery store with a loaf of bread in hand. And too many others to count. All brilliantly lifelike and done by a man who is a true artist, though he'll never let you call him that.

I turn the corner around the barn and find him exactly where I knew he'd be—in front of a massive pile of wood.

He sets another large piece on the stump and lifts the axe that belonged to his father, and his father before him, and swings it down with such sharp precision, such power, that it makes me jump, as well as clench my legs together.

Sweat trickles down his exposed back, the muscles there

working as he leans down and throws the two pieces onto the pile, then reaches for the next log to repeat the motion.

Tattoos seem to move across his skin as if they're alive; intricate artwork he's built over the years, constantly adding to it, all pieces that mean something deeply personal to him.

A few new ones have popped up since I've been gone, though I haven't had a chance to examine them closely enough to see what they are.

I inch closer, mesmerized by the man, narrowing my eyes on the ink, trying to determine what they could be as he sets the next log and swings, sending the pieces splintering and flying outward.

The smell of newly-cut wood mingles with the fresh mountain air, the scent that's all Killian. I inhale it deeply, letting it soothe the anxiety over what I'm about to ask him.

He turns to reach for another log and spots me out of the corner of his eye, turning to face me fully and rising to his six-three height. "You're awake."

I nod.

His brow immediately furrows as he steps toward me, all those slick, glistening muscles on display. "Are you all right? Did you have another nightmare?"

That.

That look in his eyes.

That concern that never seems to go away.

The constant vigil he feels he needs to keep over me.

It has to end.

I shake my head.

He rests the head of the axe on the ground and leans against it. "Then what's wrong?"

Shit.

He knows me so well.

The past two weeks have proven that.

Killian hasn't forgotten a single thing.

All my favorite foods keep appearing on the kitchen table each night because he remembers each and every one of them exactly how I like them. And in the morning, my tea, with exactly the right amount of honey in it because he knows I like it super sweet.

He's given me everything I need before I can even ask for it.

Except this...

Because he thinks I can't handle it.

I shift nervously on my feet. "I need to ask you something."

His eyes immediately darken, and I know what he's thinking—what he believes I'm going to ask for.

The truth about what happened between us.

"Not that."

I watch the tension ease out of him with the reassurance that I'm not going to question him about our breakup.

Neither of us is ready to discuss it at this point, and that's probably for the best. It's easier to live in this semi-dream world, where he and I are still *something.*

That tension still radiates between us.

The kind that's always been there.

I can't seem to shake these feelings, this draw to the man standing in front of me, which makes it so hard to believe I would have walked away from him.

"What do you need, Willow?" His brow furrows. "You know I'll do anything for you. Anything to help you."

I believe his words because he's proven it over and over again over the past five years.

And the last two weeks.

Spending almost all of his time scouring the mountain, the endless wilderness, for one scrap of information that might help explain what happened to me, because the sheriff is coming up empty.

Tony Briggs is a good man.

Smart.

He was always looking out for everyone else when we were in high school, and now it's literally his job, ensuring the citizens of McBride Mountain are secure and safe, but one thing he hasn't been able to provide is answers.

He hasn't been able to locate anything that confirms I actually lived in any of the locations I sent Raven gifts from. Even my friends in Asheville, whom I intended to stay with when I left, said I never even contacted them about coming and haven't heard from me in over a year, either.

Which means I lied to Raven in those notes.

Why would I do that?

Why would I leave Killian?

Why would I lie to my best friend?

I take a tentative step toward the man who has become my savior, but who also poses one of the biggest mysteries in all this. "I need you to take me to where you found me in the river."

His shoulders tense, his massive pecs rock hard, his jaw working as he stares me down. "I don't think that's a good idea."

I take another step toward him until I'm so close I can smell the sunshine in his hair and that clean sweat smell emanating from him that makes me think of only one thing: sex.

I shiver.

Good God, this man could always turn me into a quivering mess.

"Why do you want to go to the river?"

I suck in a long, deep, fortifying breath, knowing he isn't going to like what I'm about to say. "I need to know if being there will jog my memory. If I see anything there that might, I don't know, match these flashes that I've been having."

"Are any of them the river?"

I shake my head, running my hands through my hair. "No, but they're coming more often now. Longer flashes. More vivid images."

"Still no specifics?"

"Fire. Something that sounds like thunder or a gunshot. Running, carrying something. The sound of metal dragging or clanging against something. It's all just..." I squeeze my eyes closed, pressing my fingers into my temples. The all-too-familiar throb that always comes with mining my mind for the memories returns full force. "It's all just so jumbled in this dark haze."

He closes the distance between us, capturing my cheek in his rough palm and tilting my chin up with his thumb. "Do you really think going up there would help?"

I open my eyes to meet his that watch me so intently. "I do. I have to do something other than sit around here all day or hang out with Raven while she works. I need to do something active, something that might actually make a difference, otherwise I might just..."

Lose myself.

Because that's what it feels like.

I didn't just lose a year; I lost part of what makes me *me*. Until this mystery is solved, I can't move forward, and Killian has proven we can't go back.

This is limbo.

That strange state of hanging between worlds—the old and the new. The past and the future.

I blow out a long, heavy breath, unable to explain it to him when I don't even understand it myself at times.

The calloused pad of this thumb scrapes across my jaw. "Okay."

That was too easy.

I expected some sort of objection or even an argument from him. "Really?"

He nods. "If this is what you think you need."

It isn't just about me.

That may be the way he sees it, but this is about far more

than just my missing memories. This affects him. His future. His life.

"You need it, too. You can't keep ignoring work, ignoring the business, to run off to the mountain to solve this mystery."

The corners of his lips curl up into a smirk. "I'm the boss. I can do whatever I want."

That draws a half smile from me. "But all your employees depend on you. It's not fair to take you away from them."

He snorts. "Believe me, Connor and Liam are enjoying having their chance to boss people around while I'm not there."

I chuckle. "Liam would never."

"You're right, it's mostly Connor, but they have everything well in hand. I'm not needed there."

"Yes, you are. You're always needed."

My words somehow soften his gaze even more, and his eyes dip to my lips as he brushes his thumb across my bottom one, sending a little shiver through me that's full of heat rather than a chill.

It centers low in my belly, blooming between my legs because I know that look.

I craved it for so long, relished every time I saw it in his eyes, wanted it as badly as I do him right now, despite everything that's going on.

"You'll take me up there?"

He nods. "Let's pack a bag and go. But I want you to promise me something."

"What's that?"

"That you won't push yourself too hard. I know you're feeling better, that some of your bruises and aches are starting to go away"—he slides his hand down to my side, resting it gently over my ribs—"but you're still going to be sore for a while, and where we're going is steep. A lot of hiking. We'll have to spend the night up there. You need to tell me if it's too much. You need to promise me you will."

"I will."

His lips tip down, concern drawing frown lines around his mouth and eyes. "I can't watch you hurt anymore. You understand that, right?"

I nod and lean into his touch. "I do."

He draws in a breath, his slick chest rising enough to almost brush mine. "Then let's go. Maybe we'll get lucky and find the answers we're looking for."

KILLIAN

I shouldn't have brought her up here.

After hiking for hours, navigating the unfriendly terrain, I can already see how exhausted and uncomfortable she is.

The slight tensing of her facial muscles with each step she takes. Her labored breathing. The way she keeps reaching over and grabbing her side and then quickly pulling her hand away before she thinks I've noticed.

But I see everything.

I *notice* everything.

I always did.

Because I've always been obsessed with her.

Even in high school, years before anything but friendship existed between us, it was always *her*.

She was the only one who ever caught my attention, who ever held it.

The way she laughs.

The way she smiles.

Even the way she cries is beautiful.

But I never want to see the look on her face that I have every night since she came home with me.

I never want to see her tears.

Those strange flashes of memory that she can't piece together haunt her, making her gray eyes violently stormy. A tempest rages inside her, threatening to drag her into the dark, menacing abyss of her unknown past.

And so far, being up here has done nothing to improve her situation or give us any more information that might alleviate any of her suffering.

All it's done is make her hurt even more than she already did.

Emotionally and physically, she's dancing a fine line of complete burnout.

Still, she pushes on.

Never complaining.

Hiking through the dense, treacherous foliage. Climbing over fallen trees and weaving around trunks bigger than her as we follow the river up the mountain.

She scans the bank intently, the same way that I have over the last two weeks, every damn day I have been able to get up here, hoping to find something I missed before.

And it is wearing on her.

We can't go on much farther, or she'll drop.

I trail behind her, watching for any signs that she's too wiped to continue. "Anything yet?"

She glances over her shoulder at me and gives me a tight smile that doesn't reach her eyes before she shakes her head. "Nothing new."

"I figured you'd tell me, but..."

I had hoped.

Prayed that being up here might trigger something for her that could end this ordeal.

A sigh slips from her lips filled with the frustration I share with her—though, what she's feeling must be a thousand times worse than what I do.

She reaches back to adjust her ponytail to keep the hair off her neck, now matted down with sweat, the physical toll of the hike hitting her hard.

We used to go on hikes far harder than this regularly, but this type of exertion after what she went through borders on torture. It doesn't matter that she asked for it and wanted this, or that we both had hoped it would offer her something she couldn't get anywhere else.

She can't keep going.

Any pain she's feeling now will be ten times worse tonight and tomorrow.

"It's getting late, Honeybee. We should probably set up camp soon."

We didn't get nearly as far as she had wanted to, but given how slow she has to move and the late start we got after spending time packing up what we needed to spend the night and talking to Raven, Connor, and Liam about our plans, that's to be expected.

At least *I* expected it.

But given the way Willow now looks at the water, she apparently never counted on this being so taxing. "How much farther until we get to where you found me?"

I motion up the bank. "Another half an hour or so."

Her lips twist as she contemplates the bubbling waters flowing beside us and the heavy brush we have to move through. "I want to keep going."

"Willow..."

I grab her wrist to stop her progress, and just like every time I've touched her since her return, heat flares through my body at the simple contact.

She allows me to pull her to a stop. With a gentle tug, I turn her toward me. Restless gray eyes plead before she even says a word. "Please don't, Killian."

"Don't what?"

"Don't try to stop me from doing this." She swallows thickly, as if she's trying to keep something down. "I *have* to."

"I think you've done enough for one day. There's a place just up here where we can set up camp. We can start up again tomorrow."

I hold my breath.

Please, Honeybee, just accept that you need to rest.

But the longer she waits to answer, the more sure I am that I've lost the battle.

She finally smiles at me softly, and that steely determination I always loved so much about her settles into her gaze. "I'm all right. I appreciate your concern, but I want to push on. We can camp there, right?"

I grit my jaw to keep myself from arguing with her, from trying to push what I think is best for her onto her because that's gotten me in trouble in the past, and the last thing I want to do is upset her right now. She likely wouldn't sleep anyway if we stopped here and would lie awake all night thinking about what we might find tomorrow.

"Okay, but we set up camp there. We don't push farther."

She nods. "All right."

I allow my fingers to slide off her wrist slowly, immediately missing the feel of her skin against mine.

It's ridiculous how completely obsessed I am with this woman. What she does to me...

Every waking hour is spent thinking of her.

Every night is spent worrying about what might come when she climbs into our bed and tries to sleep.

And as we start walking again, I can't drag my eyes off *her* instead of searching like I should be.

I readjust the heavy pack on my shoulders and force myself to return my focus to the task at hand.

She'll be okay.

We'll rest soon.

Comfortable silence settles over us, only the sound of foliage crunching under our boots and the birds overhead and animals in the forest breaking it.

As we near the place where I found her in the water, my stomach tenses, and even she seems to sense it, her footsteps slowing, becoming more cautious.

We turn the slight bend in the river, and my gaze finds the log and tree roots her body was tangled up in, still protruding out into the water near the rapids.

She stops and stares at that exact spot for a moment, her head tilting slightly before she slowly turns and looks at me. "Was that it?"

I grit my jaw. "How did you know?"

Her brow furrows, and she shakes her head, turning back toward the river. "I don't know. I was unconscious when you pulled me out..."

"Yes. And all the way to the hospital. You didn't wake up once."

And I didn't take a single breath the entire time.

At least, it felt like that.

For *hours*, carrying her down this mountain and then driving to Asheville to the emergency room, all I did was pray.

Seeing her vulnerable, so hurt, so near death...

Seeing her at *all* when I thought I might never again.

She purses her lips and slowly approaches the water. "I may have been unconscious, but I must have been somehow aware of what was happening."

I sure as hell hope not.

There were things I said to her, things I shouldn't have, as I held her in my arms and trekked down the mountain. Things that would be hard to explain without delving deeply into the very reason that we broke up in the first place.

She pauses beside the bank, the water rushing over the rocks, boulders, and the tree where she was hung up. Willow stares at the spot for what feels like an eternity before she starts walking farther upriver.

"Willow, where are you going?"

"I..." She glances back at me but keeps moving. "I don't know. I just need to go this way."

"The path you came down is just across the clearing, through those trees."

Her eyes cut over to the entrance to the animal trail where I found the scrap of fabric and her footprints, and she gasps, freezing in place.

"Willow?" I step up next to her, pulling her elbow to hold her upright as she staggers. "What is it?"

She squeezes her eyes closed and shakes her head. "I...I remember the feel of the branches cutting and scratching my arms and face, the rocks under my feet..."

I wince at the pain she describes, knowing I would do *anything* to have prevented it.

Fury heats my blood again.

That she had to suffer this.

That she had to endure it.

That it's all my fault...

Her eyelids flutter open, tears brimming and threatening to spill over as her gaze stays locked on that spot in the trees. "I need to go over there."

"I don't know if that's such a good idea." I tighten my grip on her. "You're exhausted."

She finally turns her head toward me, and the hurricane swirling in her eyes leaves no room for argument. This woman is ready to barrel through me if I stand in her way. "Please, Killian."

I was always helpless to resist Willow. It was impossible not to give her everything she ever wanted until that day when I fucked up everything.

No matter how concerned I might be for her at this

moment, this is what she needs, which means pushing away my instinct to protect her from anything that might cause her more pain and allow her to find her own limits.

"Okay..."

I release her elbow and slide the pack from my shoulders, leaving it near the river where we'll set up camp. Willow waits for me, and I pull her hand in mine and twine our fingers together.

She doesn't question the gesture or fight it; she simply allows me to lead her across the meadow toward the treeline and the small gap in it where various species of wildlife cuts through to make their way to the river.

Her grip on my hand tightens as we approach the trees, and she pulls to a stop, turning to scan the clearing and river again. Uncertain eyes dart back and forth between the water and the trail. "I must have run across the clearing."

I nod. "Probably. Any footprints would have been quickly washed away by the rain."

"But how did I end up in the water?"

Exactly what we've all been wondering for the past couple of weeks.

Willow knows the river can be very dangerous. Aside from fishing with Connor, Liam, or me, and occasionally swimming in the natural pool at the bottom of the falls, she rarely came near it.

I shake my head. "I don't know. The scrap of fabric from your shirt was maybe fifty yards into the trees here, and there are several footprints deeper in where the ground must have been wetter and softer from the rain to leave an impression. But as far as how you got into the water..."

She pulls her bottom lip under her teeth, and I can feel the tension growing in her. Almost as if she's anticipating what might await on the other end of the path, even though I know there are just more questions, not answers.

I've been searching almost every day for weeks and haven't found anything that can help explain where she has been or what she was doing up here.

Unless she remembers something more specific, this may remain a mystery indefinitely.

That thought has kept me awake at night as much as my concern for her and waiting for another nightmare to come.

How can she live like this forever?

I want to believe that won't happen, that *something* will spark her full memory to return, but today has left that boulder of doubt sitting in my gut.

She tilts her head slightly as she steps into the trees, allowing my hand to stay connected with hers as I trail behind her.

At this point, I couldn't stop her even if I wanted to.

We move into the foliage, and she uses her free arm to bat away low-hanging branches, wincing slightly a few times, no doubt remembering that they might be the ones that caused the still-healing marks on her bare arms.

After a few more yards, I pull her to a stop. "This is where I found the scrap of fabric."

A jagged branch shoots out at a forty-five-degree angle, clearly snapped by something big plowing through here rapidly.

Her gaze narrows on it. "I must have done that..."

I nod. "Yes."

"What was I doing out here in a storm like that?"

The crack in her voice, the way her hand tightens on mine, it feels like my heart is being ripped from my chest.

"I don't know, Honeybee."

God, I'm so sick of saying those words.

I want to give her answers. I want to give her comfort. I want to give her exactly what she needs—the truth of what happened to her—and it's all out of my control.

Something I'm definitely not used to on McBride Mountain.

The one thing I so badly want to fix is the one thing that's completely out of my hands.

Willow draws in a shaky breath and then pushes on. I point out the few places we found her footprints, though they're mostly gone now, animals and the weather either washing them away or covering them. By the time we reach the clearing where her trail ends, she's trembling.

She stops, her body tensing, and I slide behind her, wrapping my arms around her waist to hold her steady.

A tear trickles down her cheek, and I press my face into her hair, breathing her in and wishing so much I could take away her pain. "Anything else coming to you?"

It takes her a few seconds before she responds. "No. None of this looks familiar, but..."

"But what?"

She turns her head sideways until her eyes meet mine. "I feel like I've been here before. You and I never came up here?"

I shake my head. "Not this particular clearing. I've been through here a few times over the years hunting, but never with you."

Her lip disappears beneath her teeth, and she points to the west. "Then why do I know that way will lead me up to a small canyon?"

What the hell?

I freeze as my back tenses. "You shouldn't know that."

Her gaze goes unfocused, like she isn't seeing what's right in front of us but something else entirely. "I can see it in my head."

"What?"

"The canyon. It's narrow, barely wide enough for a human to get through. I think the animals use it, though, as sort of a bypass instead of going up over the peak or around the mountain the long way."

I turn her slowly in my arms and tilt her chin up. "You're describing the gorge. Maybe you saw it on the maps. Those old ones that my dad and his dad before him drew for McBride Timber. You looked at them hundreds of times over the years in the office."

Her lips twist. "Maybe, but I'm not visualizing a drawing of it. I'm seeing the gorge itself. High rock walls..."

Which doesn't make any fucking sense.

The dogs never made it up that far, nor gave any indication that she had come from that way. They lost the scent right around this clearing.

So, how the hell does Willow know about the gorge?

10

KILLIAN

Willow shivers in her sleeping bag that's laid out next to mine in the tent.

Though it's hot when the summer sun is high on McBride Mountain in the afternoons, once it goes down and the mists roll in, the temperature at this altitude can drop into the fifties this time of year.

A chill definitely permeates the air, but it isn't merely the weather that's causing her physical reaction.

The entire hike back from the clearing, Willow didn't say a word.

She barely spoke as I set up the campsite near the river, well away from the wildlife trail in case any animals come down in the night to drink from the water. Her eyes never left the flames burning in front of the tent while I cooked our simple dinner. She only muttered a "thank you" as I handed her some of the food.

It's as if she were in a completely different place, rather than sitting across from me underneath a canopy of trees and the sparkling, clear night sky that hangs over the mountain she knows so well.

But maybe she doesn't feel like she does know it anymore.

Everything must seem different to her now.

The life she knew is gone.

What we had, long buried beneath regret.

I can't even imagine how confusing it must be not to remember, not to know where you've been for such a large chunk of time. To *know* something happened, that something's very wrong, and not be able to piece anything together.

It makes me *furious.*

It makes her *terrified.*

Her trembling continues, and I reach over and slide my hand onto her shoulder, where it sticks out of the top of the sleeping bag. "Are you okay?"

She rolls onto her back and looks at me, and the shimmer in her eyes tells me that she's been fighting tears for a while now, not wanting me to see. "Not really." Willow pauses to try to gather herself. "I could lie and say I am, but you know me too well..."

I gently brush away one of the drops trailing down her cheek with my thumb. "I do. Have you remembered anything else?"

Hope and dread war within me as I await her response.

There are so many reasons we need her memory to come back, but her very real fear that she is suppressing them because of how awful they are quells any excitement I might have had for their return.

She shakes her head. "No, but I've had this...just deep sense of dread and a franticness ever since we found the game trail and saw the clearing. Almost like my body's remembering how I felt even if my mind can't."

"You were running from something. Or someone."

Her lips press together, as if she's fighting a sob, but she fails and releases it, the sound filled with so much anguish it rips my heart apart. "I th-think so."

Oh, hell.

I can't bear to see her like this, to see her falling apart, to see the strong woman I once knew collapsing under the weight of so much uncertainty.

There are so many things between us.

Time.

Secrets.

The few inches that separate us now seem like miles.

I unzip my sleeping bag, then hers, and drag her carefully into my arms, careful not to squeeze her still-healing ribs.

Willow buries her face against me and cries.

And I let her.

There's nothing else I can do.

I failed at every turn to help her, to make things better, to find an answer for her, and if this goes on much longer, I don't know that she'll survive it.

Or that I will.

The only thing I can think of to help take her mind off what's going on in her head possibly also means opening the door to the memory I've been trying to keep at bay and the conversation I don't want to have. But I have to do something, and whispering placations to her that don't really mean anything won't cut it tonight.

I twirl a strand of her hair around my finger. "Do you want to play Twenty Questions?"

She tenses and then draws away from me slightly, wiping away her tears. "Are you serious?"

A grin pulls at my lips. "Sure. What else are we going to do up here all night?"

Before, we would have been wrapped up in each other with far less clothing by now.

Before I could have occupied her racing mind by getting her to concentrate on something else entirely.

And the corners of her mouth curve as she realizes her thigh is pressed squarely between my legs and against my cock. "Who goes first?"

"You can have the honor."

She grins and bites her bottom lip. "Okay. Gosh, what is there to ask that I haven't during our many rounds?"

Considering how many times we've played this over literally decades, I can see her brain spinning to come up with something.

And it's exactly the distraction she needed.

"I'm sure you'll think of something, Honeybee."

Those eyes that have been so filled with turbulent uncertainty shift to an almost sadness as she examines me, and a stone settles into my stomach.

Shit.

I knew this might open the door for questions I don't want to answer, and the look she's giving me now suggests I was right.

She chews on that lip again for a moment before she finally musters up the courage to ask whatever is on her mind. "What have you been doing for the last year?"

I force myself to hold her gaze, even though I want to drag my eyes away. Because I'm embarrassed to admit it to her. "I already told you. I've been an asshole, apparently."

"Yeah, but..." She runs her fingers through my beard, scraping her nails along my cheek in a way that makes me bite back a groan and wish her knee wasn't wedged up against my cock. "But you must have done something with all your free time, not having me around."

Wallowing in self-pity.

Berating myself for losing the only woman I ever loved and the most important person in my life.

Beating myself up physically.

Pushing myself to the brink until I'm ready to collapse as penance.

Chopping down tree after tree by hand until my palms bled, rather than use the equipment that would make the job so much easier, just so I could feel the physical pain that matches what I feel inside.

But I won't tell her any of that.

Not now.

Maybe not ever.

When we do finally talk about what happened between us, I won't give her any reason to feel sorry for me because I deserved every single thing I suffered.

"I mostly spent time alone in the cabin or out in the barn working on my carvings."

Her eyes flash with interest. "What have you created since I left?"

"It's *my* turn to ask a question."

She presses her lips together, fighting a smile. "Okay, go."

I probably should have thought this out, planned something that wouldn't lead us down a dangerous road, but staring up into her gray eyes, I can't help but wonder about how she ended up in my arms in the first place. "Why didn't you walk away from the bonfire that night?"

If she had, it might have saved both of us a lot of heartache.

She might have been happy instead of suffering right now.

Willow's brow furrows deeply. "What?"

"The night we first kissed." Even six years later, the memory still lives vividly in my head. Every brush of my lips over hers. The way her hands clung to my shirt. That little sound she made in the back of her throat. "Everyone else left the fire and walked to their trucks to head home, but you lingered with me..."

"I did."

And sealed our fates.

"Why didn't you leave? I'm pretty sure Raven was trying to drag you away."

In fact, I distinctly remember the feisty blonde physically grabbing Willow's arm and trying to lead her to where the trucks were parked rather than allowing her to sit around the fire where I lingered, staring up at the mountain sky.

"Oh, she definitely was." Her lips curl into a little knowing grin. "Because she knew *why* I was going to stay."

"Why was that?"

No other woman even tried.

The couple who had in high school and the few years following, before Willow and I got together always left cursing my name and threatening violence because I wasn't interested.

And I wasn't exactly known for letting them down easily.

But Willow was different.

Not scared away by my reputation or attitude—probably because of all the time she spent with Mom and us on the homestead when she was younger.

Or maybe just because she always saw me in a way no one else ever could.

Her cheeks pinken slightly, almost as if she's embarrassed to reveal something I've wondered about for so many years. "Because I'd had a crush on you since we were like, twelve years old."

"Really?"

She nods, and I picture that little dark-haired girl sitting quietly in the front of the classroom, raising her hand with every answer and sticking her nose in a book during recess.

Somehow, I missed it.

The way she must have looked at me...when I wasn't busy looking at *her*.

I didn't notice it until *that* night.

Her steely eyes warmed as she looked through the flames at

me, where I sat on the log on the other side of the fire pit on the far side of our property.

"You talked to me when no one else really did..."

"Talk?" She slides fully across me, settling her pelvis against mine, and my cock aches where it's pinned between us. "As I remember it, we didn't end up talking."

Heat sizzles across my skin at her sultry tone and reference to what went down that night.

"No, we certainly didn't, Honeybee."

"And we would have gone all the way had we not been interrupted by the crack of thunder and the skies opening up on us." Her lips twist slightly, her playfulness doused by some thought I can't read. "Do you think it was God trying to tell us something?"

I slide my hand up her side. "Is that your question?"

She scowls at me. "Does it have to be?"

Our "fun" game just took a very serious turn I never anticipated. But Willow has always had a strong belief in something bigger than us. A creator who gave us this mountain and all the beautiful things on it.

I wasn't sure I believed in it until I pulled her from that water and immediately began praying...

The fact that she could think we were doomed from the beginning makes emotion clog my throat.

I shake my head. "No, I don't think it was any kind of ominous warning that our future was going to be complicated, if that's what you're asking. Just a freak summer storm."

Willow doesn't appear convinced. "That lightning and thunder came right after you kissed me."

I grin at her, but it's filled with a deep sadness that has seeped into my bones. "Maybe it was a sign that we're so electric nothing would be able to keep us apart..."

If only that had been true.

Instead of looking sad like she should, given the fact that we aren't together anymore, her eyes heat in a way I recognize that both terrifies me and reignites that flame that could never completely stop burning for her.

"Don't look at me like that, Honeybee..."

"Why not?"

"Because you can't."

Her dark brows draw low over conflicted eyes. "Why can't I?"

"Because you still don't know the truth. In your head, we're still..." I release a long, heavy sigh, taking her face in my hands as she looks down at me. "In your head, we're still on solid ground, and in reality, we're far from it."

It's more like quicksand slowly sucking us down...

"You've always been my rock, Killian. Don't tell me you're not solid ground."

"I'm not, Honeybee."

She shifts slightly against my cock, making it spring to life, remembering what it feels like to be deep inside her. Her slick cunt wrapped around me. Squeezing, pulsing. Accepting me no matter how I took her.

And God...

I want to take her now.

I want to wipe away any awful memories with better ones. Ones centered on the pleasure I can give her. Ones rooted in the connection we've always shared. I want to take control so she can stop searching for it when she can't find it in this impossible situation.

"Even if things were different, you're hurt. We can't—"

Willow leans down and kisses me, silencing my protest. Her lips move over mine. Heavy. Hot. Desperate.

There's nothing tentative in the way she kisses, nor in the way her hips roll with mine, fully hardening my cock between us.

"Fuck." I tear my mouth from hers, even though all I want is to keep going. "Your ribs—"

"I'll be fine."

I shake my head. "I'm not going to risk hurting you. Not again."

"Please, Killian." Her eyes glisten with unshed tears, desperation in her wavering voice, and trembling body pressed to mine. "I need this. I need you. I need things to feel normal. I need to feel alive again."

Fuck.

This is wrong.

The wrong time.

The wrong place.

The wrong circumstances.

Wrong.

Wrong.

Wrong.

But I can't say no when she needs something from me.

WILLOW

Killian battles with himself.

That part of him that wants to protect warring against the other half that has always tried to rule him. The *primal* part. The part that binds him to this wild mountain.

His eyes darken to an almost navy, his desire as molten as my own.

He releases a frustrated growl before he fists a hand in my hair and rolls me onto my back, keeping one arm around me in an attempt to absorb any potential jostling that might cause me pain in my ribs.

But any discomfort is immediately swept away by his mouth

crashing down on mine, hard and insistent, his tongue demanding entry in the way I hope his cock will be soon.

God, yes.

My body hums in anticipation, heat simmering low in my belly, moisture pooling between my legs.

This.

This is what I needed.

It's been torture for the last two weeks.

Not only because I still can't remember what happened to me, but because being around him and not being able to act on the way I feel, on the fact that, to me, this is how we should *still* be, was so *wrong*.

He tears his mouth from mine and brushes his thumb across my cheek reverently. "I know what you want, Honeybee, and you know I would never deny you anything..."

His other hand slides down and slips beneath the waistband of my pants to cup me between my legs. My body bucks under him at the brush of his palm at the apex of my thighs, and the twinge of pain in my side is well worth it for the flare of heat that courses through me.

He dips his head low, kissing his way across my cheek until his warm breath tickles my ear, making me squirm.

Killian supports his body on one elbow, ensuring the pressure doesn't hurt me, even as his other hand shifts until the meaty part of his palm rubs against my clit.

The slightest touch makes me twitch.

"I'm going to help you relax." His lips feather across my earlobe. "And warm up." He nips gently, the flash of pain so fucking good. "Because you need to do both. But that's all that's going to happen, Honeybee. Do you understand me?"

I whimper, a devastated, pathetic sound that I wish hadn't just come from my mouth.

He isn't going to give me what I want.

He isn't going to give me all of him.

I try to pull my head back to see his eyes, but he keeps his face buried along my neck and then shifts his hand to slip my panties to the side and glide his fingers through my wet core.

"Fuck." His chest rumbles with his approval. "I've missed the feel of you."

Fingertips play in my heat, barely touching, gentle strokes and feather-light brushes.

I gasp at the sensation, heat flaming up and tension swelling so easily with the simplest of touches from those familiar calloused hands.

It isn't enough.

Not nearly enough.

Those light stroking fingers will be the death of me.

"Please, I need..."

He finally draws his head back, his eyes meeting mine, and I see the icy determination there. Killian wants me. I can feel the evidence of it pressed to my thigh and witness it in the way he looks at me. But there will be no convincing him tonight.

It's too soon.

There's still too much standing between us, too many things unspoken.

I won't get all of him tonight, even if it's what I so desperately want.

But Killian would never leave me hanging.

He will *always* give me *exactly* what I need—most of the time knowing what that is even before I do.

He slides one finger into me easily, and I groan, my eyes rolling back at the sensation as I clasp around it. *Not enough.* He thrusts in and out of me slowly a few times, still grinding his palm against my clit to increase the pleasure before he slides a second finger in, spreading me wider.

"Oh, fuck."

With a slight shift of his position, his hard cock presses into my belly, assuring me he isn't unaffected by what's happening between us, even if he is going to deny me *that*.

He would deny himself rather than risk doing something I'm not ready for.

Fuck, I love this man...

And I want to scream it.

I want him to *know* it.

But Killian's hand moves against me, those long, strong fingers stroking the perfect spot deep inside, stealing my ability to speak. His breath hitches near my ear. "Christ, you're so beautiful like this, Honeybee. Do you know that?"

I nod, knowing that's what he wants, what he needs—the validation that what he's doing is working me up, that his praise is only going to build me up higher faster.

It's always been a rush, knowing Killian McBride wants *me*.

That I can do *this* to him—have him hard and wanting when I haven't even touched him.

But something about tonight, being in this tent on a desolate part of the mountain, makes each stroke, each glide, each touch ten times more powerful.

He tilts his head and ghosts his lips over mine as he starts a slow, grinding rhythm with his thumb against my clit and his two thick, rough, calloused fingers thrusting in and out of me, curling deep inside and dragging along my G-spot with each retreat. "You know I dream about how you taste..."

"What?"

I let my eyes open to meet his and find absolute burning sincerity there.

The blue that shifts from warm and inviting to sharp and icy with his emotions now swirls like molten flame.

He nods, his tongue snaking out across his lips. "I still remember it vividly. Think about it every time I take my cock in my hand at night. I can't wait to lick it off when I'm done touching you, once you've come all over my fingers."

Fuck.

Killian. Fucking. McBride.

This man always had a way with words.

A skill to make me unravel in his arms so damn easily.

Other people are intimidated by his bluntness, by his aggressive and demanding nature.

But not me.

Never me.

He uses it to command me when we're like this, and it's exactly what I need. For him to take control, for him to pull away all the uncertainty that surrounds me.

In the beginning, it was the lack of stability in my life—Mom's addiction issues, uncertainty about whether I had a safe place to land—that led me to the McBrides' door and eventually Killian's arms as a safe haven. Now, this mystery about why I left and where I've been has me lost. But his strong hands, commanding words, and the praise that lifts my heart also stir every fiber of my being and bring me home.

His lips move over mine, capturing another gasp as he increases his pace. "Are you going to be a good girl and come on my hand, Honeybee, so I can get a taste of that sweetness I crave?"

Fuck, yes.

That's what I want.

What I need.

I whimper and nod, and he increases his pace as I grip his shirt in my fists, clinging to him like the lifeline he has become for me.

And not just in the last two weeks, but always.

My body starts to tremble uncontrollably, and not from the chilly air.

Each breath I take comes harsher.

Heat centers on where he moves his hand inside me.

I'm about to unravel.

And he *knows* it.

Killian grins against my lips, kissing me softly at each corner, then slowly flicking his tongue across them. "I want to hear you when you come. There's no one else up here for countless miles. It'll just be for me. So that I can hear it again, to have another memory that I can store away for when I need it."

"Fuck..."

Is that what he's been doing for the last year?

Thinking about me?

Thinking about us?

And this?

That coiling low in my belly borders on painful as my release builds and builds.

Each expert glide of his fingers draws me tighter.

What the fuck happened between us?

That question drifts away as my orgasm finally hits me.

He swirls his thumb rapidly, pushing down on my clit, and I jerk against his hand, my pussy clasping around his fingers as he thrusts into me. Dragging it out. Catching my gasp with another kiss before I let out another long, slow scream of relief that seems to echo across the mountain.

Not just in our tent, but *everywhere*.

It consumes me the same way the fiery rush of the orgasm does, my release ebbing and flowing, rolling through me like the rapids do in the river a few yards from us.

The rapids that brought me back to Killian.

By the time I finally come down and sag onto the sleeping bag, a low rumble of approval vibrates his chest against mine, and he kisses each cheek, my nose, my eyelids, my lips.

"Fucking stunning. Every time, Honeybee."

He pulls his hand from between my legs and out of my pants, and I let my lids flicker open in time to watch him slide his glistening fingers into his mouth.

Good God.

I've seen him do it hundreds of times, but watching him now might be the most erotic thing I've ever seen. His blond hair, disheveled from the hike today, hangs around his shoulders. His eyes sharp blue and wild, reckless, like he knows that what we did is going to have consequences.

He licks his fingers clean, groaning, and then grins at me just like I remember him always doing after getting me off— smug and satisfied. Then he leans in and drops his lips to my forehead, letting them linger there, his eyes closed, his body pressed to mine.

Time seems to stop as I live in the post-orgasmic haze.

Until he pulls away and rolls onto his back, tugging me into his side and settling my head on his shoulder. Several minutes pass in comfortable silence as I try to catch my breath.

His fingers stroke up and down my arm, a soothing, consistent rhythm that helps me drift back to reality slowly.

"Now, go to sleep, Honeybee." He kisses my forehead. "You need the rest, and we have a lot to cover tomorrow."

He means the hike down the mountain to the cabin.

A return to that limbo I've been living in for weeks.

No.

The thought of doing that makes me shiver.

Something is drawing me farther up the mountain, the opposite direction...

Another flash of towering stone walls flickers through my head.

"Will you take me to the gorge?"

He releases a long, heavy sigh that I think will lead to a "no" that I don't want to hear, and continues to drag his fingers down my arm. I can practically hear him considering my request, the cogs turning in his head. The internal debate between not wanting to push me too hard and needing answers. "Do you think it'll help?"

It has to.

I nod, giving my heart a few moments to calm to a more normal beat before I even attempt to explain it to him. "I have to know why I keep seeing it."

It's too clear.

Too *real.*

I must have been there at some point.

And I need to know why.

Even if I pay for it—one way or another—later, I can't pass up this chance when I'm so close to another potential memory.

Killian buries his face in my hair, breathing deeply and tightening his hold on me for several minutes. Considering all the options. Debating with himself rather than arguing with me. "Then we'll do it, Honeybee."

KILLIAN

The bonfire rages in front of me, flames leaping higher and higher into the crystal-clear night sky. Smoke billows against black, and I follow it up to the expanse of stars spread out above me.

On the mountain, without any sort of light pollution, millions of them twinkle brightly, winking at me as if they know something I don't.

And they do.

They've been there for millions of years.

They witnessed it *all* since humans took their first steps on McBride Mountain, and they saw whatever happened to Willow.

Wherever she was over the past year...

Whoever she was with...

What she might have suffered...

They *know*.

Far more than *we* do.

Somehow, the fact that a massive ball of gas burning

millions of miles away in an infinite space has all the information when we have none pisses me the fuck off and prevents me from being able to enjoy the simple, pristine beauty of my view tonight.

That would be impossible with Willow inside the cabin, passed out, dead asleep after the last two days. The physical and emotional drain should keep her asleep, and hopefully, her memories and nightmares won't haunt her for at least an hour...because I need space.

Time to think.

Pine.

After being with her like that last night, feeling her pressed up against me, her tight, hot cunt clasping around my fingers, coating them in her sweet release, my entire body thrums with this pent-up...

Something.

A horrible conflict between what I want and what I know is right for Willow—especially after what happened at the gorge today.

And alcohol isn't helping me solve anything.

I take the final sip of my beer, letting the cool, hoppy liquid slide down my throat as I lean back in my chair and stare at the stars. *Those smug fuckers.* The empty bottle in my hand isn't going to cut it tonight. I set it beside my chair with the two other empties, the glasses smacking together with a light *tink.*

Snagging another one from the cooler, I release a frustrated sigh, then pop the cap off on the built-in opener.

"That bad?"

The voice from the darkness makes me flinch.

Shit.

I turn my head toward the sound of approaching footsteps and find Connor and Liam almost to me.

And I didn't even hear them coming.

God, am I fucking out of it...

Up here, always being alert, always being *aware,* is what keeps you safe and alive. Any number of threats linger in the darkness. Bears. Bobcats. Poisonous snakes.

My brothers...

But that woman in the cabin has *all* my focus.

Which could be very dangerous.

I scrub my hand down my face as Connor takes a seat to my left, and Liam settles into the one on my right. Connor reaches into the small cooler near my feet, grabs two beers, and pops the tops off on the arm of the chair, rather than using the opener.

"Hey, man! What the fuck?" I point to the wood Liam meticulously crafted into the beautiful custom piece of furniture. "You're going to leave gouge marks in that."

Liam smirks at me from my other side, leaning forward to snag a beer from Connor. "I'll make you a new one."

Connor hands it to Liam, and they sit back, both releasing a little sigh at finally getting off their feet after what was undoubtedly a long day at the lumberyard.

Where I should have been.

Just like I should have been there yesterday.

And all the other days I've spent on the mountain, completely ignoring my responsibilities to the company and our employees.

Thank fuck I have them to pick up the slack...

Still, guilt eats away at me for having my attention split between my responsibility to McBride Mountain, my employees at the timber yard, and my obsession with solving this mystery for Willow.

Because it definitely hasn't been split equally.

Not even close.

Since the moment I dragged her from that river, my entire focus, all my energy, every waking moment has been about *her.*

My knee bounces uncontrollably, the tension twisting

inside me seeking any outlet it can find, and a peaceful silence stretches between us as we enjoy our beers and the evening.

But it won't last with these two sitting with me.

Liam finally clears his throat, and I can feel his gaze on me. "Was it that bad?"

Hell.

He doesn't know when to leave well enough alone. If he even remotely suspects someone is keeping something in that's eating them alive, he'll dig until he reveals whatever it is. Like it's somehow his role on this planet to ensure no one wallows in their own misery.

I take a long sip of my beer, staring up at the sky, ignoring the heat of his eyes on me. "Was *what* that bad?"

He snorts. "Being up there with her. That's what has you all messed up in your head and sitting out here looking like that, isn't it?"

Too damn perceptive.

The kid always saw too much, even when he was little. And as he's grown into a man, so has his intuition, and his desire to fix everyone else's problems.

I shake my head. "It wasn't just that."

It was everything.

Every word she said.

Every look she gave me.

Every move she made.

But what happened today pushed me over that very narrow edge I've been balancing on between controlling my anger and frustration and completely losing it.

"Then what?"

I drag my gaze from the sky and return it to my brothers, first glancing at Liam and then Connor. "I took her all the way up to the gorge today."

Connor's jaw drops. "You're shitting me. That's like a five-mile hike from the river."

Nodding slowly, I remember every labored breath and step she took to get to the gorge this morning. How her face pinched in pain. But she wouldn't stop, despite how utterly exhausted she was after hiking to the river yesterday, then pushing farther today.

That strength she's always had and always demonstrated also makes her stubborn, and she had her mind set on seeing the gorge.

Willow wasn't going to fail, even if she was miserable.

Which meant I spent the entire day with the taste of her release still on my tongue, my cock still aching to be inside her, and my breath catching each time she stumbled or struggled at all.

"Probably longer than that from where we were..."

Liam shifts forward, resting his elbows on his knees. "Why did you go all the way up there?"

Because she asked me to.

Because I couldn't say no to that woman.

"She could describe it to me. In detail."

His brow furrows. "When would she ever have been up there? Did you ever take her?"

I shake my head. "No. Which made her think that maybe it was a memory from the past year returning. I took her up there to see if it triggered anything else to come back."

Connor taps his beer on the chair arm, raising a brow as I look over to him. "And?"

My hand tightens around my own bottle until my fingers ache, and the desire to chuck it into the fire makes my entire body tremble. "And fucking *nothing*." I take several more gulps of my beer, and even though I'm on my third one, the alcohol hasn't helped quell any of the churning turmoil threatening to drown me. "She didn't remember a goddamn thing. It felt familiar to her. We spent an hour exploring it, walking back and forth to both sides.

But absolutely nothing new came to her that might help us."

"Shit." Connor runs his hand over his thick hair. "And you didn't see any evidence that she came through there?"

I shake my head. "You know nobody lives up there. It's too steep to farm. And it's fucking chilly. The days don't get much warmer than, what, forty-five, fifty that high up even in the summer?"

They both nod.

"So, how could she have been in the gorge?" I concentrate on the fire, the flames flickering in the darkness. "The only thing past it is endless rough wilderness and a bunch of wild animals."

And to get from there to the river during a storm would have taken...

An act of God.

Liam shakes his head. "I don't know, man. This whole thing..." He shudders. "It gives me the creeps."

Connor nods his agreement. "Me, too. Something just isn't right."

Liam's eyes drift to the cabin, where Willow hopefully continues to sleep soundly. "Is she okay, though?"

A loaded question if I ever heard one.

I shrug. "As okay as she can be, I guess. Physically exhausted, sore as hell from the hike, even though I made her take it easy and went as slow as I could."

His gaze returns to mine. "And mentally?"

"Fuck"—I scrub a hand over my face—"I don't know how she is."

And given what happened in the tent last night, where she is mentally and where I am mentally are definitely *not* on the same page. They might not even be in the same *book*.

Hers seems to be some second-chance romance, while mine feels more like a tragic love story that ends in despair. She wants us to go back to how things were before she left, before I ruined everything, and that's just not possible, no matter how much I might want it, too.

I never should have touched her.

I never should have given in.

But seeing her so desperate, so needy for something only I could give her, made it impossible for me to say no, even when I knew it was wrong.

Which made today awkward as fuck.

The way she kept looking at me. Watching me, when she should have been paying attention to where her feet were going. Like she was expecting me to say something or do something. As if she wanted me to bring up the fact that I made her come all over my hand and that she wanted so much more than that.

Willow *wanted* to have that conversation.

And I was nowhere near ready to delve into it.

Coward.

Liam releases a long sigh, his own frustration as thick as my own. "So, what's the plan going forward?"

I rub the back of my neck and watch the flames again. "Sit out here and drink. That's my current plan."

Connor kicks up his feet on the cooler. "I can get behind that."

Good.

Because I am done talking.

I am done thinking for a while.

For a few blissful minutes, it's silent, only the crackle and pop of the fire and the occasional rustling of an animal in the trees break the moment of serenity.

But just like when they first arrived, it won't last long, not with these two doofuses.

And I know who will speak up first because he always does.

He can't help himself.

The three of us may not be brothers by blood, but since the day someone dropped him on Mom's doorstep with a note that said, "Please take care of him," he was ours. He was a McBride.

And he got the best of Mom.

All of her kindness, her caring, all of her ability to read people.

All the things I suck so much at, despite what Willow may think.

Liam's voice cuts through the night. "You need to tell her."

I slowly turn my head and look at him. "What?"

"You need to come clean with Willow. Tell her everything. If you don't, things are just going to continue to get more awkward between you the longer this goes on."

More awkward?

I snort and take a swig of my beer. "I don't think that's fucking possible."

"It is." His gaze softens. "I've seen the way she looks at you."

So have I.

I squeeze my eyes shut and see it behind my closed lids.

She looks at me like I'm her hero, but she should see me as the villain.

Before I can argue further with what was a good-intentioned suggestion to finally clear the air between us, the sound of the cabin door and soft footsteps on the porch freezes all of us.

Willow approaches, blanket wrapped tightly around her shoulders, now in a loose pair of sweatpants and a T-shirt she slipped into after the bath she took when we got back.

Connor and Liam both push up from their chairs.

Liam smacks my shoulder. "It's getting late. Time to hit the sack."

"You're abandoning me?"

They both give me a knowing smirk before they stalk off in

the direction of their cabins deeper on the property—just as she reaches me.

Fucking perfect.

She stands at the edge of the fire, eyes locked on it instead of me.

The flames cast light and shadows across the mostly healed bruises on her face. She tugs the blanket tighter, despite the warmth she must feel being so close to the pit.

"Are you all right?" I scan her, taking in every detail, searching for any signs of the distress that usually wakes her at night. "Did you have another nightmare?"

Those stormy orbs finally cut over to meet my gaze, and she shakes her head. "No. I just figured you'd be out here." She slowly makes her way around the bonfire pit and lowers herself into the seat Liam recently vacated next to me. "You always came out here when you needed to relax and think at night, and I figured you'd need to."

"Yeah, well, it isn't doing me much good." I drain the rest of my beer and set the empty down next to the cooler. "You want one?"

She shakes her head. "I'm good."

I pop open another and take a sip.

Her eyes return to the fire, and I know I should stop staring at her, should stop watching her, but I can't tear my gaze away.

Even after everything she's been through, she's still the most stunning thing I've seen in my life. The only woman who has ever held my heart, who's ever even gotten close to it, and yet, I destroyed her.

"I need you to do something for me, Killian." She finally glances over at me again. "Please."

It isn't like her not to just *ask.*

That tightens my gut.

"What?"

Her fingers twist the edges of the blanket. "I think it's time you told me the truth. I think it's time you told me what really happened between us. Because you spent the day avoiding me..."

"How could I avoid you? We were hiking together the whole day."

"And you barely met my eyes once." She huffs. "You barely spoke ten words to me the entire day. And as soon as we got here, you disappeared as quickly as you could."

"To take care of things around the homestead. We've been gone for two days—"

"We both know Connor and Liam were taking care of things, weren't they? So, stop bullshitting me. You were avoiding me because of what happened in the tent last night, and the only reason for you to be upset about *that* is because of whatever I can't remember. So, it's time you tell me. Now."

WILLOW

Killian stares at me—the strongest man I've ever known now looking like a deer caught in the headlights. He's never been afraid of anything in his life, has always taken on any challenge, any adversary, head-on and full-throttle.

The man never backs down from anyone or anything.

But right now, he looks ready to run.

I knew pushing for this, pushing *him*, might stir up some things that he would rather leave buried, but I can't take it anymore. Not after the way he looked at me last night. Not after the way he touched me. Not after the words he said.

It told me everything I need to know.

He still loves me.

He still wants me as much as I do him.

Which means I need to know what the hell happened to

tear us apart, to break what we had that was so fucking solid for so long in a way that he believes is irreparable.

"Please, Killian. *Talk*." I try to keep the tremor out of my voice, but waking up in that bed alone—again—after spending the night in his arms only twenty-four hours ago has pushed me to the point that I can't sit back anymore and pretend. "I may not be able to remember the last year, but I remember all the ones before that. I remember what we had together. I remember who you are, so none of this makes any sense to me. And the longer I go on without answers about *this*, the harder it is to live with the fact that I may never have answers about the last year. So, please, give me this. Give me *some* of my memories back."

I realize how desperate it sounds, but it's impossible to keep the plea from my voice at this point.

He scrubs his free hand over his beard and releases a long, heavy sigh, holding my gaze with his intense one. "I don't want to hurt you again. I don't know if you're ready to—"

My hands fist in the blanket. "Stop treating me like I'm going to fucking break, Killian."

"Fuck." He finally sighs and stares up at the stars above us, his clenched jaw working as he considers how to start. "You remember the Memorial Day Festival."

"Yes. Watching you carve..."

He nods, still not looking at me. "And *after*?"

Heat floods my cheeks as I turn more toward him, drawn closer like the man has a tractor beam locked on me, and he finally drags his gaze to meet mine.

The flames simmering there aren't the ones reflected from the bonfire in front of us. They're the heat of what happened in the cabin when we got home that night, just over a year ago. We both remember it. We both still *feel it.*

My pussy throbs at the memory of how completely he consumed me. "I remember all that, too."

Vividly.

He raises a brow. "And the next morning?"

No matter how hard I've tried over the past two weeks, nothing will come. He fucked me senseless. Tucked us into bed. And then...

Nothing.

I shake my head. "All just black."

Concern furrowing his brow, Killian nods slowly. "We woke up..."—his throat bobs on a thick swallow—"and had sex again. And you made pancakes, hash browns, eggs, a whole spread for the boys and me."

Which sounds like a pretty typical morning.

I would wake up and make them a monster breakfast to fuel them for the day before they went out to the timber yard, or out onto the mountain to fell trees with their men.

"They came and ate, then they headed to the yard, but...I stayed behind."

Killian doesn't offer anything else, just keeps watching me, as if he hopes my memory will decide to come back suddenly so he won't have to continue coming clean.

"Why?"

He releases a little mirthless laugh. His eyes heat again, that trepidation melting away into a burning desire I feel through every inch of my body. "I needed to get you alone again. Give you one more kiss. I wanted to feel you pressed up against me and under me before I left for the day..."

My heart aches at the sincerity of his words. "And?"

His Adam's apple bobs again as he gulps, then takes a few chugs of his beer.

Liquid courage, I guess, for whatever he has to tell me.

I tighten my grip on the blanket wrapped around me, burrowing deeper in it, cocooning myself in, and protecting myself from what he's about to say.

"You stared up at me after we kissed, and you said that by

this time next year we could have a fifth mouth to feed at the table, and it was like a bomb went off in my head."

My chest tightens, the words ringing in my head. "I said *what*?"

His gaze cuts to mine. "You'd spent the whole festival playing with Jenny and her kids, remember?"

I nod. "Yeah, we sat together for the parade while Raven was busy covering the festival."

Jenny Bellman has the cutest kids in town, and they're always a handful. She needed the help while her husband was busy running the smoker in the food tent.

"Well, apparently, it gave you baby fever because that morning you wouldn't stop talking about how we should start trying, even before the wedding." Acid churns in my stomach as he continues, "And I don't know how to explain it, but I saw this flash..."

"Of what?"

Killian hesitates for a second, afraid to reveal what he saw. "Of a beautiful, tiny version of you..."

Tears burn in my eyes, blurring his face.

His voice wavers slightly. "Of our daughter screaming and crying and me not knowing how to make anything better..."

My chest aches, as if a vise is closing around it, restricting my breathing.

Each breath gets harder to drag in.

"Of not knowing how the hell to be a father and failing miserably at it because I never had one."

A hot tear slides down my cheek.

"I had this vision of the kind of life she deserved, the kind of father she needed that I couldn't be, all the things that I couldn't provide, and...I don't know, I panicked."

The pain in his admission slices through my chest, and I swallow through the emotion choking me. I swipe at the tears, trying to see him through them. "You don't panic, Killian McBride."

His jaw sets hard as he stares at me. "I did."

"But we had discussed having kids before…"

He nods slowly. "In the future. Somewhere far down the line that wasn't immediate. We weren't even married yet, and…I thought everything was going to change. You wanted a baby"—he takes a long inhalation—"and you'd see what a shitty father I was." His icy gaze holds mine. "And I'd lose you." Killian shakes his head. "Saying it out loud now sounds fucking absurd, but at the time, it made me feel like I couldn't breathe, the thought that giving you what you wanted would mean the end of us. And I pulled out of your arms…"

Tears flow freely down my cheeks now, a tidal wave brought on by the panic I can still feel in his words.

And the terror I see in his eyes.

He's holding something back.

There's more.

The worst part.

"What did you say, Killian?"

The whole mountain knows to give Killian a wide berth.

They understand he can be short-tempered.

Quick to react.

Even mean, when he wants to be.

But no one has ever seen him *panicked.*

Panicked, Killian McBride would be downright volatile.

Maybe even to me.

His eyes shimmer in the firelight, unshed tears threatening to spill over. "Fuck." He shoves up from the chair and paces closer to the fire, staring down into it and giving me his back. A second passes. Then another. Then he chucks his beer bottle into the blaze, the glass shattering as the flames flash up. "I said the thing that made you leave."

My blood chills as I wait for him to continue.

He glances over his shoulder, and the regret and apology in his gaze are already enough for me to suspect where he's going with this.

It's the most obvious path to take when he wanted to hurt me in order to take the pressure off what *he* was feeling.

My biggest weakness.

He went for the jugular.

Killian doesn't look away, watching me as he prepares to shatter me all over again. "I asked you why you'd want to have kids after you'd had such a shitty mother. I asked you why you thought you'd be a good one when you never had one yourself."

A gasp slips from my lips, and the pain that hits me is ten thousand times worse than anything that was ever physically done to me before I woke up in that river.

He finally turns to face me fully. "I don't know why I said it. Because I'm a fucking prick. Because I felt cornered, and that's the one thing I've never been on this mountain before. Because you were always the only one who could ever get through to me, and that scared the fuck out of me. Because I took my own fear and threw it back at you so I didn't have to *feel* so much. I don't know—"

"Fuck you, Killian McBride."

The tears burn hot, sliding down my cheeks.

His hands fist at his sides. "I deserve that. And I knew it as soon as I said the words. I knew it was unforgivable." He sighs. "So, I stormed out of the cabin and disappeared into the woods with my axe, to take all that agony and frustration out on something other than you." He shoves a hand through his hair, pushing the long blond strands from his face. "And when I came back to explain, to beg you for another chance, you were gone. Without so much as a fucking note. Just my mother's ring on the nightstand and all your things gone." His body trembles. "I drove into town, figuring you were at Raven's, but she said you'd left."

I gape at him.

My brain can't process the fact that the man who was always there for me, was always my everything, could have been the one who hurt me the most by hitting me in my weakest point.

The relationship I had with Mom was difficult at best, horrible at worst, and she was never someone who should have had custody of a child in her state.

He was right when he said I didn't have a good mother, and he's right in knowing that saying *I* couldn't be a good mother because I didn't have one would cut me to the core.

To anyone else, it might not have stung as badly.

But for me...

"I knew you would probably never forgive me for what I said, but I tried to go after you. I got on the highway, and I drove and drove and drove, but I didn't know where you had gone because Raven wouldn't tell me..."

God bless that best friend of mine.

"I eventually had to come back, but I tried every day for a year to get Raven to tell me where you were. I begged for any information. But she stood her ground. She told me you were happy." His voice wavers again, and he clenches his hands. "Away from me. Away from the mountain. And I believed her. What you do, your candles, I always knew they'd be a great business beyond McBride Mountain, and I figured you'd found that...and maybe someone who could give you what you wanted."

A sob climbs up my throat as I stare at the only man I've ever loved. "All I've ever wanted is *you*, Killian."

He shakes his head. "That's not true. You wanted a family, and I wasn't sure I could give that to you."

"But *why*?"

None of this makes sense—his fear of being a father.

The panic it caused.

Killian throws out his hands. "I don't fucking know!" He shakes his head again. "Because I never had a father. I don't know how to *be* one. I don't know how to be gentle, or control my temper, or—"

I push out of my chair and march straight over to him, my entire body vibrating with anger. "Bullshit! You *had* one—it just didn't look like everyone else's. Your dad may have died when you were young, but your mother! Good God, she was *both* parents for you. And then she took in Connor and Liam, and I've never seen a family that was as happy as you guys were together. She welcomed anyone into your home and to your table as if they were family." I fight another sob as my tears rush out completely unbidden. "How many nights did I call your mom to come get me so I could sleep on your couch when my mom came home drunk or high and I didn't feel safe there?"

He winces, squeezing his eyes closed.

Stepping forward, I shove a finger into his hard chest. "You *had* a role model, you had a family, so why didn't you want one with me?"

His eyes flutter open again. "That's just it. I *did*. Every time I thought about your belly swelling with my child, holding him or her, watching our baby grow up, I couldn't stop smiling. I was just terrified that I would fail our child and *you,* and it would be the end of *us.*"

The fire crackles beside us, its heat warming me while the chill of his confession still tingles my spine.

"Killian McBride, you've never failed at anything in your life."

"I failed to protect you—"

A twig snaps loudly in the trees to our left, and both of us whirl toward the sound.

Killian's arm snaps out and wraps around me, urging me

behind him. "Get the fuck back in the cabin. Lock the door. You know where I keep the shotgun and shells. Load it."

"It's probably just—"

"Go!" He glances over his shoulder for a second to ensure I see how serious he is. "If anyone else comes to the door, use it."

His body radiates with tension that leaves no room for argument.

Whatever he's sensing, he doesn't want me anywhere near it.

And no one knows what dangers lurk on this mountain better than Killian.

12

KILLIAN

The sound of the cabin door clicking closed and Willow throwing the lock, safely securing herself inside, finally sets me in motion.

I back away from the fire slowly, keeping my eyes on the trees where the sound came from while sinking into the shadows toward the barn. Willow has my shotgun to protect herself, and I taught her how to use it. But I need a weapon, and there's only one that will do.

My axe...

It leans against the wall inside the barn where I left it when I unpacked our gear after coming down the mountain earlier this evening.

I just have to get to it before whatever is in the woods gets to me.

Another twig snaps in the thick foliage, and I freeze, tilting my head to listen better. Taking in all the sounds of McBride Mountain at night.

Darkness has fully descended.

Only the moon overhead casts any light onto the homestead, but I keep to the shadows, working my way across the clearing toward my favorite weapon.

Because something tells me I'm going to need it.

It wouldn't be unusual for one of the black bears to get near the homestead, but they're typically bedded down for the night by now. Rarely seen after dusk. And a coyote or bobcat wouldn't have been big enough to make that sound, plus they move far too stealthily to alert anyone that they're near.

Which leaves one other predator I can think of that exists on McBride Mountain that could be in the trees...

The worst kind.

And the hardest to best.

The closer I move to the barn, the harder my heart thunders under my ribcage.

Thud. Thud.

Thud. Thud.

Thud. Thud.

I step backward through the still-open doors and snag my axe from where it leans against the wall, then cautiously make my way toward the fire pit and the direction of the noise.

Step by deliberately slow step.

Circling to the east along the treeline to remain in the deepest shadows and away from where the moonlight might reveal my location.

Something rustles in the darkest part of the forest.

The easiest place to conceal your presence if you were trying.

But whatever is back there, it doesn't sound big enough to be a bear.

They lumber.

They often crash through things.

This is more deliberate.

Intentional.

Almost as if something *wants* us to know it is there while remaining hidden.

Come out and play.

My hand flexes on the axe handle, the familiar weight helping to calm my heart rate and smooth out my breathing. But it can't prevent the churning in my gut, the feeling I've had that there's something worse than black bears on McBride Mountain. Something far more dangerous. Something that could hurt her and take her away from me again. Something we have to be prepared for.

I freeze and listen, waiting again for any sound that doesn't fit the normal nightly chorus on the homestead.

Only dead silence greets me, as if whatever is there has frozen in place, too, waiting for me to make a move. Time ticks by as I loosen and tighten my grip on the axe in anticipation. The worn shaft and heavy head comfort me with the knowledge that I can decimate anything that comes at me with one swing.

Seconds become minutes.

I don't know how long I stand staring into the trees, scanning, watching, and listening. Long enough that it seems as though the shadows stretch differently in the moonlight as it makes its way across the sky.

Shit.

And Willow's in the cabin alone, probably terrified with me out here.

The longer I stand still, listening and waiting, the more it becomes clear that whatever is in the trees has no intention of being caught tonight. If it weren't for Willow, I could stay out here until sunrise, waiting for whatever—or whoever—it is to make a move, to make one wrong decision so I can act.

A single sound could guide me into the woods without hesitation, but I can't wait forever.

I'm not going to let her suffer any longer. I'm not going to let her worry when there's any way I can prevent it and make it better for her. And after what has already happened, the conversation that got interrupted, she's already in an emotional place.

Staying here to wait out the enemy in the dark will only make it worse.

I slowly ease away from the treeline and move back toward the cabin, continuing to listen and watch, though the night remains eerily silent.

Not even the usual chirping of crickets to break up the monotony.

They know something is there, too.

Not good.

And if I try to make it to Connor or Liam's place across the homestead to warn them of what might be happening, it would leave Willow alone even longer.

Once I'm inside with her, we'll be safe.

Nothing will get through that door or through me.

I finally make it to the porch, rush up the stairs, and knock, still scanning the property and taking in every detail visible in the moonlight. "Willow, it's me."

The click of the lock opening is quickly followed by the door flying open. I push inside and nudge it closed behind me, throwing the deadbolt back into place before turning to face the main cabin.

Willow stands merely a foot away, clutching my grandfather's shotgun tightly, her knuckles white. The blanket that had been wrapped around her now lies on the floor, discarded in haste as she ran into the cabin. "Are you okay?"

I nod and set my axe next to the door, then slowly step forward, holding out my hand. "Give me the gun."

Her bottom lip quivers as she stares at me, almost as if she doesn't understand the request. "What was it?"

Bad.

"I don't know."

Not true.

I know *exactly* what was out there tonight, but I refuse to scare her more. We're safe in the cabin, and I would never let anything happen to her. She *has* to believe that if she's ever going to feel secure again.

Her dark brows draw low over her eyes, her hands trembling. "A bear?"

"Maybe."

It isn't a complete lie.

It could have been, and I could simply be overreacting, reading far too much into a simple sound because I'm paranoid now, but after everything that's happened, I don't know that I have the luxury of believing that.

"Likely just a bear. Maybe a coyote." I motion again for her to hand me the weapon. "Please give me the gun."

Willow may know how to use it, but the way she's shaking right now, I don't want it in her hands. She presses her lips together firmly, like she's about to argue, before she finally steps forward and passes it to me. I unload the cartridges and slowly set them and the weapon beside the door next to my axe, where they will be easy to get to, should I actually need them.

But something tells me the intruder on the homestead doesn't want a confrontation right now.

If they did, it would have happened while I was out there, unarmed and vulnerable, not while I'm safely in the cabin where everyone knows I have a gun.

We're missing something.

Something crucial.

Some piece in a game she's a part of.

I need to fill in Connor and Liam, then call Tony on the sat phone and tell him to get up here at first daylight so we can investigate whoever was on the homestead, but all that can wait.

All that matters now is Willow.

She trembles in front of me. Her eyes remain unfocused, like she's having trouble processing everything that's happened tonight.

"Willow, look at me."

Tears start to stream down her cheeks...

Shit.

"Willow..."

"I thought...I thought something was going to happen to you—"

"I'm okay."

She shakes her head, and I can see the second she switches from concerned to downright frantic. A sob slips from her lips, her body shaking violently. "What if it attacked you? What if—"

"I'm fine." I step forward and pull her toward me, knowing damn well that only a few minutes ago she wanted nothing to do with me. With one arm firmly wrapped around her waist, I tilt her face up until she's forced to look at me. "Listen to me, Willow. I've lived on this mountain my entire life, and nothing has gotten me yet. You're safe. *I've* got *you*."

"Do you?"

The way she asks it slices through my heart.

After what I just revealed to her, she has every right to want to push me away, to want to rail and scream against the person who hurt her the most, the person who sent her running from this place, from her home.

But she doesn't.

Either because she doesn't want to or because she lacks the strength to do it at this moment.

She collapses against me, and I bury my face in her hair, pressing her close. All the tension that's permeated the air between us since what happened in the tent seems to boil over as she stares up with tear-stained cheeks. "I need to know something."

I brush my finger across her skin softly, wiping away the tear that trickles from the corner of her eye. "Anything."

"Do you really believe that? What you said to me that day?"

Wincing, I immediately shake my head. "Of course not."

I've regretted saying those words since the moment they left my mouth, not merely because they hurt her but because they were categorically untrue.

Willow is the most caring, compassionate, loving person I've ever met. She'll be an incredible mother one day—and hopefully make up for my inadequacies.

Every second of every day she was gone, I contemplated what would have happened if I hadn't said them.

How different life would have been if I hadn't completely lost all sense of myself and gone for the jugular because I didn't want her to see *my* flaws.

Her eyes shimmer with tears as she stares up at me, clutching the front of my shirt tightly in her hands. "Do you really believe you'd be a bad father?"

Hearing those words out of her mouth feels like having my own axe driven straight through my heart.

The very few memories I have of Dad flash through my head. Him showing me how to swing an axe. Cuddling with him on the chair that still sits near the fireplace. Going to the timber yard with him and spinning in his office chair until I felt dizzy.

They've faded over the years, but I know deep in my gut that he was a great father.

And once he was gone, Mom did everything with us that he would have.

Took us fishing and hunting...

Taught us how to run the lumberyard...

Most importantly, showed us what love really meant.

I may not have a clue about children and have no idea how to even hold one, but the woman in my arms could teach me.

Willow wouldn't let me fail.

"I told you I realized how absurd it was, how stupid I had been, but by the time I did, it was too late. You were gone."

She stares at me for a few moments longer before she finally sighs, releasing so much of the frustration she's held on to for the past two weeks. "I understand why I would have been upset. Why I would have felt betrayed and lost. But..."

Her eyes glaze over slightly.

"But what?"

She tilts her head slightly, her face still angled up at me, but she's not looking at me.

Willow is somewhere else.

Her brows draw low together, and she frowns. "But I didn't leave you."

"What?"

That tempest-filled gaze clears, snapping back to meet mine. "The whole time I was in here, I was thinking about what you said. About what you told me that day, and how I packed up everything and left. And it felt...wrong. Like I was hearing a story that didn't make any sense and was missing pieces."

Missing pieces.

"Your memory is still messed up—"

She shakes her head. "No. I remember now."

"Remember what?"

"Not everything. God, I wish I did. But enough about that day." She chews on her bottom lip, thinking. "I *did* pack up. I *did* intend to leave. I had even started down the mountain, intent on spending a few days, maybe even a few weeks, away from this place, away from you, somewhere I could think and process what you said and how much it hurt me. But then I stopped."

"What do you mean?"

She stares up at me, her eyes wide as the memory floods her. "I *stopped*. I didn't make it to Asheville. I turned around, and I came *back*."

My heart stutters.

My hands tighten on her.

My knees tremble.

"Are you positive?"

Willow nods adamantly. "Yes. I realized you only would have said that if something else was wrong, if you were terrified. You've never intentionally hurt me, with words or otherwise, in our entire lives. And I didn't believe you would have for any other reason than that you were scared. So, I came back so we could talk, so I could figure out why you felt like you needed to say that..."

"But you never made it."

"No." Her body tenses. "And I can't remember why." She squeezes her eyes closed. "There's something else there. Something important I can't remember."

WILLOW

Killian holds me steady, silent. Giving me time to sort through the flashes of memory assaulting me.

When I finally open my eyes, he stares down at me, his jaw locked hard, his eyes glinting in the moonlight streaming in from the windows. "Maybe you changed your mind and turned around again to leave because of what I said, because you couldn't forgive me."

His words just don't feel true.

Deep in my heart, I *know* that didn't happen.

What he said was awful.

It was a personal blow that did exactly what it intended—drew my attention away from *his* insecurity. But it wasn't something that should have sent me running from the mountain *forever*.

A piece is still missing.

Something vital.

Yet even with that gap still there, I *know* I came back that day.

I shake my head. "No. I remember driving back through town, up the mountain. I was coming *home*. There was something I needed to tell you..."

Killian lifts his other hand to cradle my face between his palms. "Why? You had every reason to hate me that day, to want to leave me. I took the worst thing in your life, the thing I knew would hurt you the most, and used it as a weapon against you. You should have wanted to get away from me."

Hot tears streak down my face. "Because I *know* you, Killian McBride. I had already forgiven you before I even made the decision to come back and turned the car around."

"Christ, Willow." His thumbs brush across my cheeks, wiping away my tears as his own threaten to fall. "I never deserved you—"

And that's *always* been his problem.

Killian has never believed he deserves anything.

He's always working. Always pushing himself. He never thought he did enough for his mother, his brothers, or the town. There was always more he could be doing. More he could be giving.

He took on the weight of caring for McBride Mountain and its residents when his mother died and let it crush him.

That's what led him to believe he wouldn't be a good father.

That's what made him panic.

His need to give *everything* yet somehow never believing it was enough.

It's the reason I've always loved him.

The reason I *still* do, despite everything.

I push up onto my toes and feather my lips across his, desperate for the one thing he hasn't given me since I've been back.

Us.

That ignitable spark that's crackled there since the moment my eyes met his in that hospital. That magnetic pull that's dragged me to him and his arms each time the darkness releases another memory. That heat and passion only he has ever given me.

The small taste of it in the tent last night proved it all still exists.

For *both* of us.

He tunnels his hands into my hair and tugs me back from him, halting the kiss, but I can *feel* how much he's trembling. Hear the hitch in his breath. "You don't want to do this, Honeybee."

I slide my hand over his heart. It beats rapidly under my palm. Solid. Strong. Like the man who lives by it and sometimes lets it get the best of him.

"I do." I nod. "I miss you, Killian. My heart knows how long it's been, even if my head doesn't, and it knows I forgave you a year ago, before whatever it was interceded and stopped me from getting back to you." Pushing my hand tighter against his chest, I emphasize my point. "This is where I belong. Where I'm meant to be. This mountain, this cabin, with you. The rest we can figure out."

"Fuck..."

The word comes out more growl than spoken.

A rumble beneath my palm.

I can feel his resolve breaking.

The tension and the way his body vibrates along mine.

He's close to giving in.

To handing over what I really, truly want.

He's so.

Damn.

Close.

I tug against his hold on my face until I can kiss him again, pressing my lips to his in a greedy taking that usually comes from him. He hesitates for a moment before he returns the kiss, his hand sliding to cup the back of my head and angle it so he can glide his tongue across my lips and delve deep in, tasting me, consuming me the way I've longed for.

Every nerve ending in my body flares to life.

A low whimper slips from my lips, and he captures it, slowing the kiss and then pulling away.

"Fucking hell, Willow." He pants wildly, his chest heaving against my own. "I'll spend the rest of my life making it up to you, I promise. Every fucking minute. Whatever you want, whatever you need, I'll give it to you."

I cling to his shirt, clutching the soft fabric in my hands. "You always do."

"I thought you'd hate me after I told you what I said." He drops his forehead to mine and heaves out a long, uneven breath that's as shaky as he is right now. "I thought...God, when I found you in the river, I prayed maybe it was God giving me a second chance to make up for what I'd done. But then I thought there was no forgiving that."

"There wouldn't have been, if I actually believed you meant it. If I didn't know *you* and how you react...often badly."

His temper, shortness, and volatility toward pretty much anyone always stemmed from his desire to just get things done quickly, efficiently—*right*.

No bullshit.

No wasted time.

It scared people, but the time I spent in this cabin with him and his family showed me who he *really* was.

"I've always known that about you, Killian. Impolite in public, rough with anyone who disrupts your day, volatile when someone crosses a line."

I thought he had never been that way with me, but he was right.

He did cross a line that day.

But he didn't say what he did to hurt me; he said it because he was scared. Because he was hurting himself. Because he didn't know what to do with all the feelings he had of his own potential inadequacy.

He hates to fail.

And failing at being a father would have been the *ultimate* failure for him.

After losing his at such a young age, he undoubtedly thought he wouldn't know *how* to be a good one, but he couldn't have gotten it more wrong.

It was stupid, idiotic, but he never stopped loving me.

He did it because he loves me, because he thought he would lose this.

Us.

He kisses me again, his groan rumbling through his chest and into mine as he reaches down and grasps my hips, lifting me easily. I wrap my legs around his waist, the dull ache in my side at the motion barely even registering anymore. How can it with his hands buried in my hair, his mouth moving over mine, our breaths mingling with each desperate meeting of our lips.

Killian stalks into the bedroom, laying me down across the comforter gently as he settles above me, kissing his way across my cheek to my ear.

He nips at it gently, making me twist and arch under him. "Don't move." His hand glides down to my rib cage, pressing against it. "I don't want you to hurt yourself."

Is he fucking joking?

Don't move when he does something like that to me?

Fucking impossible.

Hot, urgent lips glide down my neck, and I tilt my head away, giving him better access. He makes his way to the *V* of my T-shirt, then grasps the hem, lifts it from my arms, and tosses it aside, exposing my bare breasts to him.

They pebble instantly under his heated gaze.

Anticipating what's to come.

"Fucking hell. Even more beautiful than I remember them."

He dips his head and sucks one taut nipple into his mouth.

"Oh, God..."

I arch into him, pressing against his hips where his hard cock is now pinned between us. He groans his approval, lathing his tongue across the turgid peak as his other hand slides down and finds the waistband of my sweatpants. He toys with it, slowly dragging his fingers along the sensitive skin of my lower belly, making me spasm under him.

He releases my nipple and glances up at me as he moves to my other one. "I told you to be still."

"That's...not going to happen."

It comes out breathy, desperate, not sounding like me at all, and a slow, lecherous grin spreads across his lips.

"I won't do anything to hurt you, Honeybee." He dips his head and slowly circles his tongue around my nipple, refusing to give it direct contact. "Maybe we should stop so I don't risk it."

I tunnel my hands into his thick blond hair and jerk on the long strands harshly. His eyes flare with an intense heat I know I'm going to feel burn me.

"Don't you fucking stop, Killian McBride."

This is all I've wanted besides *answers* since I first came back to the cabin.

Him.

Us.

Like this.

The way we used to be, all fire and passion, heat and desperation, the need for each other overpowering our good senses.

Because he's probably right.

It's probably too soon for my cracked ribs to handle whatever he has planned, but I can't find myself caring as he slowly releases my nipple and sinks down lower, tugging my joggers and panties with him.

He pulls them off my feet and tosses them onto the floor, leaving me sprawled out naked in front of him. Fully exposed in front of the man who has always made me feel like a queen. Searing heat flickers through his gaze as it rakes over me. "I didn't think it was possible for you to get more beautiful, but somehow you have."

Slowly, he reaches out and reverently trails his fingers over the almost-healed bruises that are turning an ugly color of yellow and green, with a few places still mottled spots of purple.

Many of the scrapes and scratches have healed, only the deeper cuts still visible.

He catalogs each one, bending down to feather his lips over them.

"I'm so sorry this happened to you." Another soft brush of lips. Warm breath fluttering over goosebumped, marred skin. "I promise to make whoever is responsible pay for what they did to you."

And I know he will.

I trust him implicitly because, despite what he said to me, I know he didn't mean it, that my flight from the mountain was temporary, that I was always coming back to him, no matter what.

He finally reaches the apex of my thighs and nudges them wider, brushing his thumb lightly over my slick core. I groan and fist my hands in his hair as he slowly lowers his head and buries his face between my legs.

Fuck.

My back arches as his tongue glides over me with intense focus and determination.

Heat curls low in my belly and spreads to every limb, every nerve ending, as he explores me as if he's never been there before, as if he needs to relearn what to do and how I like it.

Like he could ever fail at this.

Killian always had a brutal mouth, as brutal as the hands he uses, both to cut down trees and to carve such beautiful creatures from them. He brings pleasure and delicious pain. Torture and release. He's a man of juxtapositions. The way he lives his life, the type of person he is, and how he is with me in bed.

All of it mind-bending.

But somehow it's all Killian.

And as he thrusts his tongue into me, all the air is sucked from my lungs.

He sets a slow, languid rhythm, licking and sucking and nipping but never giving me exactly what I want.

"Killian, please."

He always loved to hear me beg.

Loved to have me like this, writhing and desperate underneath him.

Sometimes he would make me wait until I thought I might actually die from the need. But not tonight. His mouth settles over my clit—*finally*—and I release a massive sigh of relief before his tongue flicks over it, sending sharp bolts of electricity shooting through me.

His hands slide up my thigh, and he easily slips two fingers into me, spreading me wide and filling me.

"Oh, God."

I clench around them as he curls them up and starts to drag

them down in a come-hither motion that has me arching into him over and over again as his tongue slowly decimates me.

Killian may have seen himself as the villain in this story, but at his heart, he's still my hero. Giving me exactly what I need. Rescuing me from whatever chases me in the night. Slaying my demons. Giving me home.

He'll always keep me safe, like this, as long as we're together.

As long as we don't let anything come between us again.

He sucks my clit between his teeth and grazes them slowly across it, and that low heat blasts into an erupting volcano, my orgasm swirling and cresting, making me writhe on the bed beneath him as his strong body pins me down.

All my injuries are forgotten on the waves of pleasure I ride out as he continues to thrust his fingers and work his tongue and lips over me.

His groan of approval fills my ears, mixing with the rushing sound of my world melting away, carrying along with it every concern I had.

At least for now.

13

KILLIAN

W illow twitches under me, her body sagging deep into the mattress as I swallow the last of her release, savoring the taste, relishing getting to experience it with this woman again.

I wasn't lying.

She's somehow grown more beautiful in our time apart, and I'm even more desperate for her, my cock aching, pressed against the zipper of my pants, begging to drive home to the place I always felt I belonged.

With her.

So close that nothing could get between us or separate us.

I thought it would always be this way until I said the stupidest thing I ever have in my life. The one thing I thought she could never forgive me for. But somehow, this impossibly strong, stunning woman did.

She's giving me another chance, and I will spend the rest of my life on my knees for her to prove to her that she made the right decision.

Her eyes flutter open and watch me where I still sit between her legs. I start to dip my head again to savor her one more time. To feel her come apart on my tongue and fingers.

But she threads hers through my hair again, halting my advance. "No. I need you."

Hell.

Those are the words I always loved to hear from her mouth, but tonight, they mean so much more.

They mean forgiveness.

They mean a second chance at what I lost.

They mean a belief that things *will* be okay even if it feels like they won't be.

"Are you sure?"

Her eyes narrow on me. "You won't hurt me, Killian. You never could."

That absolute faith and unwavering voice simultaneously shatters me as it puts the broken pieces of my heart back together again.

Something I never thought possible.

I slowly climb up over her, bracing myself on one elbow at the side of her head, hovering above her and staring down at her thick, dark hair spread out around her like a halo. It's beautifully poetic because she's always been an angel to me and everyone else she meets. "But I did." I trail my fingers across her flushed cheek. "Badly."

She turns into my touch. "And you've suffered for it long enough."

"I don't think I have."

There isn't enough time or space or physical pain that could make up for what I said to her and the results of it.

Willow gives me a sad smile. "Well, for tonight, just pretend you have so that you can let it go." She reaches down between us and wraps her small, soft palm around my cock, cupping me through my pants, eliciting a groan as it jerks against her hold. "Please, Killian."

Just like when we were in the tent, I can't deny her.

When this woman wants something, it's impossible for me to say no. The one time I did, my entire world fell apart, and I won't risk that again.

I ghost my lips across her forehead. "Okay."

She grins and starts to reach for my fly, but I catch her hand, squeezing her wrist.

"But I have a few rules."

Her eyes flare with heat and interest. "What kind of rules?"

I grin at her. "We take things slow. I don't want to hurt you."

She opens her mouth to protest again, and I silence her with a languid kiss. It has her squirming under me almost immediately, but I drag it out. Slowly exploring her mouth and reveling in her taste. Working her up until she can't take it anymore and tugs on my hair harshly.

God, she needs this almost as badly as I do.

To re-cement our connection. To reaffirm everything we just said to each other. To make up for time lost. To feel like life isn't spiraling out of our control by *taking* it in this moment.

I force myself to pull away so I can undo my zipper and slip off my pants and boxer briefs. They hit the floor, followed by my T-shirt, before I climb back onto the bed, settling over her again, my cock pinned between us.

Every fiber of my being aches for her.

Time hasn't done anything but make me need her more.

I kiss her again, and her hand wraps around my shaft, stroking it gently. Light fingertips glide across the head, slick pre-cum spreading over it. My hips buck as pleasure shoots through me, and I almost come all over her belly before we've even started.

"I'm not going to last long, Honeybee. It's been a year, and

I've thought of nothing every time I took my cock in my own hand except being with you like this again."

She shudders, arching into me, her grip tightening. "Did you do that often?"

Her question comes breathy, full of desire and annoyance at how slow I'm taking things.

"Every fucking night. Every time I thought about you, I either snuck out into the woods and chopped down trees until my hands bled or came in here and stroked my cock until I came, wishing it was inside you." I shift back and cup her breast, flicking my thumb across the nipple. "Or across these beautiful tits." I slide my hand down her smooth stomach. "Or over this belly."

She spasms as my palm cups her pussy.

"But especially right here."

I slide my other hand around her, then roll onto my back, taking her with me. She yelps slightly at the quick movement, and I shift until I'm settled half-propped against the pillows and she's draped across me.

"You're going to take the lead tonight, Willow."

Her eyes flare. "What?"

"You're going to ride me, Honeybee. You're going to take what you need at your own pace, so I don't hurt you."

It's a complete one-eighty from what she's used to with me.

Willow loves to relinquish control. To let me lead and allow her to go to that headspace where she doesn't have to think, doesn't have to do anything but *feel*. But tonight, I need her to *take*.

She seems to consider my demands for a moment before her gaze fills with intent, and she strokes my cock again, harder this time, twisting her wrist around the head and spreading another bead of pre-cum across it.

It throbs in her grip, aching to be inside her, to feel the warm clasp of her cunt.

All I want is to watch her come undone on my cock and know it's because of me.

When she dips her head and kisses me as she shifts back, settling herself directly over my length, I hold my breath.

Waiting.

Watching the way she catalogs my tattoos and every inch of my body the same way I have done hers. Her eyes linger on my right arm, where the new tattoo of the bleeding heart with the very important words is now inked permanently.

Her fingers trail over it. "What does *'Veni, vidi, amavi'* mean?"

I slide my hand to her hip, holding her steady. "I came, I saw, I loved. Only you, Honeybee. Always only you."

The love reflecting at me momentarily allows all other considerations to float away on a cloud of need, and Willow sinks down slightly, taking just the head inside her.

I swallow a hiss, my eyes closing and my head tipping back at how hot and tight she is.

Good God.

She stills, and my eyes fly open to find hers.

I search for any signs of discomfort. "Are you all right?"

Her mouth opens slightly. She pants and nods. "I'm okay."

Slowly, she starts to ease herself down onto me, inch by inch. Her tight, wet core cocoons me, and by the time she fully seats herself, my entire body tremors with the effort it takes to hold back.

My hands find her hips and squeeze gently, afraid of hurting her, then I glide my palm up to her ribs and press against the healing bruise there. "If this hurts too much..."

Willow pushes up, allowing me to slide out until only the tip remains in. Squeezing, she sinks down slowly, her mouth falling open on a silent cry. "Oh, God, it doesn't!"

She's lying.

I've cracked enough ribs in my day to know it has to hurt.

But whether she's lying or it's merely the adrenaline and endorphins, all the hormones raging through her that allow her to keep going, it doesn't seem to matter to her.

She starts a slow rhythm, and I slide my hands lower to help lift her so that it isn't so much work. Leaning forward, she braces her hands on my bare chest, one directly over my heart, the other over the top peak of McBride Mountain.

Her hips roll as she glides back down, squeezing me so tightly I grit my teeth to keep from coming immediately.

"Fuck, Willow. I'm not going to last. I'm not—"

She silences me with a kiss, rocking forward, the change of angle allowing me to brace my feet and push up into her even deeper.

A gasp falls from her lips against mine, the sound so heady and filled with so much need and emotion that tears start to pool in my eyes for the time we lost.

For how I hurt her.

For whatever she suffered while she was gone.

For the situation we have found ourselves in.

For all of it.

She lowers her forehead to mine and starts moving again, meeting each of my cautious upward thrusts with a down-slam of her hips, grinding her clit against my pelvis, exactly the way I know she likes it, the way that will build her up and allow her to fly.

Her arms start to shake, and her thighs quiver along my sides.

"You're close, baby?"

She nods and whimpers, pulling her lip between her teeth and biting down as she continues to roll her hips against mine.

I slide my hand up around her neck, and she whimpers, that needy mewl that I know means she's about to come tumbling out of her.

Yes.

She's almost there.

So close.

I squeeze gently, the way I know she likes it, not hard enough to restrict her breathing, just enough to let her know it's there, and she detonates, her body spasming as I continue to pump into her, her breath catching, her pussy squeezing my cock and finally drawing out my own release.

My breath rushes out of me, along with my orgasm, and I drive into her four more times, releasing deep inside her before she finally comes down and collapses on top of me, both of us finally letting go of all the things that have been holding us back since her return.

Not anymore.

The worst thing I ever did was not be completely honest with her, not give her the opportunity to talk me off the ledge I was balancing on in my own head when it came to our future together.

I may have tried to hold on to my secret, tried to prevent her from knowing what I'd done, but coming clean appears to have been what I should have done from the beginning.

And maybe it will be all she needs to help bring her memory back so I can keep her safe.

So I can keep her mine.

***

WILLOW

Excruciating pain bands around my abdomen, and I gasp, trying to find my breath through the agony. I wrap my arms around myself, curling inward, seeking any relief from the pain.

It doesn't come.

Someone tries to grab my shoulder, but I bat the hand away with all the force I can muster up.

Not wanting the touch.

Not wanting it *at all*.

"Don't fucking touch me!"

My stomach roils, and I barely manage to get the words out before another scream rents the air, ripped from deep in my chest, filled with my anguish and rage—

No. No. No.

Not like this...

Panic wells.

Choking me.

Suffocating me.

The agony comes again—stronger, more intense, unyielding.

Blinding.

There is no escaping it, no hiding, no relief.

I bolt upright in the bed.

Soaked in sweat.

Lungs seizing.

Head spinning.

Vision unfocused.

A hand reaches for me, sliding across my bare shoulder, but I slap it away, my body violently shaking as the nightmare, or memory, or whatever it is, still lingers.

It's there.

That pain.

So *real*.

So *intense*.

The touch of the hand on my shoulder that *wasn't* Killian's...

But I sense him beside me in the bed. "Willow?"

"I...I just need..."

I don't know what I need.

I can't...

I can't...

Darkness encroaches on the edges of my vision the longer I struggle to draw air into my lungs.

I can't breathe.

The vise around my chest refuses to budge.

I throw off the comforter and stumble from the bed, still naked after falling asleep in Killian's arms.

My feet hit the hand-hewn wood floor, and I stumble slightly, grabbing the nightstand to keep me upright long enough to find my bearings and work my way to the bathroom.

Heavy footsteps come fast behind me, and by the time I grip the counter and look up in the mirror, he's flipped on the light and is right there behind me, his blue gaze full of panicked concern as he watches me in our reflection. "Willow, tell me what happened."

I squeeze my eyes closed, unable to look at him as the memory assaults me like a branding iron driven straight into my brain. "I was in a lot of pain. And...and th-there was someone there. Someone I didn't want touching me. Maybe the one who hurt me. I don't..." I grit my teeth, my head throbbing as I attempt to force the memory to come clearer through sheer will, even though that's never worked before. "I don't understand it. I don't know. I..."

Killian steps forward and wraps his arms around me, tugging me back against his naked body tightly, holding me steady, taking my weight, and supporting me fully.

I may not have wanted him to touch me a few moments ago, but he knew that was what I need now, to ground me, to bring me back when I'm unraveling.

His familiar scent wraps around me as he grazes his lips over my neck. "I've got you, Honeybee. You're safe."

"I can't"—I struggle to take a breath—"I-I can't breathe."

"You can." He rests his hand flat over my chest, the other across my stomach. "Take a deep breath in."

I do it slowly, following his command, sucking air in

through my nose, my body filling with the much-needed oxygen, pressing out against his hold.

"Good." His warm breath flutters across my neck. "Now, let it out...slowly."

Instead of the rush that wants to flow from deep in my chest, I concentrate on doing as I'm told.

Slowly.

Air floats from between my lips, a long flow as his hands move with me.

"Again."

Another command I have to follow.

Over and over.

Deep.

Slow.

Breaths.

Directed by the man who holds my life in his hands.

Until my heart finally slows.

Until my lungs stop feeling like they're unyielding stone.

Killian's even breathing and rough palms on my skin guide me back to finally feeling like I'm *here* in this moment with *him* again.

"Come on." He murmurs the command against my skin, then slides away, dragging me toward the shower, cranking on the hot water. "Shh."

He holds me as I cry, waiting for it to heat up.

Steam finally starts to fill the room, cocooning us in a wraithlike fog that matches the one that covers McBride Mountain.

He walks me in under the hot spray.

I flinch when it hits me at first, but the warmth starts to seep into my skin, washing away the goosebumps, the tremors, the lingering memory of that pain.

Killian runs his hand up and down my spine gently, letting the water rush over us. The longer he holds me, the more it starts to feel normal, like the way it always used to be when we were like this *before*.

He drops a kiss to my forehead, then tilts my chin up. "Better?"

I nod and wrap my arms around him, clinging to him tightly, not wanting even an inch of space between us that might allow those dark memories to infiltrate again.

The heat of his body does as much for me as that of the cascading water.

Soaking into my bones.

Solidifying the reality of this moment and the safety Killian provides.

He pulls one arm from around me, then slowly moves the other, then returns with a loofah full of the body wash Raven brought for me. My favorite scent—honey and lavender.

Killian lathers it up and starts washing me slowly, dragging it over every inch of my body he can reach with my arms still looped around him. I close my eyes, my cheek laid on his chest, and let the water pound against my back as he does it.

When he gently pulls on my arms, urging me to let go, I don't fight it, and as soon as he's sure I'm steady on my feet, he drops to his knees in front of me and ensures every single inch of me is clean.

Cleansing me of the nightmare.

Of that darkness I can't seem to escape.

He rises to his feet, keeping his intense gaze locked with mine. "Tip your head back."

Threading his fingers through my hair, he urges me farther under the spray, fully wetting the long, tangled locks. Then he grabs the shampoo and begins to work it into my scalp the same way he did when we first returned to the cabin. Massaging gently. Lulling me into that space where all I can feel is his magical fingers and the brush of his body along mine.

"Mmm. That feels good."

"Good."

He wraps his arm around my waist again and pulls me back against him, letting the stream of hot water rinse the lather from my hair.

We remain under the spray for a few moments before he repeats the process with the conditioner, then he holds me to him, brushing his lips across my forehead, running rough palms over me soothingly.

"Do you want to talk about it?"

I shake my head, keeping it pressed into his chest. "No."

"You know I'll be here when you do."

I nod.

Killian isn't going anywhere.

"You're going to come to the lumberyard with me tomorrow."

I finally lift my head, tilting my face to gaze at him still behind me. Water cascades down his sculpted shoulders and chest as he stares down at me with concern. "How come?"

"Because I don't want to let you out of my sight after tonight."

The noise outside.

My back stiffens.

I had almost forgotten about it.

"You think a bear would come onto the property while I was here?"

He stiffens behind me, then drags his lips across my collarbone slowly. "I don't know, but I'm not going to take any chances. And I don't want you alone with Raven in town. I want you with Liam, Connor, or me at all times."

The way he says it, the tension in his voice and arms, makes me turn and look up at him. "Why?"

Killian takes my face between his palms and suddenly looks very serious. "Because that was a human in the woods. Someone was watching us by the fire."

Acid churns in my stomach and starts to crawl up my throat. "Are you"—I swallow—"are you sure?"

He nods. "We've suspected for a while that you were not alone on the mountain. Then we went up there to the area where we found you, and suddenly, someone's in the woods on my property? It isn't a coincidence, Honeybee."

"Shit."

Someone followed us...

I start to tremble again, and he drags me against him fully, until every single inch of our bodies touches.

"It'll be okay. I promise. We're going to figure this out."

"How?"

"I don't know, but we'll find a way." His voice doesn't waver. It never breaks. The steely determination lives in each word. "I'm not going to let this drag on anymore, not going to leave you to be a victim to these flashes of memory and not knowing what happened to you."

Over the past couple of weeks, he's promised me answers, and he hasn't been able to deliver, but this time, I believe him.

I feel his resolve.

If there really was someone in the woods tonight watching us, if it really was someone who might have answers about where I was and what happened to me over the last year, Killian will burn down the whole fucking mountain to find them. He will eviscerate anyone who played a role in my missing time. He will do it all without regard for what it might cost him.

And that's what terrifies me.

He'll destroy his home, the only place he's ever loved, for me.

Anyone on this mountain who gets in his way is going to be collateral damage.

14

KILLIAN

The signs are everywhere, readily apparent to anyone who knows what to look for—like *me.*

A snapped twig.

Deep boot impressions in the soft soil in several places.

Disturbed leaves in the underbrush.

From where I squat, examining the area where I heard the noises from last night, I can see it all with vivid clarity.

This is the spot where whoever was in the woods watched us from.

I glance over my shoulder to the fire pit and the surrounding chairs visible through the trees. A clear line of sight to anything happening on that portion of the homestead. From this position, he could've seen *everything.* And more disturbingly, he was close enough to have heard every word I shared with Connor and Liam and what Willow and I said to each other before I forced her inside the cabin.

What the fuck was he doing here?

Why loom in the darkness, watching and listening but not acting?

A shudder rolls through me at the likely answer.

Whoever it is was stalking his prey. Gathering intel. Planning the same way I do a hunt before I head out onto the mountain.

Only his prey isn't deer or bear.

It's Willow.

I push up to my feet, my hand tightening on my axe, and turn toward the approaching sound of footsteps. Connor and Liam make their way toward me through the trees, each wearing a grim expression. Even without having revealed what I've found to them yet, they know.

"Where's Willow?"

Liam motions behind him toward the house. "In the cabin with Raven. She just arrived."

Connor sneers in that direction, his jaw clenching. "I can't believe you trust her in there alone. Who knows what she might be digging into, looking for more dirt to—"

"Look"—I hold up a hand to stop his familiar rant—"she isn't my favorite person, either. But—"

The sound of tires pulling across the gravel interrupts my intent to argue that since Raven is important to Willow, then we need to forget the animosity that the past year only grew and accept that she's going to be part of our lives as long as Willow is part of mine.

Which means Raven will be around *forever,* since I have no intention of ever letting Willow slip away again.

We all start making our way back toward the clearing the cabin sits in and step from the thick underbrush as the sheriff's SUV pulls to a stop.

Tony climbs out, adjusting his hat and gun belt as he nudges his door closed, and gives me a dark look. "Did you find something?"

Unfortunately.

I had hoped I was wrong about what was out here last night, but seeing the confirmation of my gut feeling has affirmed that things are far more dangerous than we initially knew.

All the unease I've felt since Willow's return about what might have happened to her suddenly feels suffocating. Coupled with how violent her nightmare was last night and the intensity of her response to it, I know we need a plan of attack.

Waiting for something to happen isn't an option when it means Willow will be at risk.

I run a hand through my beard as I glance toward the front window of the cabin, where Willow watches us. Our eyes meet, and a million questions swirl in her squally gaze. Ones I can't answer when I don't have them.

That woman has put her trust and life in my hands, and I'm as lost as she is.

I turn away slightly, unable to look at her while I'm telling Tony exactly what I think happened. What I'm more convinced of than ever. "Someone was here last night, watching us. Probably for a while."

His eyes widen slightly. "How did they get onto the property?"

I shake my head as all four of us scan the area. The clearing that houses the main homestead—cabin, barn, Willow's workshop, animal pens, and a few other smaller outbuildings isn't large. But it's always been *safe*.

Mostly because there's only one road up or down to it.

Connor's gaze drifts to the gravel drive Tony just came in on that leads to that sole access point. "He must have parked farther down the mountain and hiked up on foot. Coming in from any other direction, he would have had to use an ATV, and we would have heard that on a quiet night from miles out."

He's right.

Whoever did this knew the mountain well enough to understand how to get up here undetected. This was *planned*.

Tony nods and pulls off his hat to rub a hand through his dark hair. "Don't suppose he left anything behind that might be useful in identifying him?"

I picture the scene I discovered in the woods. "Just a pair of size twelve footprints."

Liam releases a frustrated sigh. "Which could belong to anyone."

At least we know it is a *him*, given that size shoe. That eliminates over half the population of McBride Mountain, but it still leaves us with far too many possible suspects.

Tony scowls, staring into the trees. "No point in me callin' up a forensics team from Asheville then?"

I shake my head. "Nope. He's a ghost. Long gone without leaving anything that might identify him."

A true hunter.

He blended in with his surroundings, watched, and waited. There isn't a doubt in my mind that he is experienced and knows this mountain, which only confirms my belief that the snapping twig I heard last night *was* intentional.

This man wanted us to know he's around. That he can get *close.*

Whether it was a threat or a warning directed at me or Willow doesn't matter. Either way, it was a sign that we can't sit by and wait for her memory to return.

We have to try something else.

Tony returns his gaze to mine. "Who do you think it was?"

"The person who had her."

Liam's brow furrows, and Connor's head snaps back in our direction instead of staring at the cabin where Willow and Raven now both stand at the window, watching us intently.

Connor shifts closer to me. "What do you mean, *had* her?"

"Look, we've all been thinking it, right? That she couldn't

have been up there alone. Someone held her up on the mountain. Who the fuck knows for how long? But she's adamant she returned that same day she left."

Tony's brows draw low over his eyes. "Explain."

I slam the blade of my axe into the ground, embedding it there. "She was on her way back to me after our argument. She didn't leave town permanently. She didn't leave for more than a handful of hours—at least not of her own will. Someone interfered. Someone took her before she could get home to me."

Connor recoils. "You mean she was *kidnapped*?"

"It's the only thing that makes sense."

Liam rubs the back of his neck and glances at the cabin. "What about the notes? The gifts to Raven?"

Connor sneers. "Maybe Raven's in on it."

I whirl toward him. "Are you fucking nuts?"

He holds up his hands defensively. "You got any other explanation?"

Literally anything other than that.

"She's her best friend, for fuck's sake."

Tony follows Connor's look at the cabin and steps closer, lowering his voice. "That doesn't really mean anything. I mean, you've watched those true crime shows, haven't you?"

I shake my head. "You know I don't have a television."

"Well, I sure have, and I'm tellin' ya, people do crazy shit. Even to their friends."

"You think Raven held her hostage on the fucking mountain for a year?" I raise a brow. "To what? Keep her from coming back to me because she hates the McBrides?" An annoyed snort slips out. "Now you're the one who sounds nuts."

He chuckles slightly, shifts his hat back onto his head, and holds up his hands. "Yeah, when you say it like that. Raven may be a pain in the ass, but she isn't a kidnapper. So, what do you suggest we do here?"

That question has been rattling around my head for weeks.

Even more so this morning.

What more can we do?

What more can I do?

I scan the horizon, the towering mountains that climb well above our property into the bright-blue sky. Such stunning natural beauty. But it hides a secret—one that has destroyed Willow's life and taken a year of it from her, along with her memories.

"We get way more people and put together a much larger search party. Someone dangerous is on the mountain."

Tony doesn't appear fully convinced of my plan. "How do you know where we should look?"

I turn and scan the vast expanse of wilderness around us again. "We start at the river. We head down the game trail we know she used to the clearing. From there, we follow the scent trail the dogs got to where they lost it. Then we'll send out parties of five in every direction. We cover every fucking inch of the mountain, and we keep going west until we find something since we know she was on that side of the river."

He exchanges a look with Connor and Liam. "Killian, that's thousands of man-hours and dollars you're talking. Even if we recruited every able-bodied person in town to agree to assist us, this could take weeks. Out there, you know there are places that aren't even passable—"

"I don't give a fuck how long it takes or how much it costs. You know I have the money."

More than I could ever spend in my lifetime.

"It isn't about the money, it's about—" I struggle to figure out how to express the distress she's been in and how useless it's made me feel. But I've always been awful at opening up, discussing my feelings about anything, especially what I care about. That's why I lost her in the first place. "What if it were Tonya?"

Tony freezes at the mention of his wife, his eyes hardening. "What would you do if any of this had happened to *her*? That seems to do the trick.

I may not be able to explain how I feel about the situation, but putting *him* into it allows Tony to at least consider what he would do if our roles were reversed.

He shifts uneasily, but I don't miss the way his hand drifts to his holster at his side, like subconsciously he needs to hold that weapon. "I'd like to believe I could stay rational about it."

"Bullshit. This isn't about rational." I take a step closer, pointing toward the cabin where my entire life waits. "If *anyone* laid a hand on her, I need *my* hands around their fucking throat. Do you understand me?"

He nods slowly, examining me like he's seeing a complete stranger instead of one of his closest friends since childhood.

And maybe I am a stranger to him now.

Losing Willow turned me into someone else, *something* else.

A monster that has only grown more restless and volatile the longer this mystery continues.

People should be wary of me right now.

Tony continues to stare me down like there's something he wants to say but is mustering up the courage to do it, but the sound of the cabin door swinging open draws him a step back from me, whatever he would have said in response to my very clear threat to commit murder lost.

Willow and Raven come out and stop at the porch railing, examining our standoff, with Connor and Liam looking on.

Raven raises a blond brow, crossing her arms over her chest. "What are you boys talking about?"

Connor mimics her stance, tipping up his head defiantly. "Why are you asking? So you can print another article about it?"

She stares him down in challenge, not budging a fucking

inch. "The people have a right to know what's going on, to be prepared."

Liam glances between the two of them. "She isn't wrong, Connor."

His gaze cuts to our youngest brother. "Who the fuck's side are you on?"

"The one that keeps everyone safe."

Tony gives me a look, asking for permission to reveal everything we've been discussing. And as much as I would love to ignore the fact that there is a threat out there and stay locked in the cabin with Willow indefinitely, that isn't an option.

I nod.

He clears his throat. "We believe there may be someone dangerous on the mountain."

Raven scoffs. "You guys just figuring that out now?"

I motion toward the woods. "I found evidence to confirm someone was watching Willow and me last night."

Willow's hands tighten on the rail, her breath catching at the confirmation of what I told her last night, and Raven's mix of indignation and humor fades quickly.

Her green gaze cuts to her best friend, then back to me. "Someone *was* here?"

I'm sure she—like me—would have loved to discover I was wrong and that it was just a bear or some other type of wildlife that made those noises, but sticking our heads in the sand won't get us anywhere.

I nod. "Which is why she"—I point to Willow—"doesn't leave my side unless she's with Liam or Connor."

Raven gapes. "What about me? You don't think she's safe with me?"

"It isn't about that, Raven. You'll be better protected with one of us around. And you're welcome to stay on the homestead, too, if you feel like you need protection." I grin at

Connor, already anticipating his response to my next suggestion. "You can crash at Liam's...or Connor's."

He opens his mouth to argue with me, but I cut him off with a glare.

"I'll be taking Willow to the lumberyard today, if you'd like to join us."

Raven scowls. "No thanks. I can take care of myself, and I'm better off spending my time warning people than hiding behind a McBride."

"Now, now..." Tony holds up a hand. "We're not going to cause a panic with some exaggerated story, but I do need your help to spread the word about a search party we're going to be putting together."

Raven's lips twist, annoyed at the reproach, but she nods. "Of course. Anything I can do to help."

Right now, the only one who appears to need help is Willow.

She stands gripping the banister tightly in her hands, her legs trembling as badly as her bottom lip.

We discussed my belief that whoever took her was likely responsible for the noise I heard, but apparently, confirming it has hit her hard.

I slowly make my way up the porch as Raven comes down to talk to Tony.

Willow turns to face me, still gripping the worn wood in one hand tightly. "Someone was really here? Just watching us and listening?"

To my confession.

To every painful word.

I nod. "Yes..."

"Why would they?"

I shake my head. "I don't know, but I'm going to find out if it's the last fucking thing I do."

WILLOW

The McBride Timber office swirls around me as I spin in the office chair behind Killian's desk, pushing off the floor with one foot to keep going for the hundredth time, until my stomach starts to regret my decision.

Nausea rolls through me, and I drop my feet to stop my rotation, pressing my hand over my belly.

A brief flash of a memory fills my head.

This same feeling.

Overwhelming nausea and feeling like the world around me won't stop spinning, even when I'm standing still.

I swallow back bile rising in my throat.

A low snicker fills the office. "Having fun?"

Hardly.

I glance over to where Connor reclines at his desk with his booted feet kicked up on top of it. One of his thick, dark brows rises, along with the corner of his lips.

He knows how bored I am, and that my current attempt to pass the time has left me feeling...not great.

"Does it look like I'm having fun?"

Connor snorts. "Sort of. Until you turned that shade of green."

Uggg.

"I am not *green*." I give him a saccharine-sweet smile. "I'm bored out of my mind."

I settle into the chair, staring at the same ceiling I have been staring at for almost four hours while I've sat in here with the grumpiest of the McBride brothers—at least to me. Though, that might be debatable to everyone else on the mountain. They all seem to see Killian as the gruffest, roughest of the trio, but it's hard for me to accept that when I've seen his other side.

Connor, on the other hand, rarely shows even a hint of anything but annoyance at people and life in general. He certainly has at having to babysit me all day.

A little chuckle slips from his lips. "I can tell."

I motion absently toward the front window that overlooks the lumberyard, where dozens of people hustle around, moving uncut timber from the storage area to the saw house and cut boards to stacks along the far fence wall—all with Killian at the center of it.

Checking in with everyone.

Directing traffic.

Doing the job he was *born* to do.

That man is at home on the mountain, out in the wildest parts that match his soul, but he somehow fits here, too. This business is the heart and soul of the McBride family and this town.

He would never give up on it, never stop trying to improve things, which means I'm in for a very long day, since he wants to get as much done as possible before the larger search party gets organized and takes off up the mountain.

"He really expects me to stay here with him all day?"

Connor nods slowly. "Yep."

"And you *have* to babysit?"

If I have to sit here, I can do it alone.

There isn't any reason to make Connor *more* miserable by forcing him to when he's built just like his brothers and prefers to get his hands calloused and dirty.

None of them wants to spend time in the office, which means Connor is as restless as I am by now.

The corners of his mouth twitch.

He doesn't smile much, but every once in a while, when you get a grin, you realize how truly handsome he is. If he actually showed any interest in any of the women around town, they'd be in trouble. But he's always been a quiet loner, seemingly comfortable leading the bachelor lifestyle indefinitely and ensuring his attitude keeps anyone who would chance it at bay.

Just like Killian did...until me.

Connor motions to the yard beyond the window. "I think Liam's going to come trade off with me in a little bit, so you'll have much better company."

I snort and roll my eyes, even though he's right.

Liam *will* be better company.

Somehow, he avoided picking up his older brothers' attitudes. Maybe the age difference and time he spent alone with their mother while Killian and Connor were off getting into trouble helped temper that gruffness.

Whatever it was, it's good that they have him around to keep them in check.

"Or..." Connor points to where Killian stands in the middle of the yard, deep in conversation with one of the foremen. "You could always go out into the yard with Killian."

I scowl. "And watch him tear into the employees? I don't think so."

"Oh, come on. He's not *that* bad."

"Really?" I raise a brow. "You know I read the backlog of Raven's stories from while I was gone."

He winces—either because of the content of the stories or his deep mistrust and hatred of Raven. Maybe both.

"Yeah, that's what I thought." I twirl a strand of my hair around my finger. "Quite a few in there about avoiding Killian McBride because he was on the rampage again."

His broad shoulders rise and fall. "I wouldn't call it 'going on rampages'..."

"What *would* you call it?"

He issues another slow shrug. "Trying to run a business. And to be fair, he wasn't really mad at *them*. He was mostly pissed off because you were gone...and he realized it was his fault."

My chest tightens imagining what a mess he must have been. If how anguished he appeared last night coming clean with me and reliving what he said was any indication, Killian was likely impossible to deal with. "Do *you* think it was his fault?"

From what Raven has told me, most of her hostility with Connor has come from his defense of his brother over the last year and frustration with her not giving him any information about where I might be.

Connor drums his fingers on his desk. "I will always defend my brother until the day I die, but what he said to you?" He shakes his head. "I'm surprised you're so sure you came back after that. I wouldn't have blamed you if you hadn't."

Because Connor understands just as well as Killian what my shitty relationship with Mom did to me and how much those words hurt.

"He didn't mean it. You and I both know that."

If I had truly believed he meant what he said, I never would have turned around. I would have left McBride Mountain—at least for a while—to think about my next steps. But I doubt I could have stayed away forever. Not when Raven is here. That's what makes me even more certain I was on my way back. Not the memory or the feeling deep in my soul that I didn't give up on Killian, but the fact that the only people I love in this world are all *here*.

And I would never want to leave them.

Even if I couldn't have forgiven Killian, I would have stayed for Raven. For all the other people in town whom I care for so deeply. Jenny and her kids, Claire, the Wilsons, Tony and Tonya, and everyone else who has been a part of my life.

No matter what, I wouldn't have left McBride Mountain forever.

I push myself out of the chair, unable to sit anymore, and

walk over to the wall containing various photographs of McBride Mountain and the timber yard over the years.

The one of Killian's father draws my attention, even though I've seen it probably hundreds of times over the years.

He's the spitting image of the man I love, standing next to a towering pine with the same axe that Killian still carries in his hand, ready to take it down with expert precision.

"Did Killian's dad really do all the felling by hand?"

Connor follows my gaze and shrugs. "Back then, yeah. Mostly. The really advanced equipment didn't come around until closer to when Killian was born. Before then, they would hike in on foot to the more remote areas, fell everything by hand, break it down into manageable loads, and drag it down the mountain using chains and sledges."

I raise my brows at him. "Seriously?"

Prior to our hike over the last couple of days, I never gave much thought to how much *work* truly went into this business before the modern technology we take for granted today.

He nods and lowers his feet from the desk to make his way over. Standing next to me, he points to another picture, this one of his mom. "When Mom took over, she really pushed the advancements, putting money into it because she knew what the future was demanding. I don't know that Killian's father ever would have done it if he had lived. He was kind of stuck in the old ways, believed it was always how it was done, so he should keep doing it that way—at least, that's what Mom always said."

I can't help but smile at the photo of the woman who was like a mother to me when mine couldn't be—and the woman who *did* become one to Connor. It hangs right next to the picture of young Killian and his father. "Are you ever sad that you never met him?"

Connor looks over at me. "Who?"

"Killian's father. I mean, he would have been your dad, too."

The normally stoic middle McBride brother flinches slightly and then clears his throat. "Of course, but..." He shrugs. "I missed him by a couple of years."

He gives me a sad smile and walks away, effectively ending the line of questioning, and I can't say I blame him. His history must be as painful for him as my unknown year has become for me.

While only two years old when he was brought to Constance McBride, he was old enough that he might have memories of his biological parents. The young couple knew they couldn't care for him anymore and begged Connie to adopt him. The moment she laid eyes on Connor, she couldn't say no, and she never treated him any differently than she did Killian, her own blood.

Connor is a McBride, through and through, but it has to be a sore spot for him.

I shouldn't have mentioned it.

The air thickens with tension between us, and Connor returns to his desk, absently flipping through a stack of papers on the top that he already spent hours going over earlier today.

I sit on the edge of Killian's desk and swing my feet back and forth, examining the maps of the mountain that line the walls, created by various members of the McBride family over the years.

So much history.

So much tradition.

Something I never had. Something I always envied and wanted. Something I always thought I'd be a part of when Killian and I got married.

Our children would have inherited McBride Timber, along with any kids Connor or Liam ever have. But given Connor's countenance, it seems lifelong bachelorhood would be more likely.

There's only *one* person I've ever seen him react to in any way with *any* form of passion. And even though it isn't the *good* kind of passion, since my return, it's left me wondering what I missed when it comes to the two of them.

I glance over at Connor, debating whether I should even bring it up, but if I'm going to be stuck in here with him for a while, I can't handle the awkward silence. "What's your deal with Raven?"

Connor coughs, choking on the swig of coffee he just took, and pounds his chest to clear it. "What do you mean?"

"Why do you hate her so much?"

A dark brow wings up. "You're joking, right?"

"No."

"You said you read her articles..."

There wasn't much else to do all those days I spent with her, just sitting in the bakery while she worked.

"Yeah, and?"

"They weren't exactly very complimentary, were they?"

I bark out a laugh that carries through the small office. "I mean, no, but were any of them not true?"

He scowls at me.

"Yeah, that's what I thought. She's just doing her civic duty. Keeping people informed."

"Yeah, well, it feels more like stabbing everyone in the fucking back."

Animosity taints each of his words.

He *really* hates her, and by the sounds of it, that is unlikely to change anytime soon.

"Please cut her some slack."

Because it's going to make my life very difficult if I'm going to have to referee those two constantly. It was bad *before* I left, but now, it's completely untenable.

"I won't." He tilts his cup of coffee at me. "And you better be careful. You never know what she'll print about you. Or Killian."

As if on cue, the door swings open, and Killian steps in, his gaze sweeping the room and landing on me. The corners of his lips pull up. "You doin' okay in here?"

He nudges the door closed with his booted foot and wipes his hands on his jeans, which are covered in sawdust.

I shrug. "I was just asking your brother why he hates Raven so much."

Killian's gaze cuts to Connor, and he smirks. "Oh, I'd *love* to hear this."

Connor sneers at him. "Same reason you hate her."

With an annoyed huff, Killian holds up his hands defensively. "I never said I hated her. I just...she isn't my favorite person."

I can't fight a grin at his dodging the issue. Killian won't let his issues with Raven interfere with *us.* "Who is?"

His gaze moves back to me, heating instantly. "Do I really need to answer that?"

That look tells me everything without him saying a word.

Hours spent tangled together in the sheets last night flash through my head—the kind of memories I *want* to obsess over instead of the ones that are tied to my missing year.

I push off the desk and move toward him, but he takes a retreating step.

"Honeybee, I'm sweaty and covered in sawdust at the moment."

And looking sexy as hell.

I grin at him. "When has that ever stopped me before?"

The smile that splits his face would light up the room if it wasn't the middle of the day already, and he pulls me up against him as Connor issues a gagging noise behind us and climbs to his feet.

"So, I see you two worked out everything, huh? I kinda figured after this morning..."

Killian kisses me hard, the smell of sweat and wood and the

mountain enveloping me, then pulls away and looks at his brother. "We did. Though, I'm sure I'll be making it up to her until the day I die."

Connor nods. "Agreed."

He stomps out and slams the door behind him, apparently relieved of his babysitting duties and none too soon.

Killian ignores his brother's mood and kisses me again, holding me tightly to him and reminding me of all the strength and passion I love so much about him.

This morning rattled me almost as much as what happened last night and the painful nightmare did. Killian's belief that I was held against my will by someone on the mountain, likely someone we *know*, because they directed me to write those notes to Raven to draw off suspicion, is enough to almost make me wish I didn't know.

And the way Killian is kissing me, it feels possible to completely forget everything around us for as long as we keep going.

But it can't last forever.

When we finally come up for air, Killian brushes a strand of hair from my face. "What have you been doing in here all morning?"

"Spinning in your chair."

He glances at it. "How's that working out for you?"

I press my hand to my stomach. "It kind of made me nauseous."

As soon as the words leave my lips, the feeling washes over me again, but it isn't what happened this morning. It's the *memory* of it again. Retching violently in the dirt. On my hands and knees...

"Oh, God..." I stagger slightly, my head spinning.

Killian's strong arm keeps me upright. "Another memory?"

I squeeze my eyes closed. "I can't keep going like this. These flashes don't make any sense. It's like having a quarter of a puzzle and none of the pieces fit together."

He's quiet for a moment, allowing me to get my bearings. "I had a thought about that..."

I force open my eyes to meet his. "What's that?"

"What if..." He pauses as if he's unsure what he's about to suggest is an actual option. "What if we tried hypnosis?"

"What?"

"Tony actually brought it up yesterday when you and Raven went back into the cabin. He said that on those true crime documentaries he's always watching, sometimes people undergo hypnosis to try to draw out memories of things they've buried deep down. What if you tried that?"

He raises a brow hopefully.

I wish I could share in that hope, but I'm torn between wanting the truth, wanting to know, and being terrified of what I'll find there.

Fear is a horrible thing.

It's easy to try to hide from anything that might cause it.

More comfortable only to focus on joy.

But ultimately, there's just one decision I can make, no matter *how* painful it might be.

"I'd do anything to stop this, Killian, to get my memory back and know what happened to me."

He nods slowly. "That's what I thought. Tony's working on getting a larger search party organized. It'll take a day or two. In the meantime, I'll find someone who can come up here and meet with you. Or we can go to Asheville, if we need to. Anything to make you whole again."

Whole again.

For so long, that meant having Killian, being with him, and feeling this warmth that I always do when we're here like this. And now that we're back together, and after what happened

last night, I should feel complete. Like things are the way they
should be.

But I don't.

It's like a giant piece of me is missing.

A part that is somewhere on that mountain.

Something that all these pieces of memory are leading
me to.

15

KILLIAN

A familiar scent I never thought I would smell in the cabin again hits my nose the minute I open the bathroom door. My footsteps falter slightly as thirty years' worth of memories slam into me.

Of Mom in that kitchen.

Of Willow with her.

Of the years they spent making my favorite dinner together.

Of sitting at that small table with Connor and Liam with full bellies and smiles on our faces.

I couldn't bring myself to attempt it on my own when Willow was gone.

It never would've been right, never could have lived up to what they made because it was *them* doing it. I always thought the old belief that something tastes better when it's made with love was foolish, until I tried the Wilson's version at the diner.

While delicious...it was lacking *something*.

Something I couldn't put my finger on.

It lacked *this*.

It wasn't from home.

And the cabin finally feels like one again.

My mouth waters as I pad barefoot with a towel wrapped around my waist toward the smell and the gentle humming floating through the air.

Willow stands at the small kitchen counter, swaying her hips from side to side, my headphones in her ears, clearly enjoying whatever she's listening to. I lean against the giant log support beam at the entrance to the room and watch her.

The smile tilting the corner of her lips.

How freely she moves to the music, unreserved by the cloud that has hung over her since her return.

For this moment—and maybe only this single one—she's completely happy.

I'd like to believe that I had something to do with that. That finally clearing the air and coming together emotionally *and* physically somehow lifted some of the weight that was crushing her.

But I know it's merely a fleeting blink of time.

As soon as she closes her eyes tonight, she'll be haunted by the visions of things that could be nightmares or horrific memories.

Willow won't ever truly get better, and I won't really get her back fully, until we find answers for her. Yet, this moment gives me hope.

Hope for the future I thought I'd lost.

I push off the beam and sidle up behind her, sliding my arms around her waist.

She yelps slightly and turns toward me in my hold, pulling the earbuds out and setting them onto the counter. "Christ, you scared the crap out of me."

My heart stops, my mood immediately shifting at the thought that I might have done something that could have put her back in that dark place instead of the bright one she was just in, but the smile pulling at her lips assures me she's okay.

"I'm sorry"—I squeeze her gently—"but I couldn't resist with you swaying your ass like that and looking so fucking beautiful."

Her breath catches. "How long were you watching me?"

I don't bother fighting a grin. "Long enough." My growing cock presses against her. "It smells amazing in here."

Her cheeks pinken with the most adorable blush. "I thought maybe you might want your mom's cornbread, baked beans, and ham for dinner."

My eyes burn, but I refuse to let the tears fall, even though they're happy ones. I don't want anything to threaten the light, happy mood we've managed to find in all this turmoil.

"You were right." I bend down and brush my lips over her forehead, then work my way across her cheek to bury my face against her neck. "But after seeing you dancing like that in here, I'm hungry for something else."

"Oh."

Willow curls her hands onto my chest, nails biting into the inked skin in a very deliberate way.

She understands me perfectly, feels the tension in my body, the way my hard cock strains under the towel barely confining it.

I slide my hands down and easily lift her to the edge of the counter, pushing various cans and other ingredients out of the way.

Her light laughter fills the air between us, the sound so carefree and full of joy that those tears almost fall. I cage her in with one hand on either side of where she sits, and she takes my face in her palms, dragging her fingers through my beard.

Fuuuuck.

I groan at the sensation. "God, I've missed this."

Tilting her head slightly, she examines me. "What?"

"*You* being here in my house." I kiss her softly. "Your scent." Another brush of my lips. "The sound of your laughter and those little gasps you make when you come." Another one— longer and deeper. "You touching me like this..."

She does it again, harder this time, and the low growl that rolls from my chest sounds more animal than human. My eyes drift closed as I relish the feel of her nails on my face, my neck, my chest.

My body trembles.

I open my eyes to find her watching me, waiting for me to do or say something, to make the move because she doesn't like having to be in control.

She wants me to take it.

She needs me to.

Because everything in her life feels so out of it.

"How long until things have to come out of that oven?"

She glances back at the timer. "Twenty minutes."

I issue another growl, sliding my hands from the counter up to her hips and squeezing, ensuring I'm low enough that I won't tweak her still-healing ribs. "I don't like being on the clock"— my lips drift over hers—"but I can make twenty minutes work."

Those nails score across my chest, making my entire body shudder, and Willow laughs as I tug on the waistband of her leggings and slide them down her thighs, along with her thong.

I toss them to the side, not caring where they land, before I drop to my knees, drag her legs over my shoulders, and bury my face in my favorite place in the world.

Fuck, yes.

Of all the things I've missed, this is at the top of my list.

Giving her pleasure.

Making her come all over my tongue.

Feeling her fall apart and forget everything else in the world.

Something we *both* desperately need right now.

She gasps at the first contact of my tongue against her slick core, tunneling her hands through my hair, tugging on the strands sharply.

Fuuuuuck.

The taste of her arousal.

The sting on my scalp.

The way she leans back until her head and shoulders meet the wall behind her for leverage, giving me better access, allowing me to spread her even wider.

All of it is too much and not enough at the same time.

I glide my tongue through her wet heat, savoring the woman as if she's my last meal, because she is. If I ever lose her again, I don't know how I'd survive it. This is the only place I want to be every moment for the rest of my life.

Like this.

With *her.*

I could never get enough of this woman, not in the time we've already had together and not in the future. Every moment of my life is consumed by Willow, and I could feast on her all day, every day, and still feel like I was starving. Like it was never enough.

A low groan falls from her lips as I thrust my tongue as deep as I can inside her.

"Killian!"

She twines a clump of my hair around her hand, tugging to the side, trying to direct me where she wants me.

I chuckle against her wet flesh. "Tell me what you want, what you need."

A shudder rolls through her.

Willow knows as well as I do that I don't need direction. I can make her come hard and fast or do it slow and sweet until it's practically torture for her. But I love to hear the words out of her mouth. Live to hear that she's as desperate for me as I am for her.

Her thighs tremble on either side of my head, and I lift it and peer up at her. "Willow, look at me."

She pulls away from the wall, and her eyes flutter open to meet mine, the steely gray there cloaked in a lusty haze.

"Tell." I drag my tongue across her flesh. "Me."

"I want..." She shifts restlessly, that red flush spreading up her neck and across her cheeks. "I want to come on your mouth and your fingers, and then I want your cock inside me."

Fuck.

That's the most direct response I've ever gotten from her, and I could come right now just hearing those words from her lips, ones I never thought I would experience again.

Worshipping her like this isn't nearly enough to make up for what I've caused, and determination settles deep in my soul.

I *will* give this woman everything.

Starting right now.

I'll give her something she's *never* had before.

I pull my hand from her waist to slip a finger inside her, then another, spreading her wide. She moans, tightening around me, and I curl them deep, finding her G-spot.

A throaty groan falls from her parted lips, and she drops her head back to the wall again, clamping her cunt around my fingers. I drag my calloused fingertips along her inner walls, concentrating on that perfect spot with each retreat of my hand. My tongue slides up over her clit, and a needy mewl fills my ears as her hands tighten in my hair even more.

Her hips start to roll in time with my ministrations.

She unabashedly grinds against my face, seeking more while I work her up. Build her higher and higher. Tightening the coil inside her that will spring hard and fast before too long.

The scent of her soaked cunt quickly overpowers that of the food in the oven.

My entire world becomes centered between her legs as I feast on her, frantic to give her something explosive.

Her body finally starts to shake violently, her thighs tensing and tightening around my head. This woman could rip my damn fucking head off, and at least I'd die happy, knowing I made her come that hard in my final moments on this planet.

What a fucking way to go.

I pump my fingers into her, pulsing and dragging against her G-spot, flicking my tongue rapidly across her engorged clit until she finally detonates, squirting down my throat. A tidal wave of release that I swallow greedily, desperate for more.

Willow's body pulses around my fingers as the orgasm crashes over her harder than any I've ever experienced with her.

Exactly what I wanted.

Complete ecstasy.

She gasps and sags back, pushing me away almost frantically. Her wide eyes lock on me, and trembling lips gape open on fluttered half-breaths. "Wh-what the fuck was that?"

"Fucking incredible, that's what that was." I grin at her as I lick her inner thighs clean. "You squirted."

"I *what*?"

I raise a brow at her.

Her dark eyes sweep over me with so much confusion, still glazed over from the release she never saw coming. "I've never..."

"I know." I glide my tongue across my lips, savoring every last drop. "That was hot as fuck. You think you can do it again?"

Willow's cheeks and face redden even more. "I don't...I don't know."

God, her confusion and embarrassment are adorable.

And I'd love to keep my face buried between her thighs to see if she *can* do it again.

But she reaches for me, urging me to stand between her parted thighs.

Staring up at me, spread wide across my kitchen counter, thoroughly ravished, she's never looked more beautiful.

She reaches for the towel and gives it a gentle tug, letting it fall to the floor. My gaze follows her hand as it wraps around my hard cock and guides me to her slick core.

I'm fucking done for.

WILLOW

My legs tremble.

My lungs seize.

My heart beats wildly under my ribs.

But the dull ache there is barely even noticeable anymore.

After what Killian just did to me, I'm not sure I can feel *anything* the same way again. Because that was life-altering. World-changing in a way I never knew something like an orgasm could be.

It's always been electric between us. Hot. Heavy. Sometimes downright aggressive. It's the way I've always liked him— unleashed. Unrestricted by the expectations and things in life that try to keep him restrained.

That's what I need now, too.

For this man to take me away from *everything*.

He towers over me, long, wet hair hanging over his shoulders, lips still glistening from within his beard from whatever the hell that just was that he wrung out of me. Through my lust-fogged brain, I try to focus on him, but everything's fuzzy, surrounded by this glowy haze of pleasure still making my body twitch and limbs tingle.

Killian takes my face in one hand and leans in, dragging me to him so he can crush his mouth to mine in a soul-searing kiss that screams, *mine, mine, mine.*

I am his.

He's always been possessive, protective, demanding the things even I didn't know I needed until he gave them to me.

Just like he's doing now.

He's giving me *life.*

I loop my arms around his neck, clinging to him and his strength. A strangled groan slips from his lips, and he pushes into me with one hard thrust, rocking me back slightly from the edge of the counter. I gasp into his mouth, drawing his breath into my lungs.

His tongue tangles with mine, thrusting the same way his hips do as he draws back and plunges into me again.

And *fuuuuuck* is it good.

All-consuming.

A taking.

A claiming.

Until he suddenly stills his hips and tugs his head away from mine, scanning my face. "You tell me if I'm hurting you..."

His cock stretches me so full, fits so perfectly, that it's impossible to tell where he ends and I begin.

I nod, knowing I won't tell him. Knowing that even if he does hurt me, it would be the good kind of pain, the kind that makes me feel alive, not the kind that makes me crawl back into that bed and sob like I have so many times since I returned.

He plunges deep, hitting that perfect spot inside of me that did absolutely unholy things only a few moments ago. I clutch his neck, trying to draw him closer, even though it's physically impossible, like my body still knows how long I went without him and doesn't want to risk it happening again.

But it won't.

Not again.

Neither of us will make those mistakes again.

We won't risk losing *this*.

He lowers his forehead to mine as he sets a slow tempo of long, hard strokes that allow me to feel every fucking inch of him on each drive of his hips. A languid build just so he can shatter me again.

And it's utterly divine.

Delicious torture.

Until he pulls back and lifts my left leg, pressing it up against his chest to give him a different angle, allowing him to plunge even deeper, and it feels like my soul is leaving my body with each thrust.

Every roll of his hips along my clit sends blinding electric shocks through me that fry my brain and make it impossible to do anything but just *feel*.

"Oh, God."

I slide my hands to the edge of the counter for purchase, trying to keep myself steady during his more aggressive movements.

My body heats again quickly, that slow burn that he's so good at building up already lit, but it won't ignite, no matter how hard he drives into me, no matter how deep he goes, no matter how good he is, I need more.

But I don't need to say a word for him to know it.

It only takes a few seconds before his hand slides up around my neck.

God, yes.

He closes those rough fingers around my throat, squeezing gently.

That grip.

The feel of his hand there.

That possessive hold on my throat.

Knowing that he is in control of everything finally allows me to float away, to find my second release.

I come on a strangled cry, my throat working against his palm.

"Fuck, yes." His growl in my ear reverberates through my chest as he redoubles his efforts, fucking me even harder through my orgasm, drawing it out with his free hand between us, his thumb on my clit, rolling across it as he continues to pump into me.

Each thrust cements him deeper, re-solidifies that bond we finally found again, the one that was always there, but that I somehow forgot.

Never again.

My eyes flutter open to meet his, and he stares down at me, his mouth slightly open, his breath ragged as he plows into my cunt.

He grits his teeth, a muscle in his jaw ticcing as he fights his own release. "I want you to come again for me."

"Wh-what?" My head swims, barely coming down from the last one. "I've already come twice. There's no way."

I can't.

My body already feels wrung out.

Decimated.

Ready to collapse into a pool of post-orgasmic, boneless sleep.

He adjusts his grip on my neck and tightens it. "You're going to come again before I do."

Fuck, he can't be serious.

"I-I don't think I can."

"You will."

He pulls out of me so abruptly that I gasp, then releases my leg, drags me off the counter, whips me around, and bends me down over it. My chest presses into the butcher block as he draws my hips up and back to position me how he wants me.

Warm breath flutters across my cheek as he settles his rock-hard chest to my back, tilting my head to the side until my gaze meets his. He grips his cock, aligning it with me again, and pushes in.

I groan, all the air rushing from my lungs at the feel of him this way.

In this position, he's so much bigger.

Not just his cock.

ALL of him.

He's all over me.

Completely enveloping me with his body. His breath. His scent. His touch.

His love.

It's exactly what I need.

What I've always needed.

A safe haven.

A home.

And he is it.

He stills, seated fully inside me and groans—that rumble against my back, pinning me even harder in between him and the counter. "You are going to come again for me, Honeybee. I need to feel this pretty cunt of yours squeezing my cock. One. More. Time. And then, maybe, I'll devour you again after."

I whimper.

The thought of another orgasm like *that* is far too much to bear in this moment.

He drags his hips back and plunges deep again, slamming the front of my hips against the counter, but I don't even care.

I can't when it feels like he's completing me.

Like he's filling some massive void that's been there since the moment I got back.

He pumps into me again and again, then wraps his hand around the front of me and finds my clit, rolling and pinching it until my legs are trembling so hard that the only thing keeping me upright is his large, hard body pinning me down. "Are you ready to come again?"

I shake my head.

No.

I can't.

I can't.

That low tingling between my legs, the delicious burn that always signals my impending release, seems to suggest otherwise, but I already feel like I'm going to collapse.

One more might kill me.

Killian chuckles low. "Yes, you are. Don't lie to me."

I don't want to.

"Y-y-yes."

"That's what I thought."

He twists my clit as he drags the head of his cock against that perfect spot inside me...

And I erupt again.

Just as he roars in my ear.

Killian comes hard, deep inside me, pumping into me three more times before he finally stills and collapses on top of me.

The heavy pressure of him pushing me down should feel suffocating, but it's like a comforting, soft blanket.

Darkness encroaches around the edges of my vision, but it's a warm, friendly one, not the scary, treacherous one I've been living under for weeks.

His lips find my ear, then my neck. He kisses his way to my mouth, ghosting his over mine. "I fucking love you, Honeybee."

I open my mouth to respond, to tell him I love him, too, to explain how much he means to me, but I can't form words.

We remain pinned together for several moments, each of us trying to catch our breath and come back to the world around us.

The buzz of the timer going off finally jerks both of us upright, and Killian laughs, holding me in his strong arms. His cock, still embedded deeply inside me, twitches, and I clench around it, eliciting another groan from the man who can so easily destroy me as he puts me back together.

"Are you okay?"

I nod, allowing my head to drop against his chest.

He tilts my face up to him. "Are you sure?"

I manage to bob my head again, and he drops another kiss to my forehead before he slowly releases me. Tightly gripped fingers around the edge of the counter keep my legs from giving out as he slips from me and reaches down to grab the towel.

He uses it to wipe between my thighs gently, grabs my clothes, and brings them over to me. "Get dressed. I'll get the food out of the oven."

"Okay."

I barely manage to get the word out around my labored breaths.

Killian grabs the oven mitt, pulls open the door, and removes the cornbread, ham, and baked beans, setting them on top of the stove as I slide back into my underwear and pants. As I get them up, he turns to face me in all his full glory, naked as the day God made him.

My eyes roam over the tattoos, including the new ones I love so much, but my gaze catches on the mountain that covers his chest. I've traced it so many times over the years, know every peak and valley of it by heart just as Killian does McBride Mountain itself.

Another memory flashes through my head.

A more recent one...

Earlier today.

"Wait—"

His brow furrows. "What is it?"

I step closer to him and drag my finger across the tallest peak, then drag it down the river and to where the cabin we're in now stands on the McBride homestead. "I think I might know how to figure out where I was."

He slides his hand under my chin, lifting it until I meet his concerned gaze. "How, Honeybee?"

It won't make any sense to him. It barely does to me, but somehow, I *know* it's what we need to do.

"We can't go to Asheville to see the psychiatrist, Killian. We have to do it at the timber yard."

16

WILLOW

Killian squats in front of me, sliding his hands across my knees, stopping the left one from bouncing incessantly like it has been since the moment I sat in this chair.

He catches my eyes with his and holds my gaze, the crease between his brows deepening. "Are you sure you want to do this?"

Am I?

I chew on my bottom lip as I scan the McBride Timber office, over the concerned faces of Raven, Connor, Liam, Sheriff Briggs, and finally to the psychiatrist who drove up from Asheville.

He settles into the leather chair that normally sits behind Connor's desk and now faces me in the center of the room while everyone else looks on, anxiously shifting weight, gazes darting around the room the same way mine is.

Everyone shares my nerves.

Raven appears ready to jump out of her skin, and we haven't even started yet. I offer her a smile that I hope she buys, and she returns it, even though it doesn't reach her green eyes.

Her gaze drifts to where Tony, Liam, and Connor lean against the far wall, trying to appear unaffected even as they avoid making direct eye contact.

They have reason to be worried.

This could go very badly.

It might not work.

Or it could work *too well,* and I might remember something that was better left buried.

But despite all my reservations about what I might find if we delve into this, I know I have to at least try everything at our disposal to get answers.

I lock my gaze with Killian's and nod. "Yes."

Dr. Bird offers me a tight smile over Killian's shoulder. "And you're sure you want to do this here, Ms. May? I always recommend it be somewhere quiet and comfortable."

No one would ever accuse this office of being either.

With the forklifts and saws running across the massive lot right outside the window that overlooks it and the old furniture that's likely been in this space since Killian's father ran it—if not before—it's probably the last place we *should* be attempting to delve into my forgotten memories.

But after last night, I'm more confident than ever that this is where I need to be.

"It has to be here."

My gaze drifts to the maps along the wall that go back hundreds of years. Hand-drawn by generations of McBrides who lived and breathed this mountain. They knew it inside and out. Every tree. Every branch. Every leaf. Each river, lake, and stream. All the little nooks and crannies where something—or someone—might hide.

They aren't just antiquated representations of what this mountain used to look like.

They're important.

I don't know why, but something tells me they hold the answers.

And I'm ready to find them, no matter what ugly truths they may contain.

Killian leans in to feather his lips over mine. "I'll be right here the whole time."

He slips around to stand behind me. I glance over my shoulder to find him leaning against the wall, his arms crossed over his chest, his back stiff, jaw locked tight in preparation for what might happen.

Shit.

I should have anticipated his uneasiness.

He knows how badly my memories have traumatized me. The fear they bring each time one breaks free from the abyss and lets loose in my head. Killian understands the panic and agony I may suffer if this works. And the thought of having to stand by and watch it is almost too much for him to bear—and we haven't even started yet.

But with the search party going out tomorrow, we need as much information as we can get, and I'm the only one who has it.

The answers are there.

Locked away somewhere deep in my psyche.

We need to get them *out.*

I take a deep breath in through my nose and let it slip through my lips the way Killian directed me the other night, remembering how it felt to have his body pressed against my back. His hands resting on my chest and belly, directing each inhale and exhale.

The doctor settles and gives me a smile. "All right, let's

begin. I need everyone else in the room to be quiet, if you have to stay."

Tony, Connor, and Liam all incline their heads toward him in recognition of his warning, while Raven scowls at him, annoyed that he would even *suggest* she might leave when he's about to go digging in my head.

Dr. Bird releases a little sigh. "Fine." He offers a genuine smile this time, one I'm sure is intended to put me at ease. But it will take a lot more than that to relax this tension from my body. "Willow, I need you to close your eyes, and we'll begin."

I can't help but take one last look over my shoulder at Killian. He offers me a soft smile that he reserves for me, one that shows all his love when no one else is around to witness it. The fact that he's looking at me like that and smiling that way with all these people in the room gives me the strength to turn away and let my eyes drift closed.

"I'm going to ask you to follow my directions to the best of your ability." Dr. Bird's gentle voice guides me. "Picture a safe place, somewhere that you've always felt comfortable, some place that feels like home. Somewhere you can relax and forget anything that bothers you."

Immediately, I'm in the cabin and cocooned in Killian's arms, curled up in his dad's old leather recliner.

"Where were you?"

"In our cabin, with Killian in his favorite chair."

"Good, Willow. What did it smell like?"

I take a deep breath, filling my lungs. "The logs smoldering in the fireplace. Leather, freshly cut wood, summer air. It smells like home. It smells like *him*."

It washes over me like a warm breeze, flooding my mind as my body heats, my bouncing knee finally going still.

"Good, Willow. Hold on to that feeling, to that smell. Now, we're going to focus on your breathing. Slowly breathe in through your nose and out through your mouth, concentrating on allowing your lungs to fill fully, and then releasing all the air out of them."

I do as he tells me.

That memory of Killian directing me the same way and the feel of him molded against me racing back to further help me relax into the voice's instructions.

"In...Out. Slowly."

In.

Out.

In.

Out.

The voice softens, words coming slower. "Now...hold it for a count of five."

I do, keeping Killian's scent deep in my chest.

"One... Two... Three... Four... Five... Now...release."

It slides from between my lips in a long rush, taking with it some of the tension that's been hardening my spine and aching in my shoulders.

"You're in the cabin and relaxed. You're breathing calmly. You feel good. You feel safe. I'm not going to tamper with this memory or safe space in any way, shape, or form. This is your happy place. Remember this feeling and bring it to your current moment and your memories. Remember and relax. Breathe in, breathe out. Keep the rhythm. And I want you to picture the Memorial Day Festival last year. Can you do that for me?"

My mind clicks over to that very vivid memory of watching Killian work on his carving of the bobcat. I feel my lips curl up into a smile. "Yes, I remember it."

"Good. And you were happy, relaxed."

I nod. "I was."

"Good. Remember that feeling. Now, I want you to think about that evening after the festival. Do you remember that?"

Nodding, my cheeks heat, and I shift in the chair, pressing

my legs together against the throb at the apex of my thighs. "Yes."

"And where were you?"

Bent over the couch...

"In the cabin with Killian."

"And you were happy, relaxed."

I nod. "Yes."

So, so happy...

The way he loved me that night. How thoroughly he took me and made me unravel. It would be impossible to ever forget.

"What about the following morning?"

No.

My brain tries to shut it down. Familiar inky blackness fills the space where the memory should be. Swirling around my head like a vicious tempest.

I squeeze my eyes closed tighter, fighting against the abyss.

That dull throb starts at my temples.

It slowly shifts from pitch black to dark gray, lightening.

A flash—setting dishes on the table.

Connor and Liam reaching to fill their plates a second time with satisfied grins.

"Yes, I remember breakfast."

But I didn't eat.

I wasn't hungry.

I was excited.

Nervous.

"Good. And what happened after you ate breakfast?"

"I..."

A wall of darkness.

Nothing but *onyx*.

"I can't see it." My hands tighten on the arms of the chair, and my breathing picks up, my heart galloping. "I can't see anything."

That soothing voice drops lower. "We're going to return to our safe place. We're going to breathe in and out calmly."

Yes.

That's what I should do.

Killian's voice, directing me to do the same, rings in my ears.

I center myself in the cabin. In Killian's arms. His scent invading my breaths. The long, slow ones he wants me to take.

In.

Out.

In.

Out.

"Good. You're happy and safe. It's the day after the festival. Do you remember your argument with Killian?"

I flinch.

But this time, it doesn't take as long for the blackness to part so I see Killian's face.

How terrified he was.

At the time, I didn't realize what I was seeing was panic. Because Killian *never* panicked about anything in his entire life. It was an unknown feeling for him, something I couldn't recognize because he didn't recognize it himself.

I hear those words come out of his mouth.

The ones he told me he said.

This time, they ring in my ears like a resounding gong.

I feel the stab in my chest as if he's driven his axe straight into it.

My stomach churns, and I gag like I'm going to throw up as he stalks out of the cabin and disappears into the woods.

"Y-y-yes..."

The arms of the chair creak as my fingers crank on them, my body tensing.

"Remember, you're safe here, Willow. Keep breathing in and out. Slowly."

I try to relax my grip and follow his command.

In.

Out.

In.

Out.

A minute passes.

Another.

"What happened after Killian left?"

The memory comes easier this time, with barely a gray haze surrounding it.

"Raven helping me pack." My body starts to vibrate. "I was panicking. I packed, and I left."

"Why did you leave?"

I wince as the tears start to burn in my eyes, even with them closed.

None of this is anything Killian and Raven haven't already told me, but it's as if I'm experiencing it for the first time. All those agonizing feelings twist my gut and tighten my chest.

"I couldn't tell him..."

Couldn't do it.

"Tell him what?"

"He didn't want—"

I suck in a sharp breath, trying to stop myself from hyperventilating. It gets harder and harder to process the memories.

"He didn't want what, Willow?"

"He told me I'd be a bad mother, and I had to leave. I drove away, but...I turned around."

"Where?"

I squeeze my eyes even tighter, trying to get the picture of the road to clear in my head. "I made it out of town, an hour or so, then turned back, came through town, and was headed up the mountain to Killian's."

My fingers tighten on the arms of the chair the same way they did the steering wheel as I navigated the road.

"What happened?"

The sound of tires crunching on gravel.

A clunk.

Smoke.

"My...my truck overheated. I pulled over."

It was always doing that. We were going to buy a new one soon. I was annoyed that it was going to delay me getting home.

"And then what happened?"

I tilt my head, trying to see the road more clearly, but it was raining. A summer storm. It made it difficult to see through the deluge.

But I could *hear*.

The sound roars in my ears.

"I heard another vehicle, someone stopping to help me."

"Good, Willow. And who was it?"

I attempt to picture the face, to see who stopped, but I can't. A form approaching through the driving rain. A knock on the window. Rolling it down to talk. "I don't...I don't know."

"Was it a man or a woman?"

Pain slices at my temples, and I reach up and rub my fingers into them. Darkness sweeps across my vision, blanketing what should be a very clear image of the person I'm speaking with.

"Remember, you're in a safe space, Willow. The cabin with Killian. Nothing can hurt you. Breathe in. Breathe out. Keep it *slow*."

I struggle with his command.

Trying to get my lungs to cooperate.

The cabin.

Killian's arms.

Safety.

His scent.

It melts away the anxiety and pain in my head.

Clears the clouds covering the memory.

"A man. It was a man's voice."

"What did he say?"

"He...he called me Bobby."

"Bobby?"

I nod.

Squeezing my eyes closed.

Trying to stay in the memory.

"And then he..." A sharp crack of agony hits the back of my head, and I place my hand there, the echo of the pain coming through vividly before blackness takes over again. "I think he hit me with something."

KILLIAN

It takes every single ounce of restraint I possess to keep from launching myself across the room and pulling Willow into my arms, dragging her out of the horrific memory she's recounting and back to safety.

Tears stream down her face from her squeezed-closed eyes.

Her knuckles whiten where they grasp the armrests in a death grip.

My nails dig into my palms as I clench my fists so tightly that they sting. I grind my jaw so intensely that my teeth actually ache, threatening to crack. Every muscle in my body vibrates with the self-control it takes me to stay in place.

Liam inches closer to me along the office wall, like he's about to intervene, if necessary, but I give him a little shake of my head to tell him I'm good, even though I'm not.

Not at all.

The doctor glances up at me as if he, too, shares Liam's concern.

Then, I meet Tony's gaze briefly across the room.

His jaw is locked tight, just like mine, his brow furrowed as he jots down notes into his little notebook. Documenting every word she says while under hypnosis.

All of our worst fears coming true as her memory unravels.

Willow wasn't gone by choice.

Willow was *taken*.

We had pieced it together, suspected as much, but hearing it in Willow's own unsteady voice. Having to stand here while she recounts the reality of her own abduction...

It's too horrific.

Too real.

Dr. Bird returns his focus to Willow, apparently appeased that I won't be a problem when I'm trembling almost as badly as she is. "Remember, you're in the cabin. You're happy and safe. You're breathing slowly. In and out."

Come on, Honeybee.

Breathe.

I remember how she was two nights ago when she woke in a panic—unable to do it on her own. How she needed me to help her through it.

The soft, soothing tone Dr. Bird uses as he guides her seems to help Willow relax slightly, her labored breaths evening out.

I want to scream that she shouldn't have to do this right now. That it can wait. That she needs time. That we can't keep doing this to her. That we can't keep pushing her to remember something that hurts so much.

But if I intervene, she won't ever be free.

Willow won't ever be herself again until we find out who did this to her and make them pay.

Which means I have to control my most basic instincts to protect her from this pain. I have to trust the doctor to keep her safe.

Dr. Bird reminds her of that as her breathing seems to return to normal. "Willow, remember you're safe."

She nods almost imperceptibly, that death-grip loosening slightly from the arms of the chair.

"What's the next thing you remember?"

"Pain." She winces. "I had such a bad headache."

My stomach twists violently, and I shift my stance, leaning my other shoulder against the wall because I just can't remain still anymore when she's hurting so badly.

"What did you see when you opened your eyes?"

Willow squeezes her eyes closed tighter. "A cabin."

Acid climbs my throat.

Dr. Bird jots notes in his own notebook. "Did you recognize it?"

She shakes her head. "No, it looked..." Her head tilts to the side slightly, as if she can see it in her mind and is searching for the proper way to explain it. "Strange."

"Strange how?"

"Old." A pause. "Very rundown." Then another as she examines the image in her head. "Not like any cabin I've been in around McBride Mountain, where people live now. Barely livable."

Her description piques my interest, and I push off the wall, narrowing my eyes on her before allowing my gaze to meet Liam's, Connor's, and Tony's.

We know this mountain better than anyone—every resident, every property, every damn *cabin*.

Which means we *have to* know whoever was holding her.

Even Raven seems to have switched into full-on reporter mode, the intensity of her focus on Willow and every word she's saying like a laser.

Dr. Bird keeps pushing her. "What did you smell?"

Willow clenches her eyes closed, taking a long inhalation. "Burning wood. A fire."

"What did you hear?"

"Footsteps."

I tense as if I can hear them, too. Anticipating what she'll say next. What she might reveal. The identity of the monster who took her from me.

Who is the bastard, Honeybee?

"Someone's saying the name 'Bobby' again."

Who the fuck is Bobby?

Something tells me that name is important—essential to unraveling all of this.

Tony glances up from his notes to meet my gaze, raising a dark brow, asking if I know who she might be talking about. I shake my head. Unfortunately, the name doesn't ring a bell.

Dr. Bird assesses Willow, giving her another moment to regain control of her breathing. "And can you see his face?"

She shakes her head. "No."

"What does his voice sound like?"

"Low, rough, older."

"And what did he say?"

Her body starts shaking, her hands moving to the armrests again, fingers curling around them. A sob slips from her mouth, so filled with anguish I feel it radiate through my own body. "Welcome home."

The doctor glances at me. "You're safe. Go back to your safe place. Remember where you were in the cabin with Killian in the chair."

She shakes her head, her lips trembling. "I can't." Another sob rents the air. "I'm..." Her breaths shorten, punctuated by soul-crushing pain. "He's..."

No.

My control *snaps*. "That's enough!" I finally stalk away from the wall. "Get her out of it."

Dr. Bird opens his mouth to argue, but one look at me and he shifts forward slightly in his seat toward her. "Willow, remember you're safe, you're warm, you're comfortable. You're in Killian's arms in the cabin."

I step closer to her, afraid to do anything that might hurt her while she's still under hypnosis, but needing to help. Needing to do *something*.

The doctor motions for me that it's okay to touch her, and I wrap my arms around her, dragging her up out of the chair and into my embrace.

Willow buries her face against my neck and sobs as I hold her, keeping her upright because her legs won't do it on their own.

Dr. Bird continues to direct her. "Keep breathing in, out. In, out. And when you wake up, you're going to remember everything that you told me, but you'll feel safe. There will be no panic. No more fear." He watches us for a moment, allowing her to breathe deeply a few times. "Willow, open your eyes."

They flutter open, and she tilts her head to look up at me, tears streaming down her face.

"I'm so sorry, Honeybee." I swallow through the giant lump in my throat. "I've got you. You're safe."

She presses her cheek to my chest, and I exchange a look with the doctor.

Raven approaches from where she waited and rests her hand on Willow's shoulder, rubbing it gently, whispering something I can't hear.

I scowl at Dr. Bird. "I think we're done for today."

He nods, sliding his notebook into his bag and grabbing it from the floor. "You know how to get in touch with me if she wants to try again. Make sure she gets lots of rest tonight."

Something tells me that won't be happening.

Not now that she remembers.

It may not be everything.

But it's enough.

He slips out of the office, leaving her trembling in my arms.

I tighten my grip on her. "Let me take you home, Honeybee."

We can discuss all this later, when she's up for it and ready to. I won't force it now. Not when she's so shaken.

Willow pushes away from me, takes a step back, and shakes her head. "No." She swipes at her tears with determination, looking from me to Raven to Sheriff Briggs and Connor and Liam. "There's a reason I wanted to do this here."

I try to pull her into my arms again, but she holds up a hand, stopping me. "Why?"

"Because when I was looking at your tattoo last night..."—she walks over to where all the old maps hang—"it made me think about something."

Liam pushes off the wall. "What?"

Connor, Tony, and Raven join us in front of the maps.

Willow tilts her head, examining all of them. "I was in here the other day with Connor looking at these. And I realize they're all a little different."

I nod. "Of course, they are. Some of these are two hundred years old."

"Right..." She points to one of the older ones on the far left. "And this one has a lot of things on it that these"—she motions to the newer ones—"don't."

"Yeah." I nod, scanning the oldest of the maps. "Old logging trails, places we can't work anymore, where we've planted and need to wait for regrowth."

She turns back to face me. "I had to be somewhere there aren't a lot of people, somewhere very remote, if no one saw me for a year, right?"

Everyone bobs their heads in agreement.

Her lips twist. "But all of those gifts and notes that went to Raven had to be from someone who knew that if I just disappeared, she would call on the cavalry. Someone had to get me to write them to keep her from looking for me...which means it had to be someone who was close enough to town to know about my relationship with her."

Tony nods. "She has a point."

Willow paces, chewing on her bottom lip as she works through whatever is churning in her head. "And that's the only explanation for why all those notes and gifts showed up. Someone went out of their way to ensure I wouldn't be missed, which should limit the search somewhat."

Connor sighs. "It's still hundreds of miles."

She shakes her head. "It's not." Moving over to one of the newer maps, she taps her finger on the gorge. "I noticed this the other day. I know I have a memory of the gorge, of going through it, but there's nothing up that way, not on the newer maps, but look at this." She moves to the oldest one and drags her finger northwest of the gorge. "What's this?"

I step over to it and squint, narrowing my eyes on the fading ink that my great-grandfather—or maybe even *his* father— drew. "An old logging area that hasn't been used in generations."

That doesn't appear on any of the newer maps.

Willow looks at me, her dark brows rising. "How would they have gotten logs through the gorge?"

Shaking my head, I drag my finger down the map on the opposite side of the mountain from town. "They didn't. There was likely a trail that went up the backside of the mountain that's been abandoned just as long as that area has been."

She follows where I'm pointing, but this map barely shows it, almost completely faded out. A faint line running up the most remote side of the mountain, near the far edge of the gorge, and up to the old logging area. "But...there would've been a cabin up there, right?"

My spine stiffens as I exchange a glance with Connor, Liam, and Tony. "Probably." I turn back to her. "They certainly weren't coming down here every day. Even for an experienced hiker, it would be at least a ten-hour hike from there to town, depending on where they built it. Even taking the trail wouldn't have helped because they would have had to loop around to this side of the mountain, which adds several hours. They would have burned all their daylight just getting home."

Raven nudges me out of the way, examining the maps probably for the first time since she's never been in this office before, as far as I know. "They must have stayed up there for days or weeks at a time to make it worthwhile."

Nodding, Willow refocuses on that old trail, her eyes glazing over slightly, as if she isn't really in this room with us anymore. "I was in an old cabin northwest of the gorge. Near this area. I'm positive."

The determination in her voice sends goosebumps skittering across my skin.

She glances over at me. "I'm sure, Killian. This is where I was."

There's a plea in her voice for me to believe her, for me to *act*.

I nod. "Then that's where we'll go."

Tony bobs his head in agreement. "That's where we'll focus our searches."

Willow squares her shoulders. "I'm going with you."

My back stiffens. "Like hell you are."

She turns to face me slowly, standing her ground. "I'm not going to sit back here while you all go up there to face God only knows what. I need to see it, see whoever this was, know what happened to me. Maybe I'll get the rest of my memories if I do."

I open my mouth to argue with her again, but Raven steps up, inserting herself between Willow and me. "She needs to do this."

It doesn't mean it makes it any easier to accept putting Willow in that kind of position, but I know Raven's right.

"Fine." I lock gazes with Willow, her eyes red-rimmed from crying but unwavering in their intensity. "But you don't leave my side. You understand me?"

She nods.

Tony lets out a long sigh. "We've got thirty-four people ready to come out with us tomorrow. That's a good number, and now, we know where to go."

We all turn and look at the map, at the tiny squiggle of a line, barely there, that represents the old logging trail.

Hopefully, it's where we're going to find our answers.

17

TWO DAYS LATER

WILLOW

Going up the mountain feels different this time. When Killian and I did it less than a week ago, we had a purpose, but we might as well have been looking for a needle in a fucking haystack the size of Rhode Island.

Now we have focus, a destination, and a glimmer of hope of finding the rest of my memories and whoever the mystery man is who haunts my dreams. Because ever since the hypnosis session, the visions from the last year keep coming in waves, as if Dr. Bird somehow opened a dam that's now allowing a rush to work its way out.

More nightmares.

More flashes during the day.

This morning, as we gathered with the large group from town to organize and then set out for the river, it felt like all the suffering of the last several weeks, all the turmoil and tears, were designed to bring me to this point.

So many things that were surrounded by darkness are now seeing the light.

Pieces falling into place, helping me create a true picture of what happened.

I did come back to Killian that day because I knew he didn't mean what he said. That was *fear* talking, not the man I love. And I was intercepted by someone when the truck broke down. He hit me, took me somewhere, and must have somehow disposed of my truck so no one would be suspicious.

My captor kept me for the past year, somewhere no one would hear me or see me. Somewhere so remote there would never be any hope of anyone stumbling upon us. He must have made me write those letters to Raven. Whoever it is knows McBride Mountain well enough to understand she would miss me, that she would question where I was if she didn't hear from me regularly with assurances that I was okay.

Those are the things I *know*.

But what I still don't get is why it feels like there's something waiting there for me beyond my still missing memories.

The recurring dream came again last night.

More vivid than before.

That memory of running, of holding something, clutching it to my chest, as I stumbled down that game trail through the woods that rainy night. Cutting my feet. My lungs burning. Thunder rolling and lightning flashing, illuminating my way through the dark forest.

It all feels so important.

Essential.

Just as taking every step up the mountain right now is.

Killian pauses in front of me and glances back, his brow furrowing as he scans me over—like he's been doing every few minutes since we set out. "Are you all right? We can stop if we need to."

I shake my head. "No. I want to get to that spot on the river as early as we can today."

Our hike has already moved slowly enough, far slower than even mine did with Killian when I was still in far more pain physically than I am now.

The addition of some of our friends from town to help with the search meant a delayed start, the sun almost directly overhead by the time we established the plan, reassured we had all the proper supplies, and set out today.

Those who are strong hikers moved ahead to set up a base camp near where they found me in the river, while all the slower hikers—including *me* now—trail behind to meet up later.

Almost three dozen residents of McBride Mountain banded together.

The sheer number of people willing to help amazes me, as does the level of rage that seems to permeate the air from everyone who now knows what we're looking for out there.

A monster of a man.

Someone who was willing to kidnap me and hold me against my will. To do things to me I can't think about without collapsing in on myself again.

Killian stops, despite my objection, waiting for me to catch up to him so he can rake his assessing gaze over me and search for any signs that I need a break.

I reach him and offer what I hope is a reassuring smile.

The minor delay gives Liam and Connor time to reach us, and they take the momentary stop to snag a sip of water. I do the same, trying not to appear winded or give away the fact that I'm exhausted already.

We're pushing harder than we did during our last hike, and even though I'm feeling better physically, I haven't regained my stamina. And I don't want Killian to worry any more than he already does.

But I can't hide from this man.

Killian gives me a tight smile.

It shows every ounce of his concern.

He doesn't believe me that I don't need a real break.

And maybe he shouldn't, since he's the one who held me last night while I sobbed as the memories came rushing back every time I tried to close my eyes and sleep.

Of being taken.

Of being touched...

Even now, I have to shut my eyes and struggle to breathe through the nausea rolling through my stomach.

Killian's arms wrap around me, and he tugs me against his chest. "Don't lie to me like that. It's okay to not be okay."

I sense Liam and Connor slip past us and continue up the trail, giving us some privacy.

Birds chirp in the trees above us, fluttering from limb to limb, enjoying the beautiful day that I should be able to—but I can't. Not knowing our reason for being up here.

Killian skims his lips across my temple. "Do you want to talk about it?"

I shake my head and suck in a long, slow breath. "No, not again."

His words from last night still ring in my head.

Crystal clear.

Because he ensured I would hear and remember them. Repeated them to me at least a dozen times as he held me through my tears.

"Nothing he did to you changes who you are to me. Nothing. And none of it was your fault."

It's hard to believe that when I'm the one who left. If I had stayed that day to talk things through with him, none of this would have happened. But I know he believes it's his. That if he hadn't said what he did to me, if he hadn't panicked, we would have had the life we always planned.

We could go on blaming ourselves, or each other, forever, and it wouldn't change where we are right now, though.

It would just drag us into an even darker place.

Neither of us wants that.

Moving forward is the only option.

I pull out of his arms and stare up at him—the man everyone in McBride Mountain gives a wide berth. The one they're afraid to upset or cross. But Killian is my avenging hero, on a mission to seek and destroy whoever caused me so much pain. I know he won't stop until he does, and that gives me comfort that his words never could.

He brushes a thick strand of dark hair away from my eyes and gives me a hard smile. "You ready to keep going?"

I nod, and he takes my hand in his and leads me along the barely discernible trail.

We weave through the thick, towering forest, hiking for hours in comfortable silence. Just having him with me, knowing he will always be here for anything I need, watching my back, and giving me his protection, makes it possible to keep moving.

It keeps the darkness at bay.

Somehow out here, it's easier to concentrate on my breathing, drawing in the fresh, clean air. To feel my feet falling on solid ground that's been here for millennia, knowing it will remain long after we're gone. And to watch how confident Killian is as he stalks through the trees with sure steps, carrying his pack on his shoulders as if it weighs nothing, axe strapped across it in case he needs it.

All of it lulls me into an almost trance, allows those things that haunt me to float away as the sun arches overhead and finally starts to lower in the west.

It quickly disappears behind the treetops, dropping the temperature and the mountain into darkness.

Time passes, though I lose track of how long we've been

hiking or how far we've gone, until the smell of a campfire and food cooking finally hits my nose. By the time we break through the treeline and into the clearing near the river, camp is established, dinner already in full swing.

Sheriff Briggs sits on a log on one side of the bonfire, his wife, Tonya, beside him, laughing at something he whispers in her ear. A handful of others mill about the dozens of tents already set up near the center of camp.

It isn't far from the spot Killian and I stayed the night we came up here alone, seeking answers we couldn't locate but finding something else just as important.

That was the start of us figuring out a way to come together again. To forgive and allow ourselves to feel all the things we had been trying to tamp down since my return.

"Are you hungry?"

Killian's question breaks my train of thought, and I shake my head as he twines his fingers with mine and leads me toward the encampment. Concerned blue eyes watch me. "You need to eat something."

"I know..."

But now that we've stopped moving, that we've reached this spot, the fear of what we might find up there, of what I'll have to see and what memories will come with it, turns my stomach until bile climbs my throat.

I force it back as Killian releases my hand to let his pack slip off his shoulders. He rests it beside our tent that someone set up for us before we arrived, then directs me toward the fire.

My feet move, but I barely register what's happening, my mind already slipping into the dark place I avoided on the way up here.

Connor and Liam approach us with two plates in hand. Liam slips one into mine without a word but offers a knowing half-smile. Connor does the same for Killian, clapping him on the shoulder before they return to the makeshift kitchen area to get their own dinners.

I stare down at the food someone carefully prepared to ensure it would be hot and ready by the time the rest of the searchers arrived, but I can't muster up the appetite to even consider eating any of it.

Killian urges me over to an empty log along the side of the bonfire and settles beside me. Connor and Liam return, dropping down on the opposite side of their brother. They all dig in, friendly chatter filling the night air along with the sound of the river not far to the east.

Millions of stars blanket the clear sky above, a canopy of sparkling lights.

I tear my gaze from them and watch the men and women around the fire, the flames flickering across their faces, which are mostly filled with humor, but there's an underlying hum of trepidation and restless anticipation.

No one knows what we might find tomorrow.

But everyone expects the worst.

That much is evident based on the looks being cast in our direction.

Only the rest of the search party finally entering the clearing breaks the attention from me.

Additional tents go up.

People come and eat. Drifting around. Chatting. Then returning to their spots to settle in for the night.

All while I sit frozen in place, unable to move.

I have no idea how much time passes.

An hour.

Two, maybe.

Killian finally leans over, dipping his head toward my ear. His long hair tickles my cheek. Even with the fire burning close, the scent that's all Killian still fills each breath I take. "You didn't touch your food. And I've been trying to give you some space and time, but we have a hell of a hike tomorrow. You need to eat something."

I glance down at my plate.

He's right.

Today was the *easy* part of the journey—physically and emotionally.

Tomorrow gets steeper. Even less traveled. Into the complete unknown as far as what we might find.

I lift the piece of cornbread and take a bite. Despite how delicious it is, it still feels like chalk going down my throat.

Killian returns to his conversation with his brothers. Not hovering. Continuing to allow me to move at my own pace. But I still catch him watching me out of the corner of his eye.

I force myself to keep eating—the bread, some pasta salad, a few bites of beans and ham—until I feel like I might throw up.

And somehow, Killian *knows.*

That I've reached my limit.

That I'm on the verge of collapse.

He takes the plate from me, passes it to Connor, then pushes to his feet, holding out his hand to me. "Let's go."

I slide my palm into his, and he tugs me up, murmurs "good night" to a few people, and leads me over to our tent on the edge of camp. Stopping outside, he pauses to take my face between his palms, the moonlight glittering across his eyes as he stares down at me.

He doesn't say anything, but he doesn't have to.

The way he looks at me is enough to speak volumes.

What happened to me on this mountain doesn't matter to him, but it does to me. I left something up here, something important, something I have to find.

And hopefully I will tomorrow.

KILLIAN

I wake to an eerie silence and a foreboding sense of dread.

Over the past couple of weeks with her back, I've gotten used to the sound of Willow's breathing. Even before I started sleeping in our bed with her, I was always aware of the sounds coming from the bedroom, always listening to see if she needed me. And since we got back together, I've become accustomed to the feel of her in my arms, her shifting in her sleep, the comfort of knowing she's safe with me.

None of that exists in this moment.

I open my eyes to an empty tent, the sleeping bag next to mine already cold, like the dread that sits like a stone in my throat.

"Willow?"

It goes unanswered.

I push up on my elbow and scan the tight space as if there'd be somewhere else for her to be instead of at my side, but she's gone, as are her hiking boots that had sat just inside the zipper when we fell asleep.

"Shit."

Somehow, I slept through her waking, putting on her boots, and leaving, even her re-zipping the tent closure.

Where the hell did you go, Honeybee?

Unease clamps around my throat, squeezing until it makes it hard to breathe as I throw open my sleeping bag and climb out. I quickly tug on my boots before I unzip the tent and step out into the darkness of the night.

An almost full moon overhead gives off some illumination, as does the bonfire raging to the left, but the tents block most of that, casting long, ominous shadows in places. Low voices float through the air from that direction, and I approach the center of camp, weaving between the other tents where the rest of the searchers sleep soundly, scanning for any signs of her.

I quickly make it to the voices.

Flames climb high into the sky from the bonfire people have kept going, sending out a warm glow and welcome heat into the night, though it isn't nearly as chilly as it has been in the evenings now that we're nearing July.

The Winslow brothers sit on one of the long logs, staring into the fire and sipping coffee from metal cups. They both raise a brow at me as I approach, obviously surprised to see me up and around this late.

Everyone is tired after that hike, and they probably haven't seen anyone else since all the searchers retired to their tents after dinner.

"Did you see Willow come this way?"

Ned's brow furrows as he looks to his brother, Daryl. "She didn't come this way."

Daryl shakes his head. "Sorry, Killian. Haven't seen her since we took over the watch about two hours ago."

"Shit." I run my hands through my hair as that unease I felt back in the tent now races through my bloodstream, chilling every inch of my body. "Okay…"

Where is she?

The brothers push up from the log, suddenly on high alert.

Daryl starts to reach for his shotgun propped up next to him. "Should we be worried?"

I hold up a hand before he grabs the weapon. "Give me a minute to look for her before you wake anyone else."

The last thing I want to do is start a panic in the middle of the night when everyone needs to rest up for tomorrow. If I can locate Willow quickly, there won't be any reason to stir up the rest of the camp.

They both nod, their suspicious gazes now roaming over the campsite illuminated by the fire and moonlight.

Where the hell would she go?

If she went toward the game trail that we know she ran down to get to the river that night, she would've had to walk past the Winslows or at least close enough that they would have heard her, which means she went the other way—toward the water.

Hell...

I stalk off in that direction, scanning the deepening darkness for any signs of her, with the moonlight the only thing to guide me this far away from the fire.

The sound of the water bubbling over the rocks in the center of the river reaches me before I can see it, bringing with it the vision of her floating there, limp, cold—

No.

I refuse to consider that possibility.

Each step across the clearing feels like it takes hours, even though it can't be more than a few hundred yards to the water's edge. I scan it frantically until a heavy, relieved breath rushes from my lungs, my heart finally beating again.

There she is...

Willow stands not far from where I found her in the river, just above where the rapids start, where the water is calmer and swirls gently in a naturally created pool near the bank.

She stares at it, her head tilted slightly, arms wrapped around herself protectively. Her thick, dark hair floats around her shoulders in the light breeze, but if she's cold, she doesn't show it.

Her eyes stay locked on the small pool, like she can see something there I can't. She doesn't hear my approach, doesn't seem to even sense that I'm here until I'm right up on her.

"Hey..."

She startles and whirls toward me, her eyes wide, hand pressed over her heart. "You have to stop sneaking up on me like that."

"I didn't mean to." I shift closer, trying to see if she's been crying, but her eyes seem clear, no telltale streaks down her cheeks. "What are you doing out here in the middle of the night? I woke up, and you were gone. I was worried."

"Oh, I'm sorry." She closes the distance between us and rests her hands on my chest. "I didn't mean to scare you. I..." Her head turns back toward the river. "I couldn't sleep, and I thought maybe if I came out here..."

My heart breaks for the thousandth time over what she's suffered, what she *continues* to suffer because of some psychopath who decided to keep her from her life, from *me*.

Willow rotates in my arms to face the river again, and I press in tightly behind her, wrapping my arms around her waist and resting my chin on her shoulder. "You thought maybe you'd remember something else?"

She nods, her focus still completely on the water.

Moonlight reflects off it, creating a cascade of diamond-like sparkles across the surface with the movement downstream.

I nuzzle her neck. "Have you?"

It takes her a few seconds to answer. "No. I just keep staring at the river, wondering why I would've jumped into it."

"Maybe you were trying to get across it and got swept away in the rapids."

She shakes her head, threading her fingers with mine across her stomach. "That doesn't seem right to me." A little frustrated noise comes from her throat. "I can't *remember*, but I *know* that's not what happened. I can't explain it."

Her struggle slices at my chest, her pain a living and breathing thing I wish I could hunt down and eviscerate with my axe.

"You don't have to, Honeybee. You don't owe me any explanations for anything you feel. Maybe you were pushed in."

She tilts her head slightly, considering it. "Maybe. But if he went through all the trouble to keep me up here for a year, why would he then push me into the river in a way that would probably kill me?"

It would have, if I hadn't randomly been up here because of Liam that day.

I will never complain about him dragging us out in the early mornings on his hunts for the perfect tree specimens *ever* again.

"That doesn't seem right, either, Honeybee?"

A hard sigh falls from her parted lips, and she leans back against my chest heavily, giving me all her weight. "Something is just drawing me toward it, the water..."

"Then let's get in."

The words come out before I really have much of a chance to consider the suggestion. Pros. Cons. How she might react...

She glances back at me. "What?"

I scan the small pool in front of us. "Let's get in the water."

"Killian, it's *cold*."

"Not *that* cold, and we won't stay in long. Just a quick dip."

A little laugh falls from her lips. "It's like 2:00 in the morning."

I grin at her, her laughter signaling that maybe I'm on the right track. "Which means no one else is out here."

And if I don't do something to drag her out of her own head, she won't get any sleep tonight, and that will spell disaster for what we need to accomplish tomorrow.

Even as a child, Willow struggled to separate herself mentally from the emotional trauma she was experiencing at home. She found a safe place with us, a refuge from the uncertainty, but getting her to relax, to allow herself space to just *be,* was harder.

Somehow, I became that for her. I discovered ways to break the cycle that would inevitably end with more pain for her. And that's what I have to do now.

Stepping back from her, I grasp the hem of my T-shirt,

tugging it up and off, and letting it fall to the ground. I reach for the waistband of my pants.

Her eyes widen. "You're serious."

I nod, popping the button. "I'll be with you the whole time."

Considering what happened the *last* time either of us was in these waters, I understand why some trepidation may linger, but just like the memories that stay hidden in her head, the ones she so desperately wants to confront to find the truth, she needs to confront this river.

With me holding her steady, she can do that without fear of drifting away in the water or her own mind.

Hopefully.

She turns and looks at the pool again, her lips twisting as she considers what might be a really stupid idea on my part.

This could backfire—big time.

It will either draw her from inside her head and back to the moment...or it will send her spinning further away.

Willow slowly turns to face me.

The trust shining in her gaze answers before she does. "Okay."

Her hands move to the zipper of her lightweight jacket. She lowers it, then tugs the fabric free, doing the same with her T-shirt, leaving her standing in the moonlight in her bra. Shivering, she scans the darkness before kicking off her boots, pulling off her socks, and shimmying out of her pants.

I do the same, refusing to even speak in fear that I might make her change her mind.

This will work.

This will help.

I keep telling myself that as she strips off her underwear and bra.

My bare feet sink into the grass along the riverbank, and I reach out a hand for her. She doesn't hesitate in allowing me to lead her toward the quiet, small pool, away from the rapids and current that swept her downriver and almost took her from me permanently.

I dip my foot in.

Shit.

She shivers watching me. "How bad is it?"

Honestly, colder than I remember.

But I'm not about to tell her that and give her a reason to back out.

Wrapping my arms around her, I tug her body against mine with a grin. Heat radiates between us—both from the meeting of our naked flesh and the sexual tension that always seems to exist whenever we're together. "Not so bad."

Before she can respond, I step sideways and drag her down into the chilly water with me.

A gasp falls from her lips as it engulfs us up to our chests. "Shit!" She shivers and clings to my neck. "Speak for yourself; it's freezing."

Her teeth chatter, and I trail my lips over her neck and tip backward, dunking us both fully under.

Willow comes up sputtering and playfully smacks my shoulder. "Why'd you do that?"

Because sometimes a shock to your system isn't a bad thing.

"I just like to see you wet, Honeybee."

She gives me a half-grin, half-smirk, scoring her nails down my neck, pressing her naked skin against mine even tighter. "I see what you're doing, Killian McBride."

I raise a brow, doing my best to appear innocent. "Oh, yeah. What's that?"

"You're trying to distract me."

And apparently I'm not doing a good job of hiding it.

"Am I?"

Her head bobs, dipping closer to mine. "You are."

There doesn't appear to be any anger in her words, rather a playfulness I hadn't expected after finding her out here.

I shrug, settling my hands on her ass and tugging her up against me tightly, pinning my growing cock between us. "Maybe I am. Is it working?"

She smiles and brushes a kiss across my mouth. "It might be."

"Might be?" I nip at the corner of her lip. "I must not be very good at my job, then."

Distracting Willow from every reason she has to disappear into herself will always be my top priority. This woman means more than anything else to me. More than McBride Timber. More than my role as the unofficial patriarch on the mountain. More than any personal desire I might ever have.

She can have whatever she wants right now—and always.

I kiss her deeply, and Willow groans and lifts her legs to wrap them around my waist, aligning my cock along her scalding core. Even the cold river water can't douse her heat or my need for this woman. After everything she suffered, the memories that continue to come back and haunt her, she's still the same woman I fell in love with all those years ago.

The one I've missed.

The one I prayed would return and give me a second chance.

Strong. Determined. Stubborn as hell at times.

And now that I have her back, I'll do anything to ensure she's safe and happy.

I squeeze her ass, moving her so she can feel how impossibly hard she has me. "Everything's going to be okay, Honeybee. I promise."

She murmurs against my lips. "I know you believe that."

"I don't believe that; I know it. You and me. I won't make the same mistake again. I told you once, and I'll say it again until you believe it—whatever you want, whatever you need, I'll give it to you until the day I die."

Her gaze softens, and she runs her hands through my wet hair. "I know you will."

"What do you need right now?"

She shivers and laughs. "I need to get out of this cold water." Her legs tighten around my waist, and she rubs against me, letting the head of my cock catch just inside her cunt. "And I need you."

18

KILLIAN

W*ell, fuck.*
I intended to distract her. To draw her from the depths of whatever darkness woke her in the night and brought her out here. I hadn't set out to fuck her. But with her in my arms like this, needy and begging for it, she knows damn well I won't deny her.

Like I ever stood a chance to resist...

It hasn't happened yet.

And I'm not about to start letting this woman down when my entire purpose in life is to see her smile, to watch her enjoy life, to be happy and content.

That won't happen here in the river with the chilly water lapping at our naked skin, raising goosebumps across every inch of our bodies.

I need full, unfettered access to her.

We need this moment.

The moon shines down on us as I stalk out of the water with Willow in my arms. Her legs stay wrapped tightly around my waist, keeping me pinned to her. Every step rubs my cock along her slick, hot core, and she groans into my mouth as she kisses me hard. A greedy taking of precisely what she asked for.

All of me.

She already has it.

It's been hers for so long that I barely remember what it felt like *not* to love Willow May.

The sharp bite of the cool night air hitting our wet skin doesn't seem to faze her, and I couldn't give a fuck right now.

Not with her crushed against me.

Not with her devouring my mouth.

Not when she seems to have completely forgotten whatever brought her out to the river tonight, which was my only purpose.

There may be almost three dozen people merely a few hundred yards away, but we might as well be a thousand miles from anyone else, with the way the world seems to disappear.

All that exists beneath the mountain sky, littered with stars, is the two of us.

Our slick bodies.

Our all-consuming desire for each other.

Our commitment to *this,* no matter what else may come.

Willow kisses me with reckless abandon. Grinding along my length. Clinging to my neck and tunneling her hands into my hair as if she can't get close enough. Twining her tongue with my own. Frantic in a way I've never seen her before.

If I adjusted my hold and slid into her right now, she would accept me.

She would take me into her body, giving me her soul again and again, the same way I do mine to her.

But I force myself to keep walking.

To ignore the burning animal instinct to take her this very second.

I head for the treeline, the farthest away from the camp as I can get without delving too deep into the forest. The last thing we need is a damn search party coming out here, finding us naked and in a very compromising situation because we got ourselves turned around in the darkness.

All I need is a solid surface.

And this woman.

My Honeybee...

That sweet scent of lavender and honey clings to her, coats my tongue as she tangles hers with mine.

I step into the trees a few feet, ignoring the bite of twigs and whatever else lies on the forest floor on my soles, until I can press her back against the rough bark.

She gasps into my lips at the contact, and I groan my approval at finally being able to pin her to something, to get the leverage I need to well and truly fuck her.

But I would never cause this woman additional pain. "Does that hurt?"

Willow shakes her head, twining her fingers through my hair. "No, but I don't care if it does."

I drag my head back and see the truth in her gaze, the heat there flaring at the *many* ways I can make it hurt so damn good for her.

She has always liked a little bit of pain with her pleasure, a little bit of adventure mixed in with the mundane. My hand at her throat. Having sex in the McBride Timber office, where anyone might walk in on us. The sharp sting of my hand across her ass...

But only in my wildest dreams did I imagine I'd be taking her like this.

Rough.

Hard.

Out here where we're completely exposed.

"You're sure?"

She nods.

I dip my head to her neck, kissing my way along the smooth column until I get to her ear, and sucking on the lobe until she groans and rubs her cunt along my cock even harder. "You're going to have to be quiet, Honeybee. Because if anyone hears you, they might take your screams for something else and come running."

She issues the tiniest whimper. "I will."

Somehow, I don't believe her, but I don't fucking care if they see anyway.

This is what she needs right now, in this moment, to forget all the ways her head is wrapped up in the past, all the things she can't remember.

She needs me.

She needs to feel alive again.

And with the moon shining brightly overhead, the rough bark at her back, and my cock inside her, I don't know how she could possibly think about anything else.

I reach between us, align the head at her slick entrance, and glide into her in one long, smooth stroke.

She gasps, her breath catching as I seat myself fully inside her.

Her hands tighten around my neck, nails digging into the skin, and I freeze, allowing her to adjust to my size. Giving her a moment to consider what the hell we're doing and to change her mind if she wants to. But she squeezes around me tightly and scores those nails across my shoulders. "Move."

Fuck. Yes.

Her wish is my command, and I drag my hips back and slam into her again. The gasp that falls from her lips this time is louder. Needier.

My cock throbs deep inside her. "Told you, you need to be quiet, Honeybee."

She nods.

"And hold on tight."

Keeping one hand on her ass to support her, I pin my chest to hers and slide my other up around her neck, pinning her head to the tree.

Her eyes roll up, and she swallows hard against my palm.

Fuuuuuuck.

It never gets old.

This feeling of being inside her.

Of every little noise she makes vibrating along my hand and knowing they're because of me.

Because of what I can do for her.

I squeeze gently, her heartbeat thrumming rapidly under my thumb as I pull my hips back and plunge into her again.

This time, I don't pause.

I don't hesitate.

I don't stop.

I set a driving rhythm.

Harsh.

Demanding.

The type designed to bring us both to release quickly.

I crash my lips to hers, inhaling her gasps. Her tiny mewls. The frantic pants that fall as I pound into her. "I'm going to catch your scream, Honeybee."

She whimpers and nods, clenching around me, rolling her hips to meet mine on each thrust. Taking me deep. Clinging to me on each retreat, trying to keep me inside.

The sound of the crickets, the water rushing across the rocks in the river, her desperate pleas, and skin on skin fills the air.

A symphony so beautiful I can't imagine anything else ever coming close.

My harsh breaths flutter her dark hair across her forehead, and I capture her mouth again, greedily devouring her. Needing to taste her. Needing her to know it's me, that my touch is the only one that matters. That it's the sole one she should be dreaming about, thinking about forever. To wash away everything else but the two of us at this moment with a crashing wave of ecstasy.

Her hands shift up into my hair. She grips the back of my head, holding me in place, urging me to keep kissing her. Those luscious thighs tighten around my hips, imploring me to keep driving into her. I flex my palm around her throat, feel the vibration of her response against it.

Fuck.

Yes.

I dig my fingers into her ass, probably hard enough to leave bruises, but those are the types she always liked, the type I always loved to see on her skin. The ones that are evidence of how fucking *explosive* we are together.

She clings to me like I'm her lifeline, when really, she's mine.

I've been lost without her for the past year, a shadow of myself with no direction. But now, in the shadow of the night, I reclaim her fully out here, where we always felt like we were most at home, where we belonged.

On our mountain.

I can't let what happened to her take that from her.

I have to let her take it back.

"Please, Killian..."

Those words rumble against my palm.

A plea that makes my balls draw up tight and my cock throb inside her.

And I know exactly what she wants.

I squeeze her throat tighter, looking at the way my tattooed hand so perfectly fits around that fragile column. My thumb brushes over her pulse, and tremors shake her body.

Not from the cool air, but from that release she always finds when I take control, when I force her to focus on only the moment and my touch.

This moment.

I pound into her relentlessly. Demanding she take all of me and give me all of herself in return. Each thrust reassures me that this second chance I never thought I'd have isn't just a dream.

Willow is here.

Willow is mine.

Willow isn't going anywhere.

And I need to feel her come apart the way she completely undoes me. "Open your eyes and look at me, Willow."

It takes a moment before her lids flutter and those half-lidded, steely gray eyes meet mine.

I keep thrusting, grinding my hips in the way she loves. "You're going to wait for me to come."

Her lips part on a whimper, and she shakes her head. "I can't. I need—"

"You're going to wait." I drive into her again, pinning her and holding still until I get what I want from her. A promise. "You're going to do that for me."

WILLOW

It should be a relatively simple request.

One Killian has made of me hundreds of times over the years.

He loves to come with me, to feel me clenching around him as he empties himself deep inside me. As he completes *both* of us in an earth-shattering explosion of pleasure.

But I don't know if I can tonight.

I don't know if I can give him what he needs, even though he's giving me what I do. Because I'm so close, right there.

My orgasm hovers on the periphery of my vision. A glowy

flame encroaching on the edges. Promising something only he has ever been able to give me.

Release from pain. Release from worry. Release from all the wrongs of this world. Release from anything that holds me captive in my head. Release of those dark shadows that the blinding light of ecstasy will blast away.

He's about to give it to me.

Exactly what I need.

The way he took control, brought me into that river, and shocked my system into forgetting the reason I was out there in the first place. The way he dragged me up here without hesitation. The way he told me what was going to happen.

All of it took the pressure off me, off my mind, off the necessity of thinking when it was sending me down very bad roads.

I always felt like my life was so out of control until he and I finally got together, until he helped take it and put it back in my hands. Until he showed me how to let go by letting him show me *this.*

The past year, someone else took control of my life from me, but Killian is giving it back to me right now by allowing me to hand it to him. And there's something heady about knowing that I can trust him with my heart and my body and everything else. That he will never let me down. That he will always finish what he starts and do it beautifully.

Whether that be work, one of his carvings, or the way he makes love to me.

Killian McBride doesn't half-ass anything.

His entire focus is on this moment. Our connection. The movement of our bodies so perfectly in tune and sync.

And that's what he's asking for.

What he's demanding.

That we come in perfect unison.

He buries himself deep inside me, stilling his hips as he

waits for my answer. For my confirmation that I *will* wait for him the same way he waited over the last year for me.

I whimper at the painful request.

Needing him to keep moving.

Needing the friction.

And I attempt to grind against him, squeezing around his hard length, trying to urge him to get moving again, but he holds absolutely still, controlling every tiny movement I make, ensuring I can't squirm away.

"I need you to answer me, Honeybee." His strong hand at my throat tightens briefly, his thumb brushing over my thudding pulse, making my cunt contract around him again. "Can you do that for me? Can you wait?"

The base of his cock hits my clit as I try to move, but he presses into me harder, preventing it, keeping me absolutely trapped between him and the tree and at his mercy.

Rough, cold bark abrades my bare back and shoulders, a sharp juxtaposition against the smooth, warm body pinned to my chest.

I can't move.

His fingers squeeze my ass, reaffirming his control. He dips his head and trails his lips across my collarbone to my neck, then nips playfully at the spot his thumb just caressed. "I'm not going to move until you answer me."

This man knows exactly what he is doing.

The longer he stays like this, unmoving, with me dangling over the precipice with only his hold keeping me from slipping over, the more time it gives me to collect myself, to bring myself back from the brink of orgasm, to get *that* control so that I can wait for him.

I take a long, deep breath and release it, tamping down that frantic need just enough to grasp the first threads of my release and keep them at bay.

He lifts his head, grinning at me. "Good girl. Now answer me."

"I'll wait."

"Thank fuck, Honeybee, because I need your sweet cunt clenching around me when I finally unload into you."

Another wave of need washes over me with his words, rippling through me the same way the water does over the boulders in the river.

Wild.

Completely untamed desire.

The kind I only feel with him.

He pulls his hips back and drives into me again, rocking me against the tree. "Fuuuuck..."

I dig my nails into the back of his head, and he groans, the rumble of his chest pressed to mine a reminder of how close he is to the edge himself.

At least I won't have to wait long, not with the way he's vibrating.

Hard muscles ripple under my hands.

He rolls his hips and grinds against mine with each plunge, rubbing my clit and giving me the friction I need as he tightens his hand around my throat.

Not enough to restrict my breathing, just enough to remind me that he could, that he's in control, and I let him take it because he's so much better at directing me to what's important than I've been at recognizing it myself.

I let him give me intense pleasure.

I let him own me because I know I own him, too.

His whole heart.

He's proven that to me since I've been back.

That he's exactly the man I always knew he was.

That he's *mine*.

Finally, his thrusts become erratic, frantic, more animal than human. My head spins. My body tenses. We both know what's coming, and he lifts his head and takes my mouth as he brushes his thumb across my pulse point and squeezes.

I erupt at the same time he does.

He catches my scream, and I do his groan as he pumps into me, emptying himself into my core, driving himself into the deepest part of me that only he could ever reach.

Bright lights flash against my closed lids.

The world melts away.

Heat flares out through my limbs, a blast of sheer bliss that steals my breath.

And Killian is right there.

Giving it to me.

His mouth molded to mine.

His kiss giving me life again.

He finally stills his hips, and his lips slow over mine. But they don't stop. Featherlight kisses bring me down from cataclysmic heights. Floating gently rather than crashing back to earth.

I sag against the tree, only his grip on my neck and ass and his hard body keep me upright. And somehow, even out here in the wild of McBride Mountain, with so much uncertainty and danger, I've never felt more safe. More loved. More at peace.

He kisses me gently.

So softly it's barely a brush of his lips across mine.

Once.

Twice.

Then he slowly lowers my feet to the ground. They sink slightly into grass and leaves damp from the evening dew and the water dripping from our naked bodies.

My legs tremble as he slides his hands from my ass and slowly pulls his head all the way back. He shifts, and the loss of his body heat lets the chilly night air hit me, raising goosebumps across my still-damp skin.

I open my eyes and find him on his knees in front of me,

staring up with so much reverence. Like a man in church about to confess his sins...or worship his god.

The pure adoration in his gaze sends fire licking over my entire body before he even touches me. By the time he dips his head between my legs, I'm burning alive, caught in this inferno of lust.

His tongue glides through where his cock just was greedily. "Fucking beautiful. Fuck, Honeybee...so damn sweet."

I groan and tunnel my hands into his hair as he licks away the evidence of what we did.

His tongue drifts over my inner thighs, across my cunt, delving deep inside.

He groans, the vibration along my flesh making my clit throb, until his tongue flicks up over it, and I flinch at the contact with it so oversensitive after just coming. "Christ, Killian. You—"

My head spins, stealing any words I was about to say.

"We taste so fucking good together."

He murmurs the words against my core, devouring me, licking and sucking and nipping until he has guaranteed the only thing that exists is the feel of his mouth on me and that pulsating heat right between my legs.

My thighs quiver and tighten around his head, and he chuckles, then plunges two fingers inside me.

I gasp at the intrusion and clench around him as he begins to work me up again with skilled ministrations. "Killian, I don't think I—"

"You can."

Every time he has said those words to me, he's proven them to be true.

All the things I thought I couldn't do, he's assured I can, whether it was make it through another rough interaction with Mom, survive another nightmare, or come apart in his arms again.

By now, I should know not to doubt him.

He dips his head and attacks my clit again, flicking his tongue rapidly back and forth over it as he pumps his fingers into me. Curling them. Dragging them along my pulsating inner walls. Catching on my G-spot and concentrating all his focus there.

I sag my weight completely against the tree and over his shoulders, that bright heat centering between my legs now starting to blast outward until I finally come again.

This time, Killian isn't there to catch my cry.

It rips out of somewhere deep in my soul. Echoing off the trees. Across the rushing river. Drowning out the sounds of the night animals and the pain I felt only minutes ago when I was standing out there, wondering what had become of my life over the last year.

Ecstasy courses through my veins as I grind my cunt against his face. Killian gazes up at me, sucking down my release and what was left of his, letting me come apart, knowing he will always put me back together.

Tears trickle from my eyes as I finally come down to earth, sagging my weight completely onto him.

He slides his arms around my waist, tugging me up to him, and slanting his mouth across my own. The taste of him and me combined is heady as his tongue glides over mine. But he pulls away far too soon.

His eyes flash with humor. "We better get back to our clothes quickly because we're about to have company."

The post-orgasmic haze finally starts to subside enough that I can hear thundering footsteps.

I jerk away from him slightly. "Shit."

They're coming.

We're too close to the camp to hope no one heard that.

He chuckles. "We're okay!" His gaze cuts over his shoulder to whoever approaches. "Go back to the bonfire!"

The footsteps halt.

Killian's large body blocks whoever it is from seeing me. I still duck my head against his chest, heat flaring in my cheeks. But even the intense embarrassment at being caught can't override the feeling filling me right now.

For the first time in weeks, and in spite of what we're about to do tomorrow, I finally feel free.

As if that missing part of me is within reach, and it doesn't matter what we find because it *will* be okay.

19

WILLOW

Cool morning mist blankets the mountain, hovering over the ground and floating through the trees. Every step we take feels like passing through some sort of fantasy portal into another world. One bathed in the cleansing fog that doesn't hide dangers but protects us from anything that might have ill intent.

Yet, the closer we draw to the gorge, the more that vise tightens around my chest. The harder it becomes to remember last night and how utterly perfect it was to fall asleep in Killian's arms after what we shared.

Even knowing Killian is at my back—like he always is—and Connor and Liam are right in front of me, leading the way, I can't help feeling alone up here.

Almost as if some residual memory of just that lingers in my heart, even if I can't remember it fully.

My anxiety increases as we hike, and our surroundings feel more and more familiar. And not because Killian and I came up here not that long ago.

Another flash of memory hits me.

This time of racing through the gorge...

The narrow walls of rock closing in on me from either side...

Bare feet on uneven, rough ground...

Pouring rain...

Lightning and thunder overhead...

Carrying something, clutching it to me as if it's precious...

My footsteps falter—

Killian's strong arms wrap around me from behind, keeping me from falling face-first on the steep incline. "I've got you, Honeybee."

I sag against him, the memories still making my head swim as much as the exertion it took to get this far up the mountain.

His lips flutter over my ear softly. "You good?"

Killian has asked that question so many times since I got back that I can't even count them.

And so many times, I lied and said I was fine. Maybe as much as I was honest with him and said I wasn't.

The last several weeks have been a never-ending roller-coaster of emotions, nightmares, memories, and struggles I wasn't sure I could get through.

But I don't have the luxury of *not* being good right now.

Not when we're this close to what could be ultimate answers, not when it feels like I'm finally going to get what I've been seeking this whole time.

Instead of letting my own head drag me into a dark place, I nod to Killian and try to pull away. "I'm good."

Have to be.

He gives me a second to get steady on my feet again and slowly releases his hold. But I can feel the reluctance in his action. His desire to keep me wrapped up in his arms, where I'm safe.

It would be easier to stay there and allow myself to get lost in his calming presence, but this might be my only chance to resolve all the uncertainties and answer all the questions.

I glance back at him and offer what I hope is a believable smile, even though I don't feel it. But this man knows me too well, knows all my tells, and can always read me like an open book.

Like he is now.

His brow furrows over concerned eyes as he watches me move forward up the trail Connor and Liam follow, made by the wildlife coming through the gorge and down onto this side of McBride Mountain.

In the distance, above the towering treetops, the massive rock formation that houses the gorge appears, looming out of the mist. Seeing it again sends a chill through me.

As the sun comes up behind us, it starts to burn off the fog, exposing the thing I saw so vividly in my dreams that I so confidently recalled, even though there's no reason I should have been up here. But unlike the first time I came with Killian, this time, I know that answers lie on the other side of it.

That allows me to keep going.

To keep pushing past the sense of unease threatening to make the few bites of my breakfast I managed to eat reappear.

By the time we reach the edge of the formation, I'm practically vibrating in anticipation, barely able to contain the anxiety and excitement mixing in my system.

This is it.

Liam and Connor wait for us, their packs lowered on the ground for a quick break before we push onward.

Connor looks at Killian as he stops beside me. "How much farther is it?"

"Another two miles through the gorge. And on the other side, based on the old maps, the logging trail appears to go for another five. The cabin could be anywhere along there."

Which means it could take us all day, or even longer, to find what we're searching for.

If we even find it.

That confidence I had when staring at the map in the office and during our climb yesterday, that I clung to even a few minutes ago, starts to fade. This is a massive mountain, filled with any number of dangers beyond the man we seek. Anything could happen to interfere with finding the cabin where I was held—and the person responsible.

Or I could be completely wrong about all of this.

Doubt creeps into my mind. That same darkness that often threatens to swallow me whole, but I'm not going to give in to the desire to break down right now or give in to the negative thoughts.

I release a long, slow breath, staring up at the entrance to the gorge. "Let's keep going."

Liam pulls a long drink from his canteen, then wipes his mouth on the back of his hand. "Are you sure you don't want to take a break?"

The look Connor and Killian both give me suggests they are wondering the same.

I shake my head. "No, I'm good."

Because if I stop, I don't know that I'll be able to get myself going again.

Killian's hand settles on the back of my neck, squeezing gently, rough callouses brushing over my skin. "I'll be right with you the entire time, Honeybee."

He leans in and kisses my cheek, then sets off in the lead this time, snagging my hand to pull me behind him. That connection offers me the reassurance I need to keep moving.

The sun continues to further illuminate the mountain as we move into the gorge, which quickly sucks up that light with its high sides that tower over us at least a hundred feet.

Gloom settles in the deeper part of the gorge where we walk.

I trail my hands over the stone walls, able to reach each side easily.

It's so narrow.

Claustrophobic even.

If Killian weren't directly in front of me, leading us through the claustrophobic channel, I don't know that I could keep my steps steady.

The voices of the rest of the search party entering the gorge behind us echo down it, and another flicker of a memory races through my head.

Someone yelling behind me...

A bite of pain in my foot.

Lightning illuminating my way through this very narrow passage.

Utter darkness falling again, making it impossible to see.

My hands trailing along these walls to keep myself from running into one.

I was definitely here.

When I came up with Killian, I didn't remember any of that. I *sensed* it, but I couldn't put it together. But ever since meeting with Dr. Bird, things have been coming back more vividly. Memories returning piece by piece, like they're being poured through a sieve and only revealing what they want to *when* they choose.

Like now.

I definitely came this way, escaping wherever I was held.

That confidence that I was *right* back in the McBride Timber office when I knew deep in my gut that I had been kept up here keeps my feet moving forward, following closely behind Killian's sure steps.

Connor and Liam keep pace behind us, well ahead of the rest of the search party now.

The far end of the gorge appears, with the bright green of the trees visible and sunlight spilling into the opening on the other side of the mountain. This is as far as Killian and I got last time, stopped by my mind's inability to release its secrets and my own exhaustion that dragged us down the mountain to the cabin.

Not this time.

I don't care if I have to camp on this mountain for a damn week; I am not leaving until I find what we came looking for.

Killian steps out into the trees, and I follow, taking in the stillness and silence of the area around us.

Connor's heavy footsteps move toward us, and he appears beside me, scanning the wilderness before he points north. "Based on the map, the logging area should be that way."

I glance over at him. "You've really never been up here before?"

He shakes his head, Liam joining him.

Killian nods his agreement. "There was never really any reason to go past the gorge. The best hunting has always been on our side of the mountain, and we can't log this side for at least another generation."

It makes sense why no one was familiar with the area, how easy it would be for someone to disappear up here without anyone noticing.

The thought is also terrifying.

Living remotely off the grid isn't unusual on and around McBride Mountain, but this kind of reclusiveness is typically reserved for people who are hiding for a reason.

Connor leads the way in the direction he pointed, the three of us following closely and scanning for any signs of human activity in the otherwise pristine wilderness.

A few minutes pass before the trees start to open up in a way that doesn't seem natural.

Liam pauses and looks to the left and right. "Is this it?"

We all do the same, turning in place to examine the trees around us. They tower high above the forest floor, creating a thick canopy, except *right* here.

A perfect strip of cleared land, without a single tree or stump to be seen, extends in either direction.

Killian lips pinch together firmly, and he squats to check something on the ground. He drifts his palm over the uneven foliage as if the land can speak to him in some way that I can't hear. "It has to be. This isn't natural."

"That should be the way down the back side of the mountain." Liam points to the southwest, then motions northwest. "This would be the way to the old logging area. Where do you think they'd put the cabin?"

Killian's mouth twists as he considers it, and he runs a hand through his hair and pushes to his feet. "Let's split up."

It's the best way to cover the most ground, but there are only four of us at the moment.

I look back toward the gorge. "Shouldn't we wait for Sheriff Briggs and everyone else?"

Connor looks ready to respond when the sound of them making their way through the trees reaches us.

Excellent timing.

With almost two dozen people now gathering around us, the rest of the searchers remaining at the main campsite to spread out and examine the area between there and the gorge more thoroughly, we can create several teams and head out in each direction.

Tony stops next to Killian and rubs his lower back. "What's the plan?"

Killian points in the direction of the old logging area. "I'm going up with Willow, Connor, and Liam. The rest of you go down the mountain in different directions in groups of five and locate the main trail they would have taken up. We'll all look for the cabin and signal if we find it."

Or anything else.

No one has explicitly said it to me, but everyone knows why most of the searchers are carrying firearms.

If whoever held me captive is still up here, he has to be considered dangerous.

And since cell phones don't work, the only real way for the sheriff and our group to keep in contact is the walkie-talkies that may or may not work or to hope old-fashioned bird calls the loggers have used for generations can carry across the distance we create between our parties.

People move here for the seclusion, but today, it doesn't play in our favor.

Sheriff Briggs considers the plan and nods. "We'll make sure we cover as much of the mountain as possible. Be safe. We don't know what we're going to find."

The comment shouldn't come across as ominous, but a shiver slithers up my spine all the same.

Killian locks gazes with him, something unspoken passing between the two men. "You do the same."

They clasp hands, say their goodbyes, and we set off up the trail.

The McBride brothers examine everything as we walk. Keen, observant gazes missing nothing. A broken branch. A shallow depression in the soil that could have been made by a bear or another predator. The one we seek now.

After another quarter mile, Connor halts, holding up his hand to ensure we all stop, too. He crouches. "Look."

He points to the oddly packed ground, and I move around him to get a closer look at what turns out to be tire treads.

Killian squats beside him. "These are fresh. Within the last week. See how all the grass is compacted here? Someone's been using this trail since Willow came back."

My gut tightens, acid roiling.

Liam surveys the area and the tracks further. "They're too

small to be a car or a truck. You couldn't get one up here anyway. ATV likely."

Connor nods, suddenly even more on alert as he scans the trees around us. "Probably the easiest thing to get up to this area."

An ATV?

The engine sound I heard the day I was taken fills my ears.

Could that have been an ATV?

Killian pushes to his feet. "Stay close to the treeline..."

He doesn't explain the order, but we all know better than to question one that comes from him, especially in the tone he just used.

The hair on the back of my neck stands on end the farther we climb.

As more and more evidence of recent occupation starts to appear...

Freshly chopped wood.

Empty gas cans.

A stack of plastic milk crates and a board laid over them, creating a makeshift workbench of some sort.

Immediately in front of me, Killian reaches for his axe, unlooping it from his pack. His fingers tighten around his favorite weapon when he could have pulled the gun he carries at his hip. Beside him, Connor does grab his, though, glancing back to ensure Liam is okay behind us.

He brings up the rear, skillfully covering our backs and searching the thick woods that could contain literally anything.

A crack cuts through the air at the exact same time the trunk of a tree seems to explode, shards of wood flying only a few inches from Killian's head.

KILLIAN

The unmistakable crack of gunfire rings through the air, echoing off the wall of stone containing the gorge and reverberating through my chest. I turn and slam into Willow, knocking her to the ground and pinning her down, using my body as cover.

Her confused yelp fills my ears, quickly followed by five more shots in rapid succession.

They hit the tree trunks on either side of us, sending splinters flying.

I try to shift to support some of my weight off her, but a sharp pain slices through my left upper arm as another crack sounds.

I hiss at the sharp burn. "Fuck."

Willow glances back with panic-filled eyes as blood drips from the wound down and onto her. "Killian! What—"

"Stay down!" I grit my teeth through the pain, trying to ignore it in favor of keeping a clear head about what's happening. "Someone's shooting..."

Connor and Liam...

I glance over my shoulder and find them pinned behind a fallen log, trying to give themselves cover from the shooter. "Where is he?"

Connor peeks up and looks, then immediately ducks down again as another shot hits the log where his head just was. "Shit."

The sound of shots will have the sheriff and everyone else in the search party running this direction to help us fast, and they couldn't have gotten very far.

But it doesn't do anything to give us a way out of this.

If we can't locate the shooter, we can't neutralize the threat.

Pushing up into a squat, trying to keep myself as small as possible while also covering Willow from the direction the shots seem to be coming, I urge Willow to crawl forward, deeper into the trees. "Let's go, Honeybee."

Trembling, she follows my command, slowly crawling through dead leaves, branches, and everything else on the forest floor. I urge her forward with my good arm wrapped around her back, continuing to act as a human shield as much as possible as we seek deeper coverage in the thicker brush.

Connor and Liam do the same with only two more shots sounding during our retreat.

Then the mountain goes eerily quiet.

I clamp my hand over my wound, wincing at the searing pain that putting pressure on it causes and quickly take stock of everyone else.

Willow trembles violently where she's crouched up against a massive pine, her arms wrapped around herself as she stares at the blood flowing out from between my fingers.

"Willow, are you hit?"

She doesn't respond, just stares ahead, tears streaming down her face. But I can't see anything that suggests she's hurt. Connor and Liam both appear unharmed, and I return my focus to the area on the other side of the trail.

Nothing moves.

Not a single leaf rustling.

No animals moving.

"Neither of you saw where he was?"

Connor and Liam both shake their heads, and my heart sinks.

Liam crawls forward slightly, keeping low. "It seemed to be from the far side of the trail to the north."

"Agreed." Connor nods. "And those were rifle rounds."

Shit.

"We have to stop him."

My arm burns, and I lift my hand long enough to examine the wound, which seems to be a missing chunk of flesh from a bad graze. But given the amount of blood flowing, it may have nicked an artery.

Liam seems to notice the same thing, unhooking his belt and bringing it over to secure around my bicep as a make-shift tourniquet. "You need a doctor."

I grit my teeth as he tightens it. "I'm *fine*."

My gaze travels to Willow. Her eyes are squeezed closed. Mouth open. Erratic breaths bursting from her lips. Her hands pressed to her belly shake as badly as the rest of her.

"Willow, what's wrong?" Any concern for finding who's responsible vanishes, replaced by panic as I try to pull her hands away from her stomach, to search for a wound. My blood smears across her, but I can't find any coming from her. "Are you hit?"

She shakes her head, her eyes opening as more tears stream down her face.

"Willow?"

I lower myself to my knees in front of her, lifting my hand to grasp her cheek, transferring more blood to her pale skin. *Too* pale. Something's wrong.

Her eyes finally lock on mine, and her pupils are so dilated that the normal gray appears almost pitch black.

Terror grips my chest, seeing it on her face. "Honeybee?"

She blinks rapidly a few times before she finally seems to see me. "The gunshots. He was shooting at me. I remember."

"What do you mean?" I tilt her chin up, forcing her to keep looking at me. "What do you remember?"

An anguished sob tumbles from her lips. "*Everything*."

The way she says the word steals all the breath from my lungs.

Her mouth opens and closes a few times without anything coming out, as if she can't form words or bring herself to speak them.

"Willow, tell me what's happening?"

"I-I remember the reason...the reason that what you said that day sent me running."

I narrow my eyes on her, my brain struggling to follow her thought process. "I don't understand."

We're up here being shot *at.*

And we already know the reason she left—because of how hurtful what I said was...

Tears continue to stream down her face, dripping over my bloodstained hand. "I had to leave because that morning I was going to go into town and buy a pregnancy test." She sobs again, the sound far too loud in the silence of the forest. "I thought I was pregnant."

My heart stops, my entire body stilling. "You thought you were pregnant?"

She nods as the sobs and tears come faster now. Her hitched breaths shorten each time she tries to speak. "I didn't... want to tell you...until I knew for sure. And then—"

Oh, God...

What she's trying to explain finally clicks in my head.

She thought she was pregnant.

She was going to find out and tell me later that day.

But then I said those horrible words to her...

Bile climbs my throat, my head spinning wildly.

Willow shakes violently, the motion smearing more blood across her cheek. "I panicked, Killian. I didn't know what to do if you didn't want the baby. And I left." Another sob wracks her body, the full-blown force of her anguish overtaking her. "B-but I turned around. I came back. And the truck overheated."

I nod. Completely unable to speak. Barely even able to draw in a breath as she sorts through the memories jumbling her head.

Her bottom lip trembles. "I remember who took me."

Liam kneels beside me, pulling her hand into his. "Who was it, Willow?"

She gulps in heavy draws of air, her gaze flicking from me to him. "It was Earl. Earl Byers."

"What?" Connor approaches cautiously. "Byers?"

The name rattles around my head, along with the information she just dropped on me.

She thought she was pregnant.

Earl Byers.

Pregnant.

Earl?

The eccentric older man had always seemed relatively harmless. Quiet. A bit reclusive, living with his sister on the far side of the mountain, so it would sometimes be months before he would come into town.

Connor snarls. "You're sure?"

Willow nods, the movement shifting my hold on her cheek, smearing the blood. "I recognized him. It's why...Oh, God." She flattens her hand over her mouth to stop another sob. "It's why I wasn't worried when he stopped to help. He was on an ATV and he...he called me Bobby, remember?"

I finally start to process everything she's saying and nod. "Yeah..."

Connor stills next to Liam. "Wasn't his wife's name Roberta?"

A vague image of a friendly woman with dark hair who used to visit with Mom at Claire's when we were in town as children flickers through my head.

I exchange a glance with Connor. "Yeah, but she left town years ago, when Connor and I were very small."

Willow shifts closer to me, her tear-filled eyes locked with mine. "He thought I was her."

"Are you sure?"

She nods. "Almost the whole time I was with him. He was adamant, got angry if I tried to argue with him about who I was and my name." The look in her eyes shifts, filling with so much pain that the throb in my arm instantly disappears. "He said he wasn't going to let me take *this* baby from him."

Her hands settle over her stomach.

This baby?

"They had a baby." Her gaze darts across Liam and Connor before finding mine again. "He showed me a picture of the three of them together, and God, I do look like her twenty years ago."

Connor raises a dark brow. "I never knew they had a kid."

I shake my head. "Me, either... So, she left and took their baby."

Willow bobs her head. "I think so. At first, I didn't realize what he kept ranting about, but I figured out enough to understand he was delusional. Lost in some memory, something in his mind."

All the bits and pieces of the puzzle we've been collecting for weeks start to fit together, but there are too many still missing. Jagged edges. Giant gaps that I can't see clearly.

I shake my head, trying to clear away the cobwebs. "So, he thought you were her and that you had taken his baby?"

She nods. "I didn't know if I was pregnant or not, but I thought maybe there was a chance and that maybe he wouldn't —"—she gulps—"maybe he wouldn't touch me if he thought I was pregnant with his baby, so I played along. I told him he was confused, and I hadn't had the baby yet."

So fucking smart.

Connor squats, bringing himself to our level while maintaining a watch on the area where the shots came from. "And he bought it?"

"He did." Willow sniffles. "Whatever's going on with him, the confusion, it helped me convince him that he was mistaken about me having the baby. I told him he would come soon enough and that he needed to be patient. I played along with him when I realized he wasn't going to let me go. I let him believe I was Bobby."

His wife.

My hand falls from her cheek, and forgetting about my injury, I reach out with both arms and drag her up, clutching her to me.

Visions of what might've happened, what he must've done to her, flash through my head.

"Did he..."

I can't even say the words.

She inhales sharply, understanding what I'm asking, and burrows against me, pressing herself so close there isn't even an inch of space between us. "The morning sickness got so bad within a few days that I convinced him it would risk hurting the baby."

Morning sickness...

I drag her head back, holding her gaze, assuring that she sees all the love in mine. "You *were* pregnant?"

She nods, her trembling growing even stronger as panic wells up inside her, matching my own. "I gave birth to our baby, Killian, up here with that man, two months ago. He kept me locked in the cabin because he was afraid I was going to run with our son. Like his memory knew that his wife had done it before, even though I convinced him she hadn't and I was her..."

Our baby.

Our son.

Those words ring in my ears as loudly as the gunshots—the pain of them so intense it's almost numbing.

We have a son...

Who was up here with a monster.

Until Willow *ran.*

"H-how did you get free?"

She struggles with another sob, fighting for control over her emotions so she can tell us the important information. "He would leave for days at a time and return with supplies like baby formula and food. I-I tried to breastfeed and couldn't. My milk never came in, so he made sure we had what we needed. Anytime he was gone, I searched every inch of that cabin for anything to help, and I found some old maps of the mountain."

My breath catches.

The maps on the wall of the office flash through my mind.

They led us *here.*

To answers.

And the ones she found helped her escape.

"I *saw* where we were." More tears spill over, soaking my bloody hands and her cheeks. "I knew I could go through the gorge, to the river, and follow it down."

"Jesus Christ, Willow..."

Every muscle in my body goes taut, anger vibrating through me so intensely that I'm not sure I can contain it.

"The night of the storm, he had gone to town... I managed to pry one of the old boards off the side of the cabin and slip through the opening. I took the baby, and I ran, only..." She sobs, and I cling to her tighter. "He came back, and he caught up to me near the river. He fired a warning shot. He tried to take our baby from me." Her voice cracks. "We struggled, and I fell into the river."

I drag her face to mine, so close I can feel every frantic breath she takes fluttering over me. "Where's our son?"

Horrible images of the rapids float through my head...

Of Willow hung up in the water, almost lifeless on that tree...

If the baby fell in with her...

"He has him." She sobs again. "He has our boy."

A rage unlike anything I've ever felt consumes me.

I begin to tremble as hard as she is.

She had our baby up here.

Alone with that monster.

He took her.

He took my son.

He took my *family.*

I brush my lips across hers, so desperate to make it all go away and redo the past year. "We'll get him back, Willow. We'll get him back, and I'll make that motherfucker pay for what he's done to you. I promise."

20

KILLIAN

My eyes meet Connor's and Liam's over Willow's shoulder.

Her rush of words.

The truths in them.

The horrific reality of what she endured crashes over me, bringing a wave of icy resolve with it.

He *hurt* my *Honeybee.*

He *took* my *son.*

I thought I was familiar with rage. That fury and I had become friends, especially over the past several weeks, but what courses through me now rivals anything I've ever felt before. The kind of biblical wrath people burn for eternity for acting on.

Liam shakes his head, his emerald eyes wide and filled with trepidation as he watches me. "Don't even think about it, Killian."

There is no thinking now.

Just *doing.*

Connor takes a step toward us, hand fisted, jaw locked. Clearly reading me as well as our little brother has. He's ready to jump in if necessary to stop me from doing something stupid. "*Don't.*"

The word means nothing to me.

I gently pull away from Willow, feathering my lips over her forehead.

Pushing to my feet, I clench my palm over my wounded arm as blood continues to seep from it despite the triage we attempted. I lock eyes with each of my brothers. "Don't even *think* about trying to stop me or getting in my way."

"Fuck." Connor advances on me, his intent to interfere with my plans written all over his face. "Killian, no!"

Liam grabs his shoulder and holds him back. "Wait for the sheriff, Killian." He pleads with that look he used to give me as a child when he wanted us to take him along on our mountain adventures. Only this time, he's trying to *stop* me. "Don't go up there alone. You're going to get yourself fucking killed."

Willow whimpers, clutching at my leg. "No, you can't…"

Her words and the panic in her voice should stop me.

But all I can see is *red.*

She struggles to her feet, then grasps the front of my shirt, forcing me to look at her.

My blood smeared across her cheeks only intensifies my rage.

The things he did to her, the things she suffered up here, *for a year.*

Willow went through her pregnancy with a madman instead of with *me*, had *our baby* here instead of with *me*…

He locked her away.

Struck her, if the memories she's had over the last several days since the hypnosis are any indication.

Kept her chained and at his mercy.

My skin flames hot with fury, and I release my grip on my

arm, reach down and tug her hands free of my shirt, squeezing her wrists. Ensuring my gaze is locked with her stormy, tear stained one so she can see my resolve. "I *will* be back with him. I *promise*."

I crush my lips to hers and step away before she can stop me, snagging my axe from where it fell to the ground when I pushed her to safety.

There isn't anything any of them can do or say to stop me now.

Nothing that could break through this red haze of wrath consuming me.

Nor would I want it to.

Earl Byers deserves whatever I do to him and then some.

I stalk toward the edge of the woods, cautiously keeping myself concealed in the heavier trees and backtracking a hundred yards or so to where the trail curves slightly.

If he's where we think he might be, he won't be able to see me cross it from back here.

Hopefully.

And if Connor and Liam are smart, they won't come after me.

I trust them to keep Willow safe.

The only people on this planet—and certainly this mountain—that I would entrust that duty to.

They won't let her into the line of fire, no matter how much she might want to rush after me, especially now that she remembers everything.

Good God...

It explains so much.

The memories of the pain she had in her abdomen, the vomiting, running away in a storm, carrying something she knew was important.

All of it fits into that puzzle so perfectly.

He was her reason.

Our son.

We were.

The family we should have been together this whole time.

My hand tightens on the axe as blood trickles down my left arm. I keep stalking through the woods and pause for a moment to listen for any movement before quickly darting across the trail.

Earl Byers...

He used to work at McBride Timber when Dad was still alive.

He had access to the old maps, likely explored this side of the mountain and the abandoned camp that was set up here.

He knew it would be secluded.

He knew he could bring Willow here and not be discovered.

Fuck.

For all I know, he and his wife were up here for years before she left, and no one knew about it—

A twig snapping somewhere to my left makes me freeze, then I quickly dart behind a massive tree trunk.

I peer around the corner, searching for the source.

No sign of anyone.

But the hair on the back of my neck stands on end.

I shift around the tree and inch closer and closer to where I heard the sound.

Keeping low.

Careful with each step.

Hunting an animal.

Finally, I see it, the flicker of movement. But the thick foliage conceals too much to clearly see what I'm up against.

You can't hide from me...

This is where I'm most at home.

Out here.

In the trees.

With an axe in my hand.

There isn't anywhere else I'd rather have this showdown with the man who ripped my family away from me.

I circle well out of the way behind him until I'm close enough to see where he's crouched, rifle set up on a log aimed directly at where we were advancing down the trail when he started shooting.

The camouflage he wears helps him blend into the heavy brush, but he can't conceal his movements.

He keeps scanning the area.

Vigilant.

Alert.

Yet too fucking stupid to know that I would just backtrack and circle around him.

Gotcha.

By the time I am close enough to grab him, it's too late.

He whirls, finally sensing me behind him, but I'm close enough to knock the barrel of the gun away with my axe and grab him by the fucking throat, tightening my hand around it and slamming him back against the fallen log he was using as a sniper's perch.

Wide, frantic eyes sweep over my face as he struggles in my grasp, his hands tightening around my bloody wrist as it seeps down from the wound in my arm that he created.

But it's nothing compared to the one he tore into my soul, knowing what he did to Willow, knowing what I lost with her.

Being there for her through her pregnancy. Watching her belly grow with my child. Talking to him. Loving them both. Holding her hand when she was in agony, giving birth. Holding my son.

All of it.

My tears burn as they leak from my eyes, but they do nothing to quell the heat of my fury. I tighten my hand around his throat and watch his face start to go purple. "Where the fuck is he?"

His nails claw at my wrist.

The bite of pain doesn't stop me from tightening my grip even more.

"Don't kill him, Killian!" Willow's voice cuts through the fog of my anger and bloodlust. "Killian! Stop!"

Frantic footsteps fill the afternoon air.

I glance over my shoulder to find her racing through the woods toward me with Connor and Liam hot on her heels.

Fuck.

Why didn't they keep her away?

"Killian, no!" She tugs at my shoulder, trying to loosen my grip on him. "If you kill him, he won't be able to tell us where Niall is."

Niall?

Another emotional blow slams into my heart.

She named him after Dad?

My hold loosens slightly.

After everything I put her through, everything she suffered up here, she still chose *that* name for our son.

Our *baby*.

Visions of her belly growing with him and of the agony she must have endured without any medical care during her delivery choke me the same way I am the man responsible.

She's right.

If I kill him now, we might not ever find Niall.

I slowly ease my grip on his throat, only enough for him to breathe. He gasps, sucking in ragged breaths of air, but I shift my axe up against his jugular, pinning him down while threatening him with my blade instead.

"Where the fuck is my son?"

Earl's glare widens. "He's *my* son. Mine. You hear me?"

I press the blade into his skin, watching the trickle of blood drip down his neck, and lean in close, snarling in his face. "I will cut you apart piece by fucking piece until you tell me where he is."

The asshole shakes his head. "No. He's mine." His eyes shoot up over my shoulder to Willow. "I always knew you were a whore. I let you take one son from me. I'm not going to let you take another."

He's rambling again.

Not making any sense.

"I should have killed you as soon as you came back."

The day he found her with the truck on the mountain...

I urge the blade deeper. "Where is he?"

Earl starts trembling beneath me, and I tighten the grip on his throat, cutting off his airway again as I ease the blade along the edge of his face to where his ear connects near his cheek, then pressing in. "I won't do this nice and easy. Do you understand me?"

He screams, or at least tries to, but there isn't enough air in his lungs as I start to sever his ear.

Rushed footsteps sound up the trail, and Tony comes into view along with several others from the search party.

"Killian, stop."

He's the sheriff.

The law.

It should mean something when he gives me an order, but this is the man who ruined my life, who ruined Willow's, who took my son, and I'm not about to let him get away with it.

Connor rushes over to Tony. "Send them up the trail. Look for the cabin. Willow had a baby. He's up here somewhere."

"What?" Tony's gaze shoots to us, and his shoulders slump in resignation.

He knows he won't be able to stop me now, that there's no fucking chance.

Instead, he gives me a sharp nod, then motions to the rest of the search party and takes them up the trail, disappearing into the trees, leaving me to do what needs to be done.

WILLOW

Over the years, I've seen Killian annoyed.

I've seen him angry, volatile, and lashing out at people.

But I've never seen him like *this*.

His entire body tenses while it trembles beneath my hand. A warm, flesh-and-blood man, yet his stone-cold, icy glare doesn't even look human. Any ability to remember who he is at his heart has vanished in a cloud of rage.

That seems to have left him the moment I told him what I remembered.

Which is why I raced after him before Connor and Liam could get in my way—because I have to stop him from doing something he'll regret if he can't stop himself.

I grip his shoulder tighter, digging my nails into him, trying to get his attention and to break this trance he's in. He's lost somewhere I might not be able to drag him out of, the kind of darkness that sucks you in and doesn't let you go. And if he kills this man, I know he'll regret it later.

I know that the good man who's truly deep inside won't be able to live with himself in the end, despite what Earl did.

"Killian..." I shift to his side until I can see his face fully. And his eyes aren't just icy, cold, they're glacial. "Please."

No recognition of my voice permeates through the chill.

I don't even know if he sees me out of the corner of his eye as he stares down the man who kidnapped me, who tortured me, who stole my child, and left me for dead in that river.

All he sees is his hate, his need for revenge, a burning desire to hurt this man the way he's hurt us.

But this *isn't* the Killian McBride I know.

"Killian, please stop..."

Earl whimpers against Killian's relentless hold, and blood seeps from his half-severed ear, but Killian stills the blade, and his gaze cuts to me. He keeps his hand at Earl's throat, and the axe doesn't budge from where it presses to his skin.

"Let me talk to him."

Killian's eyes flare. "Are you out of your fucking mind?"

I grip the axe and gently ease it away from Earl's ear. Killian lets me, never taking his eyes off me. And I can finally release a long breath.

Tears stream down my face. Hot with my anger and worry. For Killian and Niall. For what this all might mean for our future.

A future I am willing to fight for.

I turn to the man who took the last year from me, who took my life and my memories and my ability to have everything I ever wanted with Killian.

And I should hate him.

I do, but I also pity him.

He's not right in the head.

Whatever's wrong with him has deluded him so badly that he can't even process what's right or wrong, and he has lost his grip on reality completely. He didn't know who I was. Never once gave any indication that he understood that I wasn't his wife, that the child I bore wasn't his son. Even as he looks at me now, he doesn't understand that I'm not Bobby.

It doesn't excuse the abuse I sustained at his hands, the way he treated his "wife" for the past year, through physical blows and threats, but it makes it impossible for me to look at him the way Killian does.

I squat next to Killian, keeping my fingers curled around the axe handle so it's kept steady. "Earl, I need you to tell me where our son is."

Killian flinches beside me.

Please, baby.

Just keep it together for a few more minutes.

"Is he in the cabin?"

I only vaguely remember where it is.

Farther up the trail, but deep into the woods, away from where the loggers were working all those years ago.

He so rarely let me outside, save for when he needed help bringing in supplies, hanging the wash to dry, things that couldn't be done inside. And even then, he kept a close eye on me.

So I couldn't run.

But those brief moments of freedom where I wasn't shackled to a bed frame or a radiator or the wood stove with only enough rope or chain to get me around the small cabin or to the bathroom built off the side of it meant everything to me.

They were when I took in everything around us.

Where the sun rose and set. The treelines. How the old trail curved away from the cabin toward something. Every single thing I could see.

I asked innocuous questions to figure out where the gorge was, to know which direction I had to move when my chance to escape presented itself. But I knew I would never outrun him pregnant.

And I couldn't risk the baby.

I had to wait until he was born, until I was strong enough to run.

Biding my time became a game for me. I spent those months imagining the life we would have with Killian back on the homestead. All the things he would teach Niall. The love he would show him.

That was what kept me going until the opportunity presented itself.

That is what allows me to stare him down now without completely crumbling under the weight of what he did to me.

Earl looks up at me, a mixture of anger and confusion in his green eyes. His reddish hair, graying at the temples, is disheveled, just like the man himself always seemed to be.

"Please tell me where he is, Earl, so I can make sure he's okay."

"You think I wouldn't take care of *our* son?"

He snaps the words, and Killian tightens his grip on the man's throat. But I reach out and rest my free hand on the back of Killian's neck, hoping it will calm him.

Warn him not to press too far.

He seems to relax his hold enough to allow Earl to suck in a ragged breath.

I breathe deeply to steady myself again, so he doesn't hear the waver in my voice. "What did you do with him, Earl? Let me go make sure he's all right."

"He's with the only person I can trust with him because you've proven I can't trust *you*."

Months and months of conversations with him float through my head, ramblings from a man who isn't all there, and maybe hasn't been for years, a man lost inside his own head, in memories and fantasies and flat-out hallucinations.

The only person I can trust...

Other things he said to me flicker through my head. My brain pounds against my temples, trying to get my attention, trying to direct me to the right place.

"You don't trust me because I left with our son."

He tries to buck free of Killian's hold, but Killian replaces the axe, ready to push forward with what he has already started and sever Earl's ear.

"I told you I would make you pay for what you did to him."

I freeze, my back stiffening.

What the hell is he talking about?

This is the first time I've seen him since I fled. He must be referencing something to do with his real wife, Roberta.

Killian seems to sense it, too. "What did you do to her, Earl?"

Earl's gaze darts between us. Wild, unfocused, just like the man who possesses the information we need so badly. "I slit that bitch's throat and tossed her in the river."

I gasp and stagger back as his gaze lands on me.

"You shouldn't have come back. I should have done it again to you."

My body trembles. My legs threaten to give out from under me. That threat sounds very real. And with as far gone as he is, he probably would act on it.

Killian sneers in Earl's face, pushing forward. "And what about your son?"

"We never could find what that bitch did with him."

We?

"Where's *my* son?" Killian pushes the blade slightly, slicing into Earl's ear, drawing another agonized cry from the man. "Where. Is. He?"

Earl claws at Killian's hand, desperate to escape the pain he's suffering, the same way I was to get away from *him* when he held me against my will. "I told you, he's with the only person I've ever been able to trust my entire life."

My entire life...

Someone he's known forever.

There's only one person he ever mentioned during our entire time together who he would have trusted like that, one person he might have brought the baby to if he needed help after I was gone.

I turn to Killian. "I know where he is."

Killian snarls in Earl's face and pushes to his feet, releasing the man's neck and raising his axe above his head, ready to bring it down on him.

Liam steps forward and catches the handle, stopping the blade. "No."

One word from his little brother...and Killian shatters. His shoulders relax, slumping. The axe slips from his hand and into Liam's as he pulls it away.

Earl's eyes widen when he sees the youngest McBride. "You, but...I..."

He stumbles over his words, mouth opening and closing several times as he stares at him like he's seen a ghost.

And for the first time, I see it, too.

I don't know how I missed it in all the time I was staring at this man, or when he showed me the photos of his younger self with Roberta and their son, but seeing them together, it's impossible not to notice it...

The resemblance.

"Oh, my God."

I wobble back a step, and Connor seems to have the same realization, but it takes Liam and Killian another second to process what's happening.

"No." Liam shakes his head, retreating, Killian's axe slipping from his hand to the forest floor. "No."

Someone left him on Connie's doorstep twenty-one years ago with a note asking her to take care of him.

The timeline makes sense.

And they share the same eyes, the same face shape, the same reddish hair.

Liam is a younger version of my captor.

Oh, my God.

The youngest McBride's face crumbles as Earl struggles to process what's happening. Blood flows from under his hand that's clutched over his injured ear, but he seems more concerned with the young man in front of him than his own wound.

Liam staggers back a few steps, resting his back against a tree to keep himself upright on shaking legs.

Shouts come from the trail along with the sound of heavy footsteps.

Sheriff Briggs appears, running up to us and stopping just short of the log where Earl lies. He's slightly out of breath, hands on his knees. "We found the cabin, but there's no one inside it." His gaze sweeps across all of us. "What's happening?"

His eyes land on Earl and his injury, cut to a stunned, silent Liam, Connor, Killian, and me...

I open my mouth to try to explain, but nothing comes out.

Connor steps forward. "Was there an ATV up there?"

Briggs nods. "Yeah, why?"

"Good. Killian and Willow are going to need it."

21

WILLOW

The last vestiges of daylight barely touch the mountain by the time we get down the backside of it on the ATV, using the same barely passable old logging trail Earl must have traveled to get between town and the cabin beyond the gorge.

Seated in front of Killian, his strong body at my back, arms on either side of me, holding me securely, despite his injury, we traverse the final few miles of the rough terrain.

With the main road now in sight, the bubbling anxiety that's strangled me since we set out threatens to boil over.

It's taken us hours.

Endless hours spent reliving the flood of memories that now wash over me like a tsunami.

Horrible ones of a year spent with a man who had broken from reality.

Good ones of my baby—of *our* baby—the sole light in what was the darkest time of my life.

Holding him. Just staring at him and seeing all the ways he

looks exactly like Killian, even at this young an age. Telling him about his father. Describing the life we would have when we were finally free...

The tears I've cried endlessly continue to streak down my cheeks, and I so badly want to dive into that easy darkness I've let myself drift into over the past several weeks. Where I block out everything around me. Everything that's happened to me. Where I pretend it's a year ago and my life hasn't crumbled.

But Killian's warm breath flutters against my neck, his chest presses tightly to my back, his presence keeps me grounded and reminds me that we're in this together now.

We haven't even had a chance to talk, to discuss any of the revelations that came with finding Earl and my missing memories, because they don't matter at this moment.

Only finding Niall does.

Finding him and ending this nightmare once and for all.

The trees start to thin as we near the main road that wraps around the base of McBride Mountain, and eventually, the tires cross from the uneven forest floor to cracked pavement.

Turning left will take us back toward town and the road that leads up to the McBride homestead. But in the opposite direction...the one place we might find the thing we've been looking for, the piece of me that's been missing.

Killian pulls us to a stop. "You're sure about this?"

His chest rumbles along my back, his body filled with just as much tension as my own.

I turn to look at him. "Yes."

If I'm wrong, and we've wasted time coming this way, going where we're about to, instead of heading back into town through the gorge with Sheriff Briggs, Connor, Liam, the rest of the search party, and Earl to continue to question him and try to get answers, it would be a massive failure on my part.

A detour that could cost us time in finding Niall.

But I'm not wrong.

I know it deep in my soul, the same way I knew I was missing something important this whole time.

Killian quickly drops a kiss to the corner of my lips. "Then let's go get him."

His determination lifts that tiny ember of hope that's been burning in my chest, making it flame even higher, and he revs the engine and turns right, away from town instead of toward it.

The desolate, dark road extends in front of us.

Ominous.

Creepy as the sun finally sets and the mist settles in.

There isn't much on the backside of McBride Mountain. People prefer to live closer to town for obvious reasons, but not the Byers. They've been around for generations in the backwoods, far off the beaten path. Mostly keeping to themselves, save for one member of their family.

The one person I could trust.

His words echo in my head as we tear down the road for several more miles. In this darkness, it would be easy to miss the turn-in, half-hidden by overgrown bushes and trees. But Killian knows this mountain like the back of his hand, knows where it is without being able to see it, even though he probably hasn't been over this way in months, if not longer.

He slows the ATV and turns down the drive, going as fast as he dares on the unmanicured dirt road, overgrown with vines, covered with fallen leaves, branches, and other debris.

A fallen tree halfway blocks the trail. If this is where Earl left our son, he didn't come this way via car. With the gap between the thick forest and the end of the fallen tree only wide enough for the ATV to get through, it may have been intentional.

Perhaps a way to prevent anyone from getting back to the house easily.

I just hope I'm right about what waits there.

Niall...

The moment I saw his face, I knew his name.

I knew who he was and would become.

Because I know the man behind me, who always has my back.

And his son will become the same strong, reliable, confident, big-hearted person his father is.

Killian slows the ATV as the trees start to open to the clearing where the Byers' home stands. The dilapidated two-story house sits in the center of it, peeling paint, sagging roof, and porch matching the state of the outbuildings visible around it.

It all appears abandoned, as if it hasn't been lived in for years.

Doubt creeps in, chilling the confidence I had only moments ago.

Everyone assumed Earl was still living on the family property. He would show up in town once or twice a month for various supplies or to grab something from the diner or bakery, then he would disappear again to the other side of the mountain.

And no one ever thought anything of it.

A lot of people live very isolated lives out here, and the residents of McBride Mountain respect that desire for that kind of privacy.

Even the McBride homestead is well away from town, up a narrow, winding road few travel unless they need to speak with one of them and can't do it when they're at the timber yard or down on Main Street for something.

But seeing this house now, my heart sinks.

There's no one here.

Killian kills the engine and climbs off the ATV, offering me a hand to help me do the same. My legs tremble so badly that I can barely stand, but he wraps his arm around my waist, supporting me as he leads me toward the porch across an unmanicured, weed-infested clearing that can't even be called a lawn.

I keep scanning the property for any signs of life, for a glimpse of anything that might suggest I was right in my faith that Niall would be here.

A flash of blue in the half-collapsed garage to the right catches my attention, and I stop mid-step.

Killian freezes, too. "What?"

I narrow my eyes on it and slip out of his hold slowly. "Killian. *Look.*"

That hope re-surges again.

My truck.

That's why no one ever found it on the mountain. Earl must have knocked me unconscious, brought me here, returned and fixed the overheated engine, then gotten it off the road before anyone noticed it abandoned there.

Once he brought it here, no one would ever find it.

And no one was looking for it, either.

Killian mutters a curse and turns back toward the house. "The place looks abandoned, though."

He's right.

That same fear ripples through my heart—that I got it completely wrong—but so does something else.

Some instinct that calls to me.

The one that reached out in my dreams, even when I couldn't remember, telling me I had to go back up the mountain, that I was missing something important.

"He's here."

Killian offers me his hand again, and I allow him to pull me toward the house.

We step over two broken treads up onto the porch and weave around a gaping hole in the middle of the old wooden planks where it's collapsed under the weight of time.

He peers through the dirty, frosted glass on the front door, and I do the same, through a window to the right.

A flicker of movement makes me stagger back. "Someone's moving inside."

Killian nods and reaches for the door handle with his left hand and the gun he took from Connor with his right. "You stay out here."

"What?" I shake my head, my disheveled hair, blown into a rat's nest by the whipping winds during our frantic drive down the mountain, floating across my face. Shoving it out of the way so I can see him, I stand my ground. "No, I'm going in with you."

"We don't know what's in there, Willow." He practically hisses the warning, leaning closer so he can lower his voice. "I'm not going to risk your safety."

"Our baby's in there, Killian. If you think for one fucking second that I'm not going with you, then you don't know me at all."

The corners of his lips twitch, but I can't tell if it's because he's fighting a grin or a scowl. "Stay behind me."

Thank God.

I don't have it in me to fight Killian McBride right now.

It seems like that's all I've been doing.

Fighting for my life.

Fighting for my memories.

Fighting for all the things I lost on this mountain.

He tries the door handle, which gives easily. There isn't any reason to lock it out here.

No neighbors.

No crime.

Nothing to fear.

Except the man who supposedly lives here...

It springs open with a slight creak, and we take a step in, me with my hand against Killian's lower back, clinging to him the only way I can.

Despite the outward appearances, the interior of the house is shockingly clean and well-kept. Though clearly aging and not updated since likely the fifties, it's tidy. As if someone cares for it deeply and takes pride in its appearance.

I was wrong about it being abandoned, which means I was probably right in believing this is where Earl left our baby.

Dim light draws us down the front hallway toward what must be the kitchen at the rear of the house.

The sound of someone humming low floats out to us.

Killian freezes and tilts his ear toward it.

A woman's voice, humming and singing softly.

I lean in to whisper to him. "That must be her. Amy, Earl's sister. It has to be..."

Killian nods and starts to advance, but I grab his arm, stopping him.

My gaze drifts to the weapon in his hand, the one both Tony and Connor insisted he bring along, since we didn't know what we might find. "The gun might spook her."

He opens his mouth to argue with me. I know I am going to piss him off because he ordered me to stay behind him, but I step around and push past him, cautiously advancing to the kitchen, where her song fills the air.

I cautiously step through the jamb and glance inside.

She stands with her back to me, looking out a window, rocking side to side, completely oblivious that her home has been infiltrated.

Stay calm.

That's easy for me to tell myself, harder for me to actually do with so much at stake.

My heart slams violently against my ribs, blood rushing in my ears as I take another step into the kitchen.

I clear my throat, the sound shockingly loud in the peaceful, quiet space.

She startles, turning toward me quickly.

My breath catches.

Oh, my God.

Relief floods through me, washing away all those doubts, those worries.

All I can see is Niall cradled against her chest.

Apparently healthy, whole, well-cared for.

Thank God...

Her eyes widen as they land on me, and she stills, instantly on guard at seeing someone in her home.

I quickly hold up my hands. "I'm sorry to startle you, Amy. I knocked, but no one answered."

It's a lie.

But considering how far back she is in the house, if she didn't hear the ATV approach outside, she wouldn't have heard a knock, either.

Her wrinkled brow furrows deeper, and she clutches Niall even closer to her protectively. "Who are you?"

The vise around my chest tightens at the movement from the woman who helped take my life and baby. She's protecting my own child from *me.*

"My name is Willow. You know me. We met at the clinic several times when I was younger."

It's been years since she worked at the clinic as a nurse. Easily in her late sixties now, Earl's older sister looks every bit like the mother I wished I had and found in Connie.

Graying reddish hair pulled back into a loose ponytail, kind eyes locked on us. She was always so sweet to anyone who came into the clinic needing help. But now, all I can see is the woman who helped a madman.

Still, I somehow force a smile.

You catch more flies with honey than with vinegar.

That's what Connie always used to say.

Maybe that was why the bees always gave Killian so much trouble when they never did me—even they could sense his wild bitterness.

I glance back at Killian, and he steps into the light behind me.

Amy retreats a half step.

A big man like him, looking the way he does right now—downright feral—I don't blame her.

"You know Killian McBride?"

She tilts her head slightly, then nods. "Yes, I believe I helped set your arm when you broke it when you were in, what? Third grade?"

Killian nods. "Around then."

Her gaze darts between us. "What are you two doing here?"

His glacial eyes lock on the baby, and he slides the gun behind his back as he steps into the kitchen farther. He's smart enough to know that if he pulls it, this could end badly.

I take a cautious step toward her.

Please, God, don't let me be wrong about this. Don't let me be wrong about her.

"We're here for our son."

KILLIAN

Our son.

Those words still have a stranglehold on me.

My heart beats faster, my skin tightening over taut muscle and bone. But it's actually seeing him that makes my lungs seize.

The way Amy cradles him against her chest, all that's visible is his tiny face turned halfway toward us. His eyes closed, lips parted slightly as he sleeps comfortably in her arms.

Our son. Our son. Our son.

Her brow furrows as she looks at us. "What do you mean by 'your' son?"

She glances down at the baby in her arms, one that was ripped so violently from Willow's only a few weeks ago.

Willow inclines her head toward Niall. "You're holding him."

Amy shakes her head, retreating another step until her back hits the counter behind her. "No, this is my great nephew, Earl's grandson."

Willow goes completely rigid beside me.

I step forward, not wanting to startle Amy, but I also don't want to give her space to try to do something crazy like run with him. "No." I shake my head. "He isn't. I don't know what Earl told you, but..."

The older woman sputters, and her gaze darts between the baby and the two of us. "He said Roberta came back with their son and that this is his grandson."

I grit my jaw, clenching my teeth together so hard they ache, wanting to scream.

That's a fucking lie.

There is no way Amy didn't know what was happening, what her brother was doing to Willow...

I want to scream at her to get her hands off him, to rail at her for being an accessory to kidnapping, and even worse, but I can't risk something happening to Niall.

My body trembles with barely restrained rage, and Willow seems momentarily stunned, watching the woman carefully as if she's assessing how to best approach her.

Finally, Willow takes a step forward. "That's not true, and you know it, Amy." She inches forward another step, but the long counter between them acts as a barricade, preventing her from getting to Amy and Niall unless she takes the time to walk around it. "You know Roberta didn't come back. You know he thought *I* was Roberta and that *he*"—she points to our son—"was the baby she took from him twenty years ago."

A single tear slips down Amy's cheek as she shakes her head. "No."

Willow stands her ground. "*Yes.*"

We both know Earl was too far gone mentally to have realized he would need to stage a ruse as complicated as what happened with Raven. Willow said he was never lucid enough to know who he was—or *wasn't*—so there is no way in hell he could have understood how essential it would be to send those notes and gifts to Raven, to get Willow to write them in her own handwriting and reference things *only* she could know so as to not raise suspicions.

He needed help.

From someone familiar with the town and the people in it.

Someone he trusted.

Like Amy, who knows *everyone* because of her work in the clinic with Doc Broward for so many years.

She retired only a few years before Willow left, would have understood her relationship with Raven—and the fact that Raven would have investigated her friend's disappearance if she weren't convinced she left of her own accord and was somewhere else, happy and safe.

Willow glances over at me as the tears well in her eyes, her growing frustration registering in her twisted lips, as if she's biting back what she *really* wants to say to this woman, the same way I am. "We know you helped Earl, Amy. We know you arranged for the gifts and notes to go to Raven. What I need to know is *why?*" Her voice cracks. "*Why* didn't you *help* me get away from him?"

I place my left hand on her lower back, ignoring the pain in my arm, offering her what comfort and support I can, while struggling to maintain my cool, despite my vibrating rage.

Goddamn that man for what he did to her, for putting her in this position...

A sob slips from Amy's lips, and she clings to Niall, clearly having no intention of simply handing him over. "I-I..."

I barely manage to bite back the growl trying to climb my throat. "You *what*?"

The old woman's brow furrows, pain flashing across her teary gaze. "I didn't know what to do..."

It's as close to an admission as I need to confirm everything we suspected.

Willow sags slightly, then rests her palms flat on the counter to keep herself upright. "Tell us what happened."

In all the memories that came back to her, Willow *never* mentioned Amy. Never *saw* her up at that dilapidated cabin. All she remembers is being asked to write the notes...by *Earl*.

Tears stream freely down Amy's face now, and she starts rocking again, to soothe herself or the baby. Maybe both. She glances down at Niall, refusing to look at us. "He-he comes and goes on his ATV, stops by when he needs supplies and comes to town. He makes sure I get what I need out here." Her green eyes shift up to meet mine, then move to Willow. "And one day, he just...showed up with your truck. I recognized it. Knew it was yours. But he said Roberta was *back*."

Willow's hands fist on the counter. "Did you see me?"

Amy quickly shakes her head. "No. No. Never. He took you up the mountain and never brought you to the house. But I knew..."

I take a step toward her, unable to hold back. "What did you know, Amy? Why did you *help* him?"

Another sob wrenches from deep in her chest, waking Niall and making him squirm.

Willow shifts toward the edge of the counter, like she's

about to make a grab for him, but Amy inches closer to the door that leads out of the kitchen and to the endless wilderness.

I grab Willow's arm, stopping her advance.

She trembles just as badly as I do right now. I can feel Willow's frustration bubbling over in every quiver of her body against my hand, but she somehow manages to maintain her composure.

Not panicking.

Amy swallows a few times, shaking her head. "I knew something wasn't right. That Earl hasn't been completely himself for a long time, living up there alone. But I didn't know he had *you* until he came back down a few weeks later. He kept rambling about Bobby and the baby coming." Her gaze drops to the fussy Niall, and she adjusts her hold on him. "It clicked in my head how much you looked like Bobby did back then and that he hadn't bought that truck from you..."

This time, I don't bite back my growl. "But you didn't go to the sheriff!"

She issues another sob. "No." Several strands of reddish-gray hair slip from her bun as she vigorously shakes her head. "I couldn't. Earl is all I have left. My only family. My only connection to the outside world. He takes care of me. He—"

Willow slams her fist on the counter, the sound making Amy jump. "He *kidnapped* me. He abused me. He kept me captive in that cabin for a *year*. He stole my *baby!*"

I snarl, tightening my grip on the gun. "And *you* helped him."

Amy sobs, tears sliding down her cheeks. "I did. I'm so sorry. I-I..." She looks at Niall. "I just wanted my nephew back."

Liam.

This woman knows damn well Niall isn't the baby Roberta fled with twenty years ago, but she deluded herself into believing the lie. To give herself what she *wanted*.

Our son.

"Amy..." I try to keep my voice level despite my rising anger. "Tell us about the notes. How did you get Willow to write them and get them to Raven?"

Anything we can learn from her now will be useful later, when the prosecutor reviews the case and issues charges against her and her brother.

She sniffles, looking at Willow. "I remembered you two were best friends. The last time I was in town before this happened with Earl, I had seen you having coffee and croissants together at Claire's. I knew she would worry if you just...disappeared. When Earl came back down the next time, I gave him some postcards I had from some of my own travels, along with a note I said was for Bobby."

Willow shivers. "I remember it." Her gray eyes cut over to me. "She told me she would ensure I had everything I needed for the baby if I cooperated and wrote notes to Raven. She told me to include facts only I would know and that if I tried anything, like slipping in any information to indicate things weren't as they appeared, that she could cut off our supplies."

Which would risk both Willow's and the baby's life.

This woman may appear sweet and unassuming, but this was premeditated.

Diabolical on a level that rivals what her brother did.

Only she *knew* what she was doing.

She *knew* he was delusional and holding Willow against her will, yet she let this all continue.

Facilitated it.

None of this would have happened if not for Amy Byers.

Raven would have realized something was wrong when she couldn't get a hold of Willow and didn't hear from her. She would have eventually gone to Tony and asked for help in finding her. And Tony would have come to *me*.

Willow clenches her fists so tightly that her knuckles whiten. "How did you get them sent from those locations?"

Amy averts her gaze, adjusting her hold on Niall, who has resettled. "They're all close. Drivable. I used your truck to go to each location and mail them, to ensure the postmarks were right..."

This was calculated.

Cold.

She's as much of a monster as her brother.

And I've heard all I need to.

I slide the gun into my waistband to free up my hands. "Earl was taken into custody after he *shot* at us." Her gaze falls to my bloody arm. "He's going away for the rest of his life for what he did. It's over now. It's time for you to give us our son."

It's time to *end* this.

For Willow.

For Niall.

For me.

For all of us.

Amy chews on her bottom lip, considering my words, clinging to the baby she helped *steal*.

This lonely woman living in this crumbling house thought she could have a family again by taking *mine*.

Her legs start to crumple, and I rush forward to catch her before she hits the floor or drops the baby. As I hold her steady, my son pinned between us, she looks up at me. Her red hair graying at the temples, matching that of her brother's...

And Liam's.

I stare down into her eyes filled with so much confusion but also pain.

It's *nothing* compared to what she caused Willow and me.

"You need to give him to us."

I don't know what she sees in my eyes, whether it's determination, anger, or agony. Likely, all of the above. But she nods and allows me to take the baby from her arms gently.

His tiny weight settles in my palms, and all the breath rushes from my lungs again.

He squirms and lets out a squeal, apparently not happy about the change of position, the loss of the body heat, and the comforting hold he's grown to know over the last few weeks.

And I don't have a fucking clue what to do with him.

I haven't held a baby since Liam was one.

Don't know how to comfort him.

How to ensure he knows he's safe and loved.

What the hell do I do?

Willow rushes over, sliding her hands into place and taking him from me, settling him to her chest, and burying her face against his tiny head, sobs wrenching from deep in her chest.

Tears trickle from my eyes.

Amy grips the edge of the counter to keep herself upright. "I am so sorry. I didn't— I'm-I'm so sorry..."

I turn away from her as she finally collapses onto the old linoleum.

Her words don't mean anything.

Nothing she can say will take back what she's done or give us what we've lost.

Just like nothing I can do will ever make up for what I said to Willow that day that sent her running in the first place.

My fear of failing as a father, of losing her because of it, caused me to miss out on so much. But now I am one, and seeing Willow standing here, holding our son, it finally feels like the nightmare is over.

22

TWO DAYS LATER

WILLOW

Thunder rolls overhead, rattling the windowpanes and eliciting a little squawk from Niall. He squirms in Killian's hold, and his frantic blue gaze meets mine as he adjusts his hold on the baby and continues pacing the main cabin.

His attention returns to his son, examining him carefully. "Are you sure he's all right?"

I can't fight the grin that pulls at my lips as I watch them from the kitchen, making him a bottle. "He's fine. Babies cry, Killian, when they're hungry, when they're tired, when they need a clean diaper, when a loud noise startles them."

It used to startle me, too.

But tonight, the storm doesn't bother me.

Now that I remember what I did, running out in that storm to save Niall and myself, the power doesn't frighten me anymore.

I've faced things far worse.

But my placation doesn't seem to make Killian feel any better or ease any of the tense concern marring his brow.

He brushes his lips over Niall's head and murmurs something to him that I can't hear, shifting his hand gently across the baby's back with Niall's face resting against his bare chest —right over the tattoo of McBride Mountain where he was born.

No matter what I say, I know Killian won't stop worrying.

For the past couple of days, since we got Niall, it's all Killian has done.

Even though the pediatrician assured us he's healthy. Even though Earl and Amy are locked safely away and the district attorney has already filed charges against them. Even though it's finally over and our son is in his arms and safe, it hasn't stopped the constant anxiety from overriding his usually self-confident nature.

Tension still permeates his body, even at night.

He doesn't sleep, lying awake watching Niall and me. Pacing the cabin as if he can't let go of that fear that consumed us for so long.

And when Niall is awake, he barely lets him out of his sight. Always watching for the tiniest signs his son might be unhappy.

As endearing as it is, it's also concerning.

I snag the bottle from where it's been warming on the stove and make my way over to him. Killian stops his pacing as I hand it to him and searches my face as if he's trying to determine if I'm okay, even though I've assured him I am. I lean up on my tiptoes and feather a kiss to his lips, silencing anything he might say—and hopefully the voices in his head that won't let him settle.

He leans into the kiss, clutching Niall close to himself between us, letting his lips linger on mine until I finally pull away.

I tuck a strand of his long blond hair back behind his ear.

"He's just hungry, and the thunder startled him. You have to stop worrying so much."

Killian always clutches him so tightly, afraid he's going to hold him wrong or drop him or do something that will upset him—or me. It will take some time, but eventually, Killian will believe what I already do, that he's going to be a wonderful father.

He releases a little huff. Doesn't want to hear me say those words to him again, but until he finally relaxes, until he finally accepts that this is really over, I will keep reminding him.

One day, he might believe it.

Liam snort-laughs from his place on the couch, wearing a mix of concern and amusement at watching his brother melt-down with the baby in his arms. "For what it's worth, I agree with Willow."

Raven smirks from her spot in Killian's recliner and raises her hand. "Ditto."

I grin at them, hoping the other voices backing me up help Killian see it. "I appreciate the support."

Liam tilts his beer in my direction before he takes a sip. "Anytime."

His gaze lands on his nephew as Killian adjusts him in his arms to get the bottle into his mouth. Niall latches on and settles against his father's chest again, completely content, just like I promised Killian he would be.

I drag my lips across the healing wound from Earl's bullet on Killian's bicep and move over to the couch and settle next to Liam, who I'm more worried about than our baby.

He's been quiet.

Reclusive.

Hasn't spoken a word to any of us about what we discovered on that mountain a few days ago.

The shocking truth of where he came from and who his parents are has left him reeling.

Lost.

Of all the McBride brothers, he was always the most sure of himself and his role in this world.

The most comfortable with people and opening up.

And the man who always manages to find the bright side in everything, who always goes out of his way to cheer people up and make sure they're okay.

But for days, he has locked himself away in his cabin or his workshop.

And neither Killian nor I dare bring up the topic if he's not ready to talk about it.

We've both been on the *other* side of that, and forcing anyone to open up when they need time to process typically doesn't end well.

Raven exchanges a knowing look with me.

All the fallout of what we discovered on the mountain has left the reporter in her jonesing for more information. To learn whatever she can so the residents of our small town can understand what happened instead of relying on supposition and rumors.

That includes desperately wanting to talk with Liam about how he feels about the entire situation.

But she's handcuffed—both by her conscience and her loyalty to me.

Because I told her the McBrides are off limits for the community news page...unless *I* approve it first.

And I won't when it comes to Liam. His gaze remains glued on his brother and nephew, unblinking, with an almost trance-like quality to how he watches them together.

I have to imagine he's picturing himself at this age—and the man whose arms he would have been in.

Reaching out, I squeeze his hand.

He looks over at me and raises a brow. "What?"

"You doing okay?"

His eyes darken slightly, and he averts his gaze down to the beer in his hand. "I..." He shakes his head. "I don't know. I guess I'm not sure how I'm supposed to feel about any of this."

Killian wanders over closer to us, keeping his voice low for Niall's benefit. "You can feel however you want to."

It's exactly what he's said to me over the last several days, too—that I have every right to feel however I want to about Earl, about Amy, about what happened to me.

I can be angry.

I can be devastated.

I can break things.

I can cry.

I can sob and completely fall apart.

As long as you don't shut me out, you can do whatever you want.

It's been his only stipulation, his only demand of me—that I don't shut him out. And I'm doing my best not to do just that. To talk through the memories that I've already revealed to him and Sheriff Briggs, the information he needs to ensure the prosecution goes through. To explain the nightmares that wake me, the tears that come when I'm holding Niall.

All of it.

Each painful thing that could so easily send me into that abyss of darkness.

But then Killian's there to hold me, to let me cry if I need to, to pound against his chest, to let out frustration and agony in any way I need to. To distract me in the way only *he* can when that's the only thing that will pull me from the downward plummet.

I give Killian a half-smile, then turn to Liam, squeezing his hand again. "He's right. But...if you want to talk about it, you know we're here."

The youngest McBride gives me a tight smile that doesn't

quite reach his emerald eyes. "I know, and I appreciate it. Really."

But he isn't going to tonight.

That much is obvious.

He's not ready.

It's too fresh.

Too painful for him.

I can understand that.

But Killian and I won't let Liam disappear into himself. We won't let him push us away indefinitely.

Footsteps sound outside on the porch, preventing anyone from delving any further into the issue—probably for the best.

We've all been waiting for Connor's return.

And for the information he should have with him.

The front door swings open, and Connor trudges in, rain dripping from his dark hair and clothes onto the floorboards. He pushes the door closed with his booted foot and toes them off. "Man, it's brutal out there."

As if in response, another crack of thunder rattles the house, but this time Niall doesn't even react, despite Killian watching for it, worrying over it.

Raven and I share a half-grin about it as Connor approaches her with a scowl.

He glares at where she sits, occupying Killian's father's old chair—one of *his* favorite spots. "Do you mind?"

Uh oh.

I recognize the saccharine-sweet smile Raven offers the middle McBride brother all too well.

She bats her long eyelashes at him, settling back in the chair and placing her hands behind her head. "Not at all."

Killian intercedes, stepping between them and pressing a hand to Connor's shoulder, urging him back. "Let. It. Go."

The brothers stare each other down while we all hold our

breaths, waiting for the potential explosion from the younger of the two.

Connor grits his jaw, crossing his arms over his broad chest, while Killian holds the stare-down, rocking slightly side to side to keep Niall happy as he eats.

Finally, Connor rolls his eyes and stalks off to the kitchen, returning with a beer in hand that he takes a long swig from before he settles on the arm of the couch beside Liam.

Killian raises a brow at his Connor. "Any update?"

My spine stiffens even without any reference to *what* we've been expecting updates on.

Each day, we worry...

Each day, we wait...

For information from Sheriff Briggs about his interviews with Earl. For the answers that still elude us. Those little lingering questions we can't seem to answer for ourselves. And for a resolution.

Connor nods, glancing around the room at everyone except Raven. "I spoke with Tony, and he finally finished interviewing Earl."

Killian's gaze immediately cuts to mine.

Finally.

His mental state has meant they've had to be careful when interviewing him. Some sessions were pointless, with Earl descending into rants that didn't make any sense. Frustrating for us and law enforcement.

But it seems as though it's come to an end.

I clear my throat. "And?"

Connor takes a drink and shrugs. "The dude is genuinely off his rocker. I don't know the technical medical terms, but it sounds like they're anticipating his public defender arguing the insanity defense."

A low growl slips from Killian's lips.

Raven shifts forward on the chair. "That motherfucker."

I sit numbly on the couch, trying to process his words. "What? Does that...does that mean he'd go free?"

Connor shakes his head. "No. Apparently, if they try to claim it and the jury buys it—assuming he goes to jury trial—he'll end up in a mental institution, probably for the rest of his life, given what he did to you."

I release a long, uneven breath.

It isn't prison, but at least he'd be locked away somewhere where he can't hurt anyone else again.

That's...*something.*

Raven doesn't appear to feel the same way, glaring at Connor as if he's the one responsible instead of just the messenger. "And what about Amy?"

Connor sighs. "Well, that's more complicated. The District Attorney wants to use her to testify against Earl if necessary, so she may get a deal?"

Killian glares at his brother. "So, she'd get off without jail time?"

Raven climbs from the chair, coming to squat next to me and take my hand in hers. "No way. I won't allow that to happen. I don't care if I have to contact every major newspaper in the country, I will make sure the story gets plastered across every one of them until the uproar would be too much to ignore and they lock that bitch up."

Connor glowers at her. "Can I answer before you go off on one of your 'reporter saving the world' crusades?"

Her lips twist, but she nods at him.

He sighs. "I don't think they are saying *no* jail time, but she might get sent to a lower security facility, something like that." He shakes his head. "There's no fucking way the DA is letting her walk away from her role in all this."

I release the breath I've been holding.

Killian moves closer until he's towering over where I sit on the couch, staring down at me with enough concern that I think he might actually hand Niall off to Liam to take *me* in his arms instead.

"Honeybee? You all right?"

"Umm." I nod, even though I don't really *feel* all right. The last thing I need is to give him *more* to worry about. "Yeah. I guess I shouldn't be surprised. He wasn't all there..."

It doesn't excuse what he did to me.

Nothing could.

And given the way he treated me, thinking I was his wife, given the fact that she fled from him with their child twenty years ago, he's never been a good man.

They might need Amy to testify about what she knows about all of this, especially given her medical training.

I should have seen this as a potential outcome and prepared myself for it.

Liam slides his hand over my free one and squeezes. His first reaction to anything Connor has said. I look over at him through the tears, and he gives me a hard smile.

The man is his father.

His mother died trying to prevent him from suffering at Earl's hands.

And Amy is his only other living relative.

We're bonded in this for life, and the look he gives me tells me he understands completely how I feel, even if he shares blood with my assailant and his accomplice.

Raven moves out of the way, disappearing into the kitchen to get another drink while Killian squats in front of me, Niall still cradled in one large arm, while he holds the bottle to his mouth with the other hand.

Our eyes lock, and the confidence I see in his gaze is enough to steady my heartbeat.

"That man will never hurt anyone again. He will never get near you or our son again. Neither will Amy. I promise you that.

If either of them tries, I'll finish what I started on the mountain."

KILLIAN

The soft sound of the rain hitting the roof and windows creates an almost lullaby now that the major part of the storm has passed. Without the thunder startling the baby awake, we finally have a chance of getting Niall to settle down for the night.

I watch Willow bent over the bassinet in the corner of the bedroom. She leans in and kisses him before she turns and makes her way back to me.

Willow climbs into bed, pulling the sheet and comforter up over herself as I wrap my arms around her and tug her tightly against me.

"He's asleep?"

She nods and releases a relieved sigh.

It's been a long day—as have all of them recently—but the news about Earl and Amy has rattled me more than I would ever admit to her. Willow doesn't need *my* anger and frustration to compound whatever she's feeling.

That fucker deserves to die for what he did to her, and Amy is no better.

I should have ended it on the mountain when I had the chance.

Even if he had never taken Willow, he deserves to see the business side of my axe for what he did to his wife and what would have happened to Liam if she hadn't saved him.

A little shiver rolls through Willow, something that happens far too often for my liking, and I drag my lips across her shoulder blades. "What's wrong?"

She shakes her head. "Nothing."

It's a lie.

And the one thing I've told her every day is that she can't shut me out.

If Willow shuts me out, it will lead us into a very bad place, somewhere we might not ever be able to recover from.

I tilt her chin back until her eyes meet mine. "Don't lie to me, Honeybee."

Her eyes soften. "I'm okay, really. Just, you know... everything."

"I *do* know."

Even without her saying it.

It's been hard for me to maintain any level of control or semblance of normalcy. Nearly impossible to keep myself even-keeled when I want to destroy something in retaliation for what happened to her. Even taking my axe out into the woods for hours, slamming it into trees until my palms bleed, or going to my shop and carving hasn't been enough of an outlet.

Nothing can cure this pain.

Nothing can undo what's been done.

But what she needs right now is a distraction, an outlet for the maelstrom of feelings that seems to be occupying her head tonight.

I brush my lips across her cheek, over to her ear, as I push my hips against her ass until she can feel my growing cock. "I can think of a way to make you feel better, Honeybee."

It might not be a permanent solution, but in this moment, all I can do is try to fix the *now*.

She groans slightly and rolls her hips back against mine.

We haven't touched each other, not like this at least, since we found Niall.

Too exhausted, physically and emotionally.

Too distracted by taking care of him and dealing with the fallout of what we discovered beyond the gorge.

But I know what she needs right now, what I need.

We need to feel alive again.

We need to take control of our lives by giving in to the *one* thing that has always brought us the closest to each other and sheer bliss.

I nip at her ear. "I need you to be quiet."

Willow issues a little moan, her hands snaking back between us to grip my cock as I glide one down across her belly, under the waistband of her sleep shorts, into her cunt.

Rough fingertips find her slick heat, and my chest rumbles in approval. "Already so wet for me, Honeybee."

She whimpers again and bites her lip to try to silence herself.

The last time I asked her to be quiet, we were in the woods and I had her pinned against that tree. She couldn't do it then, not in the end. Hopefully, she can tonight, or Niall will wake up, and that could *really* interfere with my plans.

I still my hand, pausing to ensure he hasn't woken already.

Willow rolls her hips in my hold, seeking friction I refuse to give her. Her deft fingers stroke my cock through the soft fabric of my sweatpants, but she eagerly slips her hand beneath the waistband so she can spread the bead of pre-cum across the head.

Somehow, I manage to fight back a groan.

God, I love this woman.

Her kiss.

Her touch.

Her smile.

Her laugh.

Her tears.

How good a mother she is to our son.

How incredibly forgiving and understanding she is with everyone, especially me.

All of it.

I can't imagine life without her.

I tried that once, and it almost killed me.

"Marry me."

Her hand stills on my cock, and she peeks back over her shoulder at me. "What?"

It may have been a whisper, but she definitely heard what I just said. "You heard me, Honeybee. Marry me."

We haven't even talked about it—the fact that she left the ring when she fled the mountain—but I need it on her finger *now*.

I need that confirmation that everything we went through has brought us full circle and hasn't stolen the life we had planned before our worlds fell apart.

I need something tangible for both of us—something we can look to when times get tough and our past wounds feel too painful to bear.

I need her to say *yes*.

Her gaze softens as she holds my gaze, the sound of the rain filling the space where her answer should be. The first time I did this, she didn't hesitate. She had no reason to. But so much has happened since then. So many things that have changed both of us.

The tears shimmering across her eyes could mean so many things I'm not capable of deciphering.

But *one* emotion burns red hot—love.

Despite all the reasons she shouldn't, this woman *loves* me and trusts me with every part of her.

The good.

The bad.

The scary.

The angry.

The broken.

The same way I trust her with all those parts of me.

I slowly glide a finger up inside her, and she groans, tightening around it and arching into my hold even farther. Her grip on my cock increases as her breathing hitches.

"Is that a yes, Honeybee?"

A tiny laugh slips from her lips, and she nods as her hand clenches around my cock a second time, tugging in a way that makes my balls ache.

Sweet mother of God.

She may not have said the word, but she did agree to be my bride. To become Mrs. Killian McBride. This stunning woman, who had my baby, is going to be *my wife.*

And I can't wait another second to show her how much she means to me in the only way I know how.

I quickly pull her hand away, shuck off my pants, and pull her shorts down her legs to give us better access to each other, then settle back in behind her. My hand slides between her legs again, and I slip one finger inside her, then a second, plunging into her heat.

She rolls against my palm, gripping my wrist.

Frantic.

Desperate.

The same way my heart beats and my blood rushes in my ears.

It's not enough, not for either of us.

Pulling my hand away, I drag her left leg up and back over my thigh to open her up, then press the head of my cock at her slick entrance. "Remember, quiet, Honeybee."

She nods as I glide into her, slowly letting her feel all of me.

Her chest vibrates with her groan, but she keeps biting her lip, holds the noise in somehow, even as I struggle not to roar at the feel of her hot cunt squeezing around my cock.

Every damn time feels like coming home.

Like finding the single place on this planet I was meant to spend forever.

I drop my forehead against her hair, inhaling that scent that

I missed so much while she was away, that I craved to have back in my bed, in my house, in my lungs.

Lavender and honey...

And now I have confirmation that it will *always be here.*

Because I have everything I ever dreamed of.

This beautiful woman who wants to spend the rest of her life with me, our son, the future laid out in front of us that we always should have had.

I draw my hips back and thrust into her again, setting a smooth, slow rhythm.

Long.

Unhurried.

Strokes.

I want to savor her.

Every twitch of her body.

Every little moan and gasp she tries to fight.

Every clench around my length.

Every time the head of my cock catches at that spot deep inside of her, her legs tighten, her thigh struggling against my hold.

I slip my free hand under her and find her breast, tweaking her nipple as I continue to drive into her. Her body jolts in my hold, a tiny mewl finally falling from her lips that she can't contain, despite her best efforts.

My movements become more erratic.

My thrusts harder and deeper.

Her hips rolling back to meet each one.

I shift my palm to her other breast and twist her nipple there, giving her that little bite of pain.

She moans and arches her neck, begging for what she needs. I slide my hand up around it, tightening and angling her head until her ear is at my lips, stilling my hips to emphasize my point now that I have her where I want her.

"I fucking love you, Willow." *Thrust.* "You're a McBride."

Thrust. "You're *mine.*" *Thrust.* "No one"—*thrust*—"and nothing" —*thrust*—"will *ever* get between us again."

I keep pumping into her, keeping it slow, dragging out the pleasure for both of us as long as possible—before we both *snap* and lose control.

She whimpers against my hand and swallows hard, the motion rippling under my palm, enough to make my cock ache deep inside her. Her pussy clamps down on me, and her body vibrates harder, trembling so badly that I know she's close.

So damn close.

"I know how much you want to come on my cock, don't you?"

She nods as I roll my hips and thrust deep again, then still.

"Then do it for me, Honeybee."

I unleash that restraint I've been clinging to.

Driving into her as hard as I can in the position we're in.

Planting my foot into the mattress for leverage and to give her a different angle.

One that guarantees I hit the spot that made her squirt down my throat in the kitchen.

That's what I want.

That kind of release for her.

One that might be able to wash away whatever was weighing on her when she climbed into this bed with me tonight.

With one more flex of my palm on her throat and drive of my hips, her head arches more against my grip, and she comes.

I slide my hand up over her mouth to stifle her cry as her pussy pulses along my cock, clasping and clutching, rippling the same way her throat does.

It drags my own release free and I still, coming deep inside her in mind-bending spurts of pleasure that spread to every inch of my body.

A release of more than just sexual need.

I'm letting go of everything.

My anger at myself.

My anger at the world.

Even my anger at the time we lost.

Because I have everything I ever need right here beneath the mountain sky.

EPILOGUE

MEMORIAL DAY FESTIVAL – NINE MONTHS LATER

WILLOW

Main Street bustles with people moving in and out of the shops, stopping to look at the stands set up along the sidewalk from various local artists and vendors, enjoying all the festivities. The smell of fried foods and crisp early summer mountain air permeates every breath I take, tinged with the scent of freshly cut wood that always reminds me of Killian.

For good reason.

I stand along the edge of the crowd with Niall sleeping soundly in the front carrier, watching Killian do one of the things he does *best*.

Put on a show that *no one* can tear their eyes away from.

For a man who doesn't really "like" people, especially after the entire town has spent the last year gossiping and speculating about our lives, he still insisted on doing a demonstration at the festival.

And this year, the cute bear cub he's almost done creating has special meaning.

As he carves away with his chisels, gouges, and knives, finishing the fine detail work, his gaze flicks up to find mine, and he raises a brow. I give him a thumbs-up, letting him know Niall's still sleeping and handling all the excitement well.

The past nine months haven't done anything to help calm Killian's constant need to hover. That worry he always carries for me and for the baby just won't go away.

Always so attentive to anything and everything either of us could need.

Anticipating before I can even ask.

He's exactly who I always knew he was and would be—an incredible father, the perfect husband.

I glance down at the rings on my finger, his mother's engagement ring and the matching wedding band.

My heart still aches with the memory of waking in that hospital and finding this finger empty. But now, it's exactly where it should be.

It may have taken us longer than we had planned to get to this point.

Life, misunderstandings, and things so far out of our control that it felt like constant spiraling seemed to conspire to keep our happily ever after from happening. But we finally made it to where we should have been a year ago.

We're finally a family, finally happy.

And as he completes work on the baby bear and steps back to examine his masterpiece, the crowd roars with approval.

He tosses me a grin, returns his equipment to the large travel case near Liam, and has a short conversation with him about something before he makes his way over to me.

Watching him approach, the sweat trickling down his corded neck and over his exposed chest, the way the muscles there bunch and flex in his arms as he runs it back through his sweaty hair...

Good God, I'm going to end up pregnant again quickly.

I clench my legs together against the dull ache there.

My body remembers every touch, every kiss, all the gloriously depraved things that man does to it.

And I still crave more of him, even after this morning.

Killian finally reaches us, and he leans in and presses a kiss to my lips, then drops one on Niall's head before scanning around me. "Where's Raven? I thought she was going to watch with you."

I search the crowd, looking for her familiar mop of blond hair, and shrug. "Who knows? She disappears all the time these days."

He raises a brow. "Really?"

I nod. "She's working on a story. You know how she is. And this"—I spin my hand around—"is her favorite time of year. So many people to talk to, so much gossip to collect."

He snorts incredulously. "Well, I don't know about you, but I'm peopled out. You ready to go home?"

"Yeah. Are Liam and Connor coming?"

He turns back to where he left Liam reorganizing the tools. The youngest McBride closes the lid on the case and secures it before rising to his feet. Someone approaches him and says something, and he quickly falls into conversation with whoever it is.

But the usual smile that used to so easily cross his lips isn't there.

Instead, deep lines mar the corners of his eyes, dark circles beneath them.

I don't think he's slept well in a year.

He certainly hasn't been himself in that time...

My heart aches for him and for what he's suffering because I understand it better than anyone.

Nightmares still plague me.

Waking me with violent screams, cold sweats, and a racing heart.

Though they've grown less frequent as time has passed, they're still there—those memories that create the dark places. But I'm not as afraid of them anymore. I'm more in control of the darkness and shedding light in a way that makes it less scary.

Yet for Liam, it seems to have only gotten worse. And despite all our best efforts, his refusal to see Dr. Bird like I do, to get any sort of help to deal with the mental trauma he suffered, has become a source of argument and frustration on the McBride homestead.

But I'm not getting into it with him again today.

Not when I know Killian is exhausted from his hours spent in the sun doing the demonstration, and Niall would sleep so much better in his own crib at home.

Killian motions to Liam, catching his attention and pointing toward the mountain to let him know we're headed home.

Liam inclines his head but waves us off.

There isn't any sign of Connor.

I scan the crowd again. "Where did Connor go?"

Killian runs his hand through his sweat-dampened hair again, keeping it out of his face as the summer breeze tries to whip it in all directions. "Who knows? He's been crabbier than usual lately. Maybe he went to work off some steam. God knows he hates being surrounded by this many people almost as much as I do."

He tries to sound annoyed, but I know him too well.

Killian loves McBride Mountain and the people in it because he cares about things like *this*.

I step into him, not caring that he's still slick with sweat.

He glances down, his eyes heating.

Resting my hand over his bare chest, I trail a finger across McBride Mountain. "Yet...you still do it." I push up on my tiptoes and lean in to kiss him the best I can with Niall between us. "You take care of this town and these people, even if most of them are afraid of you."

He snorts and kisses me deeply, his tongue twisting along mine until my body heats not just from the early summer sun. Then he pulls back, issuing a low growl. "I can't wait to get you home. I have something for you."

"You do?"

He nods. "Let's go."

I'm not about to argue with that look in his eye, the promise that underlies it.

He pulls my hand into his and tugs me along Main Street, weaving between the tourists. People stop to clap him on the back and tell him how great the carving looks. Something that even a year ago, they might not have done for fear of how he would react.

Because what happened on the mountain between us, finding our son, has changed him, allowed him to open up more and accept the possibility that he can stop being a grump and still command the respect due to him as the patriarch of McBride Mountain.

We move past the old newspaper building, but instead of the usual empty glass, tan paper covers the windows.

"Oh." I pull Killian to a stop. "It looks like something might be going into the newspaper building."

He raises a brow. "Maybe?"

"I'll have to ask Raven. If anyone knows, it would be her."

Killian nods and continues to lead me through the throngs of people until we reach his truck. He unlocks the door, then turns back to me, carefully unstrapping Niall, who shifts restlessly at the change of position, but immediately settles into his father's arms.

His favorite place to be.

Mine, too.

The massive man, who intimidates so many, snuggles his

son and kisses his cheek before he settles him in the car seat and secures him.

He turns back to me and closes the door gently.

Killian tugs me up against him, now nothing between us, and kisses me long and deep again. "Let's go home, Mrs. McBride."

KILLIAN

I grip the steering wheel to keep my trembling hands from being visible to Willow.

As we complete the drive and turn onto the property, she glances over at me for what must be the hundredth time during the long trek up the mountain, her lips twisting slightly. "Why do you look so nervous?"

Shit.

Apparently, I did a pretty crappy job of hiding it.

And I don't even know *why* I am nervous.

Maybe because I've spent months on this gift for her, ensuring it was absolutely perfect. Maybe because I'm terrified that the surprise won't be what she wants and that I'll have to see disappointment on her face.

That's one thing I can never stand—disappointing this woman.

I've done it far too much during my life, and now that we have our second chance, I won't do anything to blow it.

Instead of saying any of that, I just force a smile. "I'm not nervous."

She snort-laughs. "Yeah, okay."

I can't help but grin.

When you know each other as well as the two of us do, it's

hard to keep secrets. Hiding this from her over the last several months has been nearly impossible.

Only the help of Connor, Liam, and Raven has ensured she hasn't stumbled upon my plans or the thing I've managed to keep hidden in my workshop, despite the fact that she comes out there almost every day.

I park the truck between the house and the barn and climb out, walking around to get her door and help her before I move to get Niall from his car seat.

He's sound asleep.

His head cocked sideways, breaths floating from his tiny, perfect face.

And God, my heart beats faster just looking at him.

Even now, after all this time, I could stare at him forever, spend hours examining everything about him and memorizing every eyelash, every tiny line around his eyes and mouth, every freckle and hair on his head.

Willow wraps her arms around my waist and presses her face into the middle of my back. "Are you just going to stand there, staring at him?"

I grin as I unbuckle him and slowly lift him from the car seat, settling him against my chest.

She releases her hold on me and steps away, allowing me to turn and close the truck door. With a grin, she starts to head toward the house. But I catch her hand with my free one.

"No." I incline my head toward the workshop. "This way."

"Okaaaay..." The way she drags out the word gives away her confusion, but she turns to follow me that way instead of back to the cabin.

I re-settle my hand on Niall's back as we make our way across the clearing to where I do all my carving work. My stomach churns as I pull open the sliding door, the nerves getting the better of me again.

GWYN MCNAMEE

Willow's gift stands in the center of the space, draped with a white cloth.

Her brows fly up. "What's this?"

"Part of your gift."

She grins. "Why am I getting a gift?"

"I need a reason to get my wife something?"

She laughs lightly, the sound so carefree that it lifts away any reservations I have. Just knowing that she can sound like that, that she can feel that way after everything she's been through, assures me that she'll love what I've done for her.

"You can get me as many gifts as you like. I'm just wondering why."

Shit.

I don't want to ruin the mood by answering the question, but she deserves to know.

Why now?

Months and months have passed.

And it's been done for a while.

But I waited until today for a reason.

I swallow the reasons not to be honest with her as I make my way over to the white cloth. "Because tonight marks the anniversary of our last great day together before I fucked everything up."

Her smile falters as she freezes and watches me grip the fabric in my hand, while using the other to hold Niall to my chest, his tiny body, even now, easily fitting in my massive palm.

"It is something I've been wanting to do for you for a long time. I would have if you hadn't left. But you've been busy with Niall. And if you're not up for it, I understand—"

"What are you talking about?"

I tug on the fabric, and it falls away, exposing the massive carving I painstakingly created for her.

A honeybee.

Willow's breath catches, and her hand flies over her mouth.

"Oh, my God. Killian, it's beautiful." She walks up to it and reaches out, running her fingers over the wings reverently. "How did you do this without me knowing?"

I grin as I walk over to join her, adjusting my hold slightly as Niall shifts in his sleep, tired from all the excitement of the festival earlier today. "I came out and worked on it when you were in town with Raven."

"When you should've been at work?"

Smirking, I waggle my eyebrows. "One of the perks of being the boss."

"Didn't that piss off your brothers?"

I shake my head. "No. They knew what I was doing."

Willow slowly trails her fingers over every inch of it, all five and a half feet, stepping around it to see the intricate work and the stain I applied to the natural wood, to make the black and golden stripes simmer. "Where are we going to put it, though?" She makes her way fully around it and raises a brow at me. "I mean, I love it, but on the porch?"

The fact that she still hasn't guessed, still hasn't caught on, makes me fight a grin. "Where are the rest of the carvings?"

Several people have purchased pieces for their homes, but the vast majority stand on Main Street in front of the businesses.

A fact she's well aware of.

She looks even more confused now. "On Main Street..."

"In front of each of the businesses, right?" I step up to her, staring down into her gray eyes that no longer look so stormy, that are now calm, content, filled with the steely resolve of a woman who finally has what she wants and will do anything to protect it and never let it go. "I thought it was time you finally opened your own shop. I bought the newspaper building for you to do just that. This will sit out front."

"What?" Her jaw drops, and her body starts trembling. "Killian..."

"I thought Raven could use the upstairs as her office, so she doesn't have to sit in the bakery, unless she really needs some new gossip."

That draws a grin across her face, but she still looks unsure.

I grip her chin and brush my thumb along her jaw. "Why do you look like you're not happy about this, Honeybee? Too much pressure? Do you not want to do it? Too busy up here with Niall? I thought you could just bring him in with you. We could convert one of the back rooms into a little nursery for him so he could nap during the day and—"

She pushes up on her feet and crushes her lips to mine before I can continue to list all the things I was prepared to do to make this work. Her arms snake around my neck and tangle in my hair as she kisses me hard, almost frantically. I return it, unsure of exactly what's happening. And by the time she pulls away and presses her forehead to mine, she's laughing.

"You're a good man, Killian McBride." She pulls away and grins up at me. "And I love this and the store. I just don't know that I'm ready for it."

"You are. You're going to make a fortune on those tourists. I'm just sorry we couldn't get it open in time for the festival this year. But next year, I already know what your bestseller is going to be."

"Oh?" She raises a brow. "What would that be?"

I lean in, feathering my lips across hers again. "That one you made that smells like me. You can call it McBride Mountain Lumberjack."

She barks out a laugh loud enough that it startles Niall awake, and he issues an annoyed wail.

Despite his distress, we both laugh, and she slowly pulls him from my arms and settles him to her chest, rocking him gently and trying to get him back to sleep. "I'm sorry, kiddo."

She looks so beautiful like this, holding our son.

So happy.

It finally matches the way I always imagined things would be.

And I may not be a perfect father, not even close, but I refuse to fail her or Niall.

Nothing will ever threaten anyone I love again.

Never.

This is McBride Mountain, and I'll protect anything and everything on it with my life until the day it ends.

———

I hope you enjoyed *Beneath the Mountain Sky*. Continue your visit to McBride Mountain with *Beyond the Mountain Sky,* book two in the McBride Brother Lumberjacks Series!

Available from your favorite retailer:
books2read.com/BeyondtheMountainSky

And check out five other broody, sexy lumberjacks with the Lumberjacks in Love Series, complete and ready for you to binge now! Each is a complete standalone!

https://www.gwynmcnamee.com/lumberjacksinlove

ABOUT THE AUTHOR

Gwyn McNamee is an attorney, writer, wife, and mother (to one human baby and two fur babies). Originally from the Midwest, Gwyn relocated to her husband's home town of Las Vegas in 2015 and is enjoying her respite from the cold and snow. Gwyn has been writing down her crazy stories and ideas for years and finally decided to share them with the world. She loves to write stories with a bit of suspense and action mingled with romance and heat.

When she isn't either writing or voraciously devouring any books she can get her hands on, Gwyn is busy adding to her tattoo collection, golfing, and stirring up trouble with her perfect mix of sweetness and sarcasm (usually while wearing heels).

Gwyn loves to hear from her readers. Here is where you can find her:

Website: http://www.gwynmcnamee.com/

Shop: http://www.gwynmcnameeshop.com/

Facebook:https://www.facebook.com/AuthorGwynMcNamee/

FB Reader Group: https://www.facebook.com/groups/1667380963540655/

Newsletter: www.gwynmcnamee.com/newsletter

Instagram: https://www.instagram.com/gwynmcnamee

Bookbub: https://www.bookbub.com/authors/gwynmcnamee

Tiktok: https://www.tiktok.com/@authorgwynmcnamee

www.ingramcontent.com/pod-product-compliance
Lightning Source LLC
Chambersburg PA
CBHW060812030726
47503CB00002B/460